GODS OF KIRANIS

KIRANIS BOOK 1

RONALD A. GEOBEY

Gods of Kiranis

Copyright © Ronald A. Geobey 2012

KIRANIS HAS RETURNED
kiranis.net

Cover art by Karl Kinsella

Cover design by Frank Lynam

Printed and bound by Createspace
4900 LaCross Road, North Charleston, SC 29406, USA

The Author asserts the moral right to
be identified as the author of this work.

All characters appearing in this work are fictitious.
Any resemblance to real persons, living or dead, is purely coincidental.

ISBN 978-1479124831

All rights reserved.
No part of this publication may be reproduced, stored in a retrieval system, or
transmitted, in any form or by any means, electronic, mechanical, photocopying,
recording or otherwise, without the prior permission of the author.

For my parents. Always.

Thank you to my test readers Jennifer Byrne, Christopher O'Toole, Kevin Murphy and JP Murray. Very special thanks to Kristina Wyckoff for her invaluable editing skills and for pushing a stubborn writer to make this novel what it is today.

Ronald A. Geobey, August 2012

Hail to you, lords of eternity, founders of everlasting! Do not take the reader's heart with your fingers wherever his heart may be. You shall not raise any matter harmful to him, because as for this heart of the reader, this heart belongs to one whose names are great, whose words are mighty, who possesses his members. He sends out his heart which controls his body, his heart is announced to the gods, for the reader's heart is his own, he has power over it, and he will not say what he has done.

Spell 27 from the Book of Coming Forth by Day

PROLOGUE

The future is infinite and inaccessible. As we approach it, as each of us will, it takes on a new form and moves farther from our grasp, promising and delivering, threatening and taking. Yet the future knows us. It watches us with omniscient desire, calling to us, singing to us with its Siren Song of fate. This is the line of our destiny, an ethereal path along which we are fated to travel. But like the music of hearts which are aggrieved, these lines of destiny resonate across the Universe with discordance if there is no dream at the end. To make our future real, we must first dream of it. For only through our dreams can our future find us.

Cana slept. And Cana dreamed. In a star system far from Earth and thus from Cana's slumber, an alien planet was as silent and seemingly lifeless as he. And yet, as Cana observed the planet in what he thought was his dream, it too was aware of him:

The occupants of many space-going vessels maintained a vigil around this dark planet, waiting for something they knew must one day occur. Unseen to these aliens but visible to the dreamer, red lines reached out from the planet like the probing tendrils of a hungry sea creature. They were short and lacked any direction, any purpose. Until the cage appeared, materialising around the planet to surround it with its myriad components. The vessels manoeuvred to a safe distance as these components began to move closer together, enclosing the alien planet. Before the cage had been fully formed, however, the component sections drew back. As if they had taken hold of the outer flesh of the planet, it was torn apart by their retreat. Now the red lines flailed wildly and began to reach farther out from the broken world in their thousands, their hundreds of thousands and more, anchored in countless different land masses which were held in check by the cage, floating chaotically around an epicentre of emptiness. One particular line, sourced from a great mountain on one of these chunks of the world, raced outwards from the scene, spearing the blackness across space as it sought out its dreamer. It found a distant star system and a blue and white world just the right distance from its star. It passed through the moon of this world and through a vessel hidden in its shadows before reaching a station orbiting this planet. Here Cana slept.

1

He awoke with a start, to find himself alone in his dark and silent quarters. Someone or something had touched him, he was sure of it. As the fog of sleep began to lift, he knew that his certainty was lying, and yet the sound from his dream still lingered. He was sure it was music, or certainly something of melodious potential. It soothed him, slowing his heart and mind, and allowing him to drift swiftly back to sleep:

He stood in a forest, where giant trees surrounded him. It was cool and secure here, and his nakedness did not disturb him the way he thought it should. The melody was clearer now, more confident and encompassing. It belonged to him, and he to it. He felt that he could stay in this place forever. Then he felt his feet tingle, as if there was something hot beneath him. Looking down, he saw smouldering coals, and the heat became instantly intense. He screamed and began to run, but the coal was everywhere and his feet began to burn. The flames licked up his legs, charring them as the fire climbed his body. He cried and screamed and ran as fast as he could, but there was no end to the burning ground and his flaming torture and the music was so loud now that he felt his head would explode. Finally, he stopped, burning to the music of his fate, standing with his arms outstretched and his face raised to the sky. Except it was no longer as far above him as it had been, as it should have been, and he realised that he had been growing as he ran. The forest was far beneath him, tiny trees surrounding his feet like fresh-cut grass. He was a giant now, charred and agonised and furious. He roared in anguish, and flames spewed from his mouth. People ran about beneath and around him, tiny ant-like things desperate to escape his inexplicable attack. He tried to shout for help, for understanding, but they were terrified of him, as he was of himself. They may not even have heard him, for the music was so loud now that it filled the world. And scores of people burned to death, screaming as he walked on, his massive steps crushing everything in his path…

With a real shout of horror, Cana woke again. Heat coursed through him, the terror of his dream weeping through every pore. Throwing back the sheets, he swung his legs out and sat for a moment, perched on the edge of his bed. As if in response to some imperceptible voice, he looked out of the window and, for a long time, he sat staring into the impenetrable distance. He felt as if something was watching him, hearing his thoughts, knowing him. He could not have known that his future had found him. But he could hear the melody of his fate.

PART 1
HUMAN

THE FIRST DAY

The corridor was long, silent and peaceful, the perfect place for Cana to escape from the chaos of life on the station. From here, he could fix his deep blue eyes on the Earth below and pretend that the world was perfect. But not today. As the terror of last night's dream was suppressed and stored in chambers of deep memory and deeper fears, Cana found himself transfixed by the hurricane raging far below. He imagined this meteorological event as something akin to a spiral galaxy, its arms of benign clouds birthing stars and worlds as they slowly rotated. The serenity of the orbiting station on which he stood belied the ferocity of the earthbound storm as it devastated an island chain in the South Pacific. He heard someone approaching, but he continued to stare at the event below, feeling humbled by the silent majesty of nature's wrath. 'I heard they started evacuating people down there,' the newcomer commented casually. 'There's some archaeological dig going on.'

'In the Solomons?' wondered Cana, pushing back a blond fringe from his face with habitual absence. 'Never thought of that part of the world as having anything of historical value.'

'I thought your lot considered every part of the world valuable.'

Cana glanced briefly at the other man, a friend and colleague ten years his senior who pretended to have little respect for anyone or anything in the interest of remaining in touch with the younger staff. It did not work, however, for Lyons kept his hair shaved close, his uniform neatly pressed and his mind on the job, while Cana's uniform was a mess by comparison. The buckle of his brown belt was tarnished, his work-shirt

4

was creased and his trousers, over-sized and bordering on a health and safety infringement, took the younger man pointedly across the accepted line of practicality and into that demonic world of fashion. 'My *lot*?' Cana challenged his friend playfully, turning back to observe the wonder of the raging storm.

There was a twinkle of mischief in the other's brown eyes. 'You know…that so-called church you're part of.'

Cana smiled thinly. 'That *so-called* church is fast becoming the most influential world religion since Islam,' he replied. 'We've even got people on Garran worlds these days. But, of course, you know all this already.'

'Sounds a little suspicious to me.'

'Everything sounds suspicious to you, Lyons. Maybe you could try…' Cana stepped closer to the massive window as something caught his eye. 'What the hell was that?'

'What?'

'A flash. In the centre of the hurricane. Is that…' he pointed to something between them and the clouds. 'Is that coming towards us?'

Lyons had not been focusing on the storm and it took a moment for him to see the object. 'It looks like…I think it's a missile!' He turned around and moved to the opposite wall, pressing an intercom button. There was no response.

Transfixed by the rocketing object and seeing that it was hurtling towards them at immense speed despite concerted counter-measures from orbital defences, Cana knew he should run. Shock overwhelmed him, convincing him otherwise. 'I can't get anyone upstairs,' said Lyons, his fear evident as he returned to the window. The object was larger now, mere seconds from reaching them. Cana dropped to his knees, lowering his head and joining his hands. Lyons shouted in disbelief as Cana muttered prayers for their salvation: 'What the hell are you *doing*? Get up!' In his periphery, the missile tore silently past the window, blackening outer layers of glass as hairline fractures spider-webbed ominously and threatened implosion.

The station suddenly trembled and groaned, like a sea monster woken from rest. Explosions rocked the superstructure and the station lurched violently, turning so that Cana and Lyons found themselves prostrate on the weakening glass surface. Now Earth looked far too close for comfort, and they scrambled to their feet, desperate to save themselves. An alarm began blasting with piercing urgency, and flashing red lights announced the onset of evacuation procedures. 'They're gonna seal off the corridor!' Lyons roared. 'Move! Move!'

Whatever had struck the station had destabilised the internal orientation, and Cana was struggling to keep his balance whilst also watching the nearby door begin its inevitable closure. The window which had looked out from the corridor was now a transparent floor beneath them; and it was shattering. The station rolled again, so that they had to surmount an incline to reach the door. Lyons was quickly there, holding on to the frame and bracing himself while reaching out to Cana. 'Come on!' he yelled, his voice barely audible above the still barking alarm. Cana grabbed Lyons' hand and was pulled through the opening just as the window fell apart and the vacuum of space took Cana by the legs and the lungs. For a terrible moment, Cana thought he would die, but Lyons managed to drag him through and they collapsed together as the door closed and oxygen returned. Freezing and catching their breath, the two men exchanged glances, with Cana nodding his gratitude. 'We...have to...keep going,' Lyons gasped, 'in case they eject...the domestic levels.'

Cana was horrified at the thought, but he knew enough not to argue. They found a network of service ladders in maintenance ducts and made their way upwards through the station. The twenty-minute climb was a disorienting experience, as ascending the ladders changed from a horizontal affair, to one of decline and then incline, all caused by the changing orientation of the station. Emerging from the domestic levels, they were met by soldiers gathering fleeing off-duty personnel and directing them to safe areas. 'What the hell happened?' snapped Lyons as he fell out onto the floor, the maintenance duct was sealed and the sound of automated clamps and hissing hydraulics heralded the onset of the ejection procedure.

A soldier turned to him. 'What did you see down there?'

Lyons glanced at Cana, who nodded and replied, 'Something shot up from the eye of a hurricane and came straight at us.' The soldiers around them stopped and listened. 'What are you talking about?' one of them snapped. 'What's that got to do with all this?'

'All this?' Cana looked around. 'I don't understand. Isn't that what hit us?'

The first soldier stepped closer. 'I don't think you get it, son. We're one of the few stations left. Most of them were torn to pieces when the cage appeared. It just materialised in orbit and knocked out everything in

6

its way. We might have suffered a lot more than a loss of stabilisation if we'd been anywhere else.'

'The *cage*?'

The soldier nodded. 'I'm sure everyone will be debriefed once we get our house in order. For now, just make your way to the yellow area. Follow the yellow lights along the way and you'll find it.'

Lyons shook his head and gave a mocking laugh. 'What do you mean...a cage? What sort of cage?'

No longer in the mood for idle chat, the soldier grabbed Lyons by the arm and pointed him in the direction he was to take. 'The yellow lights,' he repeated forcefully. Cana took Lyons' arm and they walked away. As they passed a younger soldier, he leaned in and whispered, 'It's around the whole planet, man. Never seen anything like it. The whole world...in a cage!' He shook his head and walked away.

Cana and Lyons followed the yellow lights, joining the rest of the refugees. Lyons was staring straight ahead when he spoke, so Cana never had a chance to learn if he had been genuine when he said, 'Now you can start praying.'

Ω

It was clearly a cage, a spherical prison currently arranged in its component sections as it enveloped the world. The hundreds of sections were of a strange, alien design, each maintaining a synchronous orbit relative to its counterparts. A guidance array sat atop one of the sections which were being repositioned as the entire device rotated. In their final position, these sections would come together to form a gigantic dome which would be situated above the North Pole of the planet. With the Earth's North Pole now darkened by the alien structure hanging high above it, the rest of the arms reached south of the equator, their apexes disappearing into the shadowed depths of the world. Each of the arms were formed of giant triangular pieces like sharpened teeth, each inverted next to its neighbour. Tube-like corridors connected them, glowing blue from internal lighting. The components of a major corridor formed the equatorial band. In a section midway between this central band and the apex of one of the northward reaching arms, a man awoke.

Disorientated at first, he soon came to appreciate the difficult circumstances in which he found himself. Clamps held his body captive in an open capsule of cold metal and sterile equipment. His ankles, thighs, neck and wrists were locked in place and he could not move his head to look any farther than his synthetically enhanced grey eyes would permit. To make matters worse, he was being watched. 'Who's there?' he snapped angrily. 'I can feel you staring at me.'

A man moved out of the deepest shadows while managing to remain in their wake. He was perhaps a handsome man, although his close-shaved hair and the purposeful configuration of his dark stubble distracted one from concluding such. It gave the impression of the shadows of wicked fangs. He smiled a cold smile, keeping his dark eyes locked firmly on the captive individual, who was currently elevated above his captor. 'What else can you feel, Conner?' he enquired. 'Are you aware of the journey you've made?'

Conner closed his eyes and took a series of long, deep breaths. When his eyes snapped open, the man in the shadows laughed. 'Amazing, isn't it? All it took was a beacon fired from the planet and the cage was able to travel across the galaxy.'

'This isn't my time.'

'No, we're four centuries before your time.'

'Why here?' asked Conner. 'Why now?'

'Do you know who I am?'

Conner tried to nod. 'They were calling you the Prophet. I heard you were dead.'

The Prophet chuckled. 'Times change,' he replied. As he moved closer to Conner, the shadows held him possessively, stubbornly refusing to let him go. 'Speaking of such things, I should give you a little warning of what's coming.'

'Just tell me how to get home. I don't understand why you need me here.'

'You will, when you see an old friend.' The Prophet retreated into the shadows of the wall opposite Conner. 'Is that *it*?' Conner shouted. 'You put me through all this and leave me with a *riddle*?' He struggled in the bonds. 'Get me the hell outta here!'

As the blackness swallowed his strange captor, the clamps holding Conner in the capsule against the wall snapped open simultaneously and he fell forward, hitting the floor hard. He launched himself into the darkness to grab the Prophet, but there was no one there. The only sound was the thrumming of machinery as the cage maintained its position around Earth. Conner lay on the floor for a time, trying to decide what to do as he caught his breath.

Ω

Within hours, scores of military vessels were emerging from the atmosphere to approach the mysterious structure surrounding Earth. Powerful energy readings were emanating from the arrowhead points of the northern sections, suggesting that these areas housed the control centre of the alien structure. Charged with leading one of the many reconnaissance missions to study the structure, Captain Adam Echad of the *Nostradamus* did well to keep his trepidation from his bridge staff. He issued orders and stood firm and confident at the forefront of the bridge, eyeing the massive section towards which he was heading. His confidence was a façade, however, for something had been nagging at his thoughts since he awoke that morning. The dream had been powerful, vivid and intense. So vivid, in fact, that the thought of turning to observe his crew caused him to relive the disturbing scene:

In his dream, he had walked onto this very bridge, only to find it staffed by skeletons. Oh, they acted as if they were alive, addressing him and each other formally and professionally with mouths devoid of tongues and perpetual grins. Their voices were normal in tone and tenor, even without vocal chords and lungs to define them. So Echad, in his dream, accepted this, even though he had his body and organs intact and he was dressed as would be expected. It was as he took his command chair that he noticed the lines. They were red, passing right through every skeleton at the point where their hearts should be, some lines running away from the crew to the exterior of the ship, others leading off the bridge through various exits. A sudden flash heralded blue lines of horizontal light which stretched across the bow window. Now, as he looked at the strange heart-lines of his skeleton crew, every one of those lines were directed at him...at his heart. And they did not pierce him as with the others. They ended with him. They began with him.

As the *Nostradamus* rose ever closer to the monstrous object above and he found himself focused once again on the real world, Captain Echad could see nothing but the blue lines of horizontal light along the blackness of the alien metal. He found himself looking down towards his heart, instinctively raising his hand to his chest as he took a deep breath. An irrational fear struck him, and he was reluctant to turn to his crew lest he

9

should see skeletons and red lines. Someone was calling him. 'Captain?' the female voice repeated.

Without turning around, he replied. 'Yes, Lieutenant.'

'We found what looks like a docking conduit, Sir, with an entrance large enough for the ship.' Should we go in?'

Echad nodded. 'Let the fleet know. Ready weapons.'

'Yes, Sir.'

The *Nostradamus* led the reconnaissance fleet of ten ships into a huge aperture between two of the horizontal blue lines, where flashing red lights on either side guided them in along strips of yellow which reminded the Captain of a runway. He inhaled slowly, turned to look at his crew, and then exhaled with relief, berating himself for his stupidity as he saw that they were all very much alive. For now.

Ω

Conner got to his feet, knowing he would have to get to safety. He could no longer sense the presence of the Prophet, and he felt more vulnerable and alone than he had ever been in his life. He knew that there was no time to waste on reflection and that people from Earth would soon be here. Feeling his way along the dimly lit corridor, he walked away from the cubicle and silently counted those he passed. Before he reached twenty, his hands touched the cold metal of a panel in front of him. Hoping it was a door, he fumbled around for a locking device. The panel was smooth and devoid of any outwards signs of a locking mechanism, so he applied a different method, closing his eyes and 'seeing' inside the door. He found the lock, a mechanism designed to be discovered and accessed only by someone with telekinetic abilities. Finally, something familiar, he thought. Upon identifying the key function, he heard the sound of a heavy bolt snapping open, and the door slid aside.

He stepped out of the narrow corridor and was greeted by plenty of light as he entered a vast room. A gigantic window before him revealed what appeared to be a searchlight moving in the space beyond. Glancing back into the now illuminated corridor, he was able to see the great height of the ceilings. As he allowed the huge door to close behind him and he reviewed the giant room, something more massive beyond the window filled his vision and gradually blocked out the exterior light. It was difficult to define it at first, but giant metal panels were visible and he realised that he was witnessing the silent passage of a ship. It was not until the illuminated designation plate of the vessel moved into view that his hypothesis was confirmed. The huge letters of the name moved slowly from left to right across his vision. Recalling events from his own history, he did not need to see all of the name before gasping in awe, 'Nostradamus!'

He moved quickly towards the window, before which was an array of illuminated control panels and equipment. None of the equipment was designed for tactile operation, but he identified a psychic interface as the ship continued to move slowly by. He braced himself and leaned over the panel as someone peering out of one of the windows of the *Nostradamus* happened to spy him. Conner sensed the gaze upon him, and he raised his eyes.

The young man on the ship stood with eyes wide and mouth open as thread-like metal tendrils pushed out from Conner's hair at the back of his head and stretched out and down towards the interface panel. The tendrils probed the panel, finding input ports and permitting Conner access to the system. And all the time, Conner held the astonished and horrified gaze of the young man on the *Nostradamus*.

Once the ship had passed and Conner had gleaned all the information he needed, he reached up to the back of his head and, roaring in furious agony, he used his considerable telekinetic strength to rid himself of the metal disc implanted therein. The flesh ripped open and the tendrils lashed at his waiting hand as his arm trembled and the pain tore through his body. As the disc shot out into his hand, the tendrils retracted and the device snapped shut. It was circular, no bigger than a coin and bulging in the centre. Its silver surface was mostly covered in blood, and Conner blacked out as the pain swamped him and the blood flowed from his scalp.

The door opened and three black-garbed figures, armed and stealthy, approached his motionless form. Their faces were covered and they observed their surroundings through green-tinted goggles. As two kept watch for unwelcome company, the third reached down. Holding a forceps in one hand while opening Conner's grip with the other, this one retrieved the blood-covered disc with surgical caution. All three left the room before Conner came around.

Ω

11

In an administrative centre on Earth, two women stood apart from the bickering crowd of government officials, knowing that none of them had any control over the situation. Cassandra Messina was an influential member of the Eurasian Council, and Nell Raesa was her political aide. Cassandra had just revealed the truth of the situation, and Nell was furious: 'You're saying you were *warned* that this would happen?' she snapped, her eyes belying her disgust.

'*This*?' Cassandra laughed ironically. 'I don't think anyone could have anticipated this...particular scenario, Nell. There's a damned *cage* around the entire world, in case you hadn't noticed!'

'There's no need to be facetious, Cassandra. You said...' Nell lowered her voice. 'You said that he told you.'

'He told me a lot of things.' Cassandra looked across to the squabbling men and women. 'Look, there's no way out of this, Nell,' she assured her. 'But you and I can be safe.'

Nell grabbed Cassandra's arm, twisting her to face her. 'How?' she demanded.

'We need to get on board a ship called *Nostradamus*. As far as I know, it's up at the cage as we speak. It's connected to this somehow.'

'So how do we get up there?'

'That's already arranged. But we need to wait until tomorrow. There'll be some kind of...radiation or something from the cage. It'll come in six-hour waves starting soon. By the time the second one's over and people become symptomatic, there'll be chaos and those idiots over there will be throwing everything they've got at the cage in desperation. That's when we leave.'

Nell nodded. 'Tomorrow,' she noted, exhaling emphatically. 'How do we avoid exposure in the meantime?'

Cassandra held her gaze, expressionless. Nell could feel the warmth of fear in her belly and she nodded again, resigned to her fate.

$$\Omega$$

Captain Echad ordered that the ship be brought to a full stop, and the other vessels following *Nostradamus* did the same. Although the area appeared to allow them access to the interior of the structure, there were no suitable docking ports and an away team left the ship using anchor lines and EVA suits. Echad's voice could be heard in their helmets:

'Remember...whatever Crewman Barnes saw...you're not alone in there. So keep your eyes open.'

This away team was part of a massive reconnaissance mission happening simultaneously on every accessible section of the structure. All information gathered from every ship was being monitored and shared as it was fed to Central Command on Earth. Each of the ten ships of the *Nostradamus* Recon sent four armed personnel into the alien docking area. They used lines, bridges and docking extensions depending on the access points and the configuration of each vessel, and they set out in varying directions. Helmet-mounted cameras transmitted live feed to Central Command, which was a hive of activity as hundreds of monitors were observed along high walls of equipment. The reconnaissance teams had been briefed on the presence of an unidentified man, and so tensions were high.

For Conner, too, tensions were high. Psychic he may have been, but scores of armed men and women on the edge and angered by the intrusion of some monstrous structure into their territory were not going to be easy to avoid. He needed to become one of them, and only by selecting the right group would that be possible. The Prophet had given him a clue as to why he was here, and seeing the *Nostradamus* had confirmed it. He stood silent for a moment in the viewing area, with blood trickling down the back of his neck and matting his hair as it dried. Closing his eyes, he listened for their thoughts, quickly finding what he was looking for. Someone was thinking of returning to the *Nostradamus*, hoping to get back there safely. Conner moved his psychic sight out into the darkness of the corridors, racing along like a hunting dog with the scent in his nostrils. He found the group of four from *Nostradamus* and he saw the man he was looking for; the right height, the right build, even the same colour eyes. 'Perfect,' he whispered.

William was nervous, and annoyed by the fact. He was highly trained and capable of conducting this kind of operation, and yet something was troubling him. He was experiencing a sensation of imminent doom, and he longed to return to the safety of the ship. The Commander of the team, Sandra Miller, turned to look at him, as if sensing his unease. 'You okay, Will?' she asked.

The voice in his helmet startled him, and Sandra saw as much as he turned to her and nodded. 'Just a bit spooked, I guess,' he replied. 'Can't put my finger on it.'

'Well, you're not alone,' she assured him. 'Let's just get our area secured and get the hell out of here.'

'Couldn't agree mo-' William stopped, gasped and looked around.

'What is it?' snapped Sandra, infected by his paranoia.

'I felt…I think…someone's watching us…' His eyes were wide and crazy. 'No, they're watching *me*!'

Another of the team members, a burly man by the name of Joshua Colle, stepped up to him and grabbed his arm: 'Get it together, Will!' he spat. 'You think you're that special they'd pick you out? If you can't say anything useful, just keep your mouth shut!'

William looked to his Commander for defence, but it was not forthcoming. 'He's right, Will,' she said. 'Just concentrate on what you're doing, okay?'

William nodded as he heard Joshua and the fourth and youngest member of the team, Jason Archer, muttering to each other about him. As they set off, he realised that the conversation could be heard back at Central Command – never mind on the ship – and the embarrassment set in. Sandra glanced at him, shook her head and followed the other two down the dark corridor as they swept the area with their torches and rifles, but William hung back until his heart stopped pounding and his breathing slowed. Just as he was about to follow the Commander, he felt a sudden and terrifying paralysis rush through his body and a wave of fear dropped him to his knees. With his mouth open, he desperately tried to cry out, but he remained silent and motionless. He did not hear anyone approaching from behind him, but his helmet was unlocked, twisted and removed before a blade was pressed against his throat. With tears of horror in his eyes, William watched the others move farther away as the blade opened his throat. The vicelike grip on his neck suppressed most of the arterial spray, and William felt the warmth of his blood inside his EVA suit as it poured slowly down his chest.

Ω

Echad was on edge as time went by, but for reasons other than the portentous alien structure and the rumours that utter destruction awaited the entire planet. It was more than the dream, more than the general feeling of doom. Something specific and centred upon him was occurring. He spent some time chiding himself for such ridiculous paranoia, but he had never experienced this kind of fear and foreboding. He felt as if the walls were closing in; not those of the bridge or the ship itself, but the unseen boundaries of the universe, affirming his significance in some great scheme of which he would rather not be part. The crew watched him pace the bridge erratically, his anxiety evident and his dread barely concealed. 'Where are they now?' he asked.

'They're approaching one of the main energy sources, Sir,' someone replied. He did not care who. He simply nodded. There was another voice: 'Sir, there's a com request from the Council. Priority Red.'

Echad turned away from the bow window, feigning composure. 'I'll take it in the Briefing Room,' he replied. As he walked to the door, his anxiety grew. Something bad was going to happen.

Ω

Encased in William's EVA suit, Conner caught up with the rest of the away team as they reached a huge door. Sandra turned to him. 'Thought we'd lost you,' she quipped. 'You okay?'

Conner decided that silence was the best option. He was surprised to see a smile reach her eyes, the only part of her face visible in the helmet. 'See you decided to keep quiet after all,' she joked, patting him on the shoulder. 'Don't take it personally, Will.'

'Commander, we're ready,' Joshua reported, unable to disguise the impatience in his voice. He and Jason had finished placing a compressed explosive device on the door and they moved back as they prepared to detonate it. Before doing so, Sandra drew Joshua close to her and said quietly, 'You got a problem, Colle?'

Holding her gaze throughout, he said nothing, lifted the detonator and pressed it. The only expression on his face was a minute contraction of his facial muscles as the explosion filled the corridor. Then he nodded, said, 'No problem,' and turned away from her.

Waiting for the smoke to clear, the team entered the room to find an array of strange equipment and technology, but there was one object to which everyone's attention was immediately and fully drawn. 'Is that what I think it is?' asked Sandra, pointing to a monitor set high into a black wall. Many things about this monitor struck the team as unsettling, and even Conner felt a shiver run through him as they moved deeper into the room.

There were parts of this momentous event which had remained secret from the people of Earth and their descendants for centuries. Standing here, looking at what could only be a countdown timer in the characteristic blue light of this place, Conner could sense the defeat emanating from these usually brave people. 'Yeah, it's a countdown alright,' said Joshua. It had just passed nine days and nineteen hours. 'And it looks like we've got just short of ten days,' he added.

'Till what?' Jason wondered aloud.

'Well, that's what we're here to find out,' Joshua reminded him.

'Ah...excuse me?' Sandra pressed, pointing up at the figures, 'but you guys are overlooking the obvious here. I mean, can't you see what's wrong with this?'

Jason saw it, and was chilled to the core by the implications. 'They're not alien numbers,' he whispered. 'They're ours!'

Ω

Echad leaned forward in his chair, infuriated by what he was hearing. 'With all due respect, Madam Councillor,' he argued, 'are you sure about this? I mean, shouldn't this be coming from Central Command?'

Councillor Cassandra Messina, the woman on the screen in front of him, replied in her soft and sure voice, 'I wouldn't order it unless I was certain, Captain. Central Command have their hands full at present, which is why I am delivering this message to you personally.'

Echad stared at the screen for a moment, and then sat back, defeated. 'Is he dangerous?' he enquired.

'I suspect he won't harm any of you,' Cassandra replied, 'but yes...he's quite capable. Simply keep him on board and stay where you are until I arrive. Can you manage that?'

Echad gave a cold smile of contempt. 'I'll switch the engine off, shall I?' Cassandra responded with a smile of a more diplomatic contempt, before severing the connection. Echad allowed himself a moment of reflection, leaning back to absorb the conversation, before returning to the bridge.

'Recon team's back on board, Sir,' Lieutenant Morris reported. 'Can I ask why you recalled them when the others still have their teams out?'

Echad looked at her for a moment. 'No,' he said. The Lieutenant could feel the stares of the crew on her and she reddened, refusing to let it drop: 'Captain, Central are asking the same question. Don't you think we should respond?'

Echad walked to the rear exit of the bridge. 'No,' he called back as he left.

Ω

Conner stood in the airlock, in Phase One of detox with his EVA suit still on, waiting for the Captain to make an appearance. He could see through the smoked glass that the other three had removed their suits in the Phase Two chamber and that they were heading for the detox showers in the Phase Three annex. 'What the hell's wrong with you, Will?' a naked Commander Miller shouted from the other side of the door. 'We're back now. Get out of there!'

Echad's voice could be heard over the intercom: *'It's okay, Sandra, I'll handle this.'* They turned to see him standing outside the detox chambers and Sandra moved to the intercom. Pressing the button, she explained: *'He was acting pretty weird, Sir. Never seen him like that.'*

Echad nodded and gestured for them all to move out. As they did and Echad waited for them to leave, he kept his eyes fixed on the man in the EVA suit. Conner opened the airlock and stepped into the Phase Two chamber, removing his helmet as Echad looked on, drawing a gun from the back of his belt. He could see dried blood at the back of the man's head as he turned away to remove the suit and place it in its compartment. Unlike the other members of the team, Conner remained fully clothed, clearly with no intention of going to the showers. Instead, he approached the door which led directly out of the Phase Two chamber into the area where Echad stood watch. 'Don't do it,' Echad warned him, raising his gun and stepping back from the door.

Conner could not have heard him anyway, and he reached out to the panel to open the door. It hissed as the pressurisation corrected itself and then it opened on its heavy hinges. Conner stepped out to see the gun at his face. 'One of my crew said you had tentacles,' said Echad. 'Can't be too careful.'

Conner grinned ironically, recalling the agony he had experienced as he had removed the disc. It would be best to maintain the discomfort these people felt. 'Suppose that's one way of describing them. I hate them, but they serve a purpose.' He made to step farther forward and the gun was brandished with more emphasis. 'Think they can stop a bullet?' Echad

17

threatened. The gun was suddenly wrenched from his grip by some unseen force and it slammed against one of the lockers before falling to the floor. 'They won't have to,' Conner assured him, moving closer still. 'Are you Echad?'

'What?' The Captain looked from the fallen gun to the man before him.

'Is your name Echad?'

'I'm...Captain Echad, yes. Who are you?'

'My name's Conner...Conner Echad.'

The Captain was thrown off guard and the man punched him in the face. He lost his balance and struck his head against a bench before falling to the floor. 'I'm sorry, Captain, but we haven't got time for the niceties.' He stood over Echad as he gradually lapsed into unconsciousness. 'The Jaevisk are coming,' he heard Conner say as his vision blurred and there was a buzzing sensation behind his eyes, 'and we don't want to be here when they arrive.'

$$\Omega$$

Having completed her duties, Anya stepped into her quarters gratefully, looking forward to relaxing for a few hours before meeting the Captain for dinner. She removed her uniform without delay, discarding it half on the floor and half on the bed and stepped into the shower to wash away the stress of the day. Of course, the stress had form and the potential to continue as such. The alien structure around the planet continued to amaze and terrify.

The heat of the shower soothed her muscles and she closed her eyes to further appreciate the water on her head. She heard a sound from the main room. Sweeping her hand across the sensor, she stopped the shower and listened in silence. 'Adam?' she called. 'You there?'

Through the glass, she could see someone approaching and she grinned. 'Couldn't wait 'til later, no?' she joked, reaching out to open the steamed-up glass door. 'I think there are more important things to do then...'

The man reached in and grabbed her roughly by the arms, dragging her out of the shower. She screamed and lashed out with her fists, feeling a sudden sharp pain as if something had spiked her from behind at the base of her neck. She lost all power to her limbs and the man caught her as she collapsed. Paralysed and naked, she was terrified of what was about to happen. 'You can stop imagining such horrible things, Anya,' he assured her as she looked up at him. She had never seen him before, and yet there was something familiar in those eyes. 'I'm going to dress you and take you somewhere out of the way,' he continued. 'I'm sorry for your embarrassment, I really am, but this is the only way he'll do what I want.'

Ω

The dream came to Echad again. This time, however, the skeletons of unidentified Humans morphed into both real people and aliens and the bridge was exposed to the vacuum of space, disconnected from everything. It was above a planet, one Echad did not recognise, and he felt that if he were to walk to the edge of the floor he could simply step off and fall into the clouds. The clouds escaped the atmosphere, rising lazily to envelop the open bridge.

The people around him – Anya, the woman he loved; Helen, his argumentative Lieutenant; Cassandra Messina, the member of the Council with whom he had recently spoken – looked at him expectantly, as if awaiting his next move as the clouds closed in. There were other shadowy figures – a Humanoid alien, more than two metres tall, clearly a Garran; another alien, even taller, with a tapered head, possibly Jaevisk, from what he had heard of them; and yet another, towering over everyone else, similar in shape to the Jaevisk but more powerful and terrifying – and they also waited. Every figure was connected to Echad via the red lines.

The last figure stepped out of the cloudy obscurity, and Echad was taken aback, for it was him. This other Captain Echad approached him with a stupid grin on his face, offering him a mirror. Echad took the mirror, but it was not his own face he saw when he looked into it. It was the face of the man he had just allowed to board his ship...

He woke with a groan, finding that he was being helped to a seated position against one of the locker rows. He heard Sandra's voice. 'Captain, are you okay? What happened? Where's Will?'

Echad took a moment. 'That wasn't Will,' he replied eventually. 'He must've killed him.'

'I knew there was something wrong with that guy!' Jason spat.

Joshua agreed: 'No way Will could keep his mouth shut that long!'

'There's a medic on the way,' said Sandra, as she examined Echad's bruised face. 'Any idea where this guy went?'

With Sandra's help, Echad was trying to get up off the floor. 'None,' he replied. 'But...I was ordered to let him on board.'

'*Ordered*?' Sandra was clearly shocked. 'By *who*?'

'Councillor Messina.'

'Oh, *that* bitch. Never trusted her...*or* voted for her.' Sandra's hand came away from Echad's head with blood on it. She looked up at the others and ordered, 'Let the Lieutenant know we've got an intruder, and that he's not afraid to use force.' They were moving away when she added, 'Oh, and guys...'

Joshua turned back, his earlier animosity dissolved: 'Yeah?'

'Get my gun.'

Ω

In the auxiliary engine room, Anya was gagged and her wrists were clamped through a railing at her back. The pulsing of the engine behind her rattled her to the bone, and she struggled to break away. 'Don't bother,' her captor told her. 'The clamps keeping your hands together have a wire running from them to the engine casing. There's an explosive trip at the end of the wire which will snap and activate if you move away too far. I don't need to explain what will happen then, do I?'

Anya's eyes widened and she stilled herself. 'Do I?' he repeated. She shook her head. 'Good.' He hunkered down in front of her. 'By the way, you don't need to try to speak. Just think what you want to say and I'll hear it.'

She looked incredulous, and he grinned. 'Try it.' He waited. 'You want to know who I am.' He stood up, noticing the sceptic look she shot at him. 'Of course, who wouldn't ask that? Or what I want or why you or something like that? All obvious questions.' He turned his back to her theatrically. 'Why don't you try telling me something then...something I couldn't possibly know?'

She did so, sure that he was lying and that her secret would remain safe. But he turned back, evidently shocked. 'You're pregnant?'

The shock was shared. How could he have known? He hunkered down again, speaking softly. 'I swear to you I didn't know. If I had, I wouldn't have boarded this ship.' He lowered his head, shaking it, while Anya stared at him in fear. 'I've put everything at risk,' he chided himself. He stood again and looked up as if some entity was watching everything. 'You put me right in the middle of it, didn't you?'

20

He looked back to Anya. 'No, I'm not insane,' he assured her, still surprising her by reading her thoughts. 'I was brought here and I've got to find a way home. Captain Echad is my only hope now, and you're the leverage. He won't want any harm coming to his girlfriend...especially if she's carrying his...' He stopped. 'Oh...he doesn't know. Well, I'll be telling him. Sorry, but it'll give me more to bargain with.'

Anya cried and lowered her head. 'I know,' said Conner. 'Why don't you just try to relax? I'm sure he'll do what I want.'

Ω

Echad waited impatiently as the bridge crew scanned the ship, deck by deck, room by room. Armed teams were being guided by those sitting at the monitors. 'Still nothing, Captain,' Lieutenant Morris reported as she joined him. 'And Sandra's asking about Will. She wants to go back for him.'

'Tell her to concentrate on her orders,' said Echad coldly. 'Any sign of Anya yet?'

Morris shook her head. 'She's probably asleep with her com switched off. You know what she's like.'

'Yes, I do, thank you, Lieutenant.'

She looked at him for a moment, moving in to say quietly, 'What's going on, Adam? I know we have our bad days, but I'm on your side here, you know.'

He was about to snap at her, but he thought better of it. He sighed, resting a hand on her shoulder. 'I feel like an idiot, Helen,' he whispered. 'I was ordered to let this guy on by a Councillor known for always having her own agenda. He stood in front of me and said he's...' He stopped himself. It was ridiculous.

'He's what?' the Lieutenant pressed.

'He said his name's...Conner Echad.'

Morris held his gaze for a moment. 'Okay, now I can see why you're freaked out.' They kept their tone low. 'You think he's got Anya?'

Echad shrugged. 'I don't know what to think.' He took her arm and led her away from hungry ears. 'Helen, he's some sort of...telepath.'

'What?' She laughed the word with nervous mockery.

'When you get a minute, run the footage from the airlock. You'll see what I mean. Can you keep an eye on this? I'm going to look for Anya myself.' She nodded and he patted her upper arm, saying, 'Thanks.' But

21

as he turned away, the port-side door opened and the black-clothed intruder stepped onto the bridge. Weapons were pointed at him, but Echad raised his hand and shouted, 'No!'

He could see that Conner was not armed, brandishing nothing more than a rolled up holosheet in his right hand. 'How did you get up here?' Echad enquired calmly, glancing at Helen. 'We've got people all over the ship looking for you…proximity detectors everywhere.'

'You don't need to know the answers, Captain,' said Conner. 'There's one thing and one thing only that you need to know.'

Echad approached him, furious at the implication. 'If you've hurt her…'

'Captain, you can read minds. Congratulations.'

'Where is she?'

'This is the part where I tell you she's safe and that nothing will happen once you do what you're told.'

Helen moved closer to him, her gun levelled. 'What do you want?' she demanded. 'And what are these things around the planet?'

Conner looked only towards the Captain. 'First of all, your people down on the surface have already figured out that these…*things*…are just one thing. It's a cage, designed to enclose a planet. Believe me, you don't want to know what's going to happen. We're gonna get out of here as fast as possible and you'll all be safe.'

'You mentioned the Jaevisk earlier,' Echad recalled. 'What have they got to do with this?' He pointed to the scene beyond the bow window. 'Is this thing theirs?'

Conner shook his head. 'I'm not entirely sure who built it,' he lied, 'but I know it's not theirs.' He laughed ironically. 'It's from the future.'

'What a load of crap!' snapped Helen, her trigger-finger tightening. Conner glanced at her and the gun snapped from her hand, firing as it did so. A smoking hole ten centimetres above Conner's head was testament to Helen's intention. As Echad shouted again that no one was to fire at the man, glances of shock were exchanged and weapons were gingerly lowered. Echad called Helen, but her fiery gaze was fixed on their intruder. 'Lieutenant!' he repeated.

She turned to him. 'You have the bridge,' he told her. 'Find Anya. Our guest and I have some things to discuss.'

Ω

'Why are you doing this?' Echad demanded as he sat behind his desk in the Briefing Room. 'Did you have to kill one of my crew? You did kill him, right?'

Conner nodded as he, too, seated himself. 'Believe me, I considered all the options and the consequences. This way I can become him. It's the only way I can keep things in balance. You should also believe me when I tell you I could have taken control of this ship by force.'

'I gathered that much.'

'Oh, really? And who told you that?'

'Told me what?'

'That I was dangerous,' said Conner. 'I heard you saying it.'

'You heard?...I was *thinking* it.'

'Makes no difference to me. Ah, I get it. It was Councillor Messina. Now that's interesting. Maybe that gives you some idea of what's happening here.'

'No,' said Echad. 'Makes it even more confusing, actually. What the hell do you want?' He pointed at the open holosheet on the desk between them. 'What are these coordinates?'

'Just get your Nav officer to input them. You'll see quick enough.' He grabbed Echad by the wrist as he reached for the flat screen. 'And stop planning ways to beat the crap out of me in that dangerous little mind of yours.'

As he let go, Echad stared at him in shock and frustration. 'I'm not comfortable with you hearing my thoughts.'

Conner shrugged. 'I come from a time where most people can either stop you from doing that or feed you false information. I'm not used to it being so easy.'

Echad laughed scornfully. 'A time?' he said, dripping mockery. 'Do you really expect me to believe that you and your...what did you call it...a *cage*...came from the future?'

'You have no idea how little I care what you believe, Captain. The cage isn't mine, nor do I have anything to do with its operation. You already know there's a countdown timer in there and it's ticking away oblivious to your ignorance. I can help you avoid what's going to happen. All you have to do is take me to those coordinates. Then I'll be on my merry way.' He even managed a smile.

Echad stared at him for a moment, and then leaned back in his chair. 'Simple as, huh?'

'Simple as.'

23

'Any chance of telling us what's going to happen? Seeing as you're from the future and all.'

Conner's smile evaporated. 'I wish it were a laughing matter, Captain.' He stood up and turned his back to Echad. 'A...sickness starts soon,' he began solemnly. 'A kind of virus from the cage. Your guys start attacking, but they'll be wasting their time.' Echad was rapt, his stomach fluttering as he leaned forward. The man's tone chilled him as he continued: 'The cage won't even need to respond, and it'll exhaust your military just trying to scratch the surface. Gradually, as the timer runs down and the people on Earth accept that there's nothing they can do, they'll realise what's going to happen. But it'll be too late, cos they were too stubborn to evacuate.'

He turned around to face Echad, who knew with all his heart that he was hearing the truth. 'So tell me,' said the Captain. 'What happens when the timer runs out?'

Conner held his gaze. 'The cage closes,' he said. 'And things go from bad to worse.'

Ω

The damaged station needed to be moved outside the cage. Two large military vessels docked with it and, upon securing their hulls to the station to prevent tearing it apart, they fired their engines and slowly accelerated. Ten minutes later, the station was at a safe distance, and the staff in the Operations Area were able to look back at the cage. 'My God!' gasped General Matthews, as he walked closer to the window. He could see a flashing blue object suspended in stasis between the many apex points of the cage, and he pointed at it. 'Activate the VR,' he ordered.

The VR imaging software activated across the window, semi-transparent so that the scene was still visible beyond it. Matthews focused his attention on the blue object as he said, 'Enhance section Alpha-6.' A green square appeared around the metallic object and the image was subsequently enlarged. The General stared at it for a moment. 'It looks different,' he noted.

'Different, Sir?' asked a man to his right, the Lieutenant immediately subordinate to Matthews in the Operations Area.

'The metal...the design,' Matthews explained. 'It looks different, don't you think? Could this be the thing that launched from the planet?'

The Lieutenant nodded. 'I suppose it must be. Some sort of beacon, perhaps?'

Matthews agreed. 'Exactly. Which means that it might have guided this thing here.'

'I'll get some people on it, Sir,' said the Lieutenant, not one to be playing catch-up. 'If we can determine the range and frequency of the signal, we should be able to find out where it came from.'

'My thoughts exactly, Lieutenant.' Matthews took one last glance at the image on the screen and then gestured for another officer to follow him as he walked towards one of the exits. 'I want to talk to the guy who saw that beacon,' he explained.

Ω

Lieutenant Morris paced the bridge as the two men spoke in the Captain's Briefing Room. A message came up from Sandra and her team and one of the crew passed it on: 'They want to go back out to get the Corporal's body, Lieutenant.'

Helen thought for a moment. The Captain would not authorise it, but she could not leave one of their crew – dead or alive – on that thing. She nodded. 'Tell them to be quick about it. Any doubts as to their route and the location of Will's body and they're back without delay.'

The minutes passed. Helen was about to approach the Briefing Room when the door opened and both men exited. She watched as Echad walked directly to the Navigation post and handed the officer there a holosheet, the one previously carried by their intruder. 'Get us to these coordinates as fast as possible,' he ordered.

'Yes, Sir,' the officer replied.

Lieutenant Morris watched in amazement. Was he actually doing what this murderer demanded? She noticed that the man was watching her, and when she thought something particularly offensive about him, he grinned knowingly as the Captain approached her. Once more, he led her away from the rest of the crew. 'Helen, I need you to do something for me,' he said quietly, 'and you're not going to like it.'

'Didn't think so,' she remarked.

He nodded, refraining from rebuke. 'I want you to take our guest here down to Sick Bay and get the Doc to check his blood. I need a DNA test done, comparing it with my file sample.'

'You think he's telling the truth?'

'Like I said, I don't know what to think, but something about all this feels...' he struggled for the word, and gave up trying. 'Do this for me,' he resumed, 'and don't bother trying to hide what you're thinking from him. It's a waste of time.'

She sighed and grudgingly agreed, glancing at Conner before heading for the door. He followed her.

'And Lieutenant?'

She turned back to the Captain. 'His safety...is our safety. Understand?'

'No,' she replied, turning away.

Ω

With his back to the wall, Cana settled down on his low bunk for some sleep. Scores of men and women who had once enjoyed private quarters were now packed into makeshift dormitories. The lights were low and Cana could see figures walking from bunk to bunk. They were leaning in close to some survivors here and there and they appeared to be consoling them. It was strange, and Cana wondered what they might say to him. Lyons called him in a sharp whisper from the next bunk and he turned to him. 'What?' he whispered back.

'How come you get the corner bunk?'

Cana smiled. 'I'm truly blessed, Lyons. You know that.'

'Come on, man. I can't sleep with space on either side of me.'

Cana blinked, fitting this piece into the Lyons enigma. 'You serious?' he asked.

'Yeah. Ever since I was a kid. Have to be against the wall.' He was quiet for a moment, perhaps recalling the reason. 'You'll swap, right?'

With a sigh, Cana swung his legs out and yawned, reaching down for his uniform. 'Don't worry, I won't steal your clothes,' said Lyons as he brushed past Cana and lay down. He edged his back against the wall and said, 'Much better. Thanks, kid.'

Cana looked at him for a minute, leaving his clothes where they lay and thinking *'Kid? Seriously?'* Then he got into Lyons' bunk and was asleep within minutes:

The broken world in the alien system whispered to him as countless masses of land collided and fused in an attempt at recreation. 'Come to me, Cana,' it said. 'Give me life.' From deep within the darkness of what would become the core of the planet, two giant red eyes observed him. 'Come, Cana,' the voice whispered. 'You can worship me.' The eyes exploded into scores of burning metal tendrils, dripping molten rock torn from the formation of the world. They snapped at Cana's naked flesh like whips of fire, searing his face and his arms and legs. 'You cannot escape me, Cana,' the voice whispered again, harsher this time, threatening. 'I am your GOD!'

He was rescued from his nightmare by shouts, which were immediately followed by a number of gunshots. The lights came on full and Cana bolted upright, looking around. At the opposite end of the room, General Matthews and a squad of soldiers were standing over the bodies of five black-clothed men. 'How did this happen?' the General snapped. 'Who *are* these people?'

It was then that Cana remembered the men going from bunk to bunk. He also noticed that Lyons was unusually quiet. When he turned to him, he saw why. The man's face was grey and his lifeless eyes stared right through Cana, who shouted out in fright and scrambled across his bunk to jump to his feet on the cold floor. 'It's alright, son,' said a familiar voice. It was the older soldier to whom they had spoken only hours before. 'It's over now.'

Looking around, Cana could see the sheets being drawn back from the dead, men and women all around the room. It was noted that there was a single puncture wound in the neck of each victim. Those who had escaped the attack, like Cana, stood as he did, scared and confused. He found himself turning back to Lyons and then focusing upon his own uniform, discarded as it was with his name-tag clearly visible. It was then that he realised what had happened. 'It should have been me,' he gasped.

The soldier placed a hand on his shoulder. 'Don't think like that, son. Be thankful it wasn't.'

Cana stepped back from him, looking around in fear. 'No...no...' he stammered, 'you don't understand. We swapped bunks.' He walked along the lines of beds, seeing many faces that he recognised, now pale and motionless in death. 'I know them,' he said as a chill ran through him. 'I know these people.'

'What are you talking about?' Matthews demanded as he closed in on Cana. The officer with Matthews leaned in: 'That's him, Sir,' he supplied. 'The one who saw the beacon.'

All eyes were now on Cana, and he felt panic rush through him. 'Everyone here...' he eventually replied. 'All the dead. I know them. They're all members of the Church.'

'And which church would that be?' Matthews asked knowingly.

Cana hesitated, aware of the can of worms he was about to open. But perhaps that was already done. 'The Church of the New Elect,' he explained.

Matthews nodded, stepping closer to Cana and saying, 'You saw the beacon.'

'The what?' Cana looked at the waiting faces. 'Oh, you mean the thing that hit us. It came up from the hurricane over the Solomons. They tried to stop it, but it just kept coming.'

'It was launched from a tract of newly exposed land off the island of Malaita,' Matthews elaborated. 'There was an archaeological dig, and they appear to have stumbled across some sort of technology that doesn't belong here. You're right...counter-measures didn't work. But it didn't hit us. It reached orbit and then acted as a beacon to guide the cage right to us, which destroyed a lot of our stations in the process. We're on one of the few left fully operational.'

Cana stared at him, unsure how to respond or what was expected of him. 'I don't know what to say, General,' he admitted finally. 'I don't understand any of this. I'm just a labourer up here...a serviceman.'

'You saw the beacon,' the General repeated, as if that mattered. 'And now you're the only survivor of a massacre of your church members.'

'We swapped bunks!' Cana declared, pointing back at the far corner. 'It was only by chance!'

Matthews regarded him for a moment, breathing deeply as he thought about all this. 'I don't believe in chance,' he said. 'You're coming with me.'

Ω

Cassandra listened to the reports on the Net. A warrant had been issued for the arrest of Captain Echad and there was talk of betrayal and collusion. Of course, what she was hearing was no more than rumour and speculation, but it would not be long before the truth was out. 'They'll connect me to Echad and they'll be looking for me soon,' she told Nell quietly as they walked along the eastern colonnade of the Council Buildings.

Nell offered a perfunctory smile to a passing colleague, before leaning in and responding to Cassandra in hushed tones: 'So what are you going to do?'

There was a beeping sound in Cassandra's ear and she raised a hand to silence Nell as she pressed the button on the com unit clipped to her lobe. 'Do you have it?' she asked the unseen caller without delay. 'And did you activate it?' The reply clearly pleased her and she said, 'Then they'll be here soon. You know what to do.' She pressed the button again to end the call and Nell asked, 'What's going on, Cass? What are you up to?'

'We can't wait any longer,' Cassandra replied. Get our transport arranged. We're going up to the *Nostradamus* within the hour.'

'That's too soon!' argued Nell. 'I need to say Goodbye to my family.'

'There's no time for that.' Cassandra's voice was cold and uncaring.

'Well, I'm *making* time, Cass.'

She turned on her. 'Have you any idea what will happen here, Nell?' she snapped. 'I've got secrets to protect, but if we hang around here too long, they'll grab Captain Echad and he'll tell them why he let that man on his ship. Both of us will be implicated in this...don't doubt that for one second. And if you're out playing happy families when they come looking for you, your loving parents will be brought in with you!'

That got her attention. 'You're a cruel bitch when you want to be, you know that?'

Cassandra sighed, drawing Nell into her arms as she purred in her ear, 'We'll get away from here, Nell, and then we can sort things out. There's no point in us all dying.'

'I'm scared for them, Cass. Dad's been sick for years now. He won't survive anything else. If this is an attack...'

'Shh! Don't think about that now.' Cassandra held her head and looked in her eyes. 'One thing at a time, okay? Think of it this way...if we can get the guy who arrived on the cage, we might be able to turn things around.' She kissed her softly on the lips, and Nell smiled: 'Do you think that's possible?' she asked hopefully.

Cassandra nodded. 'I do,' she replied, although she turned swiftly away from Nell's naïve adoration.

Ω

29

On the *Nostradamus*, there was some difficulty in dealing with Conner's demands, as Echad discovered as he approached the Navigation officer. 'Why haven't you plotted a course yet?' he demanded.

The officer pointed defensively at his monitor, saying, 'Ah...I thought I should check this with you first, Sir.'

'This better be good,' said Echad as he leaned in. However, the readings and the images spoke for themselves. 'Have you double-checked this?'

The Navigation officer nodded. 'I re-entered the coordinates three times, Sir.'

Echad pointed to the column of figures on the right hand side. 'According to these records, the fifth planet of this system should be a dead world that the Jaevisk keep tabs on. Why would he want to bring us there?'

The young man gestured to one of his colleagues, saying, 'Julia activated the Observation Post on Pluto. The A.I. couldn't explain it.' An Artificial Intelligence oversaw the operations on a number of deep space Observation Posts, massive telescopes which could be accessed remotely.

Julia nodded in confirmation: 'We're running the scope and sensor logs backwards to find the first readings. Could take a while. Oh...maybe not.'

'What have you got?' asked Echad.

Julia scanned the readings, and she was clearly stunned. 'Wow!' she exclaimed. 'This is...strange. According to this, the planet has...changed...very recently. Like you said, Sir, it should be a dead world.'

'And now?' Echad pressed.

'It's like it...exploded or something,' she replied. 'There's debris everywhere, although...' She moved the static images on to a larger monitor for Echad and he could see the problem. 'The debris field isn't expanding,' he noted.

'No, Sir. It's gravitating inwards, almost like...'

'Like the planet's forming rather than exploding.'

'There's molten rock...gravitational activity...' She pointed to some sensor readings. 'There's an increase in mass occurring in the centre of the debris field, and a build-up in electro-magnetism.'

Echad took a deep breath and stared at the evolving images for a moment. 'When did this...change start?' he asked. 'Was it about the same time the cage got here?'

Everyone on the bridge was listening and watching. Silence descended as Julia performed the necessary calculations, allowing for the distance of the alien planet from Earth and the time it took for information to reach the Observation Post. She leaned back in her chair, finally revealing, 'It happened immediately before it arrived.' The crew began muttering amongst themselves and speculating, before Julia straightened in her seat and announced, 'There's an image log coming in from the Ob Post, Sir.'

Echad stepped in closer to the monitor as Julia brought up the images of the silent world, around which the tiny specks of Jaevisk Warships could be seen. 'This was taken just before the planet changed,' Julia explained, speaking quietly. The silence of the bridge amplified her voice: 'More images are coming in...in close chronological sequence.'

'Put them on the platform,' Echad told her, turning away and waiting. In the centre of the Bridge, a holographic platform in the floor activated and the first image of the alien world surrounded by Jaevisk Warships rotated for all to see. The scores of images were displayed in static sequence, and everyone watched in horror, recognising the relative time as just prior to the terrible situation in which they found themselves. The components of the cage appeared around the planet and the tiny lights of the Warships were seen in progression to move farther away from the event. The pieces of the cage closed in on the planet, and then appeared to retreat just as rapidly. There was a flash of light and, once it died out, the cage was gone, leaving behind it a boiling and tumultuous field of rock and fire.

'And then it came here,' said Echad. He turned to the terrified crew. 'Whatever we just witnessed could easily happen here,' he told them, 'and if that countdown timer we found out there is anything to go by, we've got about nine days.'

'So what do we do?' asked Julia.

Echad thought for a moment, then looked back to his Navigation officer. The young man nodded as the Captain said, 'We go out there and get some answers.'

Ω

31

Helen walked the unwanted guest towards Sick Bay. She tried to empty her mind, considering the peculiar invasive talent of the man next to her. He deliberately kept pace with her until their footfalls were reminiscent of parading soldiers. She was sure he did this only to infuriate her.

'I'm not the bad guy here,' he said, after a long silence.

'I'll be sure to tell Will when he rises from the dead.'

He grinned. 'Stranger things have happened.'

Helen stopped suddenly, turning to slam him against the wall. 'Why don't you quit the crap and tell me what you want?' She pressed her right forearm against his throat, but she felt something press into her abdomen. Looking down, she saw her gun in his left hand. 'How...?'

She stepped back, but he reversed the weapon and handed it to her. 'I'm not the bad guy,' he repeated.

'Then who is?'

He chuckled ironically. 'Where do I start?'

'At the beginning?' she suggested.

'To be honest, I'm no longer sure when all this began.'

She looked at him for a moment, tempted to argue, but instead resigned herself to her orders. 'Eventually, you're gonna pay for what you've done.' She walked away and he swiftly caught up with her. 'Eventually,' he agreed.

Ω

The sections of the disconnected cage maintained their synchronous orbital positions without any apparent means of propulsion. Massive pulses of energy had begun sweeping intermittently upwards along the inner surfaces of the southern sections. Collector devices set at regular intervals fed upon this energy burst and used it to maintain balance and position. By releasing rapid blasts of energy, hundreds of beams fired towards the planet simultaneously, all directed towards the centre of the world. The world reacted, releasing a shockwave from its core, a powerful pulse of electro-magnetism. With this first pulse, information was being gathered on Matthews' station. A female officer on one of the Science stations relayed it to him. 'It's using the planet's own magnetic field to keep it in place, General,' she explained. 'But there's something weird in the readings. I think there's something hitching a ride to the surface.'

Matthews stood on the metal bridge spanning the lower levels of the Operations Area. As if his input might be valued, Cana stood alongside him. He could not have felt more useless. 'Can you be more specific?' the General asked.

'Yes, Sir. I can show you.' She activated a viewer above her station, within which a greyish gas could be seen emanating from the cage: 'It's a nanite cloud,' she explained. 'There could be trillions of them, but the readings suggest they're inert.'

'So what's the point?' asked Matthews.

'Hard to say, but...' There was a sudden flash of light, as if the cloud had ignited. 'What was *that*?' The officer checked her readings again, before explaining, 'Well...they're no longer inert. Looks like the EM pulse...woke them up!'

'A bit out of character for an EM pulse,' Matthews noted.

'Extremely.'

'Launch a collector drone. Once they start to disperse, we won't be able to see them, let alone track them. We need to know what they're programmed to do.'

'Yes, Sir.'

Matthews headed back to his office, with Cana in close pursuit. 'General, do you really need me up here?' he asked.

'I don't know yet,' Matthews replied. 'But until I do...you stay.'

Tense minutes passed as the General waited for a report on the nanobots. Cana remained silent, stealing furtive glances at Matthews in the hope that he might engage the man in pointless conversation to pass the time. Matthews did not once look at him, engrossed as he was in his observation of the staff. Eventually, the Science officer came up the steps from her post and approached Matthews' office. 'We can't determine precisely what they're programmed to do, Sir,' she explained, handing the General a holosheet and adding, 'at least...not yet. But we've identified what appears to be a detection system, a kind of...sniffer device.'

'To detect what?'

'It seems designed to seek out a very specific element.'

Matthews looked at her for a moment, noticing that she appeared uncomfortable with what she had learned. He glanced at the screen in his hands. 'Rubidium,' he said quietly, shaking his head and shrugging his shoulders, clearly unfamiliar with the element. Matthews was surprised to see Cana reacting to this information in much the same way as the young woman. 'I'm sorry...am I missing something here?' he asked them suspiciously.

33

They both snapped out of their mysterious reflection. Cana looked away, while the officer replied, 'No, Sir, of course not. We'll have to identify the specific isotope of Rubidium in question. Until then, we can't really speculate on their purpose.'

'So why do I get the feeling that you…*both* of you…' he turned to look at Cana, who had moved closer to the door, 'are already speculating?'

Cana caught his suspicious glare and reddened like a guilty child. 'I'm just scared, General,' Cana lied. He laughed nervously, saying, 'I wouldn't know where to begin speculating!'

Matthews looked back to the officer. 'And you?'

'Ah…the same, Sir. I'm not sure what we're dealing with here.'

Matthews nodded slowly, far from believing her, but any further attention from the General was diverted towards Cana as he resumed his approach towards the door. 'And where do you think you're going?'

'If it's okay with you, General, I'd like to try to get in touch with my family. They'll be worried.' Cana held Matthews' glare for a moment, waiting as he eventually conceded. 'Don't take too long,' he told him. 'We're not finished here, and those people in the dorms killed more than just the ones you saw.'

'What?'

'I've lost thirty-seven officers because of this little cull that went on up here,' the General explained. 'I want answers.'

Cana nodded. 'I'll let you know if I get any,' he said. 'I promise.'

With Cana gone, Matthews emerged from his office with the Science officer behind him. 'We'll talk later,' he told her quietly, before issuing orders to those around him. 'Contact the Mars shipyards. I want everything ready for an assault on this thing. Run evacuation scenarios for Earth. Military and government first.'

A senior officer approached the General and reported, 'Sir, there's a ship called *Nostradamus* breaking from the recon at the cage. Central's just flagged it. Something about flouting orders and recalling their team early. There's a warrant issued for the Captain, Adam Echad.'

'Do we know where he's going?'

'They haven't submitted coordinates. Apparently, Councillor Messina's connected, but Central are keeping tight-lipped.'

'Can't be good, then,' agreed Matthews. He looked out of the huge curved window, seeing his world obscured by the disconnected alien structure. 'This isn't exactly the time for keeping secrets. Are they outside the cage yet?'

'Just about, Sir,' the man replied. 'They're in a hurry, wherever they're going.'

'Tap their Nav system. I want to know what they're up to.'

'Team Three are on it. Do you want me to get a weapons' lock?'

Matthews shook his head. 'Not yet,' he replied, gesturing towards Team Three. 'Let's figure out what's going on first.'

As he and Matthews approached the team, the General asked, 'You guys got something for me?'

A young woman with a look of confusion on her face replied, 'We got their Nav system, Sir, and it looks like they're going to a planetary system just outside Garran territory. Someone's trying to stop us looking too closely at it, though. I think Central's attempting to shut us out.'

'Surprise, surprise,' Matthews remarked. 'Keep on it.'

'Yes, Sir,' she replied.

'Ninety seconds of weapons' range remaining, Sir,' the Senior officer reminded Matthews.

Matthews shook his head. 'Just keep on eye on it. How long 'til we get backup from Mars?'

'Twenty minutes, Sir.'

An alarm sounded and Matthews looked out the window again. 'What now?' he shouted.

'Gravity shift along Venus' orbit, Sir!' came the immediate reply from a man in Team Three. 'Looks like a Jaevisk vortex!'

Matthews felt his mouth go dry. 'Battle stations, everyone! How many ships?'

'Just one, Sir.'

Matthews addressed the entire staff when he said, 'I don't need to tell you that our priorities have changed!'

The alarm resumed, and Matthews listened as the various Team Commanders reported: 'Another Warship, Sir, shadowing the Mars fleet.'

'Another one, Sir. Just crossed lunar orbit.'

'I've got another one, General. Hundred thousand kay out, heading for the south pole of the cage.'

The station trembled as a Jaevisk vortex occurred within a few thousand kilometres and a massive vessel gradually materialised as if emerging from black fog, until it could be seen in all its terrible glory beyond the main window of the station. It was reminiscent of a massive golden hornet which had consumed too much and taken to the air. The Jaevisk Warship, however, did not appear unwieldy or overfed. It was a gargantuan engine of destruction. As if to emphasise this capability, hundreds of fighter craft erupted from the outer hull of the vessel. They moved outwards from the Warship, setting up a perimeter.

The Senior officer was quickly at Matthews' side: 'Sir, we've got battleships coming up through the cage all across the north eastern quadra-sphere.'

Matthews managed to maintain his balance on the still trembling station as he regarded the alien ship. 'Well,' he said, as the alarms stopped once more, 'at least we're not on our own up here.'

Ω

Cassandra leaned back in her chair with her eyes closed. 'This can't be happening,' she groaned. 'I needed to avoid suspicion at all costs, and now this!'

Nell was beginning to wonder whether she cared about Cassandra's problems. She looked away, where she could see a number of civilian ships, public and private, launching from the port. Many people were taking the initiative and leaving the planet, reluctant to wait for state-arranged evacuation and conscious of escaping the panic which would ensue when the government finally got around to it. 'What difference does it make?' Nell asked dejectedly. 'We could easily get on one of those ships out there and disappear with some wealthy civilians. You're not that famous that they'd recognise you!'

Cassandra opened her eyes and glared at her partner. 'This isn't a good time to insult me, Nell.'

Nell grinned sardonically. 'Well, I'm sure you'll let me know when the time's right.' She rose from her seat opposite Cassandra. 'Perhaps I could schedule it for you? *Today Nell will tell me how despicable I am!*'

Cassandra laughed with genuine amusement, but it faded as she saw Nell's expression harden. She sighed. 'Oh, I'm sorry, Nell...really.' She gestured towards the vacant chair. 'Please, sit down and I'll explain, because with or without you, I intend to be off this planet within the hour.'

'But I thought you wanted to get on the *Nostradamus*.' Nell reluctantly sat down. 'Now that it's gone, that plan's out the window.'

36

'I'll find a way of following it. But first I have to go up to a military station outside the cage.'

'*What?*' Nell threw her hands up. 'For God's sake, *why?*'

Cassandra sighed again. 'There's something I have to do. It might just save millions of lives.'

'How altruistic of you,' Nell mocked. 'The great Councillor Messina wants to be the heroine. How does that fit into your scheming? You must have an angle.'

'This crisis is really bringing out the worst in you, Nell.'

'And the best in you, Cass. Get to the point, please. I want to see my parents.'

'Okay. Now that the *Nostradamus* is gone and I'm stuck here, I need to take control of things. There are now hundreds of thousands of Jaevisk soldiers in orbit. They followed a signal which has been emitting from a device taken from the man who arrived on the cage.'

Nell was stunned. 'The same guy who's on the *Nostradamus?*'

'Yes. I was told that he would remove it shortly after he arrived. He did. And we took it from him.'

'Who's 'we'?'

'My associates. You're better off in the dark, Nell. Trust me.'

Nell chuckled scornfully. 'Yeah, right. So what happens now? Your crazy church is gonna save the day?'

'I'll ignore that...for now. I have to go and speak to the Jaevisk. If you want to know any more, you should come with me.'

'Like the dutiful pet that I am?'

Cassandra actually looked hurt. 'I need you with me, Nell. You keep me strong.'

'Only because I appear so weak by comparison, Cass. I help elevate you.'

'Perhaps, but that doesn't discount the fact. Without you, I can't do this.' She stood and came around the table to take Nell's hand. 'Please, Nell. Come with me.' Her lower lip was trembling and she leaned in close to Nell so that she could whisper in her ear, 'I'm frightened.'

Nell's eyes widened and she felt her emotions stirring. She nodded. 'I'll come with you,' she said quietly. 'I love you.' Cassandra held her head close for another few seconds. When she drew back, all traces of weakness were gone. 'I know,' she replied.

Ω

37

In the Sick Bay on the *Nostradamus*, the Doctor was looking closely at the wound on the back of Conner's head. 'You say you pulled this device out yourself?' he mused. 'What did you use?'

Lying face-down on the surgical table, all Conner could see was the floor and the shoes of the confused Doctor. 'You wouldn't believe me.'

The Doctor looked back at Helen, who grinned. 'The Captain believes this guy's psychic or telepathic or whatever you call it.' Her grin faded. 'Although something made my gun snap out of my hand.'

The Doctor nodded. 'I heard about that. Some form of telekinesis, I'd imagine.'

'Yeah, *imagine* is definitely the right word!' Helen approached the table. 'He's not to be trusted, okay? Fix him up, get me the test results and we'll throw him in a cell.'

'Not if you want to live, you won't,' Conner mumbled.

'Shut it!' Helen snapped. 'We'll find Anya and kick you out an airlock long before we're at that system.'

Conner remained quiet, but he smiled knowingly. The Doctor examined the wound again. 'There's no sign of any instrument being used here.' With a torch and magnifying lens in his hands, he shook his head, clearly impressed. 'Perfectly clean opening. It's as if the flesh opened itself.'

'How's that possible?' asked Helen. 'I mean, isn't telekinesis just fantasy?'

He shrugged. 'Space travel was once just fantasy,' he reminded her. 'Never be so swift to dismiss new ideas...' he reached for a laser bonder and smiled as he showed it to her, '...or advancements.' So saying, he sealed the wound within seconds and stepped back. 'Okay, I'll just take a blood sample and then we're done.'

When the blood was in the hypovac, Conner turned over and sat up slowly, feeling slightly dizzy. He looked at the Doctor, who turned away before he could be questioned. Conner was about to enquire about what he had just done, but something changed his mind. 'They're at Earth,' he said instead, staring at Helen. 'We're running out of time.'

'Who's at Earth?' she asked. 'The Jaevisk?'

He nodded. 'Someone or something brought them there. Probably that Councillor who wanted me kept on board.'

Helen found herself drawn in, intrigued by the implications. 'What would she want with the Jaevisk?'

'I'm not entirely sure,' he admitted. 'She must know something about the cage...or something else.' He thought for a moment, lowering his head. Helen stayed silent, glancing at the Doctor, who shrugged. When Conner looked up, his eyes were haunted. 'The virus...' he began. 'She knew it was coming!'

'What?' Helen asked. 'The cage?'

He jumped down from the table, walking away with his hand over his open mouth in shock. 'This is it,' he muttered through his fingers. 'This is why they gave it to me. They needed it brought back. God, he must have gotten to them!'

'You need to start making sense...' Helen threatened.

Conner turned around to face them both. 'The device I had in my head had a number of functions...most of which are redundant for me...but I was told that it would protect me from the radiation on Kiranis. But I never got there, so I took it out, presuming that it had served its purpose. It had, but...I think I know what its true purpose is. And it has nothing to do with radiation.'

Helen glanced at the Doctor. 'Any signs of radiation sickness?'

The Doctor shook his head. 'Nothing at all.'

'There wouldn't be,' said Conner. 'I don't think I was ever in any danger from emissions. At least, not down on the planet.'

'What do you mean?'

'It's the cage itself that's the danger. For a number of reasons. I remember learning about a terrible infection that swept across Earth just after the cage arrived. A virus released by the cage was designed to kill millions, but...' He cradled his head in shock, and said, 'They thought that an alien device implanted in the brains of the victims would be the cure.'

'Your device,' the Doctor provided.

Conner nodded. 'That's not what it's for. At least...'

'Well, what *is* it for?' Helen asked him. 'Or are you just guessing?'

'I'm *guessing*...' he replied, 'that it's necessary to have one of those things in your head if you want to survive the trip in the cage. I just travelled across space and time, and didn't even get a nosebleed!' He was pacing now, turning it over in his head. 'My people must have known this. I trusted them! Someone came up to the cage to get that thing from me, so you can be sure they've got plans for it.'

'Someone like Councillor Messina?' Helen suggested.

'She might honestly believe that it's about protecting the people of Earth from the virus,' Conner conceded. 'He must have told her as much. Why else would she take it?'

'Who are you talking about? Who told her?'

He dismissed that. 'This is complicated enough without you knowing that.'

'Look...what if you're wrong? What if it does save lives on Earth? You said yourself that you didn't get to your destination, so how do you know you didn't need protection from anything there?'

Conner shrugged. 'Maybe. Either way, Messina's using the Jaevisk to get what she wants. You've no idea what she's drawing you all into.'

'So tell me.'

Conner hesitated, recalling what he had learned of Earth's history. He was reluctant to reveal any more of the future to these people. 'What the hell,' he said. 'It won't make any difference now. It's the reason I'm taking you away from Earth, anyway. That thing in my head had Jaevisk components. And whether you believe me or not, I've come here from the future.'

'So Councillor Messina will be giving the Jaevisk their own technology centuries before they actually invent it?'

'Setting aside temporal paradoxes, yes, that's basically what's going to happen. There's more to it than that, though. I don't really know why, but the Garran are part of all this as well.'

Helen took a deep breath. 'They won't be too pleased about us chatting with their nemesis, will they?'

Conner smiled thinly. 'That's putting it mildly,' he noted.

Ω

Cana waited as the connection was made. Communication traffic was slow and restricted, and carefully monitored right now. If Cana's assumptions were correct, however, it would make little difference if he were discovered. A man in his forties was displayed on screen. 'Cana,' the man said, surprised. 'What's going on? You're taking a huge risk by contacting me.'

'I know, Presbyter.' He hesitated, before saying, 'I think it's happening. I think this is it.'

40

'And I think you're over-reacting. As...momentous as this cage is, it doesn't exactly fit the bill for salvation and rejuvenation, does it? Although one might associate this with apocalyptic imaginings at a stretch, but –'

'It's not the cage itself, Presbyter,' Cana interrupted. 'It's what's happening as a result of it being here. The structure's stabilisation mechanism causes an electro-magnetic pulse from the planet's core.'

The man sat up straight and moved closer to the screen. 'It's dangerous?'

'Possibly, Presbyter...to us. The Church, I mean. Nanites are being released into the atmosphere and activated by the EM shockwave.'

'And how is this related to the Church?'

Cana hesitated. 'They're designed to find Rubidium.'

The Church official visibly paled, missing a breath. 'What possible reason...I mean...who would do this?'

'Could it be the Garran?'

'No,' the Presbyter replied dismissively. 'They're not capable of constructing something of this scale. What we're looking at here is something completely beyond the capabilities of any race we've encountered.'

'Even the Jaevisk? They're here, you know. Just showed up without warning.'

'They've a habit of doing that. Still, I don't think this...cage is theirs. I've been in touch with friends in MI. They still describe this thing as completely alien, but what has them most concerned are the human aspects of its design. I presume you heard about the countdown?'

Cana nodded. 'It's in our numeric system.'

'Now *that* makes me uncomfortable!' He sat back again. 'Anyway...these nanobots. What are we to expect?'

'We don't know yet, but they must be designed to...infect us or something. Maybe i-i-if Church members...*inhale* them or...' Cana gasped with zealous panic. 'There's no way of knowing *what* will happen!'

'Just because we have high levels of Rubidium doesn't mean that no one else will be targeted. Everyone has the element, Cana. And it hasn't caused problems for us before.'

Cana nodded, controlling himself. 'I know,' he said. 'The Rubidium has always been resilient to biological agents, but this could be different. And if it makes a lot of us sick, we won't be able to control who attends to them, and then we'll have a whole new problem to deal with!'

41

'Cana, don't you think we've had the best Nano-surgeons on the case? Nothing has been effective in adversely manipulating the Rubidium levels...or manipulating them in any way, for that matter. So what makes you think these machines will fare any better?'

'Because all of this is too coincidental to be...' he shrugged, 'coincidence!'

'And you see this as the time of our *salvation*? Inter-galactic robots sent to kill us all?'

'It depends on who built the cage, Presbyter,' Cana argued, resenting the sarcasm. 'The nanobots may not be designed to kill us. But...things have happened up here that suggest someone on Earth knows what's going on. I thought maybe you'd be able to get some answers.'

'What do you mean...things have happened?'

'Almost every Church member up here has been murdered.'

'What?' the Presbyter gasped, his eyes alight. 'Why?'

'Why else? We're outside the cage! Someone doesn't want us to escape our fate.' Cana laughed ironically. 'And I think the Church itself is responsible!'

'That's preposterous! How can you say such a thing?'

'Because I recognised some of the men and women responsible for the murders.'

The Presbyter understood the implications, but needed to hear it before accepting it. 'What are you saying, Cana?' he asked quietly.

'They were Church members,' Cana replied.

The Presbyter fell silent. 'We should end this conversation,' he said finally.

Cana heard knocking on the door behind him. 'It's too late now,' he said. 'Can I ask you a question, Presbyter?'

'Of course.'

'Who's the most powerful member of the Church? Can you think of anyone who would be able to organise something on this scale? Someone of influence? Someone in government, perhaps?'

The Presbyter thought for a moment, and then nodded. 'There is one person,' he replied. The knocking on the door behind Cana was more forceful, and he leaned closer to hear the name. 'She kept it secret for a long time. No one knew her parentage. She came to the Church voluntarily a few years ago.'

'Who?'

'We must be careful, Cana. Where are we heading with all this?'

'Who is it, Presbyter? Who could do this?'

The Presbyter reached out to sever the Com link. 'Messina,' he replied. The screen went blank and the door burst open behind Cana. He turned around to see the General and two soldiers in the room. 'Seems you have some answers,' said Matthews.

Ω

A small private shuttle passed through the still open cage, avoided the futile manoeuvres of the defensive fleet and approached the military station. It was dwarfed by the battleships surrounding the huge station. Of course, the nearby Jaevisk Warship belittled all, adjusting the hierarchy as it seemed to glare hungrily at the station on which General Matthews awaited his visitor.

That visitor discreetly took her partner's hand, surprising Nell again with her apparent vulnerability. Neither woman said anything, for the danger was clear. One did not summon the Warships of the Jaevisk Society without cause or recompense. The very fact that they arrived in five separate vortices, expending massive amounts of energy, was testament to the significance of the signal used to attract them.

The shuttle docked in the station, and Councillor Messina and her assistant, Nell Raesa, were escorted to the Operations Area. The elevator took them upwards through nearly two hundred levels before it slowed gradually and then came to a stop. Nell watched Cassandra as she visibly drew herself up and took a deep breath, releasing it as the doors opened. She wasted no time, recognising General Matthews immediately and asserting her authority: 'Inform the Jaevisk that I'm here, General.'

Although Matthews was curious as to her presence and her potential involvement with recent events on his station, he set his concerns aside as he nodded and politely replied, 'Of course, Councillor.' He gestured that she accompany him to the central bridge, a walkway spanning the circular expanse of the Operations Area, beneath which several teams were posted at their stations. Although most did not know she was a member of the Church of the New Elect, many things were known about Councillor Messina and she attracted considerable attention from the staff. She was a woman known for always being one step ahead of her political rivals. One story claimed that, as the time for the quadrennial government rotations approached, she had betrayed her

43

entire national constituency to ensure that the one to which she was due to be appointed would benefit financially. Her successor tried to prosecute her, but she had so much incriminating information about the man that he promptly withdrew his complaint.

As per Messina's command, the message to the Jaevisk was relayed. Within seconds, a perfectly formed holographic image of a huge Jaevisk appeared beside the General on the metal bridge. Accurately displayed, it was over two and a half metres tall, with a long muzzle-like head. Its yellow, almost gold skin appeared rough and reptilian and was interspersed with black tattoos. It was partially armoured in interconnecting leather and metal, which left small patches of its lean, muscular body exposed. On its back, halfway down its spine, the armour concealed two distinct bulges nearly a metre long.

Cassandra announced herself, stepping past the General and approaching the hologram of the alien: 'I am Councillor Cassandra Messina.'

'We are aware,' the Jaevisk replied, the station's automated translator working to the slightest of delays as the alien language died away. 'Present your request and your means of summoning.'

Momentarily thrown off her guard, Cassandra blinked before reasserting herself: 'If you're aware of who I am, then surely I deserve a bit more respect.' She was playing a dangerous game, but she was convinced that she had the upper hand.

'You are as consequential as any other Human,' came the curt reply.

'Really?' Cassandra sounded mildly amused, but she ignored the insult and, removing something from a pocket in her robe, she offered it up to the hologram for examination. There was a tense silence as the creature stared at the tiny metal disc. The image abruptly flickered as the hologram was replaced by its originating counterpart, and the alien suddenly reached out, taking the device from Cassandra's hands. She stepped back, momentarily shocked.

Around the giant room, men and women of the security forces raised their weapons in perfect unison. General Matthews raised his hand to sway their enthusiasm as the Jaevisk turned the device over in its huge hands, its eyes filled with poorly disguised wonder. Then it looked back up at the Humans. 'This interests us,' it confessed. 'How does this relate to our presence here?'

Cassandra turned back to Nell for a moment, who could see her concern. 'There are...Jaevisk elements in the device,' Cassandra pointed out with confusion in her voice, focusing once again on the Jaevisk. 'Aren't you aware of *that*?'

'We are aware,' the Jaevisk lied, drawing itself up to full height as it noted the sarcasm. It did not return the disc. 'This is the device used to summon us.'

Cassandra nodded. 'We require a large number of these,' she explained. 'It is vital that we receive them as soon as possible.'

'Does your life depend on this, Councillor Cassandra Messina?' Even without appreciating Jaevisk intonation, the monotone words of the computer translator somehow managed to relay the threatening undertones of the question.

'More than just mine,' Cassandra replied, 'which is why I'm here.' Standing immediately behind her, Nell found herself wondering at the veracity of that statement, but recognised her cue as the Jaevisk said, 'Explain.'

Cassandra turned and nodded to Nell, gesturing that she interject. 'At last count,' Nell began, 'nine million, six hundred and thirty eight thousand, four hundred and three people had presented symptoms of a feverish illness. This is a result of a specifically engineered virus released from the structure surrounding our planet. The symptoms are expected to worsen.'

'You believe that these devices will relieve your people of these symptoms,' the Jaevisk realised.

Cassandra noted that there was no reference to the cage as she replied, 'We believe they will save millions of lives.'

The alien glanced down at the device, as it asked, 'What evidence do you have to support this?'

'We'd prefer not to discuss that,' said Cassandra.

'As you wish,' replied the Jaevisk after a slight pause. 'Our courtesy is warranted by the suffering of your people. We will examine this device thoroughly in order to replicate it accurately.'

'Before you do...' Cassandra stepped closer, 'there is something else we require.'

'You ask much,' noted the Jaevisk, 'even for a Human elevated above others.'

'I appreciate that,' she admitted, 'but we believe that a common goal would be in the best interests of both our world and the Jaevisk Society.'

There was a short silence. Then, 'Explain.'

Cassandra could feel her heart pounding in her chest. She paused a moment to compose herself. What she was about to say would shock those around her and she felt light-headed and nervous. 'Less than twenty hours ago, there was a gravitational disturbance in the Kiranis system. Our deep-space scopes monitored the appearance of a small craft, emerging through a phenomenon similar to your vortex technology.' Cassandra could feel the tension in the room, knowing that all eyes were burning through her for keeping this secret. Nell moved closer and discreetly placed a hand on Cassandra's back. Cassandra felt the benefit of the calming hand and continued: 'The scopes followed the craft as it travelled at immense speed towards the Sieltor system. We believe it will reach its destination within a matter of hours.'

'The vessel is piloted by a single Garran,' the Jaevisk interrupted.

Now it was Cassandra's turn to be surprised. 'You know about it?'

'We also monitor that system.'

'So you know that this...cage came from there? Very soon after the appearance of that vessel?'

'We are aware.'

Now was the time. This was where lines were crossed, where requests for help increased in significance. Cassandra took a deep breath before declaring, 'We believe that the Garran are somehow connected to the arrival of this structure around Earth.' Her lies rolled easily from her tongue. 'They may lack the capability to construct this technology, but they're involved.'

'You seek revenge on the Garran,' the Jaevisk realised, ignoring the subtle inference of blame and the question of how the other race could be connected.

'We intend to speak with Governor Ben-Hadad regarding extradition proceedings,' Cassandra responded with diplomatic caution. 'We feel it is our right to interrogate this Garran pilot. If we're unsuccessful...' she shrugged, 'we'll consider military action.'

'Military action against the Garran will fail without assistance,' noted the Jaevisk. 'Their forces significantly outnumber your own. If you decide that military action is a necessity, we will consider our position.'

Cassandra smiled, exhaling gratefully. 'Then you'll help us?'

46

'We will consider our position,' the Jaevisk repeated. 'Firstly, there is the matter of replicating this device.' The Jaevisk looked down again at the object in its hand and was silent for a moment, as if awaiting instruction. Eventually, it raised its head and said, 'They will be delivered to you by an Axcebian Transport ship. Following this, we will contact you. You must do nothing to alert the Garran to your intentions until we speak again.'

Cassandra's smile faded. 'How long will *that* be?' She turned to look at Nell, whose suspicion was evident, before regarding the Jaevisk again. 'We've no intention of sitting on our hands while this thing kills millions of people and they just watch!'

'You must follow our instructions,' the alien pressed. 'If you do not, you will need someone else to relieve you of your suffering.' Calling their bluff, the Jaevisk even went so far as to hold out the metal device in its golden palm. Had anyone tried to take it, things would have been somewhat different.

Cassandra and Nell moved away and spoke amongst themselves. Other people were growing increasingly suspicious as the Jaevisk resumed its examination of the circular device in its huge hands. After a tense minute or two, Councillor Messina turned back to the alien. 'We...will wait,' Messina agreed, sealing the fate of all Humanity.

'You are now allied to us,' the Jaevisk replied. There was no mistaking the semantics. 'The Axcebian vessel will arrive in three days' time.'

'How can we trust the Axcebians not to tell the Garran about this?' General Matthews interrupted, perhaps forgetting his place. Indeed, Cassandra snapped, 'That's enough, General!' but he ignored her. 'How do you know they're not connected to this attack?' he continued. 'They deal regularly with the Garran.'

'You will leave such matters of...faith...to us,' came the cryptic reply. 'We are friends now.' The Jaevisk suddenly vanished, leaving a bewildered and unsettled gathering questioning the path upon which they tread.

Ω

'It's done,' said Conner. 'The Jaevisk have the disc.'
'So what do we do now?' asked Helen.

The Doctor came out of his office, and announced, 'I have the results.'

Conner was smiling as he turned to the Doctor and said, 'There's no need to be so afraid of the implications.'

'Don't tell me he's telling the truth,' Helen pleaded.

The Doctor nodded. 'He's definitely related to the Captain, that's for sure. Whether he came from the future or not is beyond these tests. Although there are some quantum level processes I could apply if I had the time...'

'You don't,' said Conner sharply. 'Your people have just resigned themselves to the will of the Jaevisk Society and they'll draw you into something so big your heads will be spinning for years to come.'

Helen stared at him for a moment. 'Where are you taking us?' she asked. 'What's out at that system that's so important?'

'You can dig out images from scopes monitoring the system, if you like,' said Conner. 'You'll see that the Jaevisk have had Warships out there for as long as you've been watching...and long before that.'

'Do they have something to do with what happened to that planet out there? I mean, you said the cage wasn't theirs, but are they behind the attack on Earth in some other way?'

'They're not behind the cage, no, but that doesn't mean they won't see it as an opportunity. As for that planet...well, there's no way they would do something like that.' He walked past her, heading for the exit. 'Kiranis is their world.'

Ω

'Captain, we're receiving a distress call. Oh, my God!'

Echad turned around sharply. 'What is it?'

'It's Commander Miller!' the officer gasped. 'We left them behind!'

'What are you talking about?' Echad snapped, walking up to him. 'I spoke to Sandra myself when she boarded.'

Another officer interrupted. 'The Lieutenant gave permission to retrieve the Corporal's body, Sir.'

'What? And no one thought to *inform* me?'

'I...was distracted, Captain.'

Echad stared at her for a moment. 'Liaise with Central Command. You will personally oversee the safe return of that team to Earth. Is that understood?'

'Yes, Sir. Sorry, Sir.'

'Yes, well, the next time you get distracted, you'll be relieved of duty. Now get to work.' Echad watched the young woman rush back to her station. He was desperate to find Anya and hold her in his arms, to be sure that she was safe. Incompetent staff did little for his confidence in the situation, and he found himself recalling his dream of a skeleton crew. At least they did what they were told.

Ω

Matthews sipped a drink and gestured to a chair as Cana was shown into the General's quarters. 'Take a seat,' said the General.

Cana did so and looked around. A number of shifting VR screens on the walls displayed images of Earth from orbit, passing military and civilian vessels and the many stations and satellites which had filled the orbital belt before the arrival of the cage. What caught Cana's eye, however, was a painting, a stunning canvas with Jerusalem's 'Dome of the Rock' in the centre. One word was repeated in beautiful calligraphy, in Arabic at the top left, Hebrew at the top right and in English at the bottom centre. That word was *'Peace'*. Cana smiled. 'This is...beautiful,' he said, turning to the General. 'I didn't take you for a religious man.'

Matthews shrugged. 'One doesn't have to subscribe to organisations to have faith.'

'And do you have faith?' Cana asked he sat down and reached for a drink offered by the General.

'I have faith in mankind's ability to overcome anything that comes our way. Whether we do that by divine intervention or through our own means...' he shrugged again. 'Who am I to say?'

'Some might say that our own means are divine intervention at work. We don't need a lightning bolt to start a fire.'

Matthews chuckled softly. 'True. If we're designed to fend for ourselves, then our actions are a result of that design, and our abilities are indebted to our designer.'

Cana sipped the drink and held the General's gaze. A smile formed on his face. 'But you don't believe that, do you?'

'People say a lot of things, son,' said Matthews, feeling every inch like the wise old man. 'If I say I believe, will you believe that I do? And if I say I don't, how do you know that I'm telling the truth?'

'Why would you lie?'

'Because my mind is my own, and I feel no inclination to share it with others. Hierarchical religions suppress individuality.'

'That's a harsh statement to make!' Cana exclaimed. 'Some psychologists say that being part of something greater than yourself gives you a greater sense of purpose and potential. The possible chaos of a non-conformist or rebellious individuality would be kept in check by realising your place in a larger community.'

The General laughed again, but it was a darker thing. 'You're not on a recruitment drive, son, and I'll thank you to remember your place!'

Cana nodded, contrite, as Matthews resumed, 'Now, tell me about this man you were talking to. This...Presbyter.'

Cana relented, aware of his own place in this particular community. 'He's one of many Church leaders around the world. The title was taken as a tribute to the early leaders of the Christian movement. From your point of view, the Presbyter I spoke with was of no greater significance than any other. But he was my tutor for seven years, and I respect him.'

Matthews nodded. 'Tell me about the Rubidium. Is he in the same boat as you?'

'Every member of the Church has elevated levels of Rubidium in their body. We don't know why this is, but it's become something of an entry pass. Membership comes only with the Rubidium, and everyone with it...*everyone*...' Cana added pointedly, 'is a member of the Church.'

'I don't understand,' Matthews admitted, his eyebrows furrowed. 'Are you saying the Church tracks them down?'

'That's exactly what I'm saying, and it also monitors births. We've seen babies born to Church members whose levels are fine one day, and way up the next. For whatever reason, every member for as far back as we can examine has what should be dangerously high levels of Rubidium in their system.'

'But there's no negative reaction to it...medically, I mean?'

'No. Neither is there a perceivable benefit to any of us.' Cana laughed darkly. 'I sometimes have nightmares where I burst into flames and I'm breathing fire on everyone, roaring that it's all their fault.'

Matthews caught a glimpse of moisture at the edge of the young man's eyes. 'How has the Church kept this a secret?' he asked. 'I mean, surely it's shown in scans, or if you're in hospital for blood tests?' Now it was Matthews who laughed. 'What about metal detectors?'

Cana grinned. 'We're taught from a very early age to be careful about revealing this. If an accident happens, someone always covers it up or happens to bump into a fellow member. Private Church-assigned doctors deal with every sick member throughout their life. We've also spent a long, long time trying to find a way of reducing the levels to the norm. Radiation, lasers...even nano-technology. Ironic, I know. Everything works only temporarily and the Rubidium re-asserts itself. It may be genetic modification, or natural mutation, but whatever is...well...are you aware of our theology, General?'

Matthews said nothing, but gestured for him to continue.

'Well, the Church...' Cana resumed, 'like most religions do when faced with questions they can't answer...integrated this particular problem into our theological framework. They came to the conclusion that every member is descended from one person who first showed signs of this...deformity, if you ask me.'

'You didn't sound so dismissive with the Presbyter, Cana. Matter of fact, I thought I was witnessing nothing short of religious zeal in that conversation.'

'Yes, well, until today, we had no idea of a purpose for the Rubidium, let alone that someone out there had a plan for us. It would be nice to think I'm not going to spontaneously combust one day.'

'So that's how you see it now? A plan...with theological undertones?'

Cana shrugged. 'If the Church of the New Elect actively seeks out people with these levels of Rubidium, then the consequences of having them must be important.'

Matthews thought for a moment. 'The New Elect,' he mused. 'Didn't the early Christians think of themselves as the new elect?'

'Yes, they did, but within the context of Judaism. It was a Jewish concept of being the people chosen to survive an apocalypse-type event which was appropriated by the Christian Church. They considered it a new covenant...a new testament.'

'So you just usurped Christian theology?'

Cana laughed. 'That's putting it very simply, General. The Church believes that its members are chosen to guide Humanity towards the rejuvenation of Earth, a re-creation of our world, but not through some supernatural judgement of Humanity's good and evil.'

'You can't possibly think that a cage around the planet is the means by which the world will be re-created?' Matthews stood and

51

stretched his tired body. 'And how could rejuvenation of the chosen begin with the specific targeting of them by a multitude of nano-bots?'

Cana smiled. 'God works in mysterious ways, General.'

'*God*?' Now Matthews smiled. 'I'm not completely ignorant of your theology, Cana. I happen to know that your Church doesn't believe in any form of personified deity, abstract or particular, and that even the notion of a single god escapes your theology.'

Cana finished his drink. 'Who have you been talking to, General? The Lieutenant from the bridge? Cos I can tell you that she –'

'Look, son, I've been doing this a long time,' Matthews interrupted, shaking his head. 'I have access to lines of information you can't imagine.' Placing his hands on either side of Cana's chair, he leaned close to him, staring into his eyes. 'Speaking of lines...' he whispered.

'Please, General...' Cana begged. 'Don't!'

Matthews conceded, moving away from the young man as he realised that he needed to hear no more. 'You can go now.'

Cana rose from his chair, considerably more subdued as he made his way to the door. Matthews had hinted at his knowledge of things which had long been kept from outsiders. And still he was not finished. 'One more question,' he said. Cana turned, waiting. 'If this attack is indeed part of the great plan for your Church, what will you do?'

'I don't understand,' Cana lied.

'Of course you do. You're up here, where this...nano-virus won't get you. You said it yourself in your transmission. The people murdered up here were killed because the virus won't reach them. You'll survive whatever's going to happen.'

Cana lowered his gaze, reluctant to show his panic at the thought. He had realised since learning of the Church's involvement in the murders that he would have to get down to Earth. He had to maintain his loyalty to the Church. 'Cana?' He looked up and saw the General gazing at the picture of Jerusalem. 'If it's what you think you have to do,' said Matthews, 'you can leave. There's a shuttle going down in a couple of hours.'

Without saying a word, Cana turned to the door and walked out. Matthews sighed as the door closed, keeping his eyes on the painting. 'God bless,' he whispered.

Ω

Back in Cassandra's apartment, Nell sat watching the woman she loved as she prayed. Kneeling on the floor beside the bed, eyes closed and hands clasped together before her, Cassandra whispered her devotion like a child at bedtime. Her devotion bordered on fanatic zeal lately, and Nell had for a long time dismissed it all as either fantasy or political exploitation. Cassandra had spent some time in the major religious regions of the world over the years, speaking of searching for answers and truth and guidance and other such arbitrary paradigms beloved by the spiritual voters. However, things felt different today, and it was only now that Nell was beginning to believe that Cassandra's storehouse of knowledge extended beyond the grasp of even an influential and powerful member of the Council. 'I have some questions,' said Nell, breaking the meditative silence.

Cassandra opened her eyes, her gaze piercing Nell's soul. 'I thought you might.'

Nell walked to the bed and sat down as Cassandra rose from her knees. 'You really believe that you're talking to God, don't you?'

Cassandra sat beside her. 'I know I am,' she declared. 'Everything He's told me has happened and I know that He'll continue to guide me through this.'

'I don't mean to offend you, Cass, but what makes you worthy of divine intervention? You sent people up to the cage to get that little disc. I mean, how is it that a telepath didn't know he was being *watched*? And besides that...how did you know anything about him or what he had stuck in his head...or that he'd take it *out*?'

Cassandra smiled and nodded. 'You're right, Nell,' she said, putting her arm around her. 'God informs me and guides me and...intervenes to make sure I can do what He wants done.'

'And what does he want done?'

The arm was removed. 'I'd appreciate it if you dropped the sceptical tone, Nell.'

'It's a valid question,' Nell pressed. 'Or are you not privy to the consequences of your actions?'

She sniffed arrogantly and stood up. 'Mankind is incapable of grasping the enormity of such things, Nell. You and I are nothing but pawns in God's great scheme.'

Nell watched her walk away towards the bathroom. 'That's a load of crap if ever I heard it, Cass,' she called after her. 'Why would someone like you willingly do things without knowing or caring about the consequences?'

'Someone like me, Nell?' Cassandra called back above the sound of running water. 'Care to elaborate?'

'You've never done anything that didn't suit your own advancement in life. You forget how long I've known you...how long I've watched you.'

Cassandra emerged from the bathroom with a towel, drying her face and her hands. 'I don't forget anything, Nell,' she reminded her. 'That's my problem. In fact...' she threw the towel on the bed and walked past it, 'I remember you telling me that I could do with some religion.'

'Very funny. You know what I meant. This is...'

'Is what, Nell?' snapped Cassandra, turning on her. 'This is *what*?'

Nell stood up straight, angry now. 'It's *frightening*, Cass! You're hearing voices and having visions, following the instructions of some imaginary person. You're making decisions that will affect billions of lives every day and you just dismiss it all as something none of us simple folk would understand. That's politics, *Councillor*, not religion!'

To Nell's surprise, Cassandra was temporarily lost for words. Of course, she was shocked by Nell's fervour, but the situation called for such emotion. However, Cassandra was the sort of person who sought at all times to do the opposite of what was expected. So, to Nell's greater surprise, she smiled and said, 'Politics and religion are one and the same, Nell. They both seek to tie the hands of the simple man...or woman...by keeping the secrets of the world beyond their grasp. My situation, however, is different.'

'How?' Nell approached her and looked right in her eyes. 'Tell me how.'

Cassandra sighed, and her vulnerability showed again. This time, however, Nell was not sure whether she should believe it or not. 'I've been in politics for a long time, Nell, as you well know. Rising to my position ultimately and inevitably meant that others fell beneath me. But that's the beauty and the curse of success. You don't know what it's like to be so influential and powerful in your circle that others fear to contest you, and there is no one above you to put you in your place when you cross the line.'

Nell sneered and shook her head. 'How terrible for you,' she mocked.

Cassandra took her hand and kissed it, forgiving her attack. 'I finally found someone above me, Nell,' she explained with reverence in her voice. 'Someone whose power is beyond mine and whose understanding of the world is so far beyond my grasp that I shiver to think of the insignificance of my life.'

'And you enjoy that?'

'You know me, Nell. I'm a woman who needs to feel humbled from time to time. My position as Councillor doesn't allow that. But my work for God does.'

Nell stepped back. 'I don't believe that, Cass. Firstly, this path you took to find who you call God was through the Church of the New Elect, an organisation whose membership depends entirely upon that problem with your blood. We know they don't even think of their deity the way you do.'

'I'm not responsible for the path that led me to the truth.'

Nell laughed scornfully. 'More nonsense! I think your...*work* for God, if that's what you want to call it, gives you an even greater sense of superiority by singling you out from the rest of Humanity.'

Cassandra shrugged. 'Maybe,' she admitted candidly. 'It doesn't matter now.'

'It doesn't *matter*? Do you even *hear* what comes out of your mouth?'

'I want you to leave now, Nell.' Cassandra turned her back. 'If I need you, I'll call you.'

'Don't bother,' said Nell, her face softened only by tears. 'I've had enough of being your plaything!' She could not see the tears on Cassandra's face. 'What worries me is that when history recounts what happened here, I'll be associated with *you*.' She laughed again. 'Of course, I'll be lucky to be in a footnote!' She headed towards the door, and Cassandra turned her head to watch her leave. She wanted to stop her. She wanted to call out and tell her how much she needed her and loved her. As Nell closed the door behind her, Cassandra said quietly, 'I'm so sorry, Nell.'

Ω

Doctor Aidan Greene was finishing some reports in his office when he was interrupted by a knock on the door. 'Come in,' he called.

A very tall woman, in her mid-thirties and dressed casually, entered the room and looked around. 'Good evening, Doctor.'

55

'Good evening,' he greeted her, looking up. She must have been close to two metres tall. 'My secretary's gone home, but if you'd like to make an appointment...'

'No, thank you, Doctor. I'm here to speak to you, not to be administered to.' She sat in the chair against the wall opposite the desk and looked around again as she crossed her long legs.

The doctor shut down the computer on his desk as he asked, 'About something in particular?'

'About everything in particular, Doctor,' she replied with detached mystery. 'Are you familiar with a woman named Cassandra Messina?'

Doctor Greene held the woman in his gaze for a little while. 'Who are you?' he demanded eventually. 'What do you want?'

'I represent a group of people who are...interested in this situation in which we find ourselves.'

'Considering what's going on, that could mean anyone. I think you should leave.'

She ignored the suggestion. 'We understand that you're due to be appointed to a new position, Doctor.'

'It's hardly that,' he argued. 'The Council need my assistance in combating this...attack.'

'Is this an attack, Doctor?'

'Don't patronise me. That thing up in orbit is due to...close or activate or whatever, and some kind of virus spewing out from it has infected people all over the world. Of course it's an attack!'

'Not everyone thinks as you do, Doctor. Some believe what's happening is a good thing.'

'I find that difficult to believe.'

She nodded slowly. 'Nevertheless, it's true. Anyway, I'm here to ask a favour of you.'

'A favour? This should be good!'

'Oh, it is. You see, I want you to allow me in your operating room during the surgery on Councillor Messina.'

Greene rose from his chair, but the woman remained confidently seated. 'My appointment to that procedure hasn't been made public,' he declared.

'We're not the public, Doctor.'

He thought for a moment, wishing that someone would walk in and disturb the conversation. 'There's no way I'd permit an unknown factor in my operating theatre.'

'I assure you that I know what I'm doing, and I won't compromise the procedure. I can also assure you, Doctor, that you don't want to go against us on this.'

'I don't even know who you are.'

'And it's going to stay that way. Bigger things are happening here, Doctor, and you need to realise your role. There's always a larger picture, but ultimately it's comprised of smaller pieces.'

'An inspiring analogy, I'm sure. Perhaps if you enlightened me...?'

'Like I said, not everyone considers this virus an attack. The Church, for one.'

'Which Church? The New Elect?'

'Yes. They'll try to stop the procedure from taking place. Now, I don't need to tell you that millions of people will die if that happens.'

'We don't know that for sure.'

'*We* do.'

Greene sat down again, deflated. 'Look, I haven't even seen this virus yet. I don't know what I'm up against and the Jaevisk device I'm implanting in Messina's head has me at a loss.'

'Messina's the one who's done her homework. She acquired the device and gave it to the Jaevisk. Let her bear the brunt of the unknown. You and I have to make sure the procedure goes ahead. We can't let these people die.'

'How do I know I can trust you?'

She smiled sweetly. 'Don't worry, Doctor. We're the good guys.'

Ω

Cassandra dropped to her knees again beside her bed. Tears streamed down her face and she sobbed as she pleaded with her unseen guide. 'Tell me I did the right thing,' she called out. 'Tell me that hurting her like that was worth something.'

'It was,' a disembodied voice replied. It was a man's voice, deep and resounding, strong and sure. She felt calmed even as she heard it. 'But she still has a choice to make. Her love for you is strong.'

Cassandra nodded, smiling gratefully. 'And mine for her.'

'The virus has begun killing people and I can't protect you any longer. Many people know you're one of the New Elect, so suspicion will grow once the general population realise only members of the Church are afflicted and see that *you're* not suffering.'

57

She nodded again. 'I understand. When can I leave?'

'Not until the Jaevisk devices are here. You will volunteer to be the first subject, Cassandra, and you'll have the original disc inserted.'

'How will they be sure of that? What if the Jaevisk don't return the original?'

'They will. I have seen to it.'

Cassandra nodded once more, and she fell into silence for a time. The voice did not disturb her thoughts, but rather waited for her to articulate them. 'I'm...afraid,' she admitted. 'Nell was right. It's not like me to do things without considering the consequences.'

'And yet you accept that I cannot reveal them to you?'

'Yes. But perhaps you could...reveal yourself?'

'You believe I have form? Something you could perceive?'

'I...I'm not sure. Do you?' There was no reply, but Cassandra sensed that something had changed in the room. There was a presence behind her, and she steeled herself, breathing deeply and slowly before turning. In the dim light of her apartment, from where she knelt in supplication, she saw at eye level an even darker material rippling in the faint breeze of the air-conditioning. She realised she was looking at black robes of some kind, and her eyes followed the material upwards until she could see two creatures there, seemingly moving within and upon the garment. They were dragons, one of gold, the other silver, and she was sure they watched her with their silken eyes. A hand was offered to her but she did not take it, choosing to rise to her feet of her own volition. Then she saw him.

'You're...a man,' she gasped. His dark eyes regarded her amidst a strong face with stubble-lined jaws that seemed to mimic curving incisors. His hair was shaved close to his scalp, but his soft lips and smile and the kindness even within those dark eyes belied the severity of his features. 'What did you expect?' he asked her playfully.

'I...don't know. God?'

'Did I say I was God, Cassandra?'

'No,' she admitted. 'But I just thought...' She smiled, embarrassed, but the smile swiftly faded. 'Then who are you?' she wondered, suddenly afraid. 'Oh, no...Nell was right.'

'Not exactly,' the man told her. 'She thought I was imaginary.'

'Aren't you?' Cassandra stepped back, feeling the bed against her legs. 'I mean, you must be. I've gone mad.'

He shook his head. 'Most people call me the Prophet. I'm from a world and a time that I'm trying to help you reach.'

'Me?'

'Everyone, Cassandra.'

'Why?'

'I can't tell you that.' The Prophet watched her as she backed away from him. She glanced at the wall, seeing that the air-conditioning control was switched off. 'You're not real,' she said. 'Nell was right. *I'm* right. I've gone insane!'

The Prophet laughed. 'Consider what you're saying, Cassandra. If everything I've told you has happened...and I'm not real...then you predicted it. Do you really believe you can see the future?'

She turned around to face him. The full-length cloak of black still rippled as if blown by air. The dragons still played on it. 'That's more likely than a man turning up in my bedroom with dragons moving around on his clothes!' she snapped.

Again, the Prophet laughed. 'You're right, it is,' he said, 'so for now I'll let you go along with that hypothesis. Regardless, you need to listen to me, if only as the personification of your ability to tell the future. Shortly after the Jaevisk devices are active, you must contact them and ask them to take you after the *Nostradamus*. You'll be in a hurry to leave, and you've already arranged to have the ship tracked. The Jaevisk will help you once you tell them who Captain Echad allowed on board.'

'What will happen when they find the *Nostradamus*?'

'Do you have faith in your significance, Cassandra?' the Prophet asked, ignoring her question. 'Do you believe that everything you're doing is for a greater good?'

Cassandra held his gaze, although she could not see his eyes from this side of the room. Doubt was creeping in and flooding her confidence, but she laughed inwardly and fought it back, no longer caring whether she was insane or whether God was testing her faith, for now there was no turning back. 'I believe,' she lied, just as there was a knock on her door.

The Prophet grinned, for he knew her thoughts. 'You will,' he promised her, before he vanished.

Ω

Sandra gave up listening to the static on her Com unit and swore. 'We should get to that control room we were in last time,' she suggested. 'We might be able to get Central on the line, cos we sure as hell aren't getting the *Nostradamus*.'

'This is *bull*!' snapped Joshua Colle, as he slammed the butt of his rifle against the wall. 'How could they just *forget* about us?'

'We don't know what happened,' Sandra reminded him calmly. 'That guy who killed Will had some sort of hold over the Captain.'

'Yeah, well, Echad better have a good explanation when we see him again.'

Sandra turned to him. '*If* we see him again. Let's just focus on getting out of here, okay?'

Jason Archer was transfixed by something farther down the corridor. 'What the hell is that?' he said quietly, moving away with his rifle at the ready. A figure in the shadows darted out of sight, prompting Jason to shout, 'Hey!' before breaking into pursuit.

'Archer!' Sandra snapped as he ran off.

'Kid's gonna get us killed,' Colle remarked dryly as they set off after him.

'You were a cadet once,' Sandra reminded him.

When they caught up with him in the dark corridor, he was standing at a closed door, waiting for them. 'Someone went in here,' he whispered defensively, noting their angry glares.

'I don't care,' Sandra told him, her heart pounding. 'You don't run off like that...got it?'

He nodded. 'I just figured there's not supposed to be anyone else up here. We're the only recon team left.'

'Okay, so we've got another stowaway,' Sandra agreed. 'Let's see if this one can give us some answers.' The door opened as if on cue, and they stood looking at what had to be an elevator car.

'Oh, this looks like fun,' said Colle. As Sandra weighed their options, the corridor was sealed off on either side of them by swiftly descending doors. She and Colle looked at Jason, who sheepishly shrugged by way of an apology. Without another word, they entered the elevator and the car began its rapid ascent. With no display inside the elevator, there was no way to determine how they should proceed once they exited. It was a problem swiftly solved, and in the same way as before. Bulkhead doors to their right were sealed while the elevator closed behind them. Then Sandra heard the sound of whistling coming from down the corridor. 'This guy's playing with us.'

'He's certainly not leaving us with any choices,' Colle agreed, looking into the dark corridor. He turned back to Sandra. 'You wanna keep going?' he asked her.

She did not, but Colle was right. There was little choice. 'What do you think, Jase?' she asked, turning to the youngest of them. 'Should we go on?'

He stared at her for a moment, uncomfortable with the burden of decision. 'I want to know what's going on,' he replied carefully. 'We could be near the top of this thing, for all we know, and that's where Central was focusing all their attention.'

Colle nodded. 'Sounds like a plan to me.'

There was the sound of someone whistling again, and they all heard it this time. 'We're being led around by the nose here, guys,' Sandra argued. 'You really think Whistlin' Dixie up there's on our side?'

Colle chuckled darkly, almost tempted to correct her misuse of the old saying. 'There's only one way to find out,' he said, as he pointedly brandished his gun and took the lead. 'Onwards and upwards!'

Ω

Cassandra opened the door and stepped back in shock or, at least, a sufficient pretence of shock, as soldiers pushed into her apartment. Closely followed by a tall, white-haired man in a pale blue uniform with gold stripes on the shoulders, the soldiers spread out to surround the Councillor. She looked around at them before turning to the older man. 'What is the meaning of this?' she snapped. 'Under whose authority do you burst into my home in the middle of the night?'

'Why...yours, Councillor,' the man replied with a casual smile. 'Or rather, the authority of the Council, by way of laws you set down. My name is – '

'I know who you are, Pontifex Harrogate. I attended your appointment ceremony.'

'Of course, that's right, you did.' Harrogate beamed, looking up at the ceiling as the memories came flooding back. 'Yes, I recall that wonderful red number you wore that day.' He looked back at her. 'You were quite stunning.'

61

Cassandra attempted to dismiss his charms, but she failed and found herself grinning as she turned her back to pour herself a drink. 'Can I get you anything?' she asked.

'No, thank you, Councillor,' Harrogate replied. 'I'm quite run off my feet lately. I'm here to deliver a simple message, and I truly hope you'll appreciate its importance.'

Cassandra sipped her water and kept her back to him. 'I'm sure a man as eloquent as yourself will have no problem getting his point across.'

'Good of you to say, Councillor. With that in mind, I'll get straight to it.' He approached her and she turned to find herself looking at a completely different expression. He was glaring at her, clearly suppressing his distaste for her actions as he spoke: 'I am here as a representative of the Eurasian Council, in my full capacity as Pontifex. You, Councillor Cassandra Messina, are to remain in this property under armed guard until such time as you are brought to trial for treason.'

She held his fiery gaze with one of her own. 'My dealings with the Jaevisk Society will help save millions of lives,' she argued through gritted teeth. 'Your short-sightedness will do the opposite.'

'Your...dealings with the Jaevisk are another matter entirely, Councillor. Central monitored your communication with Captain Echad of the *Nostradamus*. You ordered him to allow an invading force onto his ship, a man who murdered one of their men.'

Cassandra laughed at the Pontifex. 'An invading force?' she sneered. 'If it wasn't for that man and the technology we obtained from him, you'd have a lot more deaths on your hands.'

Harrogate stepped closer again. 'That man was in that...thing up there,' he reminded her angrily. 'He's inextricably linked to this attack and you facilitated his escape. Don't try our patience, Councillor. You're already facing severe penalties for your crimes, but execution is always an option.'

There was a moment of silence and Cassandra sipped her water again. 'How long will this...house arrest last?'

The Pontifex took a deep breath and stepped back, smoothing the front of his uniform and regaining his composure. He smiled calmly. 'As soon as this situation has passed, you'll face trial,' he promised her. 'I'm sure everything will proceed with the utmost concern for the law and the citizens of Earth.' He turned away from her, instructing the soldiers to station themselves outside. 'You will, of course, be permitted certain visitors, Councillor,' he called back to her. 'Please submit a list to my office, where it will undoubtedly struggle to reach the top of my to-do pile.'

'You're enjoying this, aren't you, John?'

Pontifex Harrogate stopped and waited for the soldiers to exit before turning to reply, 'Please, Councillor, I'm simply doing my job.'

Cassandra smiled thinly. 'Oh, I'm sure there's a certain satisfaction in this for you.'

Harrogate moved back to stand close to her. 'Councillor Messina...' he said, leaning in so that he could whisper in her ear, 'you have no idea.'

Ω

Colle and the others had reached the top of the cage, but the enclosed corridors of the structure did not allow them the luxury of that knowledge. After spending the better part of an hour feeling like lab rats in a twisted experiment, they found themselves standing in front of a huge door with a two-metre-tall glass panel in the centre. On the other side was the figure they had been pursuing, a tall man in a long black cloak who simply stood with his back to them, waiting. 'What now?' asked Archer.

Sandra kept looking through the glass. 'This is just creepy,' she said.

'There's no control panel,' remarked Colle. 'I don't see how we can get this door open.'

'He'll open it,' Sandra said, nodding with conviction as she turned from the glass to face them. 'He wants us in there with him.'

'Well...*that's* enough reason to go in!' said Colle, sarcastically.

Sandra's eyebrows rose as she looked at him. 'What happened to onwards and upwards?'

He grinned. 'Changed my mind. Downwards and backwards sounds much more appealing.' The door hissed and there was the sound of mechanised bolts sliding open. As the door began to rise, Colle took another look through the window. 'What a surprise...he's gone,' he said. 'Friggin' cat and mouse is starting to get to me.'

Sandra gestured for them to move back as the door opened. Before it had ascended half way, they were able to enter the room. Sandra took point, switching on her rifle-mounted torch to illuminate the dimly lit room as she moved in. 'Wait,' said Archer, and they turned to him. 'What if this door closes behind us? What if we're trapped in here?'

'Valid question,' said Colle. Sandra turned around and nodded in agreement. 'Hey...I'm open to suggestions,' she told them.

Colle looked into the room, still standing on the threshold as the door completed its ascent. 'I got nothing,' he admitted. 'Everything's closed behind us and seeing this through still seems like the only way to figure out what's going on.'

'Yeah,' said Sandra, moving farther in. She turned to her left and then to her right, shining the torch in those directions. 'Looks like there are a few more exits, but this room sure goes on. It's enormous.' She turned around as Jason entered the room and the two of them waited for Colle. He took a deep breath. 'Ever get the feeling your entire life was about to change?' he asked, taking a few steps forward. The door slammed shut behind him and Sandra and Jason ran back to it. Colle did not even turn around. It was not until every possible exit from the room was sealed and the lighting level ascended that he realised just how profound his observation had been.

The figure in the black cloak was standing on a platform opposite them, at the apex of a vast triangular room in which myriad forms of equipment for monitoring, controlling and maintaining the operations of the structure were arrayed. The distant walls to the left and right of the team were completely transparent, and they realised that only an energy field separated them from the vacuum of space.

The man had short black hair, black stubble-lined jaws and dark eyes. He wore a full-length cloak upon which two dragons played, and he smiled at the three soldiers and the weapons and torches pointed at him. With outstretched arms, he drew their attention to the room and the strange equipment therein, saying proudly, 'Welcome to your future.'

$$\Omega$$

'Central's lost all thermal imaging, Captain,' one of the Science Team on the *Nostradamus* reported. Echad was about to ask for an explanation when Lieutenant Morris returned to the bridge with their guest in tow. She glanced at him, nodded, and walked to the Briefing Room. Conner made to follow her, but then stopped. 'Captain,' he called.

Echad looked at him but did not reply. Conner nodded. 'I know,' he assured the Captain. 'I'll bring you to her now.'

Helen had stopped outside the door of the Briefing Room. 'What's happening?' she asked, addressing the crew member at the back of the bridge. Echad turned to her. 'They're trying to find the recon team you left behind, Lieutenant. Maybe you'd be so good as to help them out.'

Helen stood with her eyes wide and mouth open, surprising herself by not responding as the two men left the bridge. The Communications Officer called her: 'Lieutenant?'

'Yes, Kel,' she replied, turning to her. 'What's happening?'

'I've been on with Central for the past few hours. They had Sandra and the guys on thermal imaging up until five or six minutes ago, their time.'

'What's the delay on the com feed?'

'Approaching eleven minutes. But we're about to clear the system and jump to full speed, so we'll be hours out of sync before we know it.'

Helen pressed two fingers against her right temple. 'You think we've lost them?'

'No way to tell, Lieutenant. Central losing them on thermal doesn't mean much on its own. It's just...' Kel hesitated.

'What?' Helen demanded, making her way to the Com station. Kel handed a holosheet to the Lieutenant as she explained: 'We just got this across the wire. Looks like they're about to start nuclear strikes on the cage.'

Helen read the reports from the military grapevine. 'That's it, then,' she said, returning the holosheet, 'we've lost them.' As she made her way back to her command chair, she corrected herself quietly: 'I've lost them.'

THE SECOND DAY

By the end of the first day, the virus had claimed tens of thousands of lives. As the death toll rapidly increased, Earth's military hierarchies ignored their political overlords and launched an attack on the cage. With the sun rising over western Europe on the second day, the bombardment commenced. Nuclear warheads rocketed skywards in their thousands from installations around the globe. Laser-guided tactical missiles and heavy extra-gravity artillery illuminated the vacuum between the atmosphere and the cage as they pounded the presumed weak spots of the planet-side interior of the structure. As the hours went by, the assault tactics were altered to accommodate various command suggestions. There were more intense bombardments upon specific areas of the still disconnected structure, and the passing hours saw further alterations to the attack plan as all guided weaponry, from every part of the world, targeted the apparent controlling area at the northern zenith. Although none of this caused anything amounting to structural damage, this specific targeting did not sit well with those trapped inside.

'Can you *believe* this?' Colle shouted, running to one of the energy walls as the attack began. The huge room was illuminated by the silent explosions outside. 'I mean, how much longer can this go on?' He stood at the window with his arms outstretched. 'Hey, you stupid bastards!' he shouted. 'Think you could get any closer? I got an itch needs scratching!'

'Colle, get back from there!' Sandra snapped at him. With her weapon lowered, she returned her attention to the man in black. 'Are we safe in here?' she asked.

He nodded. 'Believe me, they're not even damaging the paintwork.' He stepped down and walked over to Joshua Colle. 'An impressive sight, isn't it?'

Colle found himself laughing. Despite the bizarre and dangerous situation in which they found themselves, he could not help but agree. 'It's...something else,' he said. In addition to the many missiles impacting on the sections visible from his vantage point, he could see battleships and small strike craft everywhere, manoeuvring in the one-sided battlefield between the cage and the planet.

'Why did you bring us here?' asked Sandra, joining them at the energy wall. She was feeling inexplicably calm, with no inclination to attack their strange captor. 'I mean, that's what happened, right?'

'Yes,' he replied, turning to see that Jason was still standing in the same place, and still pointing his gun at him. He chuckled. 'It's alright, Jason,' he assured him calmly. 'The three of you are in absolutely no danger. As a matter of fact, you're currently the safest Human beings in the universe.'

'I'm not sure I like the sound of that,' remarked Colle, turning from the wall. Futile explosions illuminated the scene behind them, throwing only three shadows across the floor. 'Are you responsible for this attack?'

The man toyed with that idea for a moment, shrugging his shoulders. 'It's not that simple,' he told them. 'And it's not exactly an attack. Do you see the cage responding? You've lost no one to any weaponry.'

'I heard there's some kind of virus on the planet,' Jason argued. 'You don't have to see a weapon to die from it.'

The man pointed at him in a congratulatory fashion. 'I like that. Very profound.'

'Maybe you should quit stalling and answer the question,' said Sandra impatiently. 'Why are we here?'

'And who are you?' put in Colle.

'And how do you know our names?' Jason added, still refusing to lower his gun.

The man laughed aloud. It was an arrogant sound, but he raised his hands and shook his head. 'I apologise. You're right, I've been rude. You may call me Naveen.'

'Give me a good reason not to kill you,' Jason threatened him.

Naveen seemed unperturbed. 'You have every reason to try, Jason,' he agreed. 'But even more reason to listen and learn.' He walked back to the centre of the room. 'The three of you,' he began, with his back to them, 'are going to be here for the rest of your lives.' He turned as he reached the top of the platform upon which he had previously stood. 'And I suggest you acclimatize to that notion before dealing with anything else.'

'I don't think so!' growled Jason. He made to fire as Sandra and Colle shouted, 'No!' but nothing seemed to happen as the trigger mechanism clicked pointedly. Naveen simply looked disappointed, as if his children had shamed him. 'As I said...you need to settle in and prepare for your work here.'

Colle looked at Sandra and then at the dark man. 'Work?' he managed to ask. 'What sort of work?'

'Well, I like to think of your job title as...' he looked beyond the energy wall for a brief moment. Then he smiled, nodding and turning back to them. 'Observers,' he finished. Without another word, or time for another question, he vanished.

Jason screamed 'NO!' as he fired repeatedly at the space in which the man had stood. Sandra watched the gunfire cross the room to shoot up the monitors and consoles there, illuminating other strange equipment around the room with the light from the mini explosions. Colle turned back to watch the continuing attack from Earth, his home, the world upon which he knew that he would never again set foot.

Ω

Anya was exhausted and the heat of the engine room was slowly killing her. Her body ached and tears had long since dried on her cheeks. She was sitting in a pool of her own urine while perspiration seemed to have drawn all fluid from her body. Her humiliation was total, and her shame unbearable. She cried out as the door opened and light flooded in. 'Help me, please!' she whimpered. But when she saw that it was Conner, the tears began anew.

'Anya, it's okay.' She heard Adam's voice, but she could see only her captor. Her head dropped and she sobbed, until Adam lifted her chin and looked into her eyes. 'It's me, Anya...Adam,' he told her softly. 'Are you hurt?'

She stared at him, thinking she was delirious. But as she looked beyond him, she saw her captor standing behind. 'He's...there!' she moaned. 'Behind you.'

Adam did not look back. 'I know,' he whispered. 'It's okay now. You're safe.'

Conner turned away with guilt and shame in his face as the Captain undid the clamps at her wrists. 'No!' she gasped. 'It's a bomb!'

'There's nothing there, Anya,' Adam assured her. 'Just clamps from the Brig.'

Anya was horrified. 'But he said...' She broke down and Adam held her close. He managed to turn his head enough to see Conner. 'What the hell is *wrong* with you?' he accused him. 'How could you *do* this?'

68

Conner briefly glanced at the Captain, but could not reply. Instead, he walked away and left them together in their agony and relief.

As Conner crossed the threshold, he found that he was not on the ship anymore. Instead, he was walking across a grassy plain towards a snow-covered expanse. And he was not alone. 'I was wondering when you'd show your face again,' he said, turning to see the Prophet standing there.

The Prophet was looking up at the clear sky. 'It's always strange seeing Kiranis like this, I think,' he commented casually. 'I've become so accustomed to...a different perspective.'

'You mean with the cage around it?'

The Prophet made to reply, hesitated and chuckled softly. 'Yes...that's what I mean.' He grinned. 'Tell me, how does it feel to be the bad guy?'

'I did what I had to do.'

'You're learning,' the Prophet congratulated him. 'We're not so different, you and I. You could almost say we're like...kindred spirits.'

'I'm nothing like you!' Conner argued. 'Your actions far outweigh anything I've done or will ever do.'

'Ah, but that's only determined by the scope of your abilities. If you could do what I can...' He took a deep breath and then his body shook with mock delight. 'Ooh, the power, Conner. You have no idea!'

Conner held his gaze for a moment, trying to touch his mind but getting nowhere. 'I'll find a way,' he promised him confidently. 'I'll get home...and I'll stop you.'

The Prophet laughed with genuine amusement. 'Conner, Conner, Conner...' he taunted him. 'Look around you. What do you see?'

Conner did so. Behind the Prophet, the plains stretched off into the distance. Turning around, he followed the vista of snow to the site of a distant mountain towering above everything on this part of the planet. 'This is Kiranis,' he replied. 'That's the mountain where those...creatures are.' He turned back to the Prophet. 'And you're the one who thinks he's a god.'

The Prophet's smile faded. 'What do you not see, Conner?' he asked, his voice darker.

'The cage...' said Conner. 'But that's because it's not here. It's at Earth.'

'Is it?' the Prophet challenged. 'And are you *here*? You *think* you are.' He stepped closer. 'Don't think for one second that you are anywhere near as powerful as I am. None of your kind are. It won't be long now until you meet the Kwaios. Knowing what you know about them...and knowing that I've brought them to their knees many times...how can you possibly think you can stop me?'

Conner was silent. He had no answer. The scene faded until he once again found himself standing outside the engine room. Behind him, the door opened and Adam was carrying Anya. Conner reached out to help but Anya gasped and twisted her body away from him. 'I think you've done enough damage,' the Captain told him. 'Why don't you go to the bridge and help Helen get us to this place you came from?'

Conner watched them walk away, feeling ashamed and helpless. He could hear their thoughts, but he blocked them out as best he could. Their insults were hurtful and scathing, but he could handle it. After all, it was nothing compared to what he would have to face at the Kiranis system.

Ω

Cassandra had only really dozed for a few hours, part of her mind refusing to allow her relaxation and respite. When she opened her eyes, realising she had fallen asleep on her couch, she shivered with the unexpected chill in the room, and quickly reached for a discarded jacket. Throwing it over her shoulders, she swung her legs out and her bare feet touched the carpeted floor. She glanced briefly at the sun rising beyond the city before making her way to the bathroom. Where the mirror awaited.

A mirror in the morning is a grounding thing of humility, especially if one is regularly and necessarily consumed by one's own lies. Cassandra considered herself to be a beautiful woman, and she knew that others thought the same. However, hers was a beauty which blinded others to the truth of her character, and her morning mirror always spoke that truth. 'You are a bitch!' it would say, the words coming from a mouth so like her own. 'You are a ruthless, spiteful, selfish woman and you should count yourself lucky that anyone can bare to be in your presence!' And then that same face, so inelegantly truthful and wonderfully insulting, would smile back at her. Having swallowed its distaste for such a creature, it would then see the truth washed away and replaced by the beautiful Councillor Cassandra Messina, whose only fault was that she was so very good at what she did. The mirror today was somewhat less forgiving and Cassandra gasped as she reached up to touch the dark bruising on her forehead and right cheek. Pushing her hair back to see how far the lesions

70

had invaded, she was horrified as she watched clumps of hair drop into the sink. Tears ran down her face and she sobbed. As the minutes wore on, she slowly and cautiously undressed herself, finding more and more marks on her body as the virus, which had by now swept across the planet, attacked her from within. The shower automatically activated as she stepped into the frosted-glass cubicle, adjusting to her preferred temperature. But Cassandra had neither the energy nor the inclination to enjoy it. With the warm water struggling to rejuvenate her body and spirit, she dropped to her knees in despair, burying her face in her hands to hide her tears.

Ω

Cana disembarked from the shuttle and was met by the Presbyter to whom he had recently spoken. 'It's good to see you, Presbyter.'

'You too, son,' said the older man as they shook hands, 'but I don't see how endangering yourself will do any good.'

'I'm as much a part of this as anyone else in the Church. It wouldn't be right to run and hide.'

The Presbyter reached out to grip Cana's shoulder and nodded. 'You're a good lad, Cana, but this is about to get more difficult than you can imagine.'

Noticing that the grip on his shoulder was feeble, Cana glanced at the man's arm, seeing lesions and the signs of wasting flesh. The hand was quickly withdrawn. 'It's not as bad as it looks,' the Presbyter remarked with embarrassment.

Cana smiled with sympathy, while at the same struggling with the fear of the inevitable. 'How long until it affects me?' he asked.

'If we work fast, it may not.'

'What do you mean?'

The Presbyter gestured for Cana to follow him and he turned to walk away. They left the Shuttle Port behind and made their way to an awaiting vehicle. The chauffeur nodded to Cana, showing visible signs of illness on his face and neck. As they moved through the city, the Presbyter closed a glass partition between them and the driver. 'We need you to do something for the Church, Cana,' he said quietly. 'Something very important.'

'Anything,' said Cana loyally. 'That's why I'm here.'

The older man smiled and nodded, turning to watch the city pass by before continuing: 'Someone is monitoring the Church.'

'What?' Cana was shocked. 'Who?'

'With the help of our military contacts, we traced the signal to a ship in lunar orbit. It's hidden well, and may have been for some time. We only found it because they boosted their signal to get through the interference from the cage. They're specifically looking for Humans with elevated Rubidium levels, just like the virus from the cage. We need you to find out why they're watching us and how long it's been going on.'

'So you know who it is?'

'Yes, we do,' said the Presbyter. 'It's the Garran.'

Ω

Three hours later, Cassandra was sitting on her couch with her legs drawn up underneath her, reading a novel from an old-fashioned e-book and sipping red wine. Her hair was covered with a silk scarf of pale green, and her elaborate blue dress almost reached the floor. She had used a lot of make-up to disguise the signs of her sickness, but still it showed through. There was no knock on the door, but she heard it open and she took a deep breath. 'I was wondering how long it would take,' she said casually, setting her glass down on the table next to her and folding the e-book closed on her lap.

Standing no more than five metres from her was a tall, stocky man dressed entirely in black. Even his face was covered, and Cassandra could see only his blue eyes as she looked up. 'The others were difficult to track down,' he replied, his voice muffled by the balaclava. 'I don't understand why you're still here. They said you'd completely turned against us.'

'House arrest,' Cassandra explained. 'Haven't you heard?'

'I've been busy.'

'I suppose you have. Am I the last?' As he nodded, she smiled and said, 'Everyone else in twenty-four hours. I'm impressed.'

Not even the balaclava could disguise his grin. 'I'm good at my job. That's why they hired me. Some of my associates had to dispose of...loose threads on a military station that had moved outside the cage. I haven't heard from them, but I presume they've been successful and fingers are pointing straight at the Church.'

72

Cassandra nodded. 'Good,' she said. 'Bet you never thought you'd have to go through with all this, though, did you?'

He shrugged. 'Do I get to know why?'

'That wasn't part of the arrangement.' Cassandra set the book aside, rose from her chair and walked to the window. 'If nothing else, it would defeat the entire purpose, now wouldn't it?'

'I suppose so.' He walked towards her, brandishing a small knife in his right hand. 'Are you ready?' he asked.

'No,' she replied, turning swiftly and firing a gun. The man staggered, clutching his stomach, his eyes wide with shock as the blood seeped through his fingers. 'The...arrangement...'

'I've altered it somewhat,' said Cassandra, stepping forward to put another bullet into his head. 'I do that sometimes.'

Ω

Pontifex Harrogate and a squad of heavily-armed soldiers entered the apartment to find Cassandra standing over a body with a gun in her hand. 'Drop the weapon, Councillor!' he shouted, motioning for his men to hold their fire. Cassandra did so casually, clearly not shocked or stunned, but swiftly adopting the stance of someone who was. 'What...what happened?' she stammered, moving to a chair to sit down heavily. 'Who was he?'

'Don't play games with me, Councillor!' Harrogate snapped as he looked around the room. There was no sign of struggle, the door had not been forced and a half full glass of red wine was sitting on the table. 'Twelve of my men are incapacitated at their posts throughout the building. Not one of them was killed.' He pointed to the dead man. 'This guy knew exactly what he was doing, but *you*...you cut him down like an amateur. I'm not buying it.'

Cassandra glared at him, and there was the slightest grin on her face. 'I don't die easily, Pontifex,' she told him. 'Unlike my colleagues.'

'Your colleagues?' He paused, and then it dawned. 'Church members planted in the Council. Of course. All of them were killed in the last twenty-four hours.' He nodded. 'Did you know that some of them weren't even on the planet?'

She nodded. 'Last I heard, Councillor Marrahaim had bought a place on the Mars Habitat. I never saw the attraction, myself.'

Harrogate sat down beside her. 'Why would someone want to kill you?'

'I thought I was up for execution soon, Pontifex. Doesn't everyone want to kill me?'

Harrogate shook his head, bewildered. 'We're going to have to get some answers from you, Councillor. And believe me, that's the part neither of us will enjoy!'

Ω

Harrogate emerged into the afternoon sun and, upon hearing the sound of distant missile launches, he looked up to the sky, shielding his eyes from the sunlight shining through the available gaps in the cage. There he could see the tiny explosions which continued to mark the futile depletion of Earth's weaponry. Nothing seemed to be working, so various suggestions were being entertained. Harrogate had allowed himself to be drawn into a completely different approach, for he was a man willing to look beyond the immediate problem, a man who knew that ridding a garden of problem vegetation required first digging deep enough to locate the roots. There was a discreet beeping sound in his right ear, and he pressed the sub-dermal button behind his ear. 'Go ahead,' he said aloud.

'*It's me, John,*' said a familiar voice.

'I told you to wait for my call!' Harrogate reproached the caller briskly.

'*Yes, I know, but things are moving quickly now. I have a volunteer.*'

Harrogate closed his eyes and took a deep breath, then exhaled as he looked back up at the nightmare in the sky. 'You realise how risky this is? I'm struggling to get answers here as it is. I don't need an interplanetary issue on top of things. It would be a diplomatic nightmare.'

'*I understand that, but we need to get someone up to that ship before any more Garran arrive.*'

Harrogate walked to his vehicle and gestured that no attending staff come close as he continued his private conversation, which he did quietly. 'This can't get back to me,' he warned the caller.

'*It won't. The man in question is a young serviceman, assigned to one of the military commands in orbit. General Matthews' station. The General simply allowed him to go home, so there's no official record of his whereabouts. He's enthusiastic and eager to serve.*'

74

The Pontifex smiled. 'I'm sure he is,' he quipped. 'Make the arrangements. I'll cover things from my end.'

'*Thank you, John.*'

'One more thing, Presbyter.'

'*Yes?*'

'Don't call me again. This concludes my dealings with the Church.'

'*Of course, Pontifex Harrogate. You've been most helpful.*'

Ω

'I'm not sure I can do this,' said Cana, as he was handed a gun and helped into his body-armour. 'I've no military training.'

'Now that's not entirely true,' the Presbyter reminded him. 'Everyone on the orbiting stations receives some form of preliminary training.'

'It's very basic,' Cana argued with obvious dismay, as he picked up a small electronic device designed to keep track of his movements and transmit them home. 'And very much defensive.'

The Presbyter smiled, and Cana turned away from that rotting face as he listened to the old man: 'We don't expect you to go in all guns blazing, my boy. You'll board the ship without them even knowing…we've seen to that…and you'll simply snoop around until you find answers.' He handed Cana a nanosheet with the schematics of the vessel in question as he explained, 'This is a couple of years old, but if we're right, these plans are still accurate.'

'And if you're not?'

'One thing at a time, Cana.' The Presbyter nodded to the two men and three women attending to Cana's preparatory equipment, which was arrayed on a table next to him. As they left, Cana noted that every one of them were showing signs of physical deterioration. 'The next energy pulse is due in an hour,' the Presbyter resumed, 'and it'll bring a fresh batch of the virus. You need to be off Earth and outside the cage before that. A friend of mine has arranged for a distraction, which we're sure will keep the Garran ship from noticing your approach.'

'And how do I remain undetected while on board?'

The old man smiled compassionately. 'Have you lost your faith, Cana?'

'Of course not!'

75

'Then trust in it now.' He stepped closer, saying quietly, 'The Sentience will guide you.'

Cana was confused. 'But I'm no longer part of the plan, Presbyter. I'm abandoning everyone.'

'No, no, Cana!' the old man assured him passionately. 'You're not abandoning us. It would be foolish of us to simply sit back and allow this degradation to occur...even if it *is* our destiny...without first exploring every option. We must be aware of everything the Sentience has planned for us, because nothing happens without a reason.' He smiled again. 'You are not abandoning us, Cana,' he repeated. 'You are ensuring that the path we take is the right one. I would gladly go with you if I were capable. Discovering the truth is the most noble and exciting quest upon which one can embark.'

Cana smiled as that same excitement took hold. 'Still, I'm afraid,' he admitted.

'Of course,' said the Presbyter in a congratulatory manner. 'And why shouldn't you be? You are part of the great plan of the New Elect, and the Sentience demands our fear and awe. I envy you your significance in this.'

'Thank you, Presbyter,' Cana gushed, his smile even greater, 'I won't let you down.' He turned to address everyone in earshot, promising them, 'I won't let any of you down!' But no one responded, and the Presbyter quickly retrieved his attention. 'Good luck, Cana,' the old man said sincerely. 'The Sentience will guide you.'

Cana nodded, feeling the heat of terror in his stomach as the old man walked away. It was the last time he saw him.

THE THIRD DAY

General Matthews returned to his quarters, gratefully sinking into his chair after some sixteen hours on his feet. He did not even have the energy to pour himself a drink, and felt his heavy eyelids closing before even taking off his shoes. He woke suddenly, knowing instinctively that something was wrong. There was a stillness in his room that was almost ghostly, an absence of sound so contrary to normal station activity as to make him think of a cemetery, an orbiting graveyard long abandoned, floating around with the dead in space.

Rising slowly to his feet, feeling exhaustion leeching him of energy, Matthews blinked a few times and looked around. 'Is there someone there?' he called tentatively.

'Yes,' came the deep reply, causing him to jump and gasp. Looking around him again, he could see no one and his fear angered him enough to say, 'I'm dreaming. I'm still asleep.'

'I'm afraid not, General.'

Matthews looked towards the door, where deep and dark shadows had formed. A figure emerged from them, a tall man dressed in long, black robes with patterns of dragons on the front. The man's face remained shadowed on either side, so that the centre of his face appeared to protrude farther than the rest of his head. 'Who are you?' asked the General, returning to his desk to reach for his gun.

'You won't need that, General,' the man assured him. 'You're safe here.'

'Here?' Matthews wondered aloud, unsettled by the absence of sound and still hanging on to the idea of a dream. 'Am I still on the station?'

The man shrugged. 'In a sense,' he replied. 'Think of this as a place between times, a sort of...stage, if you like.'

'I'm in no mood for riddles. How did you even get in here?'

'I'd like you to do something for me,' the stranger told him. 'A ship on its way to the Kiranis system will need considerable assistance soon. I want you to dispatch some. It's a slow vessel, so your battleships will have no trouble catching up with it.'

'You're talking about the *Nostradamus*?'

'Yes, I am. They have a man on board in whom the Jaevisk will be very interested, once they learn of him. The ship will be destroyed, and I want the survivors rescued.'

'How will the Jaevisk know who's on board?'

The man smiled. 'I'm going to tell them,' he said calmly.

Matthews brandished his gun, aiming at the man in the shadows. 'I don't think so,' he threatened. 'We've got enough trouble with the Jaevisk as it is!'

'General, please...your gun won't work here. Nothing will.'

Not one for unnecessary conversation, Matthews tested that theory. The trigger clicked, repeatedly, but nothing happened. 'What's going on?' he demanded. 'Who the hell *are* you?'

'Oh, I've nothing to do with Hell, General. Quite the opposite, in fact.' He smiled at that. 'Now, this is all I want you to do. The cage is going nowhere for...a while, and you would be best advised to stop wasting resources on destroying it. I understand you want to board it again to begin attacking it from within.'

Matthews nodded, suitably distracted. 'I don't understand why we didn't do that from the off.'

'As we speak, your staff are realising that every access point has been sealed. No one is going back onto the cage, because I have those I want.'

'What's that supposed to mean?'

The man raised his hand. 'One last time, General. Quit wasting resources on attacking the cage here. Send a fleet to follow the *Nostradamus*. That's where your people are needed.'

Matthews stared at the man for a while, realising what he was missing. 'We should be focusing our efforts on the Kiranis system.'

'Good to see we're moving along. Now will you send the fleet?'

Matthews nodded. 'They won't like it.'

'Who cares what they like?' The man grinned like Satan on the mountain. 'You're up here and they're down there, watching a clock counting down as they tear out their hair in desperation...or it falls out. Isn't it time you took control of the situation for them?'

As if he was under some kind of hypnosis, Matthews found himself smiling dumbly and replying, 'I suppose it is.'

Ω

78

The hours wore relentlessly on. Sitting in the tiny docking module with all instruments and power deactivated to avoid detection, Cana could see the tiny shape of the Garran ship in what appeared at first to be an extremely low lunar orbit. In fact, the ship was being held in place by anchor lines embedded in the moon's rock, which allowed the aliens to keep power to a minimum. It did not, however, explain how they remained undetected when this side of the moon was facing Earth. Even to someone with only basic defensive training, this method of concealment appeared too convenient and easy. Cana surmised that someone on Earth must be assisting this hiding ship, perhaps overlooking snapshots on scopes or overseeing duty rosters in observation centres. That was, of course, if the authorities on Earth even bothered looking at something as close as the moon anymore. The Galaxy was so huge that Earth's military was forced to adopt a policy that meant missing the trees for the woods.

Cana found his mind wandering, and he considered his role in all of this. As a youngster, the idea of being part of a select group of people chosen to inherit the world following a purging of the unworthy was simultaneously terrifying and glorious. Attending exclusive schools and social groups as he grew up had invited ostracism from those with whom he would rather have associated, but the Church was strict when it came to educating its young members. It prepared them for dealing with the ignorance and prejudices of those who would throw derision at members once they reached adulthood and emerged blinking into the real world. One of the main issues of Church education was how to present oneself and one's beliefs to the majority population. This involved appropriating older religious doctrines in order to associate the Church with existing paradigms with which the people of Earth were already familiar. This apparent surrender to acculturation blurred the lines and allowed the New Elect to blossom in a non-threatening manner. It allowed them to hide the fact that they no more believed in a personified deity than they did the man in the moon.

Cana smiled ironically, for the aliens on the moon appeared to have more to do with the destiny of the Church of the New Elect than any imaginary force. He stared at their ship. The Garran were indigenous to the world known as Sieltor Prime. Cana had never been there, but knew that there were other planets in their home system which began with the title Sieltor, as if the name for the mother world was something to be used with reverence. He liked that, though. It was a pity more Humans did not think that way of Earth. His eyes closed for a moment and something

79

flashed on the inside of his lids, red lines bursting across the blank screen of his fatigue. As he opened his eyes with shock, he was sure he could see those same lines echoing as they faded away to memory. One of them speared the Garran ship, and it was this one which frightened him, for it had passed through his chest. He gasped as he touched his chest with both hands in a dream-like manner. Then a smile touched his lips as a sense of peace came over him, and he knew at once that what the Presbyter had said was correct. 'The Sentience,' he said aloud. 'It *is* with me!'

$$\Omega$$

Another hour passed before a squad of fighter craft passed through the cage and headed towards the moon. With weapons fully active and projected vectors clearly indicating their destination, they could not fail to arouse the interests of the hiding Garran. Cana watched intently, his pounding heart filling the silence in his head as the soundless journey of the five sleek vessels took them ever closer to discovering the alien ship. Surely the Garran would react?

There was no indication of activity on the Garran ship, but Cana imagined them watching closely or running around in panic. No lights came on, no engines fired, no weapons activated. However, Cana realised that this was the intended distraction as orchestrated by the Presbyter and his elusive contacts, and that it was the only chance he would get. He tapped some keys on his console and the tiny module hummed into life. He pressed the button on the device strapped to his wrist, safe in the knowledge that he was being tracked by his people.

As the fighter craft made to reverse course, the module drew closer to the Garran ship, its systems on minimal power to prevent overtly announcing its presence. Just for show, Cana presumed, the squad opened fire on the area around the anchored alien ship, making it clear that the Garran presence was known to Earth, but careful not to hit it. Still, the Garran did nothing.

Closing in from his right now on their return journey, the fighter craft shot by between Cana and the aliens. Once again, they made to reverse course and prepared to open fire. By the time they had returned to weapons' range, Cana had guided his ship too close to avoid becoming a victim of collateral damage. His module drifted close enough to launch docking lines, and they latched themselves to the hull of the Garran ship, guiding Cana to an airlock. Breathless moments passed, and Cana looked out of the rear of the module to see the squad from Earth. The module connected, the airlock sealed, and the lone traveller prepared to board the alien ship. As he did so, however, he felt a rumbling and the module began to shake.

The fighter pilots watched as the Garran ship ejected its lines, leaving the embedded anchors and their metal tendrils flailing from the moon's surface. 'They're leaving!' one of the pilots shouted across the com. 'Do we engage?'

For Cana, the experience was terrifying. The module shook so violently that he fell to the floor as the Garran engines fired and they left the moon behind, rising slowly from its surface. Getting up, Cana moved to the back of the module to see the squad inexplicably holding position. 'Help!' he cried desperately. 'Get me out of here!'

He saw the monstrous cage around Earth, and watched it moving away from him with tears in his eyes. Back at his console, he desperately pounded the keys designed to release the docking clamps. Nothing happened, and he cried out in terror. When he looked up from the console, Earth was a blue and white sphere in the distance. And then it vanished.

Ω

An hour later, Harrogate was furious as he accosted the Presbyter in the large warehouse to which he and his people had retreated. 'What in *God's* name have you done?' he roared. 'They've taken him with them!'

The Presbyter looked around at the shocked faces of the younger Church members, and gestured for them to remain calm. When he addressed the Pontifex, he appeared quite serene. 'Pontifex Harrogate, ours is not to question why.'

Harrogate stepped up to the man, grabbed him by his collar and almost lifted him from his feet. 'Quit the *crap*, Justin!' he spat. 'That kid is not your property to be used as you see fit. Now did you know this would happen or not?'

The Presbyter was unfazed. He looked down at Harrogate's hands and then back up to his face. Harrogate let him go with a friendly shove. 'I didn't know, okay?'

Harrogate shook his head. 'I don't believe you. They received a message seconds before they left. Now everything up there is a bit screwed up because of the cage, but I'm willing to bet that message came from you...or one of your lot, anyway.'

'Well, you're *wrong*, John. I've no intention of handing any of our people over to the Garran, whether they're Church members or not.'

Harrogate held his gaze and considered that for a moment. 'If that ship had ever received a communication from home,' he began, seeming to be thinking aloud, 'it would have led to our detecting it a long time ago. Since we didn't, that means it never received one. Are you trying to tell me that a message just comes out of the blue within seconds of us getting a man up there?'

The Presbyter shrugged. 'I don't know what to tell you, John. I swear.'

'Yeah, you swear,' Harrogate mocked. 'But to who?'

'That's beneath you, John. Why don't you just leave us alone to deal with this?'

Harrogate looked around at the five hundred or so Church members, as they sat or lay suffering in the vast warehouse. He laughed ironically. '*Deal* with this?' he repeated coldly, returning his attention to the Presbyter. 'You can barely *stand*, Justin. The Church is in no fit state to deal with anything.'

'So what do you suggest?'

'I *suggest*...Presbyter...that you start praying that these Jaevisk devices work when they get here. More than half a million people have died so far. Your Church is being ravaged from within...' he leaned closer to whisper, 'literally. This is no grand plan, Justin. This is murder orchestrated on a massive scale. I'll get to the bottom of this.' He stepped back and looked around again. 'And to that, *I* swear.'

Ω

The *Nostradamus* was travelling at such speed towards the alien system known as Kiranis that the crew were on a stasis roster to ensure that none suffered from prolonged exposure to the immense gravitational strains of the journey. Captain Echad had retired to his quarters, leaving Helen in charge of the bridge. Two other officers monitored multiple stations on reduced remits and lighting was reduced to priority-only levels. The bridge was a place of shadows and suggestions, and Helen had the misfortune of being left with Conner in a room where silence reigned. That, she knew, would not stop him hearing her inner voice, so she decided after a time to engage him in conversation. 'You said you weren't the bad guy,' she said.

From where he stood with his back to her, he grinned as he replied, 'And you're still wondering who is?'

'It's a reasonable question,' she said, approaching him as he turned to face her. 'I mean, if there is some grand mastermind behind all this, surely it would help to know who it was?'

Conner shook his head. 'To be perfectly honest, it wouldn't help at all,' he said.

'You mean it wouldn't help you.'

'No, it wouldn't help anyone. I'm not even sure I know what to make of what I know.' He chuckled ironically. 'I was starting to wonder if I'd gone insane!'

'I wouldn't notice any difference.'

He held her gaze for a moment, sensing her churning emotions. 'I'm sorry about your crewman...Will, was it?'

Helen nodded, keeping her emotions in check. 'He'd just asked his childhood sweetheart to marry him.'

Conner sighed. 'I think he might have been thinking about her when...' He turned his back to her again. 'I was desperate. I didn't know what to do.'

Another voice interrupted, 'Is that all I get, too?'

They both turned to see Anya, and Helen stepped aside as she approached Conner. 'You must be looking for an apology,' he said.

'If I need to ask, it isn't genuine,' she replied. He must have known her intention. He stiffened before she even made her move, closing his eyes and taking the blow on his left cheek. Helen nodded in admiration as Conner dropped one knee to the floor to steady himself and Anya flexed her hand to deal with the pain across her knuckles. 'Tell me why,' she hissed. 'I want to know!'

Conner rose slowly and caught her fierce glare. He considered lying to her, but then realised that the truth would mean so much more to her, especially in her current condition. 'They're going to kill my family,' he said.

Anya stood perfectly still. She may not even have breathed for a time, but eventually she asked, 'Where are you from?'

'I'm from a planet that isn't even inhabited yet,' he replied, 'and I'm from about...' He thought for a moment. 'What year is it again?'

'Twenty-three-eighty,' Helen supplied.

'Don't tell me *you* believe him now!' Anya snapped, swinging on the Lieutenant. Helen shrugged. 'Just listen to him,' she suggested.

So Anya listened, and her world changed forever.

THE FOURTH DAY

For more than twenty-four hours they had been questioning Cassandra, but she had given them nothing. She was not entirely sure how she had held up to the interrogation, despite breaking shamefully into tears on numerous occasions. Today, however, she was smiling as she tidied her apartment in anticipation of Nell's arrival, for it would mark the beginning of a momentous day. As though she might see Nell approaching the towering building in which she lived, Cassandra went to the window and looked down. This high above the city, she had always looked down upon the little people, those whom she had always wanted to look up to her. Now, of course, with her place in the world turned upon its head, she was the one looking up. There were times when, even in the daylight, one could see the lines of the still disconnected cage in orbit. But Cassandra was not looking at the cage. She was looking beyond it. Today the Jaevisk devices would be delivered and, with them, redemption for Cassandra. Once those victims of the virus who had not yet died began to heal, her relentless foresight and courage would be realised. Of course, that realisation would swiftly dissolve. Public opinion aside, her methods had been illegal and she would be facing trial. But all of that was nothing compared to the prospects of the ten-day countdown reaching zero.

A knock sounded on her door, and she turned away from the window, pleasantly surprised. 'Come in, Nell,' she called out. 'I didn't expect you so early.'

The door was opened by one of the guards and a man in his late thirties walked in, looking somewhat nervous. 'Good morning, Madam Councillor,' he greeted her. 'I'm Doctor Aidan Greene, the Council's new Medical Designate. I hope you don't mind me coming here.'

Cassandra stood for a moment, watching the door as it was closed. She snapped out of her disappointment and acknowledged the man. 'I'm sorry, Doctor, I was expecting someone else,' she explained. 'And they're supposed to contact me ahead of any unscheduled visits.' She gestured towards one of the leather chairs. 'I'm sure you've heard all the rumours regarding my...' she smiled, 'state of incarceration.'

Greene smiled awkwardly. 'I try to see beyond rumours, Madam Councillor. They tend to blind one to the truth...or certainly to the search for it.'

85

'Admirable, I suppose,' she applauded him. 'Can I get you a drink?'

'Some water would be nice.'

Nodding, she poured a drink for each of them. Hers was not water. 'I think I've been indulging a little too much lately,' she confessed as she handed him a glass. 'Of course, I attribute it all to stress.'

He looked at her for a moment, seeing barely disguised signs of the sickness on her face and the back of her hands. Like most women suffering from the effects of the synthetic virus, she had her hair covered. 'I think we're all entitled to...let ourselves go a little these days,' he absolved her, sipping his water. 'If I weren't so busy, I'd probably join you.'

'Any time, Doctor...Greene, was it?'

He nodded. 'I've been placed in charge of combating this virus, as well as performing the surgery on you.'

'I imagine that's quite daunting. I do hope you're up to the task.'

Greene acknowledged her anxiety. 'I will be when the time comes,' he assured her. 'I just never thought I'd have the weight of the world on my shoulders.'

Cassandra chuckled. 'Some of us aspire to such lofty goals, Doctor.'

'I've never understood that,' he admitted. 'If I may ask, Madam Councillor...is it true that you were involved in the retrieval of the alien device from a man up on the...cage?'

'Straight into it,' she said, nodding. 'I like that. Yes, it's true. I'm afraid I won't be elaborating on that.'

'I understand.' He sipped the water again. 'The people who took it...did they burn their clothes...their equipment?'

Cassandra's eyes narrowed. 'What are you looking for, Doctor?'

'I need a blood sample from that man. The people who took the device from his skull will undoubtedly have come into contact with his blood. I was hoping there may be some trace of it somewhere.'

'What good will it do you?' Cassandra sat back in her chair, looking out of the window again. Greene watched her for a brief moment, and realised, 'You know why I need it. And I imagine you know a lot more than you're going to tell me.'

Her laughter then was dark and mocking. 'Oh, I know so much, Doctor,' she said, turning to face him. 'So much that it saddens me sometimes. And the people keeping me here are trying to get it out of me.' She leaned forward, her eyes ablaze. 'Do you know they've used every drug and method of psychological manipulation at their disposal and still I've given them nothing?'

'How is that possible?' he asked. 'How can you fight it?'

She shrugged and leaned back again. 'I've no idea. But I know I'm tired of fighting it. I've been reduced to a prisoner while I sit here waiting.'

'Waiting for what?'

'To leave, Doctor. To get off this world and never come back.' She grinned like a maniac. 'I've got a great future in store for me, you know. A destiny far beyond anything you could imagine. He told me that much.'

'Who?'

'God, Doctor Greene. My own...personal...God.' She laughed aloud, the sound full of twisted humour, but Greene cut her short as he stood up and shouted at her, 'I want to know the truth!'

She glared at him. 'The truth about what?' she snapped.

'I need to figure out the purpose of this virus before signing off on the procedures that *you* say will reverse it. The device was removed from someone's head and that person is conveniently gone, so I've no idea about his physiology. So instead, why don't we start with what we've got? The elevated Rubidium levels in Church members, for one. Seeing as they're the ones dying from this thing. Who would know about it outside the Church? I know you're a member.'

'Do you now?' She drained her glass and rose to her feet, standing there silently for a moment before sighing and saying, 'I was happy before you walked through that door, Doctor. I know all about you. I know who you are, where you come from, and why you were given this position.'

'What?' Greene was terrified. *Did she know about the woman who had come to visit him in his surgery? Had Messina sent her? Or was she working against her?* He watched her walk into the next room, beyond the dining area. He heard drawers and cabinets being opened and closed as she searched for something. His heart pounded as he imagined her returning with a gun and killing him on the spot. *No*, he thought, *she wouldn't be so insane as to do such a thing. Or would she?*

'Ah, here we go,' he heard her say.

Walking back into the room, she looked at him. 'You look like you've seen a ghost, Doctor,' she mocked him. 'Sit down before you fall down.'

He did so, seeing that she was carrying two items. In her left hand was a Data Slip, in her right a black plastic pouch. She first offered him the pouch, saying, 'The device was lifted with forceps which have since been destroyed, but this is the gauze and the cloth it was wrapped in. I daresay there'll be more than enough blood for you to get what you need.'

He accepted the pouch with a silent nod. 'And this,' she continued, showing him the Data Slip, 'has the access codes on it for all the information you'll need regarding the Rubidium issue and the...selective affliction.' She leaned forward. 'I warn you, Doctor, you won't like what you find. But once you've had time to absorb this, I want you to do something for me.'

He took the proffered Data Slip, saying, 'Anything,' without thinking, too overwhelmed by the prospect of discovering the truth to argue.

'If your tests show that the man from the cage has normal levels of Rubidium in his blood, that will mean that he was never at any risk from this virus. Do you see where I'm going, Doctor?'

He was horrified by the notion. 'Oh, my God!' he exclaimed. 'I mean...we'd considered that he probably hadn't been at risk up in the cage when exposure happened down here...but you didn't even know if that thing in his head was the *reason* he didn't suffer when you called the Jaevisk!'

She simply nodded. 'But I knew it was the cure that these people needed, whether *he* needed it or not. And I'm amongst them now. Don't forget that.'

'But...' he thought hard and fast, recalling everything that had happened since the cage arrived, 'you told the Jaevisk that you wanted to attack the Garran. I don't get it. What have they got to do with this?'

She pointed to the Data Slip. 'It's all there, Doctor. The pieces of the puzzle. But as soon as you use that Data Slip to access restricted military files, you'll want to distance yourself from this...and fast. Do you understand?'

'Yes,' he replied, taking a deep breath. 'Can we go back to the tests? What do you want to know about the man from the cage?'

She nodded and walked to the window. With her back to him, she explained. 'If the device he had in his head has more than one application, which I suspect it does, then he might have needed it for something other than protection from a virus to which he would never have been exposed. If you find that his Rubidium levels are normal, then we know that he was never at risk from the virus. So we need to know why he had that device. There won't be much time, Doctor, because...as you well know...I have to be the recipient of the original device. That much is being arranged for me.'

'I won't ask,' he commented ironically.

'Good.' She smiled, and continued. 'So before I go under your knife, you'll need to examine the device more thoroughly in light of your findings. I'll make sure you have access to all the data we obtained prior to handing it over to the Jaevisk.'

'So, basically, whatever your guys didn't do…you want me to do?'

'Precisely. They missed something. They must have. And for some reason, I've been left in the dark about it.'

'By who? *God*?'

'Don't you believe, Doctor?' Cassandra countered. 'I heard you invoke him.'

'Invoke…?' He shook his head. 'Oh…no, that was just a figure of speech.'

'A pity,' she noted. 'So much is just a figure of speech these days.'

'So you really believe?'

Cassandra smiled. 'I don't need to believe, Doctor. I've seen him, I've spoken to him. He guides me and intervenes in my life. As crazy as it sounds, I've been chosen to lead Humanity to its destiny.'

Greene could not help but smile. 'You're right,' he said, 'that does sound crazy.' He pocketed the Data Slip and hid the pouch inside his coat. 'But I'm in no position to argue, cos crazy seems catching these days.'

Cassandra walked and gestured towards the door, smiling. 'Thank you for coming to visit me, Doctor. I guess we'll speak again soon. It's good to know I'm still a significant part of all this, no matter what side I may appear to be on.'

'I don't think the sides are so easily defined right now,' remarked Greene as she opened the door for him and the guard watched them. 'It all seems so hopeless with that countdown still going.'

She nodded. 'We have less than six days left, Doctor,' she told him. 'Then the world we know will be changed forever.' She offered him her hand.

For some reason, Greene found himself feeling sympathy for the imprisoned Councillor as he shook her hand. There was such despair in her eyes. 'Might not be a bad thing,' he said, before a second guard escorted him away.

Cassandra watched him go, nodding to him as he looked back, halfway down the corridor. 'I'm afraid that was your only permitted visit for today, Councillor,' said the guard next to her.

'What? No, that's not right. Harrogate said I could have multiple visitors once they'd been approved. Nell Raesa is due here soon. I wasn't even *told* that guy was coming!'

The guard did not make eye contact. 'Pontifex Harrogate ordered that this visit supersede any previously arranged visits for the day. Miss Raesa will be here on Tuesday.'

'*Tuesday*?' Cassandra was incensed. 'I wanted to see her *before* my surgery. The devices are arriving today!'

'Yes, Councillor. I believe it's because of today's events that Pontifex Harrogate has implemented these particular orders.' Still refraining from meeting her glare, he gestured to the open door. 'If you would be so kind as to return to your apartment, Councillor...'

Ω

Greene wasted no time. As soon as he returned to the research wing of the hospital, he called a colleague to him and handed her the pouch as she emerged from one of the wards. 'Here's the blood we need,' he told her. 'We'll compare it to those affected by the virus. I suppose we want it to be the same, right?'
She nodded. 'I guess so. What if it's not?'

'One step at a time,' he said amicably. 'Can I leave you to get the tests started?'

'Of course,' she said, surprised. 'You don't wanna do it yourself?'

'There's something else I have to take care of.'

She laughed as she spoke, confused: 'Something more important than *this*? What is it?'

'Ah...I can't say right now,' he replied. 'I'm sorry, Maria, I don't mean to be so...mysterious. I just need a bit of time with this, and then I'll fill you in.'

Maria nodded, clearly not happy with being left out of the loop. 'Well, don't take too long about it, okay?'

He gave her a tentative smile and walked away. She watched him disappear around the corner, knowing something was not right.

Ω

Apprehension was coursing through him as he sat at the workstation. Withdrawing the Data Slip from his inside pocket, he looked around to see that the staff members on the other five stations were engrossed in their work and research. Everyone was busy working to combat this sickness. *So what am I doing?* Greene wondered. He knew he was being drawn into something here, and he knew by the words of Councillor Messina that it was dangerous. He realised that he was staring at the Data Slip as if the answers were right there on its surface. One of the younger staff was looking at him. 'Are you okay, Doctor?' she asked.

He nodded and gave a short smile, lowering the Data Slip until the scanners of the workstation could read it. Within seconds, scores of frames were displayed, stacked as virtual folders on the metaglas. The user could tap the corner of the folder he wished to open and it would be brought forward. The opening frame had three words in its centre, confirming Greene's access: *Alpha Clearance Authorised.*

Now, Greene was hardly a military man, nor had he any experience within the intelligence network, but those words carried an unmistakable weight for even the lowliest of civil servants, even without knowing how high up one had to be to have Alpha clearance. He closed the first frame and was met with words that were even more disturbing, the name of the parent folder: *Project Sieltor 1.*

Licking dry lips and looking around to make sure he was not being observed, Greene moved to the next frame...and the next...and the next. Words like "experiment" and "cross-breeding" caught his attention as he breezed over the jargon. Phrases such as "unexpected results", "DNA splicing", "genetic mutations" and "failed attempts" leaped off the screen and seared themselves into his memory. Once the expected line, "elevated Rubidium levels" turned up, he decided he had seen enough. Pocketing the Data Slip, he hurried out of the room, dazed and shocked. He bumped into a very tall nurse, nearly knocking her from her feet. But she grabbed his arm to steady herself and squeezed tight. 'Ow!' he snapped, looking up at her. 'What are you...' It was then that he saw her face, recognising her as the woman who had visited him in his surgery. 'You!'

'I see your work is progressing well, Doctor,' she congratulated him amiably. 'Perhaps we could discuss it in more detail in your office?'

'Ah...yes, of course,' he replied, gesturing down the corridor. 'This way, please.'

Ω

Pontifex Harrogate listened to the report with gritted teeth. Pressing the tiny com device closer to his eardrum, he heard the words which made his blood boil: *'Someone has used Councillor Messina's access codes to bring up Alpha level documents. We're still trying to open the files ourselves, but they're programmed to fragment and spread across the net. It could take hours, maybe longer.'*

'Can you trace the access?'

'Yes, Sir. Our intel suggests it was the surgeon who visited Messina. He's at the hospital now.'

'Send a team. I'll meet them. I don't like what's going on here.' Harrogate shook his head and pulled his coat off a hook on the wall before closing his office door behind him. There was another call for him and he pressed the device in his ear. 'This is Harrogate.'

'Pontifex Harrogate, there is a long-range communication request for you. It's coming from Sieltor Prime.'

'I just know I'm not going to like this. Who is it?'

'A woman by the name of Eyla San Setta. She says you're old friends.'

'And you believed her?'

'Stranger things, Sir.'

'Hmm. Put her through.'

There was a tense silence as Harrogate wondered what the Garran woman could want from him. She came swiftly to the point. *'I've no time for small talk, John, I'm afraid. I need your help.'*

'Ask and ye shall receive,' he replied sarcastically.

'I wouldn't be so quick to mock if I were you. You've got a fleet headed for the Kiranis system, I believe.'

'Good to know your opera glasses still work, Eyla. What business is that of yours?'

'My son's fleet is about to be wiped out by the Jaevisk. I need my people rescued.'

Harrogate hesitated. 'Our fleet isn't equipped for that sort of operation, Eyla. I'm sure you'll agree that they've more important things on their minds than coming to the aid of those who they think are the enemy. The Council is playing the Garran card with this thing around Earth.'

92

'Look, John, you and I are people who pretend to know everything, when all we're doing is playing catch-up. Although we both know that the Garran aren't responsible for the cage. Now our forces are in danger of being completely wiped out here, but for some reason the Jaevisk have given my son a chance to escape. We're talking about a massive shift in power facilitated by the Jaevisk, and it's in all of our interests to ensure that it takes place.'

Harrogate thought for a moment. 'I can't promise anything, Eyla. You know our fleet won't stand a chance against the Jaevisk so far from home.'

'They won't need to engage the Jaevisk if they get here in time. It's Ben-Hadad they're after.'

'I'll contact General Matthews. He's directing the fleet now.'

'Thank you, John.'

'Good luck, Eyla.' He ended the conversation as another com request sounded. 'Yes?'

'You won't believe this, Sir, but there's another Garran on the wire.'

'Which one?'

'His name's Carak. An Overseer, no less!'

Harrogate stepped into his transport and ordered the driver to take him to the hospital. 'Connect me, please.'

'Yes, Sir. There'll be a short delay, as usual.'

Harrogate looked out of the window as the vehicle sped across the massive city. 'Is this Pontifex Harrogate?' he heard a deep voice ask after a short silence. He did not flinch. 'It is,' he replied. 'I understand I'm speaking with Overseer Carak, is that correct?'

'You have that singular honour, Pontifex. You're not surprised that I can speak English. This tells me that I am definitely speaking with the right man.'

The alien's voice dripped with sarcasm and no little arrogance. Harrogate smiled. 'Many of my agents are coming to grips with some of your languages, Overseer. I don't see why I should be surprised that you've learned one of ours.'

'Oh, I speak more than one Earth language, Pontifex. But since you've mentioned your agents, I can get straight to the matter at hand. I need to speak with you urgently concerning one of your agents, a formidable woman who seems to have decided to take some…delicate matters into her own hands.'

Harrogate hesitated. How did this Garran know about one of his agents? Had he captured one? 'I'm not sure I have time to discuss that right now, Overseer. You may not have noticed, but we're in a spot of bother down here.'

'*A spot of bother?*' The alien laughed aloud and Harrogate winced, pulling the device out of his ear for a moment. He missed the start of the next sentence. '*...attack and you call it a spot of bother. I like that.*' There was a pause. '*Our sensors have detected an Axcebian vessel on its way to you, Pontifex. I know exactly what it's carrying and I will destroy it if you don't agree to meet with me.*'

Harrogate was quicker in his response. 'You clearly feel that this meeting is urgent, Overseer. I don't know why you think threatening a cargo of iron ore would sway me, but I'll agree. After all, we do like to keep the construction industry going here on Earth.' He smirked. 'You might like the little decoration we have in orbit at the moment.' He quickly pulled the device out again, in time to hear the Garran laughing aloud over the speaker. '*Pontifex Harrogate, you and I are going to get along extremely well, I think.*'

'Anything's possible,' conceded Harrogate. 'There's a military station in orbit, one of the few left. General Matthews there will send you docking codes and he'll have a shuttle bring you down. You may have to wait a few hours to speak with me, though. And, Overseer...'

'*Yes?*'

'You might consider wearing protective clothing and breathing equipment. Our...spot of bother appears somewhat life-threatening to a lot of people down here, and we've no way of knowing how it would affect visitors of your...calibre.'

'*Oh, it won't have any effect on me, I can assure you. But we can discuss that when I arrive. So, until then...*'

Now Harrogate knew he was getting somewhere. He could see the pieces of the jigsaw laid out for him, but there was a problem with the edges. Right now they were all sky. 'Until then,' he replied coldly.

Ω

Maria had cut a tiny square of the surgical gauze and was running the necessary tests on the blood therein. She leaned back in her chair as the instruments worked their magic, too tired to be enthralled by the wonders of genetics. But when she saw the results, her eyes widened in shock, for the database was displaying the personnel file of Captain Adam Echad of the *Nostradamus*, describing him as the closest familial match.

'Oh,' said Maria, 'I hadn't expected a hit.' She scrolled down through the rest of the information as another nurse joined her at the workstation. They both took in the figures for the blood work, and Maria voiced their conclusion: 'Our guy wouldn't have been affected.'

Ω

Anya stood silently by the window in her quarters as the *Nostradamus* raced towards the Kiranis system. She sipped a drink, not really tasting it or caring what it was before returning the glass to an adjacent table. The conversation with Conner had left her reeling, and she could find no comfort in denial, no matter how ridiculous it all seemed. She felt a threatening sense of pressure in her head, and did not know whether to ascribe it to the velocity of the ship or the stress of the situation. After what seemed like hours, as well it may have been, Adam came in, closing the door quietly behind him. 'You shouldn't be awake,' he told her. 'There's a freezer with your name on it down on E-deck.'

She nodded absently, watching the intermittent flashes of light as they passed worlds and stars relatively close to their course. The light sources in the greater distance were nought but blurs of continuous illumination, so seemingly consistent that the eye dismissed them after a time and saw only black. 'I have a headache.'

'I'm not surprised.' He took her by the shoulders and drew her to him, feeling the soft warmth of her hair in his hand. 'You must be exhausted. Why don't you go to the cryo-chamber for a few hours? I'll come down and wake you when we're in visual range of the system.'

For a moment, she considered keeping it to herself, enjoying the comfort of his embrace and the safety of his love. But he had to know, and she looked up into his ever warm eyes. 'You need to sit down,' she told him. 'There's something I have to tell you.'

'What is it?' he asked, the embrace weakening as a chill ran through him.

'The reason we're involved in all this.'

'What do you mean? Messina got us involved when she told me to let that creep on board.'

'And you don't see any problem with your DNA matching his? He's claiming he's a descendant of yours, Adam!'

Adam sighed, and moved back to a chair. 'I know what he's claiming,' he said as he sat down heavily, 'but that doesn't mean it's true. People have been known to use illegal cloning to con others out of money in inheritance cases and the like.'

Anya glared at him. 'Are you seriously going to sit there and compare this to an inheritance case?'

'Of course not. I'm just saying that there are ways around these tests, and that it might be better to consider why he's making this claim.' He gestured for her to sit with him, saying, 'Anyway, the point is moot. I've no brothers or sisters, and I'm pretty damn sure I've no kids running around.' He laughed as she sat across his lap, leaning in to rest her head on his shoulder. Her headache was worsening and her stomach felt sick with nerves as she steeled herself to tell him. 'You will soon,' she announced.

He went perfectly still and silent. All she could feel was the rise and fall of his chest against her right side as he breathed. 'I thought he would tell you,' she continued. 'He said he would use it as extra leverage over you.'

'He didn't,' Adam replied quietly.

'Don't be scared,' she whispered, kissing his neck.

'I'm scared for you.' He turned to look into her eyes. 'You shouldn't be out here.'

She smiled softly, and his fears forgot themselves. 'None of us should be out here, Adam, but it's no safer at home.'

Their lips met and a tear fell to her cheek. Adam pulled away and went to the window, saying, 'Why is he here, do you think?'

Anya's arms encircled him as she stood behind him. 'He said that someone told him it would make sense when he saw an old friend.'

Adam turned and the embrace was broken. 'You spoke to him?'

She nodded. 'When he saw the *Nostradamus*, he recognised it...from his own history, he said. He knew you were the Captain and that you had to be the "old friend" in question. He killed Will to take his place. Something to do with keeping the time-line intact. He said that it was better for everyone that the team never came back with Will's body. Whatever happens to Conner, we have to report it as having happened to Will. Do you understand?'

Adam laughed scornfully. 'Do *you*?' he countered. 'I mean, you're taking all this on board like it was Gospel.'

96

Anya lowered her head for a moment, and then said quietly, 'He knew our son's name.'

'Our *son*? You know it's a boy already?'

'I do now.' She looked up. 'I was going to call him Rueben,' she grinned, 'if that's okay with you.'

'Ah...yeah...I like it.' Adam was too confused to decide baby names. 'And you're saying he knew what you were going to call him?'

'I told no one, Adam, I swear. I even thought it was too early to tell you I was pregnant. Only the Doc knows.'

'Conner could have read your mind.'

'I don't know what to make of the fact that you can believe one thing and not the other.'

'At this point, reading minds is more feasible than coming from the future.'

'Why? With everything we've seen in this part of the Galaxy...the Jaevisk, the Cquaston, the Sori, not to mention the advances in Garran technology...why is it so difficult to believe that Conner is from the future?'

'People believe what they want to believe, Anya. You're so desperate to accept this...not the least because us having a child confirms that we survive this mess...but because he got to you.'

'What's *that* supposed to mean?' she snapped. 'He *got* to me? Get off your high horse, Adam, and see that this guy is in serious danger and gains nothing by lying to us. There's a battleship fleet on a pursuit course and we're heading into the unknown out here!'

'The unknown for us, maybe. Conner...or whatever his name is...came from that place. Of course he's lying to us. What sob story did he pitch you that made you come around so easily? What could he possibly have said to make you melt so easily in his hands?'

She slapped him hard across the face, thinking absently that she was doing that a lot lately. 'Your being pathetic. Now snap out of it or get the hell out of my face!'

He glared at her, cowed by her anger but struggling to maintain some level of composure. Still, his question was less confrontational in tone. 'What did he tell you, Anya?'

She took a few deep breaths, seeing the bloodless hand print on his face and feeling regret. 'He said his family were in danger,' she said eventually. 'He said that he was threatened into taking a dangerous mission, that his family would be killed if he didn't. The mission must have been a lie, a trick to get him here so that his presence and the Jaevisk device in his head would lead to...all this chaos.'

Adam returned to his chair. 'But all this chaos, as you put it, is a result of the cage around Earth. He didn't bring it here.'

'No, but he thinks he was brought here to facilitate something larger, something the Jaevisk have planned. The cage is simply the catalyst for...whatever they're going to do.' She walked to him and offered her hand. Taking it absently, he held it against his burning cheek, so that she could feel the dying sting of her outburst.

'What was his mission?'

'What?'

'You said someone made him take this mission. What was it?'

She sat on the arm of the chair. 'Something to do with a Garran he called the World Killer. A crazy name, I know, but...there was something about the way he said it, you know?'

Adam nodded, recalling Conner's tone as he spoke about the cage. 'What did he say about this...World Killer?'

'Just that he'd vanished during a battle in this system we're heading for. Some sort of disturbance in space swallowed his ship and he was gone. The people Conner works for told him they'd located him in the past.' She held up her hands in anticipation of the inevitable. 'Don't ask me how it works. I'm just telling you what he said.'

'So Conner's here looking for this single Garran, who could be anywhere...even if he's in this time? How was he supposed to do this exactly?'

Anya shrugged. 'Something about them being connected and that they always found each other.'

'Connected?'

'His words, not mine. Anyway, when the cage came to Earth before Conner could even begin looking for this guy, he knew that something was wrong.' Anya knelt down in front of Adam. 'Look, I don't know what all this has to do with us beyond the fact...and I do believe it's fact...that our unborn son is connected to Conner somehow. However, I've been thinking about the fleet that's following us, and I think there's more to it than you just taking Conner on board.'

Adam nodded. 'You think they've connected him to me in the same way we did.'

'Yes. And there are people out there who'll put two and two together and come up with our baby as the answer.'

Adam was horrified by the implications, and he grabbed her passionately by the shoulders. 'There's no way in Hell that I would let anything happen to you, do you hear me? No one is going to lay a finger on you, Anya.'

She could no longer hold back her fear. 'They'll try to take our baby,' she sobbed. 'I know they will.'

Adam drew her up to him and held her close. 'Let them try,' he said.

Ω

Greene was too wound up to sit down, and his guest got straight to business. 'What did she tell you?' she snapped.

He stared at her for a moment, thinking absently that her attitude had significantly deteriorated since last they had spoken. 'You're spying on me,' he accused her.

'Of course I am, you idiot. That's what I do.'

Greene's eyebrows raised. 'You're not exactly gaining my trust here, you know.'

She stepped up to him, looking down on him. 'I couldn't care less whether you trust me or not, Doctor. All I need you to do is trust in what we're doing.'

'So the two are mutually exclusive?'

'Look, I'm no angel, Doctor, but I'm trying to do the right thing here. People are dying and others will wish to reap the PR benefits of that situation.'

Greene shook his head. 'I've been thinking about what you said before. Members of the Church are the only victims of this thing, and it's genetic, so they won't be escaping it. There's no good reason for them to stop the procedure.'

'You're right.'

'What?'

She retreated to a chair and composed herself. 'I've been lying to you, Doctor,' she told him. 'I don't work for anyone on Earth.'

Greene was visibly taken aback. 'Well, who do you work for?'

'Certain people on Sieltor Prime who don't want to see another war between our two people.'

'*Another* war?' Greene finally sat down. 'When was the last one?'

99

'Quite some time ago. Look, that doesn't matter. What matters is that Messina stood up there with the Jaevisk and suggested that the Garran were behind all this. Now, I know I've no proof to offer you, Doctor, but I swear to you that they weren't. This is far beyond their capabilities.'

He thought for a moment. 'Okay, so...let me get this straight. You work for the Garran, and you want to stop us invading them...' he paused, 'by making sure Messina gets a Jaevisk implant stuck in her brain. Am I following you so far?'

'I've a good idea of what you just found out, Doctor. There's a connection between the Church and the Garran, a genetic connection. But the Church are also our people, and if they all die because of what Messina says is a Garran biological attack, everyone will cry for Garran blood. Now, I've spent a lot of time on the Sieltor worlds, and believe me, we cannot win a war against them.'

'The Jaevisk said they'd help us.'

The woman blinked in disbelief. 'Am I hearing this from a Doctor? Are you advocating war? No matter who wins or loses in the end, millions will die. You can't possibly agree with that course of action.'

'No...no, of course not. That's not what I meant. It's just that...'

'I'm trying to stop a war, Doctor. Others are trying to make sure it happens, and when the stakes are so high, certain kinds of people are called in to make sure things go according to plan. Don't think for a minute that you're not in danger here.'

That brought him round. 'You think they'd come after me?'

'Why not? I know *I* would. But don't worry, that's what I'm here for. Right up until the last second of this procedure, I'll be at your side. I promise I'll keep you safe.'

Greene closed his eyes, nodding his head slowly. 'Okay.'

'So do I get to see this implant thing before the procedure?'

'No,' he replied. 'I'll be the only person with direct access to it prior to the surgery.' She seemed overly concerned by that, and he noticed. 'You have a problem with that?'

'Oh, no, it's fine,' she lied, comfortably. 'I'd just like to see it, that's all.'

'Yes, well...you focus on your job and I'll focus on mine, alright?'

She was about to reply, when there was a knock on the door and it opened. Maria was talking as she entered. 'It's different!' she said. 'The DNA...' She saw the other woman and laughed nervously. 'Oh, Hello,' she said to the woman, flicking her gaze then to Greene. 'I didn't mean to disturb you,' she apologised.

Greene shook his head, relieved to have been disturbed and beckoning for her to continue coming in. 'No, no...it's okay, Maria. This is...'

'Linda,' the woman interrupted, standing up to offer her hand. Clearly shocked by the height of the woman, Maria shook her hand and smiled as the woman told her, 'I'm a new nurse here, and we were just discussing the surgery that I'll be assisting with. It'll be a great opportunity for me to learn.'

'Oh?' Maria questioned Greene. 'Which surgery is that?'

'The operation this evening on Councillor Messina,' said Linda. 'I believe she's to be the first subject for these Jaevisk devices.'

Maria glanced at Greene, who was neither arguing nor helping, before turning back to Linda. 'You seem very calm about the whole thing,' she noted. 'Doesn't it freak you out a little?'

Linda chuckled softly. 'Oh, I've seen a lot,' she replied. 'Anyway, I'd better be going. I've a lot to do. You'll call me when we're ready to get started, Doctor?'

Greene hesitated, but her glare warned him. 'Of course...Linda.' Without another word, she left the office and Maria watched her go. 'What's going on?' she asked, once the door was closed. 'I thought the rosters had all been checked and re-checked by the Council. Who authorised her?'

'Who knows?' Greene replied, shrugging dismissively. Reaching out for the holosheet she was carrying, he asked, 'What were you saying...it's different?'

'Ah...yeah.' Against her better judgement, Maria shook the feeling that something was wrong. 'The blood work's different to everyone who contracted the virus. That guy wouldn't have been affected.'

Greene nodded, his mind whirling. 'So the device wasn't there to protect him, as Messina claimed. The Jaevisk are bringing something different to us, and we've no clue what it does!'

'You think Messina knows?'

Greene held her gaze for a moment, images from the files accessed by the Data Slip flashing in his mind. 'Do you have a family, Maria?'

Her eyes narrowed. 'Why?'

'Because the next stage of this conversation could put them in danger.'

She saw that he was serious, and she lowered her head for a moment, wondering what to do. After a brief silence, she looked up at him. 'Tell me.'

Ω

Harrogate closed the door of the vehicle behind him and walked towards the main entrance of the hospital. A massive complex, it could comfortably house five thousand patients and could deal with even more in an emergency. Right now, it probably had closer to seven or eight thousand patients, and Pontifex Harrogate was decidedly uncomfortable as he crossed the threshold. He knew he was not suffering from the virus and that only Church members could contract it, but there were always other things floating around in these death-traps. Going into hospital was always a risky business.

There was a call in his ear, and he sighed: 'Harrogate here.'

'Sir, we dug up what we could on that Overseer. Seems he's not exactly on good terms with the Governor on Sieltor Prime, even though his family have served the governors for generations. If there was ever a candidate for leading a military coup, it's this guy Carak.'

'What about this agent of ours?'

'We have reason to believe he's talking about one of the deep-cover boys and girls we sent out there back in '68. Don't mean to speak out of turn, Sir, but I didn't think any of them would last this long.'

'Yeah, I remember thinking the same,' Harrogate replied thoughtfully as he stepped into an elevator. 'Not easy staying out of sight on any alien world, but it's the height that usually gets them among the Garran.'

'Yeah, we figured that too, so we went through the files looking for a particularly tall candidate. We got lucky...there's just the one. Her file's in your office, but there's no photo.'

'Well, that's a great help! The price we pay for black ops, I suppose.'

'Yes, Sir. We're trying to get the people who sent her to Sieltor, but it's not gonna be easy.'

'Easy doesn't pay well. Get me what you can...quick as you can.'

'Will do. One more thing, Sir...'

102

'Yes?'

'I'm sure you don't need us to tell you this, but...don't trust a word that Garran says. If he's out here, he's not wanted back home!'

Harrogate smiled as the elevator doors opened. 'Or maybe he is!' he joked. The channel was closed and he stepped out into the corridor. There were nurses and doctors everywhere, many of them rushing around. One nurse, a tall brunette – even in her flat shoes – was walking towards him. 'Can you hold that, please?' she called, pointing to the elevator. Harrogate stuck one foot in between the closing doors and gestured with a friendly grin for her to proceed. 'Thank you,' she said sweetly, rewarding him with a dazzling smile. 'I like your uniform.'

'Oh...thank you,' he replied as he pulled the doors open and she stepped in.

'What do you do?'

'I'm a...Pontifex,' he explained. 'It's a...security term.'

'Ah...' she nodded. 'I like security.' The doors closed and Harrogate stood there for a moment, distracted. Feeling like a foolish teen, he shook his head and, chuckling to himself, he set about finding Doctor Greene.

Ω

A strange vessel had entered the solar system, intercepted immediately by military ships dispatched by General Matthews. This was the Axcebian transport ship promised by the emissary of the Jaevisk Society, the hope of millions, the dread of the rest. Yes, it signified Jaevisk commitment to the bargain made by Councillor Messina, but it also introduced the people of Earth to the intergalactic machinations of a race synonymous with secrets and lies.

Without communication, the transport vessel continued along its course, reaching Earth orbit in less than an hour. Here it was met by almost a dozen other ships, crewed by men and women with itchy trigger-fingers. Co-ordinated by General Matthews and representatives from Central Command, shuttle crews set about bringing the cargo to the surface.

Ω

Maria sat dumbstruck, and Greene wondered how much more he could say without further risking her life. He knew that he was caught up in more than he could handle, but there was no point involving anyone else. He was already beginning to regret confiding in Maria. 'I shouldn't have said anything,' he realised quietly.

Maria nodded, then shook her head slightly as if coming out of a daze. 'What?'

'I said...'

'I heard you. Sorry. I'm just...a bit shocked.' She stared at him. 'I also think there's more.'

'More?' Greene laughed ironically. 'The Council are responsible for covering up genetic experimentation with the Garran, going back centuries, and you want more?'

'I didn't say I wanted more, just that there was more. You don't think I believe what you told me about that woman in here earlier, do you?'

'I didn't get a chance to tell you *anything*.'

'Yeah, she took control of things pretty quickly. But I didn't hear you arguing with her.'

The Doctor stood up, pushing his chair back. 'There was no point. Whatever's going on here, the wheels are firmly set in motion.'

'So she's part of it?'

Greene sighed. 'Somehow,' he replied reluctantly, nodding.

'What do we do?'

'What do you mean? We can't risk exposing this. They'll have us killed. There are rumours going around that a number of Council members have already disappeared!'

There was a knock on the office door and they looked at each other. 'Who is it?' Greene called.

'It's Pontifex Harrogate, Doctor,' came the reply. 'I'd like to speak with you, please.'

They exchanged glances again, this time of fear. Maria stood up to open the door, although Greene made to stop her. 'Your mind's been made up for you, Aidan,' she told him. 'You've no choice now.'

'I'm getting a lot of that lately,' he grumbled, as Maria opened the door.

'Pontifex Harrogate,' she welcomed him pleasantly. 'Please, come in.'

'I hope I'm not disturbing anything important,' Harrogate commented dryly.

'Oh, no,' Maria replied, turning to Greene with a wry smile. 'I was just leaving.'

Ω

Cassandra finished packing her travel case while the guard watched and waited. 'I suppose I brought this on myself,' she said, unable now to even stand up straight. 'You'd think...' She coughed so heavily that she could not finish her sentence. The guard moved closer. 'Are you alright, Councillor?'

She turned to him, her eyes red and tear-filled as she nodded. He stepped back from her, knowing that he could not contract the condition, but nonetheless uneasy in close proximity to her decaying form. The skin on her face appeared almost transparent in places, and it was peeling or split in others. The bruising had given way to eruptions of swelling and blistering. Knowing that her entire body was probably covered as such, the soldier felt the guilt of revulsion as he recalled the beautiful and desirable woman she had so recently been. 'I see it in your eyes,' she accused him gratingly. 'You can drop the pretence.'

'Councillor, I...'

'Don't bother!' she snapped, adding in a defeated tone, 'My appearance is the least of my worries right now.' She looked around her apartment as they came out of the bedroom, throwing her full-length hooded robe around her and gazing out upon the city as her shoulders sagged with the weight of the world she had created. Then, finding within her the persona that was Councillor Cassandra Messina, she drew herself up with a deep breath and walked to the door as the soldier held it open for her. 'Let's get this over with,' she said, pulling the hood over her head.

Ω

'Can I get you anything, Pontifex?'

Harrogate shook his head as he seated himself opposite the Doctor. 'I'm here for information, Doctor, not coffee.'

'Anything I can do to help,' replied Greene enthusiastically.

Harrogate raised his eyebrows. 'Really? Somehow I doubt that.'

The warmth of fear caused Greene to shiver in the air-conditioned office. 'I don't understand. Why would you say that?'

105

'Where do I start? Your meeting with Messina? Your unauthorised access of restricted files? You'll be sure to stop me when you hear something familiar?'

'How could I possibly access unauthorised files?' Greene asked, conscious of the perspiration on his forehead, the heat of his deceitful face and the twisting of his stomach.

Harrogate stood up slowly, sighing. 'I really thought you'd co-operate at this point, Doctor. I guess you don't know when the game's up.'

Greene held his calm but determined glare for a while, before conceding with an audible sigh and sitting back. 'I'm in way over my head,' he admitted.

'Yes, you are. But you can redeem yourself here and now. Tell me what you know.'

He hesitated, confused. 'I don't understand. If I could access the files, why couldn't you?' Harrogate did not reply, and Greene waded on. 'I mean, why would you be asking me what I know unless you saw the same files? And I thought you worked for the Council?'

'What happened to being in over your head, Doctor? We're working on the files, but you spoke privately with Messina and I'm sure it wasn't all about the possible complications of her surgery. Now are you going to tell me or not?'

The Doctor weighed up his options, or certainly tried to imagine some. 'I'm not sure who to trust,' he admitted.

Harrogate nodded. 'I can see that,' he replied. 'So how about this? What if I told you that a Garran Overseer was on his way here right now? And that he knows something I don't about the virus?'

Greene looked beyond the Pontifex, as if he could see through the darkened windows of his office. 'I'd advise you to find out what he knows as fast as possible.'

'Why?'

'Because the Garran are connected to this...intricately. The files were about genetic experiments involving Garran and Humans. They go back over two hundred years, to when we first encountered them, and Councillor Messina is one of the...caretakers, I guess...of those files.' He looked as if he had just realised something significant. 'But she must be working apart from the Council. That's why you're not aware of it!'

Harrogate stared at him for a moment before sitting down again, clearly not happy with being reminded that he was out of the loop on this one. 'How is this connected to the cage?' he asked finally.

'I think that these...implants the Jaevisk are bringing could have more than one purpose. They may be a cure for the virus, but all that tells us is that whoever's behind the virus...and the cage...is aware of the genetic background of the Church. Councillor Messina referred to it as selective affliction, and I think...'

'Wait a minute. You're saying that the people suffering right now...every member of the Church...they're...what...descendants of genetic crossing with the Garran?'

Greene nodded. 'It appears that way, yes.'

'So what will these implants do that you haven't been able to come up with here at home?'

'I don't know,' the surgeon admitted, 'and I won't know until I get my hands on one. Even then, I can't be sure that I'll figure it out in time...not without considerable help.'

'What do you need?'

'Experts in every field of neurological and psychological medicine. I mean, we're implanting a Jaevisk device in a Human brain, for God's sake! I'll also need the best reverse engineers on the planet, preferably people from your AAT program, cos every attempt at combating the virus on its own terms has failed.'

Harrogate's eyebrows rose. 'What do you know about AAT?'

The Doctor smiled. 'Not much really. Just what it stands for and a few conspiracy theories doing the rounds. I'm also going to need to cross-reference our finds with anything you've learned so far about the cage.'

'Well, we certainly need to figure out the connection,' Harrogate agreed. 'I'll get you what you need, Doctor. But the reasons for all this stay between us, do you understand? I don't really care about exposing the AAT program, but if the people pick up anything about these experiments...'

'I know. Sickness won't be the only thing the Church has to deal with.'

'My thoughts exactly.' Harrogate stood up and turned around, hearing the beep of an incoming call as he did. 'Yes?' he responded, tapping the button in his ear. *The devices are here,'* he heard someone say. He took a deep breath before replying, 'I'm on my way.' Before he opened the door, he turned back to the Doctor and asked, 'Have you considered postponing the surgeries until after the countdown?'

Greene shook his head. 'From what I'm hearing from my colleagues around the world, there isn't one person who'll last another six days. Like I said, the implants may be the cure, but one person who didn't need one doesn't tell me that no one else will, especially when the evidence suggests he wouldn't have been affected anyway.'

'So no matter what, you still need a test subject?'

Greene sighed. 'Yes. She's on her way.'

'So are the implants. It may be time to start praying.'

'From what I've gathered, Councillor Messina will be doing enough praying for us all.'

'Good luck, Doctor.'

'And you, Pontifex. I'm sure you don't need me to tell you not to trust that Garran Overseer.'

Harrogate smiled and opened the door. 'I'm hearing that a lot,' he said.

Ω

The Garran Star Cruiser was an impressive vessel. It did not have the grace of a Sori Border Fighter and it certainly made no allusions to the sheer dominating presence of a Jaevisk Warship. However, its weaponry and armour were significant enough to warrant the shadowing of three of Earth's largest vessels. These battleships were only slightly smaller than their Garran counterparts, but they were faster and more manoeuvrable. And they were watching closely.

The Garran vessel docked at Matthews' station as Harrogate had instructed and, within minutes, a shuttle made its way down to the planet. It was an unfortunate oversight on the part of the Battleship Commanders, but none of them seemed concerned that the Garran vessel had closed its airlock and drawn back slightly from the station.

'What are they doing?' asked General Matthews, as this was brought to his attention. 'They should be waiting for him to get back the way he came.'

The officer at the monitor shrugged. 'Maybe they don't trust us to keep the lights on.'

'Hmm. Well, whatever their doing, I don't like it.' Matthews pointed out the window, to where the ship could be seen moving slowly away. 'Two eyes, boys and girls,' he ordered the staff. 'Like a hawk.'

Ω

As the sun was beginning to set and Harrogate was on his way to meet the Garran Overseer, the vast transport network arranged for the distribution of the Jaevisk devices was set into motion. Within two hours of the Axcebian ship's arrival, thousands of land and air vehicles under armed escort had begun delivering the devices to hospitals and care centres worldwide. There was only one consignment which differed from these myriad deliveries, for it contained an individually packed device, identified only by the name of its intended recipient, crudely scrawled by Axcebian hands in the Jaevisk language: *Councillor Cassandra Messina*.

It was brought to Greene's department, where the arguments began. The people from the AAT – who did not officially exist – wanted the device first. They stressed that it could be connected to a threat of invasion and that understanding the technology from that perspective was imperative. The neuro-surgeons and Tech-psychologists wanted to begin experiments immediately to determine the effect the device would have on a Human brain, while Greene's team wanted to examine it thoroughly for any traces of blood which they could compare to the sample given them by Messina. Doctor Greene, however, had other plans, and expressed them with no hesitation. 'Will everyone please SHUT UP!' he roared as he entered the large room. Silence fell, but not the sort of respectful silence one would normally afford a figure in authority. There was an almost palpable resentment towards Greene by now. Rumours had circulated regarding his meetings with Councillor Messina and Pontifex Harrogate, and the fact that he had called these specialists here and was clearly not allowing them free rein did not sit well with a room full of egotists.

'Now, this is what's going to happen,' he continued, before anyone could respond. 'Councillor Messina is on her way here and her surgery will proceed with the device intended for her. There are more than enough of these devices for all of you to experiment with. I'm sure you'll be happy to hear that the mortality rate has ensured a workable surplus!'

Maria raised her eyebrows at that, surprised by this outright insult and wondering how the others would take it. Surprisingly, it seemed to subdue them. What was more surprising to Maria, however, was that the majority of them had enough of a conscience to at least feign shame. 'If I may...' she said, spotting a man in a business-like suit about to speak and talking before he had a chance. Greene turned to her. 'Yes, Doctor?'

She smiled inwardly at the formality. 'Are you suggesting we risk the Councillor's life before we get any results from the experiments?'

He nodded. 'That's exactly what I'm suggesting. Not only is she the one responsible for bringing us to this point, but a live subject is the only way to truly understand what we're dealing with here.'

They loved it. Blaming the Councillor was exactly the right move. Blaming anyone at this point was a good move, but Messina had never been overly popular. The only group who did not fully agree were the AAT guys, of which the suited man was one. 'Inserting the device could herald an invasion,' he argued. 'You could be playing right into their hands.'

'Whose hands?' snapped Greene, sick of everything and everyone by now.

'The Jaevisk, Doctor,' the man replied dryly. 'They're their devices, after all.'

'You're AAT, right?' Greene approached the man. Holding his ground firmly, the man looked around before asserting himself: 'I've no reason to explain myself to you, Doctor. Your authority here is questionable and your collusion with Councillor Messina will be investigated thoroughly.'

Greene grinned, uncaring. 'Messina is one of the few people on this planet who has *any* idea of what's going on here, and so we need her on side. She's also not stupid enough to think that the Jaevisk Society would go to all this trouble to invade us from within when they could wipe us out from orbit without breaking a sweat. Now, I'm no security expert, and I probably couldn't fight my way out of a paper bag, but I know a cover-up when I smell one and you lot better start giving us some answers soon!'

The Suit smiled. 'Likewise, Doctor, I'm sure,' he replied, raising his hands in surrender and stepping back. 'Go ahead with your surgery. But any indication of conspiracy on your part will be severely dealt with.'

Maria stepped up and took Greene's arm, eyeballing the Suit. 'You know, for some reason, I think you're as much in the dark on this as any of us. So why don't you just let us get on with it and we'll all take it from there?'

'Sounds like a good idea,' said someone else.

'What are we waiting for?' another quipped. 'It's only Messina.'

Ω

She arrived at the hospital amidst a sea of media hounds, political enemies, defensive fans and offensive protestors. Unable to face them

110

physically or mentally, she remained silent and detached as the medical staff took over and led her inside. Security sent by Harrogate kept the hounds at bay and Cassandra was soon standing in the silence of an elevator. Flanked by two nurses – one of whom looked down at her robed and hooded figure with something other than medical fascination – and two armed men, the journey to Greene's floor was a veritable eternity of apprehension. Her heart fluttered, her stomach turned and her mouth was dry. Her hands began to shake and she felt as though her head might float away from her body. She heard the voice, calm as ever. '*I know this is frightening for you,*' he whispered, his voice sending chills through her, '*but everything you're doing is for the greater good. I hope you can believe that, Cassandra.*' She stared silently at the closed doors of the elevator. '*This is a great opportunity for you,*' he continued. '*The fate of billions is in your hands.*'

'I don't *want* that responsibility!' she snapped aloud, forgetting herself and cringing with the pain in her throat.

The guards exchanged glances with the shorter nurse until she addressed Cassandra. 'Are you…alright, Councillor?'

There was an awkward silence as Cassandra dealt with embarrassment on top of everything else. 'I'm…sorry,' she croaked eventually. 'I was talking to myself.' There were tears in her eyes which no one could see.

The taller nurse had remained silent and unflinching throughout, but she smiled knowingly as she smoothed the front of her uniform. 'As long as you don't answer back,' she said sweetly.

Ω

Doctor Greene and his staff waited at the elevator doors, and Greene felt the rising panic of one who had opened a door into a dangerous world and heard the door slam firmly behind as he stepped inside. Eyes and ears watched and listened, those who wished to learn, those who wished to accuse and those desperate to condemn. Greene was under a level of scrutiny far beyond anything he had experienced throughout his career. 'Are you okay?' Maria asked him.

'No.' He grinned. 'But once we get started, I'll deal with it.'

'I don't doubt that,' she whispered, moving closer. 'But it's what you're going to be dealing with that's worrying me.'

'You mean surgically?'

111

'Don't you?'

He chuckled softly, but all trace of humour vanished as the elevator doors opened. Nothing else registered, not the armed guards nor the tall nurse of whose secret he was aware. All he saw was Messina, and he felt a lump in his throat as he recognised the terrible progression of her condition. Yes, she tried to hide it, and the hooded robe made her look like a melodramatic portrayal of some horrific leper, but her back was more bent than it had been and her shoulders were slumped. He knew that the psychological effect of having the weight of the world on her shoulders was surely evident, but there was something else, something he had seen and heard of in only the worst cases over the past number of days. She was close to death.

Raising her head, her watery eyes registered his expression. 'You look like you've seen a ghost, Doctor,' she said.

He offered his hand. 'Not if I can help it,' he replied, waiting for her to respond. She did so, and he saw the corrupted skin of her right arm as it emerged from the sleeve. Her skin was clammy and leathery, and it was a thoroughly unpleasant experience to shake her hand. Greene shook it for longer than was necessary, and she knew why. 'Thank you,' she said, with genuine appreciation.

'Everything's ready, Councillor,' Maria informed her. 'We're doing our best to keep away those who have no business being here.'

'I appreciate that,' said Cassandra. 'Has a woman named Nell being looking for me? Nell Raesa?'

'Not that I'm aware of. Is she family?'

Cassandra shook her head. 'A close friend, that's all. It doesn't matter.'

Maria gave a sympathetic smile, for it was clear that it mattered considerably. As Greene gestured for the patient to walk with him, Maria addressed the two nurses. 'Get scrubbed up, ladies. We're prepping the patient in thirty minutes.' She watched them walk away, sure that the taller one had winked at her as she passed. Shaking it off, she turned to the guards. 'So...what's the plan for you guys?'

'Oh, we're here to watch *you* guys,' one of them replied sarcastically. For a moment, Maria considered a sharp retort, but then she looked back down the corridor, seeing the nurses. The taller one had broken away, taking a different route to the theatre. 'I'd watch closely if I were you,' she said.

'I've had to make you Enemy Number One just to keep control of this.'

Cassandra nodded. 'I'm sure you had little objection to that,' she said. They walked on a little more, until Cassandra stumbled and Greene caught her. 'Guess I'm weaker than I thought,' she groaned.

'Let's just put it down to nerves. No one saw it, so the inimitable strength of Councillor Messina remains legendary. Here, sit down for a moment.' He helped her to a chair as Maria rounded the corner with the guards close behind her. 'I'll get some water,' she offered diligently, passing them. The guards hurried over to her, but Cassandra dismissed them. 'I need to speak with the doctor alone.'

Greene sat next to her and watched them stop just out of earshot. 'Do you want to postpone the procedure?'

'Would you recommend that?'

He shook his head. 'As much as I hate to say it…it has to be you. If not, then some other poor soul who's got nothing to do with any of this.'

'Doctor, if you've done your homework, then you know that every Church member has something to do with this.'

'Possibly,' he conceded, 'but they didn't exacerbate the issue as you did. They're not even aware of their circumstances.'

'Their *circumstances*?' She laughed. 'You mean that they're half-Human, half-Garran *hybrids*?'

'Hybrid is hardly the right term, Councillor, certainly not this far down the line. They're…something else entirely!'

'Thank you, Doctor,' Messina teased. 'Or have you forgotten I'm one of them?'

Greene stood up, seeing Maria returning with water and raising his hand to stop her approach. 'Listen,' he said softly to Cassandra, leaning in close, 'you were able to tie this all together within hours of the cage arriving. You got the device, you had the technology checked for its compatibility and undoubtedly knew exactly who the virus would target. You just wanted me to do the work through more official channels so the investigation would expand without your presence. I'm sure you've arranged to disappear pretty soon.'

She held his gaze for a moment. 'That's not all I did,' she confessed.

'Go on.'

Looking around, she ensured that they would not be overheard, seeing only the guards turning people away and Maria waiting with her water. 'Someone's telling me what to do,' she told him quietly. 'I can't go into any more detail, cos I don't have any. When I was told about the Garran connection, I contacted the one person I knew could give me some insight and possibly help me get out of this mess.'

'I'm not gonna like this, am I?'

'He's from Sieltor Prime. An Overseer named Carak. I told him to use whatever excuse he could think of to get here.'

Greene stared at her in shock. '*You* called him here?'

'You know about him?'

'Harrogate left here a while ago to meet him.'

Cassandra nodded. 'Then he's handling things well. Undoubtedly he'll use the meeting with Harrogate to get to me. He and I really need to talk.'

'Why?'

'Let's put it this way. Just as I'm not exactly Human...' Again she looked around before finishing. 'He's not exactly Garran.'

Ω

Almost an hour later, Nell Raesa used a political influence rarely brandished to gain access to the floor of the hospital on which Cassandra would be treated. Having bid farewell to her parents as the civilian transport took them from the North Pole station and ascended into the clouds to pass beyond the dark and ominous components of the cage, Nell decided that she would come to the hospital to make sure that her decision to stay had not been in vain. Furious with Cassandra for allowing this terror to be brought upon them without warning, Nell wandered around the quiet corridors with her blood boiling, eager for a fight. Amidst a silence filled only by the pounding of her heart, she heard muffled voices from behind a closed door and she stopped to listen, surprised to hear a woman's voice speaking in Garran. It was a language in which Nell was well versed, and she did not expect to hear the woman talking about Cassandra with considerable disrespect: '*She's signing the death warrants of everyone in the Church. You know that.*'

'*I also know that they'll die without this thing,*' a second woman replied in English. Nell realised that this speaker was here and that the other was at the end of a Com device.

114

'*There might still be a way to prevent that,*' the first woman argued. '*At the very least, you'll push them to reconsider their options.*'

'*And what happens when Carak starts talking? He's here now and he's bound to expose me. You should have found a way to stop him!*'

'*He's far beyond our control now, I assure you. You have to do this. Millions of lives hang in the balance.*'

'*One death to save them all?*'

Nell held her breath now, and she could hear her heart pounding in her ears. She knew who they were talking about, but she was terrified to accept it. Unfortunately, it was confirmed: '*Messina agreed that she would die rather than be part of this,*' the Garran woman said. '*So, one way or another, you have to make that happen.*' The conversation was ended and Nell hurried away from the door. Farther down the corridor, she slipped into another room and watched through the open door as an extremely tall woman in a nurse's uniform passed by. Nell crept out and watched her continue down the corridor, wondering what to do. Without any sort of plan, she rushed after the nurse, desperate to stop whatever was planned for her beloved Cassandra.

Ω

On the opposite side of the city, Pontifex Harrogate rose from a comfortable seat at a conference table as his guests were escorted into the room. The long room was ringed by soldiers, who stiffened as the two-metre tall Garran Overseer and his second-in-command, a man of a slightly narrower build but a more severe appearance, walked in. 'Ah, Pontifex Harrogate,' the Overseer beamed as they shook hands, 'it's a pleasure to make your acquaintance.'

Harrogate smiled. 'I don't doubt that, Overseer Carak,' he replied, 'considering how difficult it would normally be for someone of your rank to make my acquaintance.'

'Ah, but these are...extenuating circumstances, wouldn't you say?' Carak sat down opposite Harrogate, who waited for the other Garran to follow suit before he also seated himself. 'And I hear that you're the man responsible for...building bridges, as it were.'

'That's one way of putting it, I suppose.' Harrogate looked at the other Garran, knowing a true soldier when he saw one and feeling a slight shiver pass through him. 'Aren't you going to introduce me to your second-in-command?'

115

The other Garran stiffened as Carak smiled broadly. 'Certainly. This is Tanna. He is my...First Officer, you might say. A trusted advisor, a strong and experienced soldier. All in all, a good man to have around.' Tanna nodded graciously and acknowledged Harrogate dutifully.

'He doesn't seem too happy to be around right now, Overseer. Perhaps he...advised against this little sojourn of yours?'

Carak laughed, but the humour drained from the sound. 'To business,' he said.

Harrogate nodded. 'By all means. And get to the point, cos I haven't got time to waste with diplomatic niceties.'

The Overseer stood, and the soldiers around the room raised their weapons. Harrogate gestured for them to restrain themselves, but Carak seemed not to care. Even Tanna had not flinched. 'Your agent discovered something of significance, Pontifex. However, considering that this was some time ago, we were surprised that she chose not to pass that information on to you. We believe that someone else has recruited her, although we've failed to identify her handler.'

'I see. Any theories?'

'Lots of theories, but none very convincing. What concerns me is that she came back to Earth some time ago and she clearly hasn't come to you.'

Harrogate had to concede that this also concerned him. 'We'll get back to how you know she came home. You can start by telling me the nature of this information.'

'It concerns genetic experiments undertaken by both of our governments some two centuries ago...' Carak looked down at Tanna as he visibly reacted to his commander's simply blurting out this information, raising his hand to his forehead in an unmistakably Human gesture. 'The goal was to find a genetic line capable of surviving biological attacks.'

Harrogate held Carak's gaze for a moment, and then watched Tanna, who was clearly uncomfortable with the progression of the conversation. Finally, he decided to ease the younger officer's suffering. 'Although I wasn't aware of the specific goals of the project,' he began, noting the surprise in Tanna's face as he did so, 'these experiments have recently been brought to my attention.'

Carak was also surprised, but he failed to show it, sitting down again and leaning forward. 'Do you mind if I ask how?' he pressed, delighted that his lies were working. It was true what they said about Humans: give them half-truths and they believed anything.

'Yes, I do...for now.'

'Please, Pontifex. Don't underestimate the magnitude of what you're dealing with here. The higher powers have kept this quiet on both of our worlds for a long time, handing down the information from generation to generation. And all this time the descendants of the original experiments are propagating.'

'I'm aware of the magnitude, thank you. We've had significant Councillors assassinated and members of a religious order murdered just for being outside this cage hanging over our heads. Perhaps you'd like to shed some light on that.'

Carak sat back, glancing at Tanna, who remained silent. 'We're not responsible for the...cage, if that's what you mean. We wouldn't have anywhere near the resources to build anything like that, and quite frankly, I've no knowledge of anyone who would.'

'Not even the Jaevisk?'

The Overseer shook his head. 'We're closer to their territory than you, Pontifex, and we've seen what they've got. They're a formidable race, of course, but they're more like...nomads...travellers. The only consistency to them is their observation of a system on the fringe of their space.'

'The same system the cage came from, if I'm not mistaken.'

'Yes, we saw that too, but still...'

'They know more than they're saying.'

Carak smiled. 'They always know more than they're saying. Just like a certain Councillor who happened to survive your little...cull.'

Now Harrogate hesitated. He considered everything he had learned so far, and wondered how it was all connected. Now to hear that Messina was known to this man...that gave him pause. 'I'm impressed by your intelligence gathering, Overseer. It wouldn't have anything to do with a certain vessel you had stationed on our moon, would it?'

Tanna leaned in and whispered something in their own language. It was quiet enough that Harrogate had to wait until the recording of the meeting was analysed before hearing it. He would later learn that Tanna said, '*It was called home to join the armada.*' Carak nodded. 'That ship was initially sent out on my order, Pontifex,' he explained. 'Just as Councillor Messina is one of the...guardians of the project details here, I'm her...counterpart on Sieltor Prime.'

'So you monitor the Human subjects from that ship?'

117

'Yes, and a network of information modules relays the data back to me.'

Harrogate stood, pushing his chair back. 'Are you aware of the situation we're in, Overseer?' he asked, annoyed now. 'I mean, you do realise that the descendants of those experiments are being specifically targeted by the cage emissions? It's not random. It's a highly advanced virus!'

'And Councillor Messina believes that some Jaevisk device will reverse the process, I'm told.'

'You sound like *you* don't believe that. I'm interested as to how much you actually know about all this, Overseer, because for all your attempts at transparency, you're holding a lot back.'

'I believe that's my prerogative.'

'Not anymore.' Harrogate gestured and stepped back as guns were raised and fingers were poised on triggers around the room. Tanna made to respond, but Carak stopped him. 'You're making a mistake, Pontifex. No amount of interrogation will work on me, I promise you. On the other hand, there is a way I could prove that I'm worthy of your trust.'

'I doubt that.' Harrogate headed for the door as the soldiers closed in to escort their prisoners to more exclusive quarters.

'How long ago did the Jaevisk Warships leave here, Harrogate?' Carak asked, causing the Pontifex to stop and turn his head slightly. 'What?'

'You heard me. How long ago?'

'What difference does that make?'

'Answer the question, Pontifex. It may prove costly to ignore the consequences.'

Harrogate turned around fully and looked at both Garran. The soldiers moved back as he approached them. 'I've no time for games. I asked you to get to the point, but you've so many points that I'm no better off than when I started.'

Carak nodded to Tanna, who reached slowly and cautiously amidst the soldiers into his pocket and withdrew a small touch-screen pad. He tapped the screen a few times and then handed it to Harrogate, as Carak explained, 'This is a relative time-frame between our two worlds. The Jaevisk left Earth...' he paused as Harrogate noted the time, 'and then arrived at Sieltor Prime.'

Harrogate looked up in shock. 'They went straight to your people?'

118

Carak nodded. 'Offering an alliance, Pontifex. Does that sound familiar?'

'Why would they do that?'

The Overseer shrugged. 'We're not sure of their intentions. But what we do know is that shortly after making arrangements with your Councillor Messina to have those devices replicated, they asked our Governor for ten thousand Garran soldiers, citing some vague reason or other.'

'Ten thousand...' Harrogate was lost, drawn in far beyond his pay-grade. 'Why?'

'We have no idea,' Carak admitted. And Harrogate knew he was telling the truth. 'The only thing we've got is the connection to your missing agent, and if she's here now, she's here to cause trouble. I urge you to stop her before this gets worse.'

'Stop her?'

Carak shook his head impatiently. 'You have to shoot her on sight, Pontifex. Because, believe me, she won't give it a second thought.'

'I don't know how I'm supposed to find her. We've no image on file.'

'I'd be happy to help with that.' Carak nodded to Tanna, who gestured for Harrogate to return the pad. Once again tapping some buttons on the screen, Tanna set about bringing up an image. 'It's encrypted,' he muttered in a cold voice. While he worked on decrypting the image, Carak looked at a picture on the wall, a beautiful painting of the gas giant, Jupiter. 'I've always been an admirer of your star system, Pontifex,' he said. 'I find its ecology quite...primitive.'

'How gracious of you.'

'I was hoping to visit that wonderful moon on the way home...what was it called?'

'Titan,' muttered Tanna absently.

'Titan, yes. To see the methane rivers and witness a cryo-volcano. Quite spectacular, I'd imagine.'

'I wouldn't know,' said Harrogate. 'We do our best to keep...tourists away from an evolving world.'

'Quite right. Don't worry, Pontifex. I'll be careful not to step on anything.'

Harrogate smiled thinly. 'What's taking so long?'

Tanna looked up, eyebrows raised, and then handed the screen to the Pontifex. 'Oh, my God!' he exclaimed.

119

'What?' snapped Carak. 'Have you seen her?'

Harrogate ignored him, tapping the com button at his ear. 'Get me the team at the hospital,' he ordered.

'There's no response, Sir.'

'What do you mean, no response?' He was walking away as he spoke, and he gestured for the soldiers to follow him. The two Garran visitors were left alone. 'I believe the clock is ticking, Tanna,' said Carak.

Ω

Despite the sedative, Cassandra could still feel her heart pounding in her chest and in her throat, and she doubted the effectiveness of the anaesthetic to make things any better. Her head had been shaved and she lay face-down on the trolley-bed, supported by a cut-out area to minimize her discomfort. Garbed only in a surgical gown and feeling more vulnerable and exposed than at any time she could remember, she was thankful for the presence of Doctor Greene. He had stayed by her side throughout the preparation, and they had shared a companionable banter to alleviate the tension. Someone else entered the operating room. Cassandra could not see who it was, but she could feel the draught caused by the door.

'I'm feeling breezes in places I don't care to mention,' she remarked with unfelt levity.

'It doesn't help that you're exposed that way, I imagine,' replied Greene as he watched the Anaesthetist checking the levels in the IV.

'If something goes wrong and I end up insane...' it was here that one could hear the truth of anxiety, 'can I trust you to make sure my ass isn't hanging out as I'm running round the place?'

Greene smiled sympathetically. 'I'll personally look after it, Councillor.'

She chuckled softly. 'I hope that's a professional statement.'

'We're going to administer the anaesthetic now,' he told her gently, nodding to the Anaesthetist. 'Just keep breathing gently and try to relax.'

'Doctor, I haven't been breathing gently for days.' She paused. 'Has there been any progress made with the tests?'

'Not that I'm aware of, although the way things are going, I'm unlikely to be the first to know. The AAT guys are all over this.'

'But I'm still the guinea pig, right?'

120

The tall nurse came up beside Greene. 'Would you like me to take over, Doctor?' she asked sweetly.

Greene glared at her, but then realised he was doing so and looked cautiously around. 'I think the Anaesthetist can handle this, thank you...Linda.'

She smiled thinly. 'I'll just wait for your instructions, then, shall I?'

'I believe that's how it's supposed to go, yes.'

She stepped back with a malevolent grin, joining the other nurses in their preparations. The Anaesthetist performed his duties and stood back to monitor the situation. 'Twenty seconds,' he reported, to which Greene nodded his acknowledgement.

'No...' gasped Cassandra, imagining she could feel liquid death travelling throughout her body. 'Wait...I'm not ready.'

Greene took her hand. 'You never will be, Councillor. Just relax.'

'No!' Her breathing was short and her heart rate was not as steady as it should have been. As she felt her eyes getting heavy and she drifted deeper into oblivion, she thought she heard the door opened forcefully behind her and she once again felt a slight chill. But this was not from some wayward breeze. Rather, it was caused by the last words she heard before losing consciousness. In her delirium, she could have sworn she heard Nell shouting, 'Stop! She's not who she says she is!'

$$\Omega$$

As the operation was underway, a team of AAT agents had occupied an entire floor of the hospital and were studying the Jaevisk devices. So far, no one from AAT could figure out what the thing was for, let alone the effect it would have on those to whose brain it would be attached. Sitting in a silent and secluded room, Agent Malone had dissected his device methodically, performing the standard work of a reverse engineer, until it lay in pieces across his workstation. One by one, he examined every element under the microscope and made notes regarding the dimensions, the composition and the possible applications of each. As he finished this task, he sat back and closed his eyes, yawning, only to be disturbed from his respite by the sound of a commotion in the next room. He imagined the frustrated agent in the adjacent room slamming his fist on the desk in anger.

'Hey, keep it down in there!' Malone shouted. 'We're all in the same boat, you know.' Silence fell, but a similar sound erupted from the room on the opposite side. 'What the hell?' Malone got to his feet, too quickly it seemed, as the blood left his head and he almost fell over. He reached out with his left hand to steady himself, but accidently knocked a tiny piece of the device onto the floor. 'Damn it!'

As he hunkered down with a tweezers in hand to retrieve it, he did not hear the door opening behind him. The piece in question was a tiny cylindrical rod that had been in the centre of the device. The fall to the floor must have damaged it, for when Malone brought it back up to the light on his desk, he saw that dark liquid was dripping from it. The amount was miniscule, but it did not take much for him to speculate as to what it was. 'This is blood!' he gasped, before realising that someone was watching him. As he spun round, the last thing he saw was a black-garbed figure brandishing a knife. He noticed that the blade appeared shiny and new. It was strange what one noticed.

Ω

Greene swung round, seeing a pretty and petite brunette barging into the operating theatre as if the world was about to end. 'How *dare* you come in here!' he shouted. 'Where the hell's our security?'

The intruder pointed to the tall nurse. 'Why don't you ask *her*?'

Before Greene could do so, however, Linda had levelled a gun at him, and she was no longer smiling. 'Get on with the procedure or they'll be cleaning you off the wall!' she roared.

The Anaesthetist was furious: 'What on *Earth* is going on here?'

The nurse shot him in the head and Greene felt his stomach turn as the man crumpled to the sterile floor. He backed away in terror. 'What's *wrong* with you?' he shouted. 'We're doing what you wanted, so what are *you* doing?'

'She's taking orders from someone else,' their intruder put in. 'Some…Garran woman!'

'Who *are* you?' snapped Greene angrily.

'She's Messina's lapdog,' Linda explained, turning the gun on Nell as she reached into her pocket. Withdrawing a tiny plastic case with something metal inside, she offered it to Greene. 'Take this and attach it to the Jaevisk device.'

Greene remained still. 'This is why you were so eager to see it before the procedure.'

'You've no idea what you're doing, Doctor,' she reminded him. 'You're just taking a gamble with unknown technology without considering the implications.'

'And you're aware of the implications, I suppose?'

She held his glare, wanting to tell him but knowing the dangers of doing so. If it became public knowledge that Garran elements were behind her presence here, the consequences would be catastrophic. 'You have to do this, Doctor,' she replied eventually, in a tone that told him everything.

He shook his head. 'My job is to help people.'

Nell stalked towards the armed woman, her lips trembling. 'If I lose her, you crazy bitch, I'll see you hunted down and strung up!'

Linda grinned, closing the gap so that the gun pressed against Nell's chest. 'I think the prize for Crazy Bitch goes to your lover,' she sneered. 'Don't pretend you don't know what's going on here.' Around the room, the other three attending nurses were ashen and terrified. Linda looked beyond Nell to them. 'One of you moves, all of you die, understand?' They nodded frantically. 'Look around you, Doctor,' Linda told him. 'There are enough people here for you to help. You can keep them alive by doing what I say.' Again she offered him the tiny plastic box. 'Attach this to the centre of the device and carry out the procedure. If you don't, everyone in here dies.'

'You can't expect to get out of here alive.'

'I don't. Now get back to work!'

Greene took the box and reluctantly began, setting it down next to the dish in which sat the tiny Jaevisk implant. Trying to think what he could do to stop this madness, he called for a laser scalpel and Linda permitted the assistance of the nurses with a nod. Greene took a deep breath and waited for his hands to steady before beginning the shallow incision that first allowed him to draw back the skin, revealing access to the skull. He called for the saw. As he switched it on, Nell and Linda looked away.

Aware of the gun barrel pressing against her, Nell looked up at the woman in disgust. 'Why Cassandra?' she asked, having to raise her voice as the saw cut in. 'She was just confused...and misled.'

'Two reasons,' said Linda, keeping the ensuing surgery in her periphery as the smell of the bone-saw did its work. 'She brought the Jaevisk into this and brought their technology amongst us. But she's also part of something far worse.'

'What? The Church?'

'The Church is nothing to the people she works for.'

123

'I don't understand,' Nell confessed. 'What are you talking about?'

'I was sure you knew. But by the time you do understand...by the time everyone understands, it might be too late. I have to do this now.'

There was some commotion outside, the sound of someone running down the corridor and then shouting, 'They're down!' The door burst in and Nell cried out and dropped to the floor as Linda fired at the men running in, killing two of them instantly and injuring a third. The fourth man crouched and shot her in the leg, causing her to scream in agony and collapse. Yet she fired as he did so, killing him and waiting for the next. The nurses were crying and Greene had stepped back from his patient, the little Jaevisk device resting in the palm of his hand. The other item had not been removed from its case.

Silence descended, and no more of Harrogate's men came in. Instead, the man himself could be heard from outside. 'Why are you doing this?' he called to the woman. 'You work for *us*. Damn it, you work for *me*!'

Linda ignored him, turning to Greene. 'Please, Doctor,' she implored with heartfelt urgency. 'Please do it!'

'I can't,' he told her. 'Without knowing why...I just can't.'

She was bleeding profusely from her leg wound, and it was clear that she was weakening. She took a deep breath, and then she managed to rise from the floor with her teeth gritted in pain. Then she turned her gun on Greene as she hobbled towards him. 'Then I will,' she gasped, firing at him. The bullet took him high in his left shoulder, throwing him back against the operating table. The Jaevisk device fell out of his hand, landing at the edge of the surgical gown below the nape of Messina's neck.

Linda pushed Greene aside, dropping her gun and taking up the little plastic case. She was about to take out the item she had brought when Harrogate stepped in and shot her. One shot to her left shoulder spun her around while a second shot to her chest threw her back across Messina's unconscious body, where she began to cough up blood. Somehow, she still managed to twist herself around, getting hold of the Jaevisk implant and placing the circular device on Messina's exposed brain. Before she could attach the peripheral object with her other hand, however, Harrogate hauled her back with such force that she was slammed against the monitoring equipment. It came crashing down around her as she fell to the floor, and the tiny metal device bounced across the tiles.

Nell was in tears as she went to Cassandra, seeing the horrific sight of the Jaevisk implant sitting on her brain. Behind her, Linda had armed herself with a fallen scalpel. She spat out blood and screamed in fury and determination. Nell spun around and shouted, 'NO!' as she saw Harrogate raise his gun, but he mercilessly shot Linda in the head. Collapsing to the floor in shock, Nell watched the blood pooling on the floor around the mysterious woman. Harrogate moved swiftly over to Greene as the nurses ran out, passing more soldiers on their way in. What he saw as he helped the Doctor to his feet astonished and terrified him.

The tiny circular Jaevisk device which sat on Messina's exposed brain extended from its core countless tendrils of fibrous metal. They sought out parts of the brain with programmed precision, and they latched themselves to these target areas like leeches, evenly distributing themselves across the left and right hemispheres. Once they had done so, the disc drew upon them, causing it to lift from where it was and to be drawn into its proper position inside the patient's head. It moved itself closer to the upper stem, and it was then that Cassandra's body erupted into violent convulsions. More of Harrogate's people ran in and struggled to hold her down, until she finally fell still. 'Is she okay?' Harrogate asked them as he helped Greene out of the theatre.

'She's breathing!'

Greene tried to look back, wincing from the pain in his shoulder. 'Make sure she stays that way,' he told Harrogate. 'If she dies, they all die!'

Ω

Overseer Carak walked with Tanna back to their shuttle. The waiting pilot was surprised to see them without an escort. 'I gathered there was some emergency and Pontifex Harrogate had to leave,' Carak explained. 'We didn't even get a chance to say Goodbye.'

The pilot was not amused, and pressed the button on a device at his hip as the aliens walked past him and embarked. The locator activated, sending the pilot's position to Central Command. The pilot was not the only one who sent a silent signal.

Matthews was the first to see the Star Cruiser begin its descent towards the cage. 'They're on the move, people,' he shouted. 'Get to it!' He watched as the Garran ship headed for the zenith of the cage. 'Someone talk to me. Don't tell me Central's got all the firepower.'

'I've got three Cruisers on intercept,' someone reported. 'Two Snipers coming up from the surface,' said someone else. 'I borrowed a heavy gunner from Central,' said a third. 'Everything else is wrapped up in evac.'

'Don't give them an inch!' Matthews ordered. 'Light 'em up!'

As the shuttle rose into the air and the pilot set course to return the Garran to their ship, his instruments showed him that the Star Cruiser was descending from orbit. 'What the hell?' Hearing movement behind him, he turned to see a gun pointed at his forehead. Tanna pulled the trigger and the pilot slumped over the controls as Carak said, 'Quick as you can, please, Tanna. As much as it galls me to say it on this dreadfully cold world...take us to the North Pole.'

The Star Cruiser levelled and then continued its descent between the disconnected polar sections of the cage. Standing at the energy-sealed edge of their fated section, Colle, Jason and Sandra watched the Garran ship passing down towards the atmosphere. 'Will you look at that?' breathed Colle in amazement. A missile suddenly exploded on impact with the Garran ship and the three watchers jumped back in fright. Two small and very fast-moving attack craft came into view, opening up on the Star Cruiser, which responded with its considerable array of weaponry. A stray shot struck the energy wall, causing it to fluctuate ominously just as Colle was about to step up again. He stepped back.

'They've engaged our ship,' Tanna reported.

'We'll worry about that later. How much longer?'

The ground beneath them was snow- and ice-covered, and great pieces of glaciers were sheared off as the shuttle passed them low and fast. 'Four seconds. Is the device ready?'

In the rear compartment of the shuttle, Carak was fiddling with a black cube with four-inch edges. A number of blue lights flashed as he turned the object in his hand. He nodded, but said, 'I have no idea.'

'We're here.' Tanna landed the shuttle and waited as Carak exited into the icy air. He was almost overwhelmed by the sudden cold and he hurried to a spot in front of the shuttle. Here he stood and looked straight up, watching his ship grow larger as it made its way down to him. The wind cut through him, but he managed to place the black box on the ice and activate it. Immediately, he turned and ran back to the shuttle as a

126

blinding blue beam of light shot upwards, spreading itself wider as it ascended towards the zenith of the cage. Back in the shuttle with the door closed, Carak did not need to say a word. Tanna nodded and took the shuttle up, heading for the Star Cruiser, only narrowly avoiding death as a shell was launched from the Heavy Gunner which had arrived at the scene. The ice exploded beneath the rising shuttle, enveloping it momentarily in white mist and melting debris. The shuttle continued to rise, and the Garran ship above fired down at the large Earth vessel, even as it continued to hold off the other five attack craft. But someone else was about to join the party.

'Vortex opening along lunar orbit, General. Moving in fast!'

'They're ready for a fight,' someone else warned. 'Full shields and weapons!'

'What?' Matthews felt his heart pounding. 'Get our defences up. Launch any fighters we've got down below.'

The Jaevisk Warship moved swiftly towards Earth, and fighter craft exploded from it, descending towards the Garran ship as it in turn rose through the atmosphere, bombarded by the Humans. Somehow the Garran managed to break atmosphere, the Star Cruiser looking considerably worse for wear as the shuttle docked inside it and the ship passed through a circular pool of blue light at the zenith created by whatever Carak had done. No more than a score of fighters from Matthews' station had engaged their Jaevisk counterparts. The Jaevisk, however, did not return one shot at the Humans. On the station, Matthews heard the inevitable, 'Central's ordering us to stand down!' but he ignored it.

The Jaevisk Warship, like some ravenous beast, had engaged the Star Cruiser, even as the Garran were being pummelled from every angle by the Jaevisk fighters. The Star Cruiser appeared to have lost navigation control, as it rushed along a collision course towards the Jaevisk. Then something happened which would echo across the galaxy for a long time. The massive Warship, without so much as an open wound on its surface, appeared to explode from its very heart. Debris shot out in every direction, the Jaevisk fighter craft were obliterated by the fury of their mothership's destruction, and even some of Matthews' fighters were caught in the blast.

The Star Cruiser, however, enveloped as it was in the madness, survived annihilation by means far beyond their own technology, seeming to pass through the hell and emerge from the swiftly extinguished fires of the battle to escape from the system. Matthews and his staff stared in shock as the pieces of the Warship floated aimlessly around the epicentre of destruction. 'Get someone out there to look for survivors,' the General ordered.

'General. The cage.'

Matthews saw it. Descending along the north-south lines of the cage until they could no longer be seen in the south were lines of pulsing blue light. While this phenomenon may have indicated an event of immense significance and technological complexity to any who might be versed in such things, to Matthews it simply meant trouble. 'Now what?' he said.

THE FIFTH DAY

Cassandra opened her eyes slowly, seeing bright lights on the ceiling above, hating them for their intrusion but hailing them as the harbingers of her survival. She found with relief that she could breathe slowly and deeply, feeling a strength in her lungs she had not felt for what seemed like an eternity. There was silence around her, and she tried to move her head. Something prevented that movement, and she gasped. 'What's happening?'

There was no reply, and she imagined that she might be in some kind of limbo, waiting to die. She heard a rhythmic tapping sound begin then, and thought that Death might be growing impatient with her, his long, skinless fingers tapping on the metal of her hospital bed. A door opened and she imagined the scythe for souls scraping along the tiled floor. 'How's our patient?' asked a familiar voice.

The delirium faded, and Cassandra cried. 'I thought I was dead,' she whimpered.

Greene came up to stand beside her, and she could see him in her periphery, noting the blue fabric of the sling holding his left arm against his white lab coat. 'For a while there, so did I,' he admitted with a gentle smile as he checked the monitors and the equipment arrayed around her. He placed a drinking tube against her lips and she gratefully took the water. 'I guess it's going to be tougher to get rid of you than we thought.'

'Very funny. Why can't I move my head?'

'We'll remove that in a while. It's just something to keep you safe. There were some...reactions to the implant.'

'What sort of reactions?' she gasped.

'That doesn't matter now. What matters is that it seems to have worked.'

Cassandra shed new tears. 'I'm not going to die?'

Greene shook his head. 'Your body started combating the virus within hours, but there's still a lot of it left. I'll explain it all when you're up and about, but I want you to rest for a while.'

'So it worked!' She smiled. 'Have the procedures begun?'

Greene sighed. 'I was reluctant to rush into something so widespread, but...I was outvoted. It looks like every Church member will have the device inserted. Still...' he paused, 'more will die before they ever reach an operating table. As you can imagine, theatre space is at a premium.'

'So your procedure's now the blueprint?' Cassandra closed her eyes and grinned. 'I guess that makes you the hero of the day.'

Greene stepped back and looked at his wounded arm, choosing not to reply. He could not tell her what really happened, or how the death of the mystery nurse had affected him, or that there was no standard procedure to speak of. To tell her that the device had practically implanted itself would be far from comforting. 'By the way,' he resumed, 'don't worry about the tapping sound. It's a machine regulating your heartbeat while the brain adapts to its new companion. Everything's looking good. Relatively speaking, of course.'

'So the tapping's keeping me alive?' she mused. 'That's better than what I thought it was.'

'I wouldn't think of it at all if I were you. Get some rest and I'll see you later.'

'Wait. I'd rather you explained now.'

'Explained...?'

'About the virus.'

'Well, it's more the cure I was going to explain, but I don't think you're ready to hear all that right now, Councillor.'

'I'll be the judge of what I'm ready for, if you don't mind.' She could not see him, and her helplessness infuriated her. 'And for God's sake, will you take this damned thing off my head?'

He regarded her for a moment, deciding what to do. 'You need to realise that any sudden shock to your system could be damaging.'

'You say that and expect me to just lay here clueless?' She laughed. 'I didn't take you for a tease, Doctor.'

He called for a nurse, who came over and began to undo the brace, before removing the protection from around her head. Cassandra opened her mouth wide, stretching her jaws. 'Much better,' she said. 'Now tell me.'

He pulled up a chair and sat next to her. 'The virus triggered the cumulative ionization of Rubidium, generating an endothermic reaction that...eventually...would have killed you.'

Cassandra nodded. 'So the Jaevisk device stopped it?'

'It's in the process of stopping it, yes. Intermittent charges to your nervous system are systematically combating the virus, but different parts of your system are experiencing different intensities of activity right now.

The device seems to be aware of what it's dealing with and the charges are on a regular cycle.'

'Sounds complicated.'

Greene laughed softly. 'The medical community is stunned by this technology.' His face darkened and he leaned closer to her. 'But we're also highly suspicious of the connections here. It's very convenient that this thing worked so effectively.'

'The Jaevisk aren't behind this,' Cassandra assured him.

'No, Councillor,' he agreed. 'You are. Or someone you're working for. Harrogate is pulling his hair out trying to figure out what's going on.'

'Then you should tell him he's wasting his time,' she replied, smiled sweetly, 'before he's no hair left.'

'Hmm. I can't imagine that would stop him. Especially now since he thinks the Garran are involved.'

Her eyes narrowed. 'In what sense? They couldn't have brought the cage here, and it's unprecedented that the Jaevisk would work with them against us!'

'Unprecedented doesn't mean impossible,' he argued. 'Cos not only did your good friend Carak seem completely unconcerned about you...he also seems to have done something to the cage. And to top it all off...' He hesitated, reluctant to tell her.

'What?' she asked him, scared by the look he was giving her. 'What is it?'

'There's Garran blood inside the Jaevisk device.'

She could not find the words to respond, and he continued. 'It's blood from the cranial ridge, the only part of a Garran body in which their stem cells remain in an embryonic state.'

Cassandra felt sick. 'What...why is it there?' she stammered, horrified. 'What will it do?'

Greene took her hand. 'It hasn't yet been released, and it's not entirely clear how that might happen.' He shook his head. 'Despite this, the Church has insisted that the procedures continue. But someone knew about this. Someone murdered all of the AAT agents before they could reveal it in time to stop your surgery. We have no idea what the blood is there for.'

'So maybe it's unnecessary,' she suggested.

Greene shook his head. 'According to Harrogate, the Jaevisk left here and went immediately to Sieltor Prime. They demanded ten thousand soldiers as part of some sort of alliance.'

Cassandra laughed uncomfortably. 'No...no, that can't be right. This wasn't supposed to happen.' She turned away from him.

'If you know something, Councillor, you have to tell me. Millions of lives are at stake. A highly organised group of people knew about the virus and the potential cure before it even got here. I think you work for them. What I don't understand is how you...'

Cassandra could no longer hear him. There was a buzzing sound in her ears and a warmth beginning at the back of her head. She gasped with fright, screaming then as her eyes rolled back, before she quickly lost consciousness.

'I need help here!' Greene shouted as he jumped up, leaning over her and lifting her eyelids. Only the whites were visible and Greene hit a button to his left, activating a holographic representation of Cassandra's brain which rotated above her head. What he saw scared the hell out of him. Inside Cassandra's head, at the stem of her brain where the strange new prosthetic was located, something was happening. The disc began retracting the evenly distributed tendrils, pulling the hemispheres of brain matter closer together as the outer rim of the disc rotated. Then it snapped open and Greene was transfixed by the hologram.

From the underside of the disc, where it made contact with Cassandra's brainstem, a needle-like appendage appeared and pierced the oldest and most primitive part of her brain. Now Cassandra screamed with renewed agony, seemingly awake but mercifully unconscious of what was occurring. As the nurses and other doctors rushed to Greene's aid and tried to subdue the patient, Greene himself could only stare in wondrous terror at the holographic projection as the Garran cranial fluid was injected into the midbrain.

With sudden ferocity, Cassandra's face contorted with resolute rage, and she roared as if possessed. She bolted upright in her bed, throwing Greene and the others back as the sheets fell from her body. Her chest rose and fell in her pale blue hospital gown, and she raised her hands to her head in a misguided attempt to keep it from exploding. Then she collapsed back to the pillow, exhausted as the pain passed and the sibilant suggestions of Fear taunted her in the darkness of her mind. The blackness behind her shuttered lids was swept aside, replaced by a vivid image of wonder:

At first she felt a great serenity as she found herself floating, suspended high above ground, free of all restraints, real or imaginary. An alien landscape stretched away in every direction, and before her a snow- and ice-shrouded mountain range protected the land from a turbulent ocean beyond. Many blurred shapes and images occupied this white world, on land and in the air, but nothing was defined. As she strained to look up, her vision was obscured by a dark shape directly above. Amidst a haunting absence of sound, massive black shapes could be seen pushing through distant clouds in every direction, their ominous presence threatening to fill her field of vision and every distant horizon. Cassandra recognised the pieces of the alien cage descending to enclose the world, but she knew that this was not Earth below.

A tiny but intensely bright flash of light from the surface drew her attention, and she looked down to see the Prophet, his black cloak billowing and his arms raised as he shouted up to her. His words were stolen by the wind amidst a humming sound building from the machinery above her. Cassandra reached down desperately for him, knowing that he was the only one who could save her, but a burning sensation at the back of her head drew a scream of agony and she tried to claw the device from her skull. An agonising wave of sound enveloped her, but it abruptly stopped, allowing peace to envelop her…

She was no longer suspended above the ground. She stood in a massive chamber, where the ceilings were too high to perceive. All around her, columns of black and mirror-like metal and crackling blue energy reached up into the darkness. Something approached her, something big. Towering maybe five metres above her, a bipedal creature she had only ever heard about regarded her with eyes of fierce intellect and intent. Without saying a word, it opened its upturned hybritech palms to her, and something materialised in those great hands. Here was a Human baby, silent and staring at her with its head lolling to one side, appearing stillborn with its umbilical cord hanging from the alien hand. Looking down at her chest, she saw a red line which speared her heart and connected her with that of the child. The line passed through the child and shot upwards, and she heard the roaring of engines as a vessel passed slowly above the alien's head. The red line connected her and the child to this vessel, and she read aloud the name emblazoned on its hull: 'Nostradamus.'

A man appeared before her, the mysterious individual she had allowed to board that ship; the man from whom the device now in her head had been taken. 'What's happening?' she asked him.

'You're going to die here, Cassandra,' he replied.

133

'Who is the child?'
'The birth of this child seals your fate.'

She was torn from the strange chamber and found herself suspended again above the alien world. Strange winged creatures flew by beneath her, and alien vessels were firing upon them as they gave chase. One vessel passed by in front of her, causing her to gasp as once again she saw its name.

Whatever was going to happen at this world would cause her death. For Cassandra, it was this ship, *Nostradamus*, which represented the beginning of the end.

Ω

As he lay on the bed staring at the ceiling, Conner had never felt so alone. Despite his attempts to provoke a sympathetic reaction from the crew, the atmosphere was one of distrust and anger, and many of Will's friends harboured thoughts of revenge for his death. Add to that the general confusion and fear concerning the cage and this unexplained race across the stars and most people were on the verge of mutiny.

Conner had been assigned quarters by the Captain, but had also posted guards outside his door. They were of little concern to him, for he could deal with them without breaking a sweat if needs be. He could run to the closest shuttle deck or he could take complete control of the ship if he thought it would help. But he would not do any of these things. On the contrary, he knew exactly what would happen and he appreciated the consequences of his being here. He had acted solely within the constraints of his understanding of the past, and he was obliged by intangible forces to ensure that that continued.

He looked towards the door, sensing the Captain's approach before the door opened and Adam walked in: 'I was going to knock, but...'

'I knew you were coming.'

Adam nodded. 'I've been busy. We should have spoken sooner, but...' he moved to a chair and sat down. 'Now's as good a time as any.'

Conner remained where he was, his gaze returned to the ceiling. 'I'm sorry I scared Anya,' he said. 'You had to be convinced to go where I wanted.'

'Why?'

Conner smiled, unseen by the Captain, who was sitting with his back to the bed. 'Because that's where you went.'

Adam chuckled darkly. 'I still don't know what to do with all this future stuff,' he admitted. 'You certainly have Anya convinced.'

Conner sat up and swung his legs off the bed, rubbing his eyelids with his fingertips. 'She told you. Good. I didn't want to be the one to spoil the surprise.'

Adam leaned over the side of the chair and looked back to him. 'I think "shock" is more appropriate a word, don't you? I mean, not only are we going to be parents, but apparently you're descended from our son and you're at the very heart of everything that's going on around us.'

Conner crossed the room to sit opposite the Captain. 'You think the fleet is coming to take Anya from you?'

Adam shrugged. 'I don't know what to think.'

'An entire fleet?' Conner shook his head. 'This *is* about me, Captain. And yes, they've connected me to you back on Earth, so they'll presume collusion of some kind. However, to think that they're going to take your baby...or worse...' He shook his head again.

Adam met his gaze, and seemed reassured. 'I hope you're right, because I'll die defending both of them.'

Conner looked away, too quickly for Adam's liking. 'What?' asked the Captain. 'What are you keeping from me?'

Conner laughed. 'So much,' he admitted. 'But I can't risk you knowing.' He sighed and leaned back, staring at the ceiling again. 'It's a strange thing, knowing the future.'

'The future isn't set in stone.'

'No, it's not. But the past is. You're just seeing things from your perspective. You have no idea how difficult this is for me.' He leaned forward and stared straight at Adam. 'I've seen your dream,' he said quietly.

Adam shivered. 'What?'

'The skeletons,' he explained. 'I've seen it in your mind.'

Adam was horrified. 'Why would you tell me that?' he whispered. 'Why bring it up?'

Conner sat back. 'I think you know why, Captain.'

Adam suddenly launched himself at the younger man, pressing down on his groin with one knee as Conner was pinned to the chair. 'If there's something I can do...' he hissed, 'tell me!' With nothing more than a blinking micro expression to announce his power, Conner threw his

135

attacker back from him, throwing him across the room. Adam cried out, but did not hit the wall opposite. Instead, he found himself hovering above the bed. Still, his resolve was intact: 'You have to TELL me!'

The guards burst in and, upon seeing their Captain floating in mid-air, they made to fire on Conner as he stood up. But no bullets came out of their guns, and the room was filled with the clicking sound of trigger mechanisms. 'Stop,' the Captain told them as Conner lowered him to the bed. 'Tell me, Conner. Please! What can I do to save her?'

'You will do exactly what you did,' Conner replied cryptically, before sitting back down and staring out the window at the passing stars.

Ω

'What happened to her?'

'I'm not entirely sure,' said Greene, sitting back and massaging the inner corners of his eyes with thumb and forefinger. He was in his office now, two hours after Cassandra had lost consciousness. 'Not only would I normally not concern myself with the workings of the midbrain, but I tend not to speculate on the injecting of alien blood into it!'

Harrogate sat opposite him. 'Enlighten me, Doctor. What's the midbrain?'

'The oldest part of the brain. Some would call it the reptilian brain. It deals with the most basic functions of Human physiology.'

'Reptilian brain? Now that's unsettling. I mean, have you looked at a Garran recently?'

Greene nodded. 'They certainly maintained a considerable amount of reptilian traits in their evolution. The genetic programs of two hundred years ago began at an embryonic level. This is entirely different. We're talking about a genetically altered Human who's just had Garran stem cells rammed into her brain. No wonder she's having fits and hallucinations!' His eyes widened and he jumped forward in his chair. 'That's it!

'What?'

'The midbrain has long been understood as the source of chemicals causing altered states of consciousness. Studies of ecstatic religious experiences cite these neurochemicals as the reasons for the earliest imaginings of the supernatural. It happens through...sleep deprivation, or hunger...or intense physical trauma.'

Harrogate was baffled by the implications. 'What are we talking about here? That the virus was just a...*catalyst* for this? That the Church may have *wanted* this to happen?'

Greene took a deep breath. 'I dread to think that's the case, but...' he shrugged, 'nothing would surprise me right now.' They were both silent for a moment, until Greene asked, 'What about that...agent of yours? What was she hoping to achieve?'

Harrogate nodded. 'It looks like that thing she had with her was designed to disrupt the Jaevisk device...maybe even kill Messina. As far as we can tell, she wanted the procedure to fail so that it would be discredited and the Church wouldn't survive.'

'What if she knew what was going to happen? You said she'd been on Sieltor Prime.'

'Yeah, it's possible. She might have known about the Garran...ingredient. Ten thousand dead soldiers to make the Church's cure. Maybe this is a...religious thing. Some kind of extremist group?'

Greene thought for a moment and then shook his head. 'That girl...Nell. She said she heard your agent talking to a Garran woman just before the surgery. I think we're dealing with the people behind the original experiments.'

'Could be. Maybe the Garran contingent didn't want this...next step...to happen?'

'Well, I can't say I disagree with them on that. Have the procedures stopped?'

Harrogate nodded. 'Hundreds of thousands of people too late, but...yeah, they've stopped.'

'I told them it was too soon.'

'What did you expect, Doc? When the Councillor started showing signs of recovery, everyone jumped the gun. It's what we do best. That's why it wouldn't surprise me if there are rich folk out there who are still getting those things stuck in their skulls whether we like it or not. And if the Church really believe it's a necessary sacrifice, they'll push to have everyone healed.'

Greene sighed and nodded. 'To be honest, I can't blame them. Better than dying.'

'Maybe.' Harrogate rose from his chair. 'Oh, remind me again. What was Messina saying about the *Nostradamus*?'

'Nothing specific. She was just saying it repeatedly during her last episode.'

137

Harrogate thought for a moment. 'I was in touch with a General Matthews up on one of the few stations left in orbit. He sent a fleet after the *Nostradamus* when it went AWOL. It's heading for the star system the cage came from. You know...the one the virus came out of?'

'The one Messina found her cure on,' added Greene, nodding. 'This is all too much for me. I just wanna go home and get some sleep.'

'You and me both, Doc, but with less than five days...' he shrugged.

'Until what? I mean, do we have any idea yet what's going to happen?'

'Not the slightest. It doesn't take the brightest to presume the cage is going to close, but that doesn't tell us what'll happen when it does. Central's had people working round the clock to figure that out. After the hammering they gave it, they tried everything from computer viruses to chisels.'

'Have they tried flinging rocks up there?'

Harrogate grinned. 'I'm sure it won't be long.' He offered his hand and Greene shook it. 'Good luck,' said the Doctor sincerely. 'I wish there was something else I could tell you.'

'Just keep an eye on Messina and get in touch if anything...significant happens. The Council are stepping up to full-scale evacuations, but Central Command doesn't want a panic, so they're trying to play this thing down.'

Greene chuckled. 'How on Earth do they intend to do that?

Now Harrogate looked worried. 'Something to do with collusion between the Church and the Garran Overseer.'

'You think they'll lay the blame on the Church? Won't that create more trouble?'

The Pontifex shook his head and laughed ironically. 'Doctor, I hate to be the one to tell you this, but...seeing as the world's gonna end and secrets are pretty worthless these days...' He turned and opened the door and said before leaving, 'Central Command *is* the Church.'

Ω

As Harrogate emerged from the hospital into the light of early afternoon, his peripheral vision glimpsed a flash of sunlight reflecting on a swiftly concealed surface, some six or seven storeys up on the building at the end of the street. Feigning ignorance, he entered his waiting transport and did not look back as it headed west. On another continent, someone was in for a hand-slapping.

Following centuries of uneasy and unsubstantial truces amidst the rise and fall of powers around the globe, the Eurasian Council and Central Command emerged as the only authorities of Earth worth mentioning. The amalgamation of European and Asian interests had created a more than considerable opposition to the retention of American strongholds overseas. Over time, this led to a decisive rift as the United States withdrew its military and, for all intents and purposes, fortified its position in the west while abandoning and crippling eastern and European economic allies. Absorbing South America came next, as a trading embargo enforced by the North American military forced those independent nations to submit after decades of violent opposition. While the new political body of Eurasia had its hands full trying to rejuvenate its consequently integrated economies, its leaders decided against any significant intervention in the west, making the mistake of losing allies to the American onslaught.

As the years wore on, it became clear that the tensions between this newly defined west and east would erupt into something catastrophic if nothing was done to ensure otherwise. With the creation of Central Command in the west and the Eurasian Council in the east, two political bodies divided up the responsibilities of running a world suddenly and unexpectedly introduced to extra-terrestrial neighbours. It was the way of the world that only a common enemy would bring opposing views and forces together, but it was clear to those in the right circles that these two powers were not truly together on anything. The Eurasian Council, on the surface, dealt with civil and administrative matters, while Central Command appeared responsible for the off-world military operations and surveillance. In truth, both authorities maintained covert operations to ensure that every aspect of Human life was monitored. And both authorities knew this.

What happened next could not have been anticipated by either power. A breakaway group formed by high-ranking representatives from the EC and CC became increasingly infatuated by philosophies encountered on the alien worlds of the Garran, leading to the inception of the New Elect movement on Earth. As it became more politically influential and financially powerful, the New Elect infiltrated both world powers and sought to evangelise the general population. The Eurasian Council managed to successfully combat the ensuing coup, but Central Command, hampered by internal conflict, was lost to the movement. Thus the New Elect took control of the west, and a new philosophy spread eastwards like a contagion. Once again, surface relations and appearances were maintained, but the Church of the New Elect were now a force to be reckoned with, and the general population of Earth, ever oblivious to the big picture, did not even witness the change of power. The vast majority of people considered the New Elect to be just another religion, without sufficient influence to become anything more. They were wrong.

Patriarch Mannix Relland listened to the report from his office chair. It was delivered by a young man garbed in a blue and crimson affair indicative of modern fashion. Mannix did not like it one bit, but the report was sufficiently disturbing to distract him from this monstrous faux pas, and he glanced at the senior officer standing behind the speaker. She was dressed more appropriately, in the uniform of Central Command Operations, but her demeanour was not a reflection of the confidence her uniform engendered. Mannix raised his hand. 'Stop,' he said quietly.

Once the incessant garbling had ceased, he leaned back and looked at them. 'When are you due to undergo surgery?' he asked.

The officer replied first. 'This evening,' she said. The younger man said, 'Tomorrow morning.'

Mannix nodded, aware of the fresh signs of surgery at the back of his own head. 'Perhaps when you return to my office, you'll have a greater understanding of what's going on here, and why they're now so adamant to have these procedures stopped.'

They nodded in unison, unsure of how to respond, to which he shook his head, slowly and carefully. 'Because of your blundering sniper, Harrogate is undoubtedly aware now of our surveillance, although I grant you that he would have suspected it for some time. You can be sure, however, that he is at present conducting an operation to have that sniper taken in. I do hope that you anticipated this?'

'Yes, Sir,' replied the woman. 'Our man has already left the scene.'

'Not good enough. Have him take the pill. They'll be following him.'

'But, Patriarch...' the woman argued unwisely, 'this man is not a talker.'

'He'll be a damned soprano if Harrogate gets his hands on him!' snapped Mannix. 'Now order him to take the pill. We're too close to have any loose ends.'

The officer nodded and turned to the younger man. 'Send the code,' she told him. He left the office, and Mannix gestured for the woman to sit down. 'Tell me about Matthews,' he resumed.

'On the surface, his station appears concerned with nothing more than monitoring evacuation procedures. There was the recent Garran incident, of course, but there was little he could do. As for the Jaevisk Warship, well...that was far beyond his control.'

Mannix nodded in agreement. 'And beneath the surface?'

'We think he knows more about us than befits someone in his position. I think our little members round-up on his station failed, and someone probably talked. Anyway, he managed to organise a considerable fleet and send it to the Kiranis system. It's quite out of character for Matthews, Sir. He's always been a team player.'

'Yes, well...looks like he signed with someone else. Anyway, the more protection we can call on out there the better. According to our Garran sources, Ben-Hadad is planning a major move on the system.'

The officer exhaled dramatically. 'What will that mean for us once we get there?'

Mannix smiled thinly. 'Well, for one...we won't look like the enemy. It also appears that we'll have someone else on our side.'

The woman's eyebrows raised. 'Who?'

'The Garran Overseer who tampered with the cage. He sent us an encrypted message promising backup for us and coordinates to keep the *Dragon* safe.'

'Can we trust him?'

Mannix shrugged. 'We have to. Once we're out there...there'll be no going back.'

'That's what I'm afraid of.'

'There's little else we can do now, Jennifer. All of the pieces are in place, and the Sentience knows we're going to need all the help we can get. There's just one thing worrying me.'

'This...prophet person?'

'There's more to him than we know. Messina knows more about him, but we won't get to her now. We just have to pray that he's on our side.'

141

Jennifer nodded. 'I'm sure he is, Sir. After all, he was the one who told you the real reason we'd need the Jaevisk devices in our heads. If it weren't for him, we'd all be dying and there'd be no hope for renewal.'

The Patriarch considered that for a moment. 'I know, Jennifer, but I'm not comfortable dancing to someone else's tune.' He shook the doubt away and smiled. 'Anyway, I'm sure it will all become clear in time. The Sentience is most definitely on our side. Of that I'm sure.'

She grinned. 'And the Sentience works in mysterious ways, doesn't it, Sir?'

'It certainly does, my dear.' He chuckled darkly. 'It certainly does.'

Ω

The *Nostradamus* was within visual range of the outer planet of the Kiranis system and the view was not promising. From a vortex close to the planet, Jaevisk Warships were emerging at regular intervals, and their numbers were growing with dark promise. 'I've never known a vortex to stay open so long,' Helen remarked. 'If they keep this up, there'll be more Jaevisk here within a couple of hours then I've ever heard of in one place.'

Adam nodded, letting go of Anya's hand as he rose from his chair. 'Well, if we were looking for answers, we certainly came to the right place.' He turned to Conner, who was leaning back with one foot against the port wall. 'Any recommendations now that we're here?'

He pushed himself away from the wall and shook his head. 'This isn't where you want to be,' he told them. 'The coordinates I gave you were for the fifth planet, not this one.'

Helen laughed. 'So we just sneak by a Jaevisk rallying point? You gonna make us invisible now?'

Conner grinned. 'You wouldn't keep quiet long enough for it to work, Helen.'

Despite himself, Adam found that amusing. 'Look, this might be as close as we're gonna get. The current position of the fifth planet requires us to either continue on this course or go round the block. That'll take too long. Now, I know we're here because of your threats, Conner, but I also think that anything we learn could help back home. What do you know about this planet?'

Conner approached the forward window to stand next to the Captain as the ship moved ever closer to the dark world. 'In my time, this is a solely industrial world. People don't live here. They just come here to do business or to see how their operations are faring. But I know a lot of mining goes on here, and that it was facilitated by construction and excavation going back centuries.'

'So this might be when that work began,' suggested Anya. 'There could be something of significance going on down there.'

'I've no doubt,' said Conner, 'considering the Jaevisk presence. But it's not like there's a red carpet out for us. Trust me, you don't want to go down there.'

Adam stared at him for a moment, and Conner turned in response, leaning in to speak quietly. 'I know what you're thinking, remember? You're trying to second-guess my advice in the hope that things will turn out different to what I know.'

'But you think that's impossible, so how could I do anything other than I'm supposed to?'

Conner smiled. 'You're going to prove too smart for your own good, Captain.'

Adam regarded the planet for a moment. 'My second-guessing could be exactly what I did, which would mean that you're saying exactly what you're supposed to be saying.'

Conner threw his hands in the hair. 'I give up. Do what you want.' But there was less playfulness about his demeanour now, and Anya could see it. 'Tell us what to do,' she said as she stood.

He hesitated, clearly sensing that something had changed. He quickly approached Anya and surprised her by taking her in an embrace. 'I'm sorry,' he said softly in her ear. His words then chilled her soul and Adam saw her eyes widen in terror as he whispered harshly, 'Save your son!'

The ship was suddenly struck by something and a workstation exploded at the rear of the bridge. 'What's happening?' Adam shouted as the ship was rocked again. Conner simply backed away from Anya, leaving her trembling in fear. He was woefully resigned as a bolt of blue lightning shot through the starboard side of the bridge and enveloped him. Lifting him from the floor, he was suspended in agony and Anya ran to him. 'Stop!' he warned her, shouting above the electrical crackling and the sounds of screaming as fires broke out and the ship continued to be pummelled by some form of energy. 'They're taking me, not killing me.'

'Why?' Anya screamed, as alarms sounded. 'What do the Jaevisk *want* with you?'

He looked down at her and shook his head. 'This isn't the Jaevisk!' he shouted. He vanished and Anya roared 'No!' as she ran to the space where he had been. Adam grabbed her and lifted her from her feet. 'We have to go, Anya. Now!'

The ship was surrounded by snapping blue lines of energy, like an electrical storm with otherworldly purpose. The energy whipped out to pierce and sever pieces of the *Nostradamus* and many of the crew were lost to the vacuum of space or were incinerated where they stood. Adam, Anya, Helen, some officers and staff and the remaining few military personnel were running for their lives through the corridors of fire and destruction. Bulkhead doors were sealing automatically as gaping hull breaches threatened to remove all life from the ship. Burning corpses were slumped across their stations, while living victims ran screaming in flames, their flesh seared from their bodies. For some, the emptiness of space brought peace as the fires were extinguished. Adam's nightmare of bone had come true, and he had brought it upon them.

The survivors, scattered across the burning ship, managed to get to escape pods and launch themselves into oblivion. They had no way of knowing whether the electrical phenomenon would consume them more readily in the pods, but the risk was worth taking, for the *Nostradamus* was doomed. Some of the escape pods did indeed explode as the snapping lightning sought them out with conscious ferocity, but most of them made it through and beyond. The problem now was clear. Where would they go?

Occupying one of the smaller pods with Anya seated next to him, Adam activated the minimal thrust engines, knowing that there was only one place they could go. What he did not know was whether the Jaevisk would allow it.

144

THE SIXTH DAY

Mannix knew he must be dreaming, yet every sensory nanometre of his body fought to convince him otherwise:

He found himself standing in the middle of a frozen wasteland, not unlike one of Earth's polar regions when one considered the expanse of empty blinding whiteness. What made this considerably different, however, was the enormous mountain dominating this domain. This tower of stone and eternity called to Mannix, promising him wondrous rewards if only he would enter its gaping volcanic mouth. Yes, it was dormant at present, but the Patriarch could sense its patient hostility. 'What do you want?' he heard himself ask. Immediately, he wondered who he might be addressing, but an answer was delivered: 'I want YOU!'

The top of the mountain exploded as Mannix was dragged towards it across the ice, and something rose on massive dark wings from the spewing rock. Mannix struggled to break free of the unseen grip, shouting angrily, screaming desperately, whimpering dejectedly. A black, bestial face with enormous red eyes observed him. 'You are coming to me,' it growled hungrily.

Mannix roared in terror and the winged creature raised its own head to echo the futile sound. It mocked him. 'Who are you?' the Patriarch shouted.

The head descended once more, and the beast seemed to grin. 'I am Leviathan,' it told him. 'And I will be your god!'

Mannix awoke with a gasp, his eyes wide, his breath short. Sweat rolled down his back and chest, and he shivered. His ComFone was beeping, and he composed himself before picking it up. 'What is it?' he said with a barely steady voice.

'*Patriarch, we need you here immediately!*' It was Jennifer.

He swung his legs out of bed and held his forehead. It was 5 a.m. 'What's going on? Tell me.'

'*The Tech team got the static camera working again. We can see the countdown.*'

'And?'

There was a pause, a silence of agonising unknown. 'Jennifer!'

145

'It's today, Sir,' she said, causing his stomach to turn. 'It's going to happen today!' Mannix once again heard the bestial whispering, calling him with promise.

Ω

The cage was beginning to change. All along the longitudinal lines of the superstructure, separate protrusions emerged and twisted to form horizontal bars. Every one of these bars, forming rungs of a ladder for a god, were illuminated around the edges of their rectangular perimeter with a soft blue light. General Matthews was awestruck, but he was also swift to react. 'Liaise with Central and get more teams up there. Random sweep. Look for any new access points. And don't forget that the *Nostradamus* lost a team on that thing!'

Within the hour, hundreds of recon teams were once again trying to find a way into the cage. One particular team was luckier than most, and found themselves walking down a corridor near the equatorial line of the structure. In the silence of the empty corridors, they remained alert and ready for anything. And then they heard the banging.

It was regular, like some thumping machine beating out its workload, and it was definitely something striking a metallic surface. As they continued along the deceptively curving corridor, which may have run for thousands of kilometres without end, the sound grew louder. None of them spoke, using hand signals and silent gestures to communicate intent and tactics. They passed exit after exit from the corridor, some open and illuminated, others sealed with security doors, all to their left as they continued eastward around the world. Only minutes had passed since they first heard the banging, and yet it felt like an eternity of apprehension. Until they stood at a metal door against which something was thumping. They knew instinctively that this was not a machine. Something was rhythmically pounding against it, and it mocked the rapid beating of their hearts. The Unit Commander motioned for the door to be opened, and one man reached for the handle while the others stepped back with their weapons ready, their torches lighting the way. The door was opened.

A man in a white lab coat fell backwards, his blood-covered head slamming against the floor. A head-sized patch of blood dripped its overflow down the inside of the door, and two soldiers dragged the wounded man out of the way, helping him to sit against the wall next to the door. Once they did so, he resumed his relentless head-banging. 'Make

146

him stop!' the Commander ordered. They tried, holding his head while he still moved it back and forth in their grip. The others entered the room.

Here everyone else was dead, six other men and women in identical lab coats. 'What happened to them?' someone wondered.

'Head wounds, all of them,' said someone else, as they moved around the room. There was a vast array of scientific equipment. 'It looks like…like something exploded out of them.'

'Yeah…their brains. Look at this mess.'

The Commander hunkered down beside one of the dead. 'The base of the skull,' he noted. 'Isn't that where they put all those Jaevisk things in the others?'

'You think this is gonna happen to the Church guys?'

The Commander shook his head. 'No…but I've an idea why it happened to this lot.' He stood up and took one more look around. 'Let's get out of here. Bring the head-banger. They'll wanna check him out.'

Ω

Harrogate had just finished shaving when the call came. Devoid of his usual hidden earpiece, he tapped a button on his bedside locker. 'Go ahead.'

'Good morning, John.'

The voice was familiar, although it took a moment for Harrogate to place it. He smiled thinly. 'Ah, Patriarch Relland. Good morning to you, too. I see you're still advocating suicide over capture.'

'I don't know what you're talking about. Listen, John…'

'Of course you don't. Good to see you're still playing the game, though. I thought you would have retired by now.'

'You know, I don't know why you're bothering with the superfluous banter, John. You won't locate me.'

'Am I that transparent, Mannix?'

'If only. Now, will you listen to me, please?'

'I'm intrigued.'

'We have a problem. An immediate problem.'

Harrogate could hear it in his voice. The man was scared. 'Explain.'

'We got the feedback up on the countdown clock. It's running faster now. A lot faster.'

'What? How's that possible?'

147

'*Must be whatever that Garran Overseer did. But we've no time to investigate. It's running at three times normal speed.*'

'My God!' Harrogate was dressing himself as he spoke. 'That means we've got...what, hours?'

'*By the end of the day, John.*'

'What are you going to do?'

'*I really think there's nothing we can do...except pray that we were right.*'

'Does the rest of the Church know?'

'*If you mean those in the general population, then...no, they don't.*'

'Is there anything I can do?'

'*I'd appreciate it if you could watch our backs, John. I may be something of a zealot, but there's something else going on here. This may be the last time we speak.*'

Harrogate paced the bedroom. 'Damn it, Mannix! Why did you have to keep this up? You could have dropped it after the war. I told you the Garran couldn't be trusted, but you people took their crazy superstitions...'

'*This is my life's work, John!*' Mannix snapped.

'I know,' said Harrogate softly. 'That's what saddens me the most.'

There was silence for a moment, then, '*You never really got it, did you, John?*'

'Your damn right, I didn't! Your universal god stuff doesn't work on normal people.'

Mannix chuckled darkly at the insult, but his tone was even darker as he replied, '*My...universal god stuff, as you put it, is the only reason the Garran, the Jaevisk...all of them...allow us to go on living. But don't think for a moment that the war ever ended, John. Cos it's just getting started!*' The channel was closed and Harrogate was left reeling. 'Today,' he gasped, looking out of the window. The cage was obscured by heavy clouds and rain was spitting its disdain on the glass. In a matter of hours, everything would change.

Ω

Adam had ordered all those in the escape pods to deactivate their propulsion systems and allow the gravity of the planet to take them down to the surface. Under power in a vacuum, the pods were programmed to

148

cluster, but now they were inside the planet's atmosphere and all bets were off. These were last option vehicles with technology to match. Now, Adam and Anya worked to coordinate a rendezvous. The pods would touch down in the same general area of the planet, but it was characterised by mountain ranges, cave systems, deep depressions and valleys. In short, it was a topographic nightmare upon which only a sophisticated guidance system could shed light.

'We're looking at about a twenty kay area at maximum spread,' Anya reported as she studied the readings on the monitor before her. 'I've factored in as many geological formations as I can that might cause the others to direct their pods elsewhere.'

'Yeah, well, let's hope they're all quick to respond to what's down there,' said Adam, 'cos I'm not climbing any mountains to look for them all. I think the best thing to do is send out a rally point signal and wait a couple of hours at most. We can't be sitting around indefinitely or wandering around searching for every lost soul.'

Anya was surprised by his attitude. 'I hope the rest of them are a bit more considerate than you, Adam,' she remarked.

'Look, we've got the ship's tracking system with us, so we won't be leaving anyone behind. I'll send the rally signal, and I've already sent a general distress call, but there's been no reply from the fleet that was so eager to catch us up until a few hours ago.'

'They're probably waiting for orders from home.'

'Or they've decided to leave us in the lions' den. One way or the other, we're on our own for now.' An alarm sounded and Adam tapped some keys. 'We're almost in range. I'm deploying the 'chute in…five…four…'

The escape pods hurtled downwards, passing through nought but the thinnest atmosphere. There was very little activity in the region below, but the Jaevisk were bound to be watching. As his countdown ended, the parachute was released from the lighter end of the pod. Across the dark and alien sky, some of the pods twisted and righted themselves accordingly, while others spun out of control and continued their deadly plunge. Most of the pods, Adam's included, drifted towards the surface. Within minutes, all of the pods were on land, some in better condition than others and bound to be determinate of whether those inside had survived or not. As their pod stopped rolling and came to a final stomach-settling stop, Adam and Anya looked at each other and exhaled a simultaneous breath of dramatic relief. They laughed together and Adam moved across the pod to open the airlock. Before he did, however, the ground trembled and there was the sound and sensation of large objects striking the ground around them. Anya screamed and they held each other in terror as if caught in a meteor shower. Something extremely big hit the ground and the surface beneath their pod rumbled. 'It's getting closer!' Adam shouted, unaware that a major part of a ship was racing across the ground towards them. By some miracle, the section of the broken vessel which had crashed dug up the ground and came to a stop just short of the escape pod.

When Adam eventually found the courage to open the airlock, he found himself looking out at the hull of an enormous vessel, one he had never seen before. But he recognised some of the markings on its hull. 'This is a Garran ship!' he gasped.

Anya climbed out of the airlock and Adam helped her to her feet. Moving away from the crash site, they turned to look back and Adam shook his head in wonder. They were amazed to see figures moving around behind the high and distant windows of the ship. 'You think the same thing happened to them?' Anya asked.

'I don't know,' Adam replied, 'but we're gonna find out.'

Ω

For Cassandra, reality was beginning to change. Doctor Greene had helped her leave the hospital unnoticed and she returned to her apartment in the early hours of the morning to find Nell waiting for her. They fell into each other's arms, their recent terror heightening the relief of their reunion. Cassandra had for some time expected to die. Now she was cured and more, altered beyond reverse and fascinated by what was happening to her. Senses she had for so long taken for granted seemed to have been sharpened, intensified by her experience. The slightest breeze sent waves of pleasure through her body; the general cacophony of city life was like music to her ears; flavours and smells aroused her in a way she could not define; and touch...touch was explosive. Cassandra found that she required a level of concentration bordering on meditative rhythm in order to quell the overwhelming sensations. Yet she had very recently set such discipline aside.

Now, she sat cross-legged on a large soft cushion, her eyes closed and her palms resting on her thighs. Outwardly, all signs of the infection had receded and, like a work of art, she had been restored to her

150

former beauty, seemingly by the hands of Nature. 'Thank you for the necklace,' she said softly, as she tucked it in against her chest behind her sleeveless top.

'I thought you'd like it,' said Nell.

'You know, sometimes I think I can hear your thoughts.'

Sitting opposite her in the same fashion, Nell smiled gently, feeling more relaxed than at any time in her adult life. 'So give it a try,' she challenged her. 'What am I thinking?'

'I'm not going to repeat it,' she laughed softly. 'You should be ashamed of yourself, Nell. What would the Council think if they could see in there?'

'That I was a red-blooded woman,' she replied. 'Anyway, I'm sure there isn't much different going on in your head right now.'

Cassandra smiled. 'Well...some things are difficult to forget!'

Nell chuckled playfully and blushed. 'Anyway, I think you were controlling my mind.'

'I wouldn't let you know if I was. I mean...who knows what I'm capable of?'

Nell opened her eyes and leaned forward. 'Why don't you show me?'

Cassandra mirrored the motion, hands out beside her as she balanced on her knees. They met half way, kissing softly. The very brush of lips sent an electrical charge throughout Cassandra's body, surging to all the right places, but the kiss was harshly interrupted. With her eyes suddenly snapped open, Cassandra felt a presence in the room and Nell moved back. 'What is it?' she asked quietly. Cassandra looked beyond her into the shadows, but Nell could see nothing when she turned around. 'Cass...what's wrong?'

Cassandra could not reply. She was lost in another nightmarish vision, and she suddenly threw herself backwards, as if afraid of the images before her. Nell reached out for her. 'What on Earth is it, Cass? What do you see?'

'Nothing on Earth,' replied Cassandra. 'You have to go now, Nell.'

Nell got to her feet as Cassandra was doing the same. 'What? Why?'

'Please.' Tears were building in her eyes, and her lips were trembling with fear. 'If you don't go, I'll call security.'

'Cassandra...' pleaded Nell. 'I don't understand.'

151

This time, there was nothing but resolute authority in her eyes and her voice. 'Get out, Nell!' she snapped, to which she added in a softer tone, 'It's for your own good.'

Nell held her gaze for a moment, trying to figure out what was going on in her head. She knew, of course, that such a day would never come. 'I...' Nell wanted to say she loved her, which of course she always had. But something told her that such a gesture was meaningless, that Cassandra's life was moving beyond hers to some indefinable doom. Something told Nell that she no longer belonged. She simply nodded, and then turned to leave.

'I know,' Cassandra called after her. Nell closed the door, and Cassandra was visited by the certainty that she would never she her again. The silence then was overwhelming, and Cassandra looked at the shadowed corner beyond the west-facing window. 'You can show yourself now.'

A tall shape moved out from the darkness, and the shadows were reluctant to release him. As before, the Prophet's long, flowing cloak teased the soft carpet as he walked towards her. As he moved into the light, she could see again the black stubble on either side of his face which had been shaped into the shadows of fangs. 'I'm not here to hurt you,' he said quietly. 'Your fear is unwarranted.'

She stared at him, feeling a peace flowing through her mind that was unlike anything she had ever experienced. Then she closed her eyes, breathing deeply, savouring this feeling. 'Are you doing that?' she asked him.

He nodded. 'I need you to be calm.'

She opened her eyes. 'I've been seeing you in my dreams, in some place I don't recognise.'

'One of us is going to die in that place,' he said calmly. 'I am working to ensure that it's not me.'

'So why are you not going to hurt me now?'

'I'm not going to hurt you at all, Cassandra,' he assured her. 'But I will ask you to do one thing. It will mean bringing you eventually to the place in your dreams, but it will also mean saving you from a more immediate doom.'

She turned away from him, considering this. Walking to a table by the wall, she poured herself a drink and welcomed the moisture in her dry throat. 'You want me to decide whether I should die here...or there?'

The Prophet looked at the back of her head, for she had not yet turned back to him. The signs of surgery were still fresh. 'Are you a selfless woman, Cassandra?' he tried. 'Would you like me to talk of the greater good?'

She turned around with a scornful expression. 'Is that what I'm dying for?'

'Only a person in my position can tell you that that's what everyone lives *and* dies for, that everyone is significant.'

'And what position is that? Because we had the god conversation already.'

He smiled genuinely, and she could not help but respond in kind. 'I suppose it's all a matter of perspective,' he said. 'If you believe that all it takes to be a god is to have unlimited power and sight...even foresight...then yes, I could be a god. Even *the* God!'

'But you're not.'

'How do you know?'

'Because if you were, you wouldn't need to try so hard to ensure you don't die.'

'Cassandra, you'll learn in time that gods are always struggling to survive. But first you'll have to go to the place you've been dreaming of. It's a planet called Kiranis. You've already witnessed its return.'

'Its return? Would you mind explaining that?'

He hesitated, smiling thinly. 'Kiranis, at the moment, is a forming world which will rapidly become a...dark planet. It's a world of undefined order, where chemical and biological stability have yet to take place. The way in which different individuals experience the planet can vary.'

'I've never heard of such a thing.'

'They're rare in this Galaxy. Kiranis is important for other reasons, however.'

'Such as?'

'It will all become clear when you get there.'

'And why would I want to be there?'

'Because the planet needs stability. And because I need you there. In time, I'll need you all there.'

'All? You mean...*everyone*?' She set the glass back on the table behind her without looking. It rested close to the edge.

He nodded. 'Your future is my past, Councillor. Everything I cause to happen here has already happened in my time.'

'So whatever I decide...I've already decided?'

153

'An interesting dilemma, wouldn't you say?'

'So how do I know what the right choice is?'

'There's no right or wrong here, Cassandra. Just destiny.'

'I don't believe in destiny.'

'If you could visit a point in the past, everything from there back to where you came from would be destiny. Destiny is what exists when viewed from the future.'

'So our actions and choices are irrelevant?'

'Of course not. As I said, everyone is significant, every choice that everyone makes combines to create a moment in time. It's all about perspective. All those constant choices and actions are what keeps the universe going, regardless of intent.'

'It doesn't say much for morality or ethics, does it?'

'Make the past grey, Cassandra, and keep the future black and white. Don't let old mistakes blind you. You called on the Jaevisk to help you, drawing your people into their affairs. The Garran Overseer who was supposed to support you has complicated things further, and he's beyond the control of both his own superiors and the Jaevisk Society. He's working for someone else.'

'Who?'

'That doesn't matter.'

'You mean the information would sway my decision?'

'Possibly.' He shrugged. 'You need to leave now, Cassandra. I told you to contact the Jaevisk, but you ignored me. Now Carak's also been and gone, leaving you with no choice but to come with me, because the Church is about to betray you.'

'What do you mean?'

'The cage activates today, Cassandra. The Church was relying on the support of Carak and his people once they got to the Kiranis system. What none of you understand is that I've already arranged transport for the Church. They're about to learn all about the Jaevisk devices which you brought here. And now they don't trust Carak, who sped up the cage countdown and with whom you've dealt in the past...' He spread his hands. 'Need I go on?'

Ω

Doctor Greene stood with Pontifex Harrogate, looking through one-way glass at the insane man taken down from the cage. 'They've determined

154

that it was the journey that did it,' Greene told him, 'but that's not the amazing bit.'

'Amaze me,' said Harrogate dryly.

'This man isn't from...our time. He came from the general location of that forming planet out there...the one that they say just...changed all of a sudden, but he didn't start his journey a few days ago.'

'You're going to tell me he's from the future, aren't you?'

'It's the only possible explanation for the condition of his body and the elements we found in his system. I mean, AAT were blown away by the intricacies of his prosthetic.'

'I'm sure they were. What I want to know is what blew *him* away, Doctor.'

Greene nodded. 'The brain isn't capable of withstanding the conditions within the cage when it...jumps or shifts or whatever you want to call it. It simply moves across space and time and takes everything with it. If it wasn't for this guy's cellutech-casing at the back of his skull, he would have died like the rest of them. Instead, he just went mad.'

'So the Jaevisk devices must be designed to prevent this.'

'It appears so. I think the virus was supposed to push us in the right direction. Those infected were cured by the Jaevisk device, but it's done more than that. It's changed the very nature of their brains. And if we're right about this guy, then it's like an...inoculation against insanity for every member of the Church.'

'And what about the rest of us? The cage is going to close in a matter of hours and it looks like Earth's going with it. What happens to us?'

Greene fell silent. He did not want to consider that.

Ω

'I'll talk to them,' Cassandra argued, starting to pace the room. 'I'll convince them otherwise.'

'You won't be here.'

Cassandra felt anger well up inside her. 'You mean you've already made my decision for me?'

'See it that way if you must. But you knew you'd be leaving before the cage closed. That was our agreement. Now they're coming for you, Cassandra. And they won't knock this time.'

'What about Nell?' she asked, feeling a chill run through her as she imagined Nell betraying her. And why would she not, after the way

155

Cassandra had treated her? But the Prophet's reply drew the very breath from her lungs and made her blood run cold. 'She's already dead,' he told her. 'The uprising against you and your supporters...what's left of them...has already begun. The military agree with those of the Council who disapproved of your decision. They think that the Church should have been left to suffer rather than to be indebted to the Jaevisk. They still don't know anything about Tesckyn's deal, and he won't risk exposure to help someone who broke her part of the agreement.'

'Then I'm alone,' she realised quietly. The Prophet stepped up towards her. 'No you're not,' he told her. 'Now get dressed. They're coming for you.'

She emerged from her bedroom fully clothed, and walked towards the man in the black cloak. He gestured that she should stop and she did. The gold and silver dragons were still, but they seemed to be looking up at her with some unspoken affinity, as if the emotions of the wearer of the cloak were portrayed thereupon. There came the sound then of pounding on the door, and angry voices shouting her name. 'You're running out of time,' the Prophet reminded her softly. 'Now take my hand.'

The array at the northern pole of the cage was suddenly illuminated, a red line encircling it.

'I...I'm afraid,' she told him.
'I know. I'll protect you, but you have to come with me.'
She took a deep breath and, letting it out slowly, she looked into his eyes and reached out...

Red bursts of energy erupted from the array and a single pulse of light raced downwards along each of the longitudinal lines of the cage, disappearing into the shadows of the southern hemisphere.

He was real. Cassandra's hand was in his and she could feel his warmth. Then she felt a tingling, itchy sensation begin to course through her body and she saw him grin. It was a subtle thing, but his eyes spoke of malevolence fulfilled. Suddenly, her mind was filled with flashing imagery, grand scenes of terrific moment and horrific concern, in which worlds were ravaged and civilisations were consigned to dust and flame. There were huge winged beasts and creatures of immense and indefinite proportion, of fire and metal, water and stone. Vessels in space annihilated cities from orbit and fought amidst the stars. Armies of alien origin, varied in shape and size and strength battled for supremacy on a galactic scale. All was war and death. And just as swiftly as it had come, the visions were gone, and she stood before the Prophet again, her hand in his.

'What...what was that?' she gasped. 'What have you done to me?'

'You look unsettled, my dear,' he mocked her with a twisted grin. 'Why don't you finish your wine?'

Dazed, she turned to reach out with her left hand as he still held on to her right. But her hand passed through the glass and she snapped it back in shock. 'Oh...oh, my God,' she whimpered.

The Prophet chuckled softly. 'Not even close,' he replied. The soldiers burst into the room, but they were too late. Cassandra had vanished. And all that was waiting for her would-be lynch mob was a half empty glass which fell to the soft carpet below, spilling its crimson promise.

Ω

Within hours, rumours had taken on a life of their own and life itself had taken on a whole new meaning. Someone from within the Eurasian Council had been talking, and they spoke words of betrayal on the greatest scale and nothing short of civil war. In the streets, people identified as members of the Church of the New Elect were being targeted and assaulted, in some cases murdered. One man, returning home to his family, was grabbed and beaten to death, his status identified by the scar of recent surgery at the back of his head. Central Command was powerless to protect these individuals, no matter how they tried, and significant security personnel of the Council felt no inclination to implement measures to do so. The world was truly divided.

General Matthews listened to a horrifying report from the Net: "*A vessel carrying over six hundred people as part of the evacuation procedure was shot down over the Pacific. Those responsible for the atrocity claim that everyone on board was part of the Church of the New Elect, and that normal people were being left behind.*"

'This is what we're dealing with now,' he announced to the eighty-three staff around him. 'We will do what we can to protect the evacuations. These rumours are nonsense...is that understood?'

There were compliant nods and the mumbling of acquiescence, but Matthews could see that they were becoming increasingly uncomfortable with the situation. He decided to reassure them, making a station-wide announcement: 'All hands...this is General Matthews. Listen carefully. The evacuation procedure has not discriminated depending on whether you're in the Church or not. I offer you first-hand information that the people of the New Elect don't even want to leave! I also want you all to know that it's standard policy to evacuate the families of military personnel early on in a situation...' He was going to say "like this", but thought better. 'In a crisis situation,' he resumed. 'So they're safe, you're safe...and I need you all at your best. We'll get through this.'

A senior officer approached him as he switched the Com off, handing him an open holosheet. 'Messina's personal distress codes are active,' he explained.

Matthews took the sheet and pointed at the display. 'She's on this shuttle?'

The man nodded. 'For some reason, her PDC is being patched through the shuttle's transponder. It's like she's...' He shrugged.

'One with the shuttle?' Matthews suggested with a wry smile.

'You might say that, yeah.'

'Can you bring it in?'

'There's a retrieval team on the way.'

'Good. Well done.'

The officer nodded. When he spoke again, it was quieter. 'And to you, too, Sir.'

Matthews' eyebrows raised. 'Meaning?'

'There's no record of priority evacs in the system. But I guess it was the right thing to say.'

Matthews held his gaze for a moment. 'Can you do the right thing, Mark?'

'I always do, Sir.'

Ω

Opening her eyes, Cassandra emerged from one nightmare into another as she came around. She was in the cockpit of a small civilian shuttle, and she could see the cage through the window. The first thing she did was to find a communications console, and she tried every channel as she shouted her name and called for help. Each time she did, she heard her

158

own voice replying after a pause, echoing exactly what she had said. After three or four times of hearing this, she was sure that the echoed voice was laughing at her as it spoke. 'Stop LAUGHING!' she screamed. 'I am *Councillor* Cassandra Messina!' The laughter intensified, her own laughter, mocking her arrogance, until she could take it no longer. She collapsed with the console at her back, sliding down to sit with her head in her hands, sobbing until her head ached and her heart was sore.

'Remember this,' she heard him say. Looking up, she glared at him through teary eyes and pushed herself to her feet. 'Remember how it feels to lose everything, Cassandra,' he continued, 'when everything is beyond your control and you're just another number.'

'Why?' she whispered miserably. 'What's going to happen?'

He smiled fondly, stepping forward to brush her hair back from her face. 'You're going to be reborn.'

An agonising pain, akin to electrocution, began at the back of her head. The tendrils of the Jaevisk device pushed out through her flesh, making of her head a sieve of blood. She screamed in terror as they snapped out towards the consoles, interfacing with the navigation and propulsion systems. All the while she glared at him, and her hatred was a thing of endless promise. 'You...MONSTER!' she roared at him, as tears streamed down her face.

Naveen laughed. 'Oh, you haven't even *seen* a monster yet, Cassandra.' He vanished, the engines powered up, and the navigation systems plotted a course for the planet called Kiranis. The retrieval team watched the shuttle move away at multiple speeds of light, considerably faster than the little vessel should have been able to travel.

Ω

'We're moving!'

Sandra turned to Colle, who had spent most of his time standing at the energy field and observing the activity below and around them. The vessels of the evacuation continued to pass by, some making round-trips to stations farther away from Earth, or to colonies on the moon or on Mars. But now the beacon which had been hovering in the centre of the empty space between the upper sections was drawing closer, as was every other section. It was a simultaneous motion, choreographed by the automated machinery of the alien structure, and the instruments around the room were designed to monitor it. 'Is this it?' asked Sandra. 'Do you think it's closing?'

Archer was at one of the consoles on the opposite side of the chamber. 'Looks like it,' he called out. 'The beacon's gonna fit right in the centre, like a massive wheel-nut.'

The movement was aggravatingly slow, but no structure so massive could be expected to move any faster. 'Have we got access to that clock up here?' wondered Colle. 'I mean, I thought we had days left yet.'

'Unless we've just lost track of time,' Sandra mused. She walked over to a console some three metres from Archer. 'I'll see what I can get.'

Colle watched silently, too tired to concern himself with the consequences until Archer discovered something else: 'What the hell is this?'

Joined at the console by both of his colleagues, Archer activated a hologram, which projected a slowly rotating Earth behind them. With evac ships still passing their vista beyond the hologram, they stared with abject wonder and increasing horror as they realised that signals were being received by the cage from countless sources on Earth. Every flashing red dot displayed a number above it. 'These are positioning codes,' said Sandra. 'Millions of them…like GPS targets.'

Archer nodded. 'But what are the targets?'

'Not "what", Jase,' said Colle quietly. 'Who!'

Ω

Despite the impending doom and the terror spreading across the globe, Greene had fallen asleep in his office. He was even in the middle of a nice dream when the door burst open and he was reintroduced to reality. The groan he emitted was either a result of the headache which suddenly hit him or the disappointment of returning to his own life. 'We want answers!' someone was demanding.

As the pounding in his head dissipated, he looked at his three unwelcome guests. None of them were familiar, and he stared at them with disdain. 'I beg your pardon?'

The tallest of the three men, an imposing figure with a skullcap on his bald head, slammed his hand on the desk. 'I said we want *answers!*' he bellowed. 'You met with Messina and you accessed restricted files. Tell us what you know, while we still have time.'

Greene noted that there were soldiers outside his office, presumably a personal guard for these three. 'You're Council members,' he realised.

'That's right...and you answer to us.'

'How's your hand?'

'I...*what?*'

'Your hand...that must have hurt. I've done it myself a few times.'

One of the other men stepped forward, interrupting any further engagement. 'Have you any idea what's happening here, Doctor?'

'Not really,' admitted Greene. 'I'm as much in the dark as anyone else.'

Someone else entered the office. 'Well, that's not entirely true.' It was Harrogate, and Greene breathed a sigh of relief as the Councillors turned to him. 'I've been in contact with Patriarch Relland at Central Command,' he continued. 'Whatever's going to happen, the Church appear to be as spooked as we are.' He walked around to stand next to Greene. 'All the doctor knows is that the Jaevisk devices are designed to protect people from travelling within the confines of the cage.'

'Ah...' Greene began, upon which all eyes turned to him. 'I'm no longer certain that the devices are Jaevisk.'

'But we got them from the Jaevisk,' argued the first Councillor. 'That's ridiculous!'

Harrogate shook his head, realising the truth. 'No, we didn't. Messina got the original one from the guy who was on the cage when it got here.'

'And she had no idea what it was for,' added Greene. He held up his hands. 'But her procedure showed us without a shadow of a doubt that it would stop the virus.'

'And everyone else just rushed ahead without waiting long enough for side effects or further study,' Harrogate reminded them. He held the anxious gaze of the tall and hairless man. 'Care to explain yourself, Councillor?'

For a moment, it appeared as if the man would deny it, but he conceded. 'What does it matter now?' he sighed. 'I've been a Church member all my life, and I infiltrated the Council a long time ago.' The other Councillors backed off as he removed his cap to display the signs of surgery. 'Now I'm stuck with the consequences of my birth.'

161

'Which is why you're here,' said Greene, to which the man nodded. 'Well, I don't know if...' He stopped as the floor trembled beneath them. It did not stop.

'What's happening?' Harrogate shouted out of the room. One of his men pushed past the Council guards to get in. 'Gravitational disturbances,' he reported. 'The cage must be too close now for its own technology to compensate. We're in for a bumpy ride.'

Ω

Sandra was monitoring the event closely. 'Seismic activity...everywhere,' she told the others. 'Seems relatively mild, but I'm sure they're gonna feel it down there.' The cage itself started to tremble, and an alarm sounded. Colle ran across to the monitor from which it came. 'These look like the controls for stabilisation!' he shouted. 'Maybe we're supposed to compensate manually.'

Archer joined him, nodding in agreement. 'You could be right. Unfortunately, Commander, I don't have a physics degree.'

'No need to be a smartass, Jase,' Sandra called over to them. 'Just keep an eye out for a chance to do anything.'

Unseen to the three observers at the top of the cage, thousands of apertures opened along the insides of the sections. A red glow emanated from each.

Ω

'You've got a way with words, son,' said Harrogate. 'Get me someone in Civil Emergency. I want to know how bad we're gonna be hit.'

'Earthquakes, tidal waves, volcanic eruptions,' the third Councillor mused. 'It's going to be like Armageddon all in one go.'

Harrogate eyeballed the man. 'I thought that's what Armageddon was.'

Greene stood up. 'I think it's time we all got out of here, don't you?'

'You still haven't *told* me anything!' said the Church man.

'Look!' Greene snapped. 'You're the one with the *chip* in your head. The rest of us are either going to go insane or explode! Now what the hell makes you think that I care about you?'

162

Harrogate grinned, taking his arm. 'Remember your oath, Doctor,' he quipped as he led Greene out of the office.

A pulse of red light shot out from each aperture, piercing the Earth to the core. The world trembled again, this time more violently. Now the cage components descended faster, swiftly coming together.

Ω

'I think we just ran out of chances,' remarked Colle dryly. He returned to the edge of their chamber, and the others followed him. On either side of the huge room, the walls of energy fluctuated as they came into contact with their reconnected counterparts. The team were thrown to the floor with the force of the impact, and then the walls of energy deactivated. There was a blast of recycled air across the newly-formed and expanded room, which gradually dissipated as the gigantic circular section was pressurised. In the centre of the vast chamber, which had so recently been the pointed edge of the team's strangely shaped room, was the enormous blue beacon, still flashing. Colle got to his feet and looked around as Sandra and Jason did the same, feeling their defeat as harshly as his own.

Ω

General Matthews had never felt so helpless. This was all like some terrible, ridiculous nightmare. 'A cage,' he gasped, as if he were only now realising the scale of this horror. 'Earth is actually in a cage!'

Standing next to him, Mark tried to calm his own pounding heart. 'Orders, Sir?'

Matthews was rapt, lost to the terrible wonder of the scene before him. Evacuation ships moved farther away, and military vessels gathered closer, waiting for whatever was coming next. Despite orders to the contrary and the futility they had come to understand, many of them opened fire on the structure. It was better than doing nothing. 'Orders...Sir?'

'What? No...no orders. What the hell do you want me to say?'

Silence filled the Operations Area as they watched the red lines of energy piercing the globe. It was as if some giant spider had encased the world and was setting up home. Then something happened that Matthews had dared to imagine possible, considering the intel from the alien system

163

from which the cage had come. Yet he had not dared to discuss it with anyone or make any preparations for it. How could he?

Taking Earth with it, the cage vanished.

Ω

As Harrogate, Greene, the three Councillors and anyone with any sense descended emergency stairwells and rushed out of the hospital, there was a terrible sound, a dull thing of ominous moment which reverberated around the entire world. It was only when Greene and the others emerged into what should have been daylight that they realised what had happened. 'It's closed,' said Harrogate, looking up into the sky. 'We're trapped.'

Everyone was looking up in horror, at a darkened sky broken by red lines of light joining the planet to the structure. There were no stars beyond the cage itself, only an empty blackness. The heavenly constellations were replaced by the distant flashing lights of the interior of the cage. Greene pointed to one of the red lines, along which a pulse of energy was travelling, descending towards the surface. 'I think we're about to find out what that means,' he said.

'Let's get airborne.' Harrogate rushed them to a waiting helicopter, and allowed the three Councillors to board first. There was a deafening thud as the pulses of energy along every one of the thousands of red lines reached the planet's core. It was a frightening, chilling sound, and people all over the world shuddered as if a surgeon had probed the central nervous system of the planet.

Greene shivered as he secured his seatbelt and the helicopter lifted from the hospital grounds. Soldiers around it forced people back, and one man was shot dead as he tried to hang on to the ascending aircraft. The Earth began to rumble beneath them, but there were no quakes now. Instead, the entire planet was vibrating as one entity. Monitors in the helicopter indicated what was happening. 'There's a shockwave coming from the planet's core, Sir,' one of the crew called back to Harrogate. 'We may not escape it.'

All around the world, computer consoles displayed the advance of the spherical shockwave, but no one was watching them. People were running for their lives, without knowing where to go. Those living on the lowest lying land were hit first, and that was when the true nature of this horror became clear. Most people were not affected at all. This was not an explosive shockwave, or some seismic echo. It was something entirely different. It was a collecting device. And yet only certain people were collected, vanishing from sight in front of their friends and colleagues. The wave of energy was a visible thing which passed through the floors of homes and places of work, rushed up hillsides and mountains, relieving the world topographically of those who were marked for removal.

The occupants of the helicopter watched in horror, realising what was happening as some people vanished from below…yet most did not. The wave was rising fast, getting closer. 'No, No, No!' screamed the Church man. 'You can't have me!' Before anyone could respond, the Councillor reached out and grabbed Harrogate's gun. With one swift motion, he pressed the gun under his chin and made to pull the trigger…

The wave of energy rushed up to his head and he disappeared as it reached the base of his skull. The gun dropped to the floor. Greene was transfixed in horror. Harrogate retrieved his gun and sat back in silence, watching the red wave continue towards the black sky as the helicopter turned and headed back to base.

$$\Omega$$

Time ticked slowly on as Matthews and his people monitored the decaying orbit of the moon and searched frantically for any sign of the presence of Earth. 'No activity out at the Kiranis system,' someone called.

'Keep watching!' snapped Matthews. 'That's where it came from. That's where it's going.' But even as he said it, Earth reappeared. Time was lost in orbit, the damage to the moon was irreversible, but not cataclysmic. And nothing appeared to have changed. 'Report!'

'I'm getting distress signals from…everywhere!'

'Central's down!'

'The Council's online.'

Matthews hurried to that station. 'Get me someone there.'

'There's already someone on. Pontifex Harrogate.'

Matthews pointed upwards and the officer broadcast Harrogate over the main com: '*General Matthews? Can you hear me?*'

'Yes. What happened?'

'*Scan the cage for life-signs. Either it took them all or they're dead.*'

'Took who?' The scan was running.

165

'*Everyone who got one of those things in their heads. Everyone in the Church.*'

Matthews watched the team running the scan. They either shook their heads or shrugged. 'We can't penetrate it,' Matthews replied. 'There's no way to know.'

'*Then you'll have to board it. Whatever it takes, General. We're talking about millions of people.*'

'I'll put every available man on it. Can you send people up?'

'*They're on their...*' Harrogate stopped as shouting was heard around him: '*It's going! It's going!*'

Matthews could see it happening and his heart sank. The cage was breaking up once more into its identical sections. The beacon was released and it floated aimlessly above the atmosphere. Rising higher and higher until Matthews was sure that his station would be struck again, the cage components moved farther from each other. One of them was approaching the station, looming towards the giant window. 'Brace for impact!' shouted Matthews, as alarms sounded. But the impact never came. Each section gradually vanished, as if swallowed by space itself. Within a minute, the cage was gone. And Earth was left silent, and alone.

Ω

Cassandra felt the shuttle come to a sudden stop, and the tendrils were torn from the consoles, causing her to cry out in pain. She dropped to her knees and looked around while the metal appendages retracted to her brain. 'Where are you?' she whimpered desperately. There was a moment of silence, until something slammed against either side of the shuttle and she looked out of the window. Without having to look too far up, she could see the underside of a large vessel, and she realised that she was being taken up into it.

Metal walls appeared in front of the window, passing by as the shuttle continued its ascent. She then heard voices in her head, but they were not in a language she could understand. She did, however, recognise it. 'Oh, God, no!'

The shuttle began to move to one side, swaying slightly as it was lowered to a deck. She found herself trying to hide like a frightened child as she kept her eyes on the window, seeing her captors move into view. Seeing the Jaevisk.

166

Ω

Harrogate had never felt so helpless. As he walked solemnly back to his office, he went over the rush of events and the desperate attempts to do something to stop them. Millions of people taken, possibly dead. He opened his office door and did not even make it around to his own seat. In silent despair, he fell to the couch set opposite his desk. But peace was not permitted even here, as he realised that someone was watching him. He reached for his gun as he stood up. 'You don't want to do that,' said a voice from the shadows as a man stepped out. But the gun was raised as the suited man came slightly into view. He was older than Harrogate, grey-haired and wrinkled, yet his eyes showed strength and confidence as he spoke in a deep voice. 'With the collapse of the Eurasian Council and this sudden...removal of Central Command, I imagine you perceive a general lack of authority, Mister Harrogate. I suppose that's to be expected.'

'It's Pontifex Harrogate.' The gun remained high. 'Who the hell are you?'

'Ah, yes, the bridge-builder. A hilarious play on words, I'm sure. But being the...Minister for Foreign Relations doesn't afford you complete autonomy simply because there's no visible command structure.'

Harrogate was tired and confused, but luckily he was also irritated. 'My position as *Interplanetary Mediator* supersedes any currently active post right now. If you can think of someone else qualified to call the shots, I'd gladly pass the ball.'

The man smiled. 'I can assure you, Mister Harrogate, that you never had the ball. Since the inception of Central Command, there's been a unified organisation operating under the radar, its operatives pervading every aspect of world government, ensuring that the petty squabbles of the other two parties didn't bring us all to ruin. The people I represent know at all times exactly where the ball is and how it should be played. Do you understand?'

'I've worked for the Council for over twenty years,' argued Harrogate, 'and I've never even heard whispers about anything of the sort!'

'Testament to our competence, I'm sure. You're a highly visible figure in government, Mister Harrogate, and yet you run operations using invisible people. You know secrets can be kept, even when one is out in the open.'

167

'Of course, but you're talking about centuries operating behind the scenes. It's crazy. There would have been signs, conflicting policy shifts...orders that made no sense!' He paused, lowering the gun. 'That's if you were neutral, of course.'

'Neutrality is nothing more than an ideal for public relations. We formulated our...policies, as you call them, in conjunction with those of the party we favoured at any given time. We served a greater purpose, which is why we're aligning ourselves with you now. Your dealings of late have highlighted some conflicting issues with regards to our primary goal.'

'Which is?'

The man hesitated, and Harrogate noticed in the darkness the flash of a tiny light in his right ear. Someone was directing him. 'You might like to return to your seat for the rest of this conversation,' he said eventually. 'People don't usually take this very well.'

Harrogate found himself complying, exhausted and curious as he was. 'What's going on?' he resigned.

'All that has happened in the past few days...the cage, this strange new world in the Kiranis system, the Garran military manoeuvring, the Jaevisk and so on...it's all part of a greater issue for us, a problem we've been hoping to remedy for centuries.' He took Harrogate's chair and seated himself before continuing. 'What do you know about our first contact with the Garran...with anyone in the Galaxy, for that matter?'

'You're going off base now, and I'm losing patience fast.'

'Then I'll have to ask you to find some more, Mister Harrogate, because this will take some explaining. You asked about our primary goal.' Harrogate nodded. 'In fact, it's our only goal,' said the visitor, before leaning into the light. 'You see, for quite some time now, what we've been trying to do...all we've been trying to do...is get us all back where we came from.'

Ω

In a silent office, a burly, middle-aged man with a pockmarked face was sitting upright in the chair behind his desk, trying to maintain some semblance of composure in light of the sudden appearance of his visitor. 'I presume you've heard of me,' said Naveen.

'There's very little I haven't heard of,' the man replied. His name was Anev Tesckyn, and he was the Head of Operations for an organisation that did not exist. Naveen grinned. 'It's one thing to obtain

168

knowledge, Mister Tesckyn,' he told him, 'but quite another to apply it correctly. People like you mistakenly apply the word...*intelligence*...to the gathering of information. The two are quite different.'

'Are you really here to lecture me on the principles of covert operations?' Anev mocked. 'I have a lot of work to do.'

'Indeed you do,' Naveen replied, unfazed. 'Now that you've deemed it necessary to embrace Harrogate with your death-grip of naivety, I thought you and I might have a little chat.'

Tesckyn glared at the Prophet. 'From what I've heard, your...little chats have a habit of ending in revelations we'd rather do without.'

'That's true, yes. But wouldn't you rather be kept apprised of the situation than be kept in the dark? After all, you thrive on information.'

'Just get to the point,' said Anev, frustrated now. 'Because you're not going to change our minds on this. We don't belong here and we need to get back.'

'You've been here for over two hundred years, Anev. And trust me, there's no one missing you back home. In fact, the Earth back there is getting along just fine without you.'

Tesckyn visibly deflated, sighing with resignation. 'Why did you bring us here?' he asked. 'What possible reason could you have for moving an entire civilisation from one universe to another? What purpose does it serve?'

Naveen stepped forward and leaned slightly over the desk. 'Do you really think you can deceive me, Anev?' he whispered harshly, ignoring the questions. 'Believe me, there is no one with greater...intelligence-gathering skills than I. And I know who you've been talking to.' He straightened and shook his head like a disgusted parent. 'What you're doing won't work. Surely you can see that by now.'

'We'll never give up. The cage incident was a...minor setback.'

Naveen straightened up as he laughed aloud. 'A minor setback?' he mocked. 'Your manipulation of Church fanaticism has just facilitated the kidnapping of hundreds of thousands of people. Your organisation is directly responsible for the deaths of those Church members who couldn't survive the virus long enough to wait for the Jaevisk devices. What would the people think if they knew that you had launched that beacon?'

Tesckyn paled and swallowed nervously. 'Don't pretend you didn't have a hand in this,' he retorted quietly. 'I heard about Messina's ridiculous ravings about God. Yes, she was working for us, but her loyalty to the Church confused her. If it wasn't for her, those devices would never have come amongst us.'

'If they hadn't, the Church would have been wiped out, Anev. And you'd have been left with nothing to even begin bargaining with.'

Tesckyn went silent for a moment, trying to work his way around the twisting conversation. Then he remembered something. 'They said that…you needed this to happen just as much as we did. But that your reasons were…beyond us.'

Naveen nodded. 'Oh, I didn't say I wasn't happy with the way things turned out.' He grinned. 'I simply said that your plan isn't going to work.'

'And how do you know that? I don't believe for one minute that you're omnipotent, just as they don't.'

Again, Naveen leaned in closer. 'Why don't you ask them, Anev? Ask them if they can do it now. After all, you've given them what they asked for.'

'We need to wait for confirmation from our fleet out at Kiranis. I have two hundred ships out there and they'll be returning with the cage.'

Naveen shook his head. 'They won't, Anev. They won't be returning at all. Even if they had the Garran support you'd hoped for…it's not going to happen. Ask them. Ask the Kwaios if they can do it now. Ask them who controls the cage.'

Tesckyn held his gaze for a moment and then reached out to a drawer on his left side. Opening it, he removed a black box, measuring four inches on each of its six sides. Naveen stepped back as Tesckyn held it up in both hands. He could not see what the seated man saw in his mind as the communication link was activated, but he had enough experience with the species at the other end to imagine the sight. The conversation took place in Tesckyn's mind and it was significantly abrupt. Dropping the box as if it seared his flesh, Tesckyn looked up at the Prophet with terror in his eyes. 'They lied,' he gasped. 'I sacrificed those people for nothing!'

Naveen remained silent, suppressing a smile of true intelligence.

INTERVAL – CREATION

Cana awoke with a start, trying to calm himself after his nightmare...only to find he had not escaped it. In the claustrophobic confines of the module, he was weak from depleting oxygen. Instruments arrayed around him flashed sporadically, perhaps just as disoriented as he was. The journey across space was terrifyingly glorious, and Cana had experienced an altered view of space and time before finally succumbing to the psychological and physical stresses of such an unnatural odyssey. The console informed him that less than a day had passed since his untimely departure from Earth.

The Garran ship had come to a full stop, orbiting a non-planet that appeared to Cana to be nothing more than molten rock, gas and swirling, frenzied matter. From the rear window of the module, he observed this strange world with a fascination that gripped him totally. There was something here that he was supposed to see, something he was destined to experience. He could feel the truth of that deduction in his very soul. There were no red lines, no Sentience calling him on, but he knew it was here. He knew it was everywhere, all the time. There was no place or time in which it did not exist.

He felt a breath on the back of his neck, and he spun around in terror. The forward section of the docking module had vanished, replaced by the dark and deadly volcanic expanse of the world below. Cana edged closer to it, reaching out with his right hand. 'Not yet, Cana.'

Twisting back around so quickly that he stumbled to one side, he blinked in wonder as he regarded his visitor. The man was tall and dark-haired, his face a pretence of bestial character. Two dragons appeared to move around the ethereal fabric of his night-dark cloak, and Cana was reminded of his dream, the one in which he was one of these fire-breathing beasts. 'Who...?

'My name is Naveen,' the man replied. 'Some people call me the Prophet, others call me names which are not so...respectful. In the end, it doesn't matter. Our names are irrelevant, wouldn't you say?'

'I...I'm not sure what you mean.'

'Well, the Sentience cares little for our petty labels and titles...correct?'

Cana nodded, enthralled. 'You know about the Sentience?'

Naveen smiled softly. 'Oh, the Sentience knows about me, Cana. We have...an understanding, you might say.'

'What am I doing here? What's that planet down there?'

'It's called Kiranis. It's one of the most important worlds in the universe.'

'But there's nothing on it,' argued Cana. 'I mean, it's lifeless. It's not even formed.'

'That's why you're here, Cana. You're going to bring form to it. You're going to give it life.' The creatures on the black cloak grew until Naveen could no longer be seen. Cana stumbled backwards, reaching out for the instrument panel that should have been behind him. It was not. The burning world reached out for Cana, drawing him into its embrace of liquid fire.

Seconds later, the forward docking hatch below the instrument panel exploded inwards, and a Garran soldier cautiously entered the module and ascended the three-rung ladder. Looking around with his gun raised, he saw no evidence of occupation. 'It's empty!' he shouted back down the ladder. 'Then get back down here and we'll release it,' came the reply.

Ω

Cana lay on his back, feeling cold and alone. There was no fire, no lava, no molten rock. There was no heat to speak of, no motion, no sensation at all. There was no sky above him, unless one considered the storm of greys a sky. Yet one could not, for there was no apparent horizon. Getting to his feet, he looked around to see that the land and sky were as one. There was no definition in this place. Even the ground on which he stood swirled around his feet and reached up for him from time to time. It had no substance, however, and could not envelop him as he walked away. Dispersing like fog as he moved, he realised that he could not see a horizon because everything he saw only existed in the place from which he observed it. There should not have been a surface for him to walk on, and perhaps there was not. He tried stamping his feet, but there was no physical resistance to his descending limbs. He may as well have been floating and walking through air, and it was an altogether disorienting experience. 'Help!' he roared. But he was shouting into an abyss, his voice lost to the greater mass of existence. He looked all around him again, feeling like he was spinning, although with no point of reference to confirm it. 'What do I do here?' he wondered.

Feeling lost and helpless, Cana dropped to his knees in the all-consuming fog and began to pray. As he did so, images from his childhood nightmares merged with his most recent memories and he envisioned fire-breathing creatures rampant and destructive, ruling a world where Humans struggled to survive. Something moved beneath him. He stumbled backwards, getting to his feet as the greyness darkened in front of him and a thick black mist opened up a space of definition. In the centre of this huge and growing dark circle from which Cana continued to retreat, a shapeless form rose from what was gradually becoming a solid surface. Once again, the brimstone of creation could be seen, but it appeared to be cooling rapidly. The surface continued to solidify until the black form was forced to break through it, sending debris upwards and scattering it all around. Cana had now retreated almost a hundred metres from the event.

Not unlike the hurricane he had witnessed in the Solomon Islands, which was so fresh in his memory, the black mist rotated as it ascended into a newly forming sky, still grey and yet now boasting clouds. The furious mist was extending its circumference, and an arm of black reached out to envelop Cana. He cried out in shock and tried to scramble away, quickly realising that he was now lost in the centre of the event. He heard a bestial growl, and he found himself looking up into huge red eyes. They backed away from him, and rose high into the lightening sky. Cana jumped in fright as he heard a voice next to him say, 'It's quite a sight, isn't it?'

Turning to see the man called Naveen, Cana tried to calm himself. 'What's happening? What is it?'

Naveen smiled. 'This...' he gestured with a wide embrace, 'is order from chaos, my boy. Don't you recognise a creator god when you see one?'

'A creator...' Cana was horrified. 'What about the Sentience? I'm here for the Sentience!'

'You need to learn to see the bigger picture before experiencing the Sentience,' said Naveen. The black mist was forming a creature – an enormous, towering monster whose wings blocked out the sky as they unfolded. Cana knew then what he was seeing, and came to understand his part in it. 'A dragon!' he gasped. 'That's not possible. None of this is possible!'

The giant head, still not physically connected to the body, came down to observe the two Humans. 'Where is my sacrifice?' a nightmare

173

voice demanded. 'You brought this torment upon us. Where are the hosts you promised?'

Naveen stepped forward. 'They're on their way,' he said calmly. 'Hundreds of thousands of them.' Cana could not believe what he was hearing. And he almost fainted when he heard the rest: 'And this is the first.'

The black dragon seemed to laugh, and Cana was rooted to the spot with terror. As the dragon opened its mouth, he felt a hold on his chest like a vacuum and he was lifted from his feet. His body-armour split and fell apart, his clothes began to tear, removing themselves in shreds until he was completely naked and suspended above the ground. Then he felt a further pull on his flesh, and he watched in horror as blood began to exit his body like a crimson mist. In slow and exaggerated virtualisation of events, he watched as metallic elements were separated from his blood and drawn into the mouth of the beast. Then Cana was dropped to the ground and the monster raised its fully formed body, rearing its head to breathe flame into the sky, the combustible element now part of the beast.

'Are you beginning to see the bigger picture, Cana?' asked Naveen. 'Do you realise why the New Elect are coming to Kiranis?'

Cana felt as if his life had been drained from him, but he had just enough energy to respond. 'Rubidium,' he said. As his heavy eyelids closed, he was unaware that he was sinking into the forming surface. Kiranis embraced him.

PART 2
GARRAN

TWO HUNDRED AND THIRTY YEARS AGO

The campaign had been hard fought, but a final victory was now in sight. Although relatively primitive and in an early state of industrialisation, the inhabitants of Earth had found military support amongst the species of neighbouring systems. The Garran Empire had learned that the genocide they had planned for Earth was considerably unpopular in this neighbourhood, and they had been forced to commit every available resource to the campaign. Borders were invariably weakened and the Sieltor worlds became a lot less secure. Many a skirmish had been fought in the Sieltor system itself as the supporters of the Humans' cause sought to hamper supply lines and to cripple vital communication networks. For almost twenty years, the Garran military battled a coalition of sympathisers and traitors as they sought to cleanse Earth of its infection. Humanity could not be allowed to develop into a space-faring threat, so close as it was to the extent of Garran borders.

Now, with so many Garran dead and the coalition of enemies destroyed or weakened beyond the point of resistance, the Humans who remained on Earth were facing their final annihilation. Governor Ral-hadad, an ageing Garran with white and grey flecks in the dark hair of his cranial ridge, watched from the bridge of the armada flagship as the last of the nuclear bombardments began, witnessing the vaporisation of entire cities, the fiery consumption of pre-industrial towns and villages, the radiation of outlying settlements and tribal holdings. The end of Humanity was nigh, and he felt strangely numb as he oversaw the destruction from the stars. Everything was going according to plan, and the Elders back home were awaiting his report of the same. For some unfathomable reason, he chose to delay that report, sensing without comprehending that something was about to go wrong. When it eventually did, it was so far beyond anything he could have imagined that he was left reeling.

Everyone on board felt it, and for years to come many would even claim that they had heard it. A shockwave struck every ship in the armada at once, knocking out power across every system, from the major to the minute. The ships began to lose their relative positions in orbit, many slowly drifting towards each other and impacting with silent conclusion. On-board gravitational systems stopped working, and hundreds of thousands of Garran found themselves floating around inside their now useless vessels. They tried not to waste what breathable air was left by shouting in panic, and a ghostly silence soon descended upon the Garran crews. Ral-hadad grabbed hold of a railing before him and, as his view of Earth was altered through the window of the bridge by the rolling of the battleship, he saw something happen to the surface of the planet which he would never forget.

A pulse of white light, mere seconds in passing, appeared at first to have caused the instantaneous extinguishing of every nuclear fire on the planet. But the continents were then alight with a different source of illumination, countless points of light stretching across every landmass. In the areas of greater concentration, these beacons of industrialised significance indicated massive population centres. Holding white-knuckled to the rail, Ral-hadad realised that he was looking at a heavily industrialised world, with greater levels of energy production and inhabited by many times more people than the world so recently facing annihilation. This was an impossible scenario, and he considered for a moment that the depletion of breathable air on the bridge may already be causing hallucinations.

As swiftly as it had been taken, power returned to the armada and the gravity kicked in. But the ships remained silent and inactive. All weapons' activity had ceased, an order Ral-hadad would have given had it been necessary. The scale of this bizarre phenomenon had sufficiently stunned everyone so that they awaited word from higher up the food chain. With his feet once more on the deck, Ral-hadad took his hand from the rail and steadied himself. He felt light-headed, but there was no time for such indulgence. 'Scan the planet,' he ordered one team. 'I want a population estimate.' Turning to another officer, he said, 'What hit us?'

'The shockwave seemed to come from within the planet itself, Governor,' the man replied. 'But it disrupted our atomic clocks, and that's...'

'Unusual?'

'Unsettling,' the man agreed. 'For as long as we were without power, the autonomous clocks seem to have...waited for us to catch up with them.'

Ral-hadad stared at the man. 'Catch up with them?'

The officer nodded. 'Almost as if we experienced a kind of stasis.'

'Governor?'

Ral-hadad turned to the first team. 'Yes?'

'According to these readings, Sir...not only are there approximately eight billion Humans down there, but...there's no sign of any nuclear damage whatsoever. It's like we were never here. As if the war never happened.'

'How is that possible?' the officer asked. 'We were watching them die.'

Ral-hadad rested a palm on his stubble-lined cranial ridge. 'Run the scans again,' he ordered. 'Be absolutely sure of what you're saying before I report this to the Elders.'

'Yes, Governor.'

The results were the same, and more information was gathered as information networks on the planet were tapped. Ral-hadad reluctantly contacted the Elders, sitting before the monitor in his office with trepidation as the channel was opened. 'Your report is late, Governor.'

Ral-hadad nodded without apology. 'The situation has changed.'

'Explain.'

'Some sort of...event has occurred. Whatever it was, Earth is different. An enormous population, advanced industrialisation. No vessels in orbit, but facilities on the planet indicate at the very least the possession of ships capable of interplanetary travel. There are thousands of nuclear power generators, as well as launch facilities for extra-atmosphere weapons.'

'You're making no sense, Governor. Are you suggesting that Earth has been somehow...repopulated...reinforced...what?'

'I'm...suggesting, Elder Goram, that this planet out here has just experienced a technological and evolutionary transition which makes its inhabitants capable of withstanding our attacks without any of the assistance it took us years to eliminate!'

'You should be wary of your tone, Governor,' the Elder warned.

'I apologise, Elder,' Ral-hadad said sincerely. 'I'm...stunned by what I have witnessed here.'

The Elder nodded and then conferred with his unseen associates as the Governor leaned back and waited. Finally, they appeared to leave the decision to him, as Goram came back on. 'How do you recommend we proceed, Governor?'

Ral-hadad thought for a moment, knowing that there was only one viable option, the correct tactical move. 'I recommend a retreat,' he said finally. 'We need to assess the damage we sustained as well as determining precisely what happened here. We need more detailed reconnaissance...before resuming our attack,' he added cautiously.

He was sure that they would relieve him of his command and find someone else to do his job, but Goram surprised him. 'Report to me as soon as you arrive home, Governor.'

'Yes, Elder.' The channel was closed and an officer knocked on the door. 'Come in.'

The man came swiftly to the desk and presented a Tablet to the Governor. 'The Humans contacted us, Governor,' the man reported. 'The language they used is called English, and there are phonetic affinities to some of the Earth languages already in our database, so...'

Ral-hadad raised his eyebrows. 'They contacted *us*?' he asked, taking the Tablet. The officer nodded, saying, 'We decided it would be best not to respond,' as Ral-hadad perused the message on the screen. It made for disturbing reading, and he looked up at the officer: 'Did you read this?'

'I heard it, Sir.'

'So you realise what this means?'

'Yes, Governor,' said the officer. 'These people not only have no idea who *we* are...'

Ral-hadad was nodding, and he glanced at the screen again as he added, 'They don't even know *where they* are!'

TWO YEARS BEFORE ARRIVAL

Carak Tae Ahn woke early that morning, with no idea of what the day had in store. For a Garran who craved adventure, it was the perfect start to any day. He dressed himself in his civilian clothing, but strapped his gun to his left thigh in the hope that he would need it. He ate with his beautiful wife, Senneya, and his delightful daughter, Kera, setting his mood for the morning, and he greeted his colleague and friend, Tanna, with a smile as the man stood waiting for him at the front of the military transport vehicle. It was an urbanized vehicle, desperately and unsuccessfully trying to disguise the ugliness of being equipped for battle. Tanna smiled in return, but he failed to disguise his trepidation in much the same way. 'I don't see why you're so anxious, Tanna,' Carak told him. 'You know the Setta like to call these little meetings.'

'This one is different, Carak.' They both stepped into the vehicle and closed the doors. 'Eyla called this one herself, and demanded the presence of every military and intelligence operative.'

'I see,' said Carak, as the vehicle sped towards the city. 'Maybe the Humans are doing something she doesn't like.'

Two hours later, almost a hundred senior figures from those High Families of the Garran race who had allied themselves to a common cause were gathered in a secret location and Eyla San Setta had taken a position at the top of the room to address them. Carak recognised many military and government figures, revelling in the notion that Governor Ben-Hadad would give half his empire to possess this guest list of anti-government conspirators. The topic of this meeting, however, was not that of the government: 'I've called you all here to talk about a situation which has developed on Earth.'

Eyla allowed the muttering to die down before resuming, while Tanna smiled inwardly at Carak's expression as he congratulated himself for his prescience. The old lady continued. 'Our counterparts on Earth were contacted by a race called the Kwaios Council.' She raised her hands to quell the inevitable response, saying, 'I know. I've never heard of them either. However, from what I can gather from Tesckyn's people on Earth, these...Kwaios...are an immensely powerful species, long absent from our galaxy. Tesckyn believes that it would be in our best interests to consider them to be at least as powerful as the Jaevisk, which is why he has negotiated a...type of alliance with them.'

'What do you mean...a type of alliance?' someone shrewdly asked.

Eyla nodded. 'Tesckyn has made a deal with them. Apparently, the Kwaios have promised to do for the people of Earth the one thing that no other species in the galaxy has the technology to do.'

Carak leaned forward now, listening intently. Tanna noted his interest as someone else asked, 'They can get them home?'

'They certainly claim to be capable, yes,' Eyla replied. 'But their price...' She paused, and looked around the room, trying to gauge the consciences of her conspirators and allies. 'Their price is high.'

'What is it?' asked Carak, surprising Tanna as he did so. Normally, his friend would remain silent at these meetings and simply absorb the information.

Eyla clearly wished to make eye contact with the man, and she moved across the room to look back four rows to where Carak was seated. 'Good to see you again, Overseer.'

'And you too, Lady Setta.' Carak stood respectfully, and pressed beyond the formalities. 'What is the price?' he repeated. 'What do the Kwaios want?'

Eyla held his gaze, feeling an unfamiliar chill run through her as she looked into those eyes and replied, 'They want the Church. Every single member of it. Every one of the descendants of the experiments.'

'How do they know about them?' another voice asked. Eyla could not identify the speaker, because she held tight to Carak's steely gaze. 'Tesckyn didn't say how they knew. All he said was that this was the best opportunity they were ever going to get, and that the people of the Church were a small sacrifice to make.' She could see in Carak's eyes that he agreed. And she watched his confusion manifest itself as she said, 'But I don't agree.'

Moving back to the centre of the room, she addressed everyone again, this time leaving no illusions as to who was in charge. 'We will not allow this to happen. Our goal was always to protect the secrets of our genetic contribution to those people. We might say that they are an extension of our race, and as such, they deserve our protection. I will set in motion events to ensure that Tesckyn's plan fails, and I will contact you all in due course with precise instructions as to the role you will play in this.'

Carak was incensed, but he remained calm. Instead, he asked pointedly, 'If these Kwaios are as powerful as you and Tesckyn believe, do you really think it's wise to go against them?'

Eyla suppressed her outrage at being questioned in such a fashion. '*We* are not going against *anyone*, Overseer!' she reminded him. 'We are not subordinate to Tesckyn's operation, nor are we held to any agreement with any other species. We...Overseer...are our own people!'

The majority of the room audibly agreed, inspired by the flagrant patriotism. Carak was ready to gather up his dignity and leave the room, but Tanna leaned in towards him and whispered, 'Not here, Carak. Not now.'

Of course he was right. Carak took a deep breath and briefly nodded, and then nodded towards Eyla to signal his acquiescence. She acknowledged and the meeting continued. She spoke about something that was going to happen in two years' time. The Kwaios had not said what it would be, but that the means by which their terms would be met would be brought to Earth at that time. But Carak had stopped listening, for his curiosity regarding this mysterious and powerful species had been piqued. And, in the mind of one constantly seeking adventure and secretly lusting for power, other possibilities had just presented themselves. To top it all off, Eyla San Setta had humiliated him in front of his peers. It was an error she would come to regret.

TEN HOURS AFTER ARRIVAL

A small vessel with a hull of shimmering metal arrived at the massive planet of Sieltor Prime, the home world of the Garran. There was a single Garran occupant, and he had made the journey rapidly from the Kiranis system. He was more than a little concerned to see that three Jaevisk Warships were in orbit around his ancestral world, considering that the Jaevisk had monitored his arrival at Kiranis. He was oblivious to the fact that certain people on Earth were also aware of his mysterious materialisation in the distant system and his subsequent odyssey, but he would care little had he known.

This Garran was different from others of his species, for numerous reasons, the most immediate of which was his appearance. His skin was similar to others of his kind, the rippling sheen of green and brown indicative of his Northern Prime ancestry, but he was shorter than the average adolescent male. The only hair on his body ran along the peak of his cranial ridge, a protruding line of cartilaginous material that was never more than a centimetre high amongst his species. Severed at the base of the neck immediately after birth to permit mobility of the head, this ridge began just above the eyes, where it split to form a heavy brow ceasing just short of the ears, to run back down along the entire length of the spine. The only hair on the bodies of Garran males was along this ridge, while females had no hair whatsoever, and the cranial hair of this particular male was a fiery red, a colour unheard of on any Sieltor world. A Human might call this Garran one of a kind, and in another time and place, they had. But this was a new time, one which called for a new man.

Satellite surveillance around Sieltor Prime monitored the descent of the shuttle. There was a succession of beeping sounds from the console to the pilot's left and he watched as he was scanned. Those observing him would not be able to identify the ship, but they would recognise its composition as having derived from Sieltor minerals and they would identify its occupant as Garran. That placated them temporarily, and the ship was permitted to pass safely through the weapons ring of the planet. It descended towards its destination, its advanced propulsion systems making not a sound in the still air.

The area of land towards which he headed was empty save for one large dwelling. There were patches of farming soil arrayed in a semi-circle at the rear of the house, ready for the next seeding, and in the distance the great city of Khas choked the horizon to the northeast. The small craft righted itself for landing, heading for a stone strip just beyond the outer curving line of dark soil fields. It was coming down too fast, but the pilot seemed unconcerned. The single occupant of the house might have fled from the place had the ship made any noise. Unaware of her arriving guest, she continued her work inside and the craft somehow passed through the stone to vanish beneath. Although there was no one down on the surface to witness this strange phenomenon and Garran attention was focused elsewhere, the Jaevisk observed with interest. And in a dark and hidden vessel orbiting a lifeless moon, representatives of another species monitored the event with justifiable concern.

Ω

As the sun began to set beyond the agricultural zones of Khas, a hooded Garran man returned to his home. He usually enjoyed the walk from the city, spending his time assessing his past and planning his future. He looked forward to the meal which would always be waiting for him, the company of his wife and the ever peaceful sight of his sleeping son. He loved to return home.

This night, however, something was wrong. There was a subconscious warning in his head, the anxiety of impending danger. He struggled to explain it, to define it, to understand how it was possible that he knew something was about to happen. Reaching the beginning of the path to his door, he paused and looked around. The air was still and humid, the red sun inflaming the horizon as darkness descended. What was it about this night? What was different?

'I know this night,' he said aloud. 'I've seen it in my dreams.' The fiery sun was quenched by the universal dance, and the man found himself standing in silent darkness. He waited while his eyes adjusted, seeing the lights of his home ahead. His heart was pounding in his chest, and there was a ringing in his ears. He felt nausea building in his stomach and the air before him seemed to ripple as if he were immersed in water. Recognising the phenomenon for what it was, he knew what was about to happen with horrifying dread. 'WAIT!' he shouted, throwing back his hood.

'No,' said the familiar voice of his fate. He turned from the light to see a figure holding a gun to his face in the darkness, and there was no more time to reflect. The killer maintained the stillness of horrific shock as the body dropped before him. He had instinctively pulled the trigger, even

183

though the face before him was the most familiar one of all. He could not bring himself to look at the body, and kept his eyes averted as much as possible as he dragged the lifeless form up the path, hauling it to the back of the house.

A short time later, his clothing switched with that of the dead Garran, he entered through the back door of the house. There was a meal on the table, and he sat down to eat. A woman came into the room, her face filled with concern. 'I thought I heard someone shouting,' she said.

He shook his head, keeping it low. 'I didn't hear anything.'

She came to him and kissed his cheek as he ate, running her fingers through his red hair. 'Maybe you had one of your episodes,' she told him softly. 'You're safe now.'

He looked up at her with haunted eyes, wondering how she could care for one such as he. 'I know,' he replied quietly, unsure of what she meant.

As she headed out of the room, she turned to look at him. 'You look...different today.'

He hesitated, his heart pounding. 'What do you mean?'

'I'm not sure.' She smiled, and he felt tears building in his eyes as she said before leaving the room, 'You look...younger.'

Ω

A large, twin-decked Jaevisk shuttle launched from the lead Warship and descended towards the planet. It headed for the city of Khas, and then veered off to the agricultural land on its outskirts. It landed at a large farm, an airlock opened and a ramp descended. But no Jaevisk emerged from the vessel. In the dark and peaceful night, all that could be heard was the hissing of settling hydraulics and the silence of patience. The door of the house opened, and light poured out.

Slowly, reluctantly, the red-haired Garran stepped out and pulled the door shut behind him. As he walked down the path, the woman opened the door behind him. 'Malik!' she called frantically. 'Where are you going?'

'Go back inside,' he told her, without turning around. 'I'll be back soon.'

Too frightened to argue, she watched him walk towards the alien vessel. He stepped onto the ramp, and turned to look back, perhaps intending to make a farewell gesture. A huge, dark shape filled the doorway behind him and he was hauled into the shuttle, struggling in a powerful grip. As the shuttle fired its engines and lifted from the ground, there was a flash of weapons' fire from high above. It did little damage to the shuttle, but the horrified woman was sure she saw it change for the briefest of moments, from a vessel clearly Jaevisk to something else. It had been black, blue and silver in colour, and was a single-deck vessel, unnecessary large for the Jaevisk. It moved away, racing towards the west, and Malik's wife now saw Garran battleships descending through the night clouds, opening fire in a concerted attack on the shuttle. 'No!' she shouted, running down the path to watch the distant event. All she could see were tiny flashes of light from the attack. Then, as three concentrated bursts of weapons' fire tore through the sky from orbit, there was a massive explosion on the horizon. 'Malik!'

But he was far from her now.

Ω

On a much smaller planet in the Sieltor system known as Promies, Jakari San Setta took deep and welcomed breaths as he walked through the Yre fields belonging to his family, the purple and yellow fur-lined pods brushing against his bare arms. He found himself laughing at the absurdity of his recent thoughts, when mere hours ago he imagined that the potent odours of fuel in the military hangar would linger, burning his senses and thus diminishing his ability to appreciate the marvellous scents of nature around his family home. Service to one's world did that to a mind. Trapped in a relentless melee of psychological disconnection where memories could be both strengths and weaknesses, proud Garran men and women of loving families could sometimes lose their individuality in favour of the obedient capitulation of the mass-produced soldier. The enemy in sight was not half as dangerous as the enemy within.

Jakari knew that he was more than an ordinary soldier, but believed that he was less of a man because of it. For him, the bravest thing a man could do was raise a family, see it through times good and bad, and retain respect throughout. Had he the courage to do such a thing, he would care little what other people thought of him. It was by the respect of his family that he would measure his worth, and by extension…respect for himself. But there was no time for such dreams. Courage was redefined these days, stamped with the burning mark of

185

weapons' fire and denoted in the achievements of military bureaucracy. Courage, Jakari knew, was an illusion.

His mother, Eyla, opened the door of the seventeen-room house, waving to him as he quickened his pace. 'Hello, Mother,' he called to her, realising as he did so that he had spoken in English. She shot a warning glare at him and he conceded with a nod and smile of apology, repeating the salutation in Garran as he reached her. She laughed and embraced him, reaching up to throw her arms around his shoulders: 'You know I don't like any of the Human languages. We should never use them amongst ourselves.'

'I know,' he replied, as she took his hand and they entered the house. 'I find it hard to switch it off when I get home.'

'Yes, well...repair the switch.'

Jakari laughed. 'Yes, Mother.' He kissed her on the cheek, thinking how much older she looked. How long had it been since he had seen her? Six years? Seven?

'Don't stare at me, Jakari,' she told him. 'You know I don't like it when you stare.'

'I was just thinking how beautiful you look.'

'And you know I don't like it when you lie to me.' She pointed to a large leather chair, suppressing a grin. 'Sit down. There's something I need to tell you before your father gets home.'

'Where is he?'

'There was a meeting about extra land benefits for Civil War veterans.'

Jakari laughed. 'So he's probably drinking and singing by now.'

'He's not singing yet.'

'How do you know?'

'The hill dogs aren't howling!' Eyla San Setta sat opposite her soldier son, and her eyes were sad. Jakari leaned forward and took her hands. 'What is it, Mother? Are you ill? Is Father well?'

She looked into his eyes, and smiled softly. He saw a galaxy of love in that smile, and he felt that his heart would break if she said she was dying. 'How long have you served the Governor, Jakari?' she asked.

He withdrew his hands, sighing in dismay. 'Not this again, Mother. Please!'

'No, no...Jakari, you have to listen to me. In all your years of service...with all the fighting you have seen and all the death you have experienced, have you ever considered the reasons behind it?'

'I'm a soldier. I obey commands.'

'But now you obey Carak, correct?'

Jakari got to his feet. 'Overseer Carak is not my superior officer. My fleet doesn't come under his...'

'Yes, yes, I know all that. But I also know what he's planning.'

'Well, if that's the case, then you're better informed than I, Mother. Our family must still be pulling the strings of power in some quarters.'

She smiled, but there was no warmth there now. 'There's acid in your tone, Jakari. That's good, because you're going to need all that anger and strength very soon.'

Jakari paused, gauging her. The Setta family was powerful and influential, its extended genealogy permeating almost every aspect of political concern on the Garran worlds. 'What do you mean?'

She reached out for his hand again. Allowing her to take it, he was surprised to feel the strength in her grip. There was no weakness here, no frailty or decay. The woman was as dangerous as she had always been. 'Something has happened at Earth. I'm sure you've heard the reports.'

He nodded. 'Some nonsense about a cage surrounding the planet and their defensive ring practically annihilated in one strike.'

'It's not nonsense, Jakari.'

'What? How can you believe it?'

From behind the cushion at her back, she withdrew a projector sheet and activated it, handing it to him as the three-dimensional hologram of Earth was displayed. He watched in silence as alien structures materialised in Earth orbit, obliterating the military stations and vaporising any vessels which had previously occupied their position. He estimated the initial loss of life at just short of two million. 'Where did you get this?' he whispered. 'We were told there was no data available.'

'Our own probes recorded it.' She took the projector pad from him and switched it off. 'Jakari, we are about to be drawn into something beyond our understanding and our capability to survive opposing it.'

'Are you talking about Carak? Do you want me to speak with him?'

She shook her head. 'Carak's mysterious behaviour is certainly troubling, especially since it appears that he's been communicating with a species whose power is...unfathomable. But Carak may be the lesser of two evils right now. I'm sure you've heard that the Jaevisk are at Prime. Ben-Hadad is meeting with them, and we've no idea of his motives. As much as it galls me to say this...you must initiate contact with everyone loyal to our family and inform them that Overseer Carak's plans...whatever they are...' she paused, lowering her head and then raising her eyes, 'are our plans. I want you to follow his instructions, Jakari, as if your life depends upon it.'

'I don't understand. If he's working with someone who threatens us...another powerful race...how can you want me to continue my alliance with him, let alone make myself subordinate to him? What are you not telling me?'

She closed her eyes and leaned back in her chair. He waited in silence, until finally she said, 'I know you have never believed in a god, Jakari.' He said nothing, for it was not a question. 'But defining a god is something we mortals...Garran, Human, Jaevisk, Sori...none of us agree, except on one matter.'

'Which is?'

Opening her eyes, she replied, 'That a god exists and operates outside the realms of our comprehension of space and time. Reality, as we know it, is less of a boundary for such an entity than it is a challenge, waiting to be redefined.'

Jakari knew that his mother was no fool, and had not lost her mind. This sounded like so much nonsense, and yet he felt a shiver run through him. 'What are you saying, Mother?' he asked her quietly. 'How is this relevant?'

'It is of the utmost relevance, Jakari,' she told him, reactivating the projector to once again display the alien cage around Earth. 'Because such an entity is at work here.' He looked at her through the slowly rotating image as she said, 'You know that it's my job to keep secrets, don't you?'

He nodded. 'I know. I trust you.'

'Good,' she assured him. 'Because whatever's about to happen here, secrets will be our most valuable weapon.'

THE SECOND DAY

There was blood on the hands of Overseer Carak, a lot of blood. But great men are born of blood, and drown in a sea of blood. It bothered him very little that he had achieved so much by the suffering of others, mainly because the others in question had spilled at least as much blood as he. The day of reckoning was close at hand, though, for soon he would awaken his most powerful enemy, if indeed the man had been asleep to Carak's treachery.

Carak was a Garran of imposing physical stature, a man as proud of his body as of his mind. He worked hard to ensure that both of these assets remained in peak condition. Unlike some men who considered physical strength to be the only thing of import, Carak knew that unless the brain was kept actively challenged, entire aspects of character and mood would be severely altered. Boredom was a killer, the deadliest and subtlest of all, creeping in while the world spun on and life drained from the body, no matter how physically strong one was. With this philosophy, it was inevitable that the ever-taxing and winding paths of deceit and conspiracy would seduce a man of Carak's military and political position.

He stood now in silence in the quarters assigned him by Governor Ben-Hadad during his visit to the capital city of Khas, breathing slowly and inducing calm before reaching down for the black cube on the table beside him. Measuring four inches across every side, the icy surface of the box cut through his thoughts. The daylight streamed in through the windows, everything to his right thrown into shadow. It was a beautiful day, and would remain so. Regardless.

Carak heard his heart pounding in his chest as darkness swept over him, creeping out from the wall beyond to enshroud everything in the sunlit room. He gritted his teeth as he heard the first words spoken to him, an agonising affair that almost brought tears to his eyes.

Ω

When Tanna had been appointed to the position of First under Overseer Carak, he had been elated, filled with pride. That was almost five years ago now, and his feelings on the matter were currently a complex war of resentful contradictions. Raised on Sieltor Thuros to believe in the comforting ideals of the Governorship, Carak's dissent scorched Tanna's

189

sensibilities with the tempting fires of empowerment. Of course, such conflict would not have been possible had the seeds of doubt not already found purchase in the verdant soil of his enlightenment. Tanna was a convert to Carak's treachery while still refusing to define it as such. On the contrary, it was Governor Ben-Hadad who was destroying the core of Garran greatness and prosperity, and the Jaevisk Warships in orbit were testament to this treason.

Slightly slimmer than the broad and muscular Carak, Tanna was an athlete turned soldier whose exercise regimen involved honing skills at hand-to-hand combat. His cranial hair was dark and almost absent, shaved so tight that it gave only a hint of contrasting colour to his scalp. Upon arriving at Carak's apartment, he tapped lightly three times, knowing how much the Overseer hated to be disturbed in the middle of the day. Following no response, he applied slightly more force to the door, wincing with immediate regret. He waited, but became worried as the silence continued, for although Carak could be meditating as he often did at this time of day, he was also aware of the delicacy of the current situation and would therefore maintain vigilance. Taking a deep breath, Tanna made his decision, reaching out to turn the handle...

Carak spun around as the door opened, and Tanna saw him quickly return a black box to the table next to him. Forcing a smile, the Overseer came towards Tanna. 'I was meditating,' he explained, as Tanna had expected. 'I must have been somewhat more detached than usual.'

'I apologise for intruding, of course,' said Tanna, relieved that he had not angered the man, 'but someone has requested our immediate presence in the hangars of Niera.'

'Someone?'

'The communication was encrypted, accessible genetically by only you or I.'

'A trap?' Carak turned away to retrieve some personal effects, throwing on his jacket and strapping his gun to his waist.

'Possibly,' said Tanna.

Carak smiled. 'Interesting,' he said, passing his First as he made for the door. Before Tanna turned to follow, he glanced at the black cube on the small table, its right side thrown into shadow by the bright light of day streaming in through the windows. For some indefinable reason, he shivered.

Ω

A shuttle brought the two men up to Niera, the inner moon of Sieltor Prime. There was very little activity up here at the hangars, mainly due to the landmark proceedings underway on Prime. Governor Ben-Hadad knew how to put on a show, and often did so with little excuse. Quite a display would be missed if one failed to get within even a hundred kilometres of Khas when Ben-Hadad's political theatre was open for business.

Once the shuttle set down on the outskirts of the main hangar assembly, the pilot turned to Carak. 'I'll be waiting at Departure 8, Overseer.' Carak nodded, and he and Tanna rose to disembark. 'If you need me,' the pilot called after them.

Outside the shuttle, with the door closing, Carak wondered, 'What did he mean...if we need him?'

'Perhaps we're not expected to leave.' Tanna made no show of emotion at this prospect, and Carak smiled. 'Such a relief from the monotony of Ben-Hadad's ceremonies, Tanna. Do you feel the air in your lungs?'

'I think that's battleship fuel, Carak.'

The Overseer shrugged. 'Whatever it is, it smells like excitement to me!' He marched away, determined to make the most of whatever awaited them.

Tanna shook his head, allowing himself a little smile as he caught up with Carak, who sparked up a completely unnecessary conversation: 'So...will you be glad to return home, Tanna?'

'Surprisingly, yes,' he replied. 'This may be the great seat of power, and all that Garran civilisation holds dear, but to me it is no more than a wounded beast refusing to die.'

Carak chuckled softly and shook his head, feigning disgust. 'You've spent too long in my company,' he chided him. 'You need to take a trip around the great city of Khas, or fly through the Canyon Falls of Lacstel, or jump from the Magnetic Heights of Orellin. You might then appreciate the wonder of Prime.'

'With my luck, I would probably suffocate in the sprawling mass of the city, drown in the Falls or find myself too full of some vital bodily element for the magnetic field at Orellin to slow my descent!'

'Yes, you truly are a wonder amongst Garran.' Carak slapped him on the back. 'Cheer up, will you? As the Humans say...it could be worse.'

'I doubt they are saying such a thing at present.'

'Yes, of course. I'd like to see this cage the Jaevisk mentioned. It sounds quite spectacular!' As they spoke and walked, it became increasingly evident that there was no one around; no crew amidst the scores of vessels waiting in the hangars, no maintenance staff, not even a minimal security detail. As their conversation died away, they became aware of their destination in the sporadically illuminated hangar. 'This area should most definitely be guarded,' noted Carak, looking around and instinctively drawing his gun. Tanna followed suit, and the two men moved apart from each other, stepping off the marked path onto bays on either side. Up ahead, the officer's boarding area of a massive ship came into view, and a tiny fraction of the hull could be seen beyond the glass. Carak whistled in admiration. 'This must be the Governor's new Star Cruiser,' he realised, making some sense of their summoning. 'Do you think someone wanted us to see this for ourselves? Perhaps to show us the error of our ways?'

Across the path, Tanna heard the question and called back. 'To what end? As far as I know, it doesn't even have an engine.'

Carak was about to reply when a figure stepped out from one of the gigantic columns flanking the boarding area and said, in English, 'Oh, it has an engine.'

Both men raised their guns, to be met by laughter. 'Not the best way to greet your newest recruit, Carak,' said the stranger. A Garran man dressed in a military uniform stepped out from the shadows. He had a shock of red hair along his central ridge and he carried an array of weapons. 'I know you speak English, Carak,' he added.

Cautiously, Carak replied in Garran, 'Why did you call us here?'

'I come bearing gifts,' the red-haired Garran quipped, refusing to speak in his native tongue as he gestured behind him to the massive ship. 'A gift for Carak and Tanna in their quest for domination, their desire to kick Ben-Hadad's considerable ass from his worthless throne.'

Startled by this blatant candour, the two men moved closer, keeping their guns high as they looked around cautiously. 'Who's with you?' Tanna shouted. 'And where are the staff?'

'I'm alone,' the stranger replied, 'with no need for anyone else. As for the staff, I killed them all.' He raised his right hand with the index finger extended. 'One moment, please.' He moved back to the column and reached behind it.

'Another move and you're dead!' Carak shouted in English.

The linguistic shift delighted the man. 'Now we're getting somewhere!' He grasped something behind the column, saying as he pulled it, 'I was told that Carak was a clever man.'

'*Was?*' noted Carak.

The stranger grinned as he dragged the mysterious bundle from behind the column. Acting on instinct, Tanna fired as Carak shouted, 'No!'

But it was too late. Tanna shot a bound and gagged man held upright by the stranger, the bullet piercing the throat. 'That's the Governor's personal *envoy!*' Carak roared as he ran forward. The stranger dropped the dead body and stepped away as Carak desperately tried to staunch the blood pooling onto the floor of the hangar. But there was too much and Carak witnessed the last breath leave the man's body. He turned to look at Tanna, and then beyond to the red-haired stranger. 'Why?' he asked him. 'He was a good man!'

'*Why?*' the stranger laughed, spreading his hands. 'So there can be no mistake, Carak,' he explained. 'So there can be no turning back. You just murdered Ben-Hadad's top man. He'll never let you get away with it, so we should probably get going. You might want to get a crew together.' He turned to head towards the Star Cruiser as the boarding portal opened.

Carak and Tanna looked at each other, and Carak asked, 'Get going where? I don't even know who you are!'

'My name's Malik,' the man called from inside the passageway. 'And your friends in the black box already told you where we're going.'

Tanna's curiosity was piqued at the mention of the box he had earlier seen, and he looked at Carak expectantly until he explained. 'Earth.'

Ω

A suitably ostentatious ceremony was underway in the great Hall Of Governors in Khas City. Representatives from across Garran territory were present, Garran Governors who lorded over conquered underworlds and alien vassals subject to Ben-Hadad, Governor of Sieltor Prime, who afforded them varying measures of token courtesy. The Sieltor Confederation had acquired some economically and strategically valuable worlds, and relationships were always strained to keep the people of those worlds from either revolting independently or requesting external assistance. Humanity's continued expanse into the stars meant that they

193

were an option for such requests, and that was a threat which could not be allowed to surface. An empire under Earth was the last thing any Garran wanted, the irony of the power shift the least of their concerns. Of course, a mere three years ago, following the massacre at Thuros, this alliance with the Jaevisk Society would have been unthinkable. *Sometimes, a sacrifice or two is necessary,* Ben-Hadad reminded himself. Besides, he was aware that this was only a temporary arrangement, even if the Jaevisk were not. After all, they had come to him, and the prize for this ambitious reasoning was about to be displayed here in the Hall of Governors once the guests of questionable honour arrived.

There was panic amidst the spineless as four huge Jaevisk warriors suddenly appeared in the middle of the Hall. As ordered, the military Guard around the room remained motionless and impassive and Ben-Hadad laughed to himself as he retreated casually and absently to his seat – he liked to call it a throne, but only in the playground of his mind – on the raised platform which ran along the wall. Usually in darkness, the area was now well illuminated and everyone could look upon their immediate ruler.

The Governor was a large man, horizontally speaking. He was significantly shorter than two metres tall, the height at which Garran boys were sent to military school. He was dressed in voluminous robes of stained leather, a gaudily coloured ceremonial outfit dating back to the Age of Kings, a retrospectively troubled time in Garran history. Of course, kings had not worn the outfit in those days. The colours had, in fact, been worn by the court entertainer, and they were used on occasions such as today's gathering to remind people of the folly of having leaders who sought absolute rule.

To expect an entire nation to emulate the desires of one man is truly the dream of a fool.

The inscription on the wall above Ben-Hadad often made him laugh, as even now he sought to convince the population of the falsity of such words. When a strong man sat at the head of his world, Ben-Hadad believed, his desires should indeed be reflected amongst the population. After all, they agreed with what he had to say before they put him there. Such thin lines between democracy and dictatorship could only be walked by men with the charisma to draw them himself. And Ben-Hadad was such a man, blinding the people with great victories and wealth while making

194

decisions for them that they did not even have the chance to question. It was a dangerous path for any leader to take, and there were already signs of threatened insurrection amongst those who recognised his manipulation. Ben-Hadad had already taken steps to stop a threatening revolt, and his methods were as intricate as the plans devised by his enemies to incite it. Hence today's pageantry.

'Welcome to Sieltor Prime,' he called out expansively, as he stood up and extended his arms to encompass, it seemed, the entire Hall. From his perspective atop the platform, everyone did indeed fit snugly within his grasp, and this metaphorical delight was not lost on the Governor. Indeed, it served only to enhance his false smile with genuine contentment as the four Jaevisk representatives came closer. One of them carried a large black box, and it seemed that even he struggled with its weight. Ben-Hadad smiled still, realising that he thought of every Jaevisk as male. They all looked exactly the same to him, and probably to each other. Copulation amongst the Jaevisk was not something with which Ben-Hadad tended to occupy his mind. And if he did, he would probably awake screaming.

The Jaevisk with the black box lumbered forward and set the object down on the polished stone floor. It was made of a mysterious dark metal, alien and unobtainable to every other species, a trait synonymous with everything Jaevisk. Their biotechnology was testament to their obsession with metal. Stepping back from the box, the Jaevisk – its height allowing it to look straight into the eyes of the Governor on the raised platform – indicated that Ben-Hadad should approach.

Secretly trembling and perspiring beneath his flowing robes, the Governor smiled and nodded, descending the steps to the floor and stopping at the sealed black cube. Without his intervention, the box clicked, the sound of an opening lock echoing throughout the hushed gathering, and the square lid rose to open before him. The crowd shuffled forward in unison, like some great stalking creature, scores of feet whispering across the smooth golden floor. They were enthralled.

So too was Ben-Hadad, as a red glow pulsed deep and slow from within the box. Vapour rose from the container, and the Governor felt a chill air accompany that eerie mist. He glanced up at the waiting, watching Jaevisk quartet, his white tongue sliding nervously across his dry lips. This was the moment he had waited for, the prize for which he had played his political and military games. This was the result of many long years of murder, deceit and – most difficult of all – patience. He looked into the

195

box. Here, set into a square mould surrounded by a silver circle, four glowing stones of crimson taunted him with their power. It was too much to bear any longer and he reached down, plunging his greedy hands into the freezing cold of the box and grabbing one of the four stones. When he rose up again, a shadow had fallen over him, and one of the Jaevisk stood directly before him, its hands out...expectantly.

Ben-Hadad stared up at its face for a moment, feeling the burning cold of the red stone in his hand, his face aglow with its eerie luminescence. It was clear that he was reluctant to relieve himself of the object, thinking that this was no more than Jaevisk deception. Around the room, he heard the clicking and humming of weapons, as his Guard prepared to defend him.

'*If you wish to know the power of the crystals,*' the voice was in his head, in his language, '*you will allow us to show you.*'

Slowly, carefully...almost reverently, he offered the stone to the waiting alien, who stepped back once he had received it. Then each of the other three Jaevisk were given a stone by the same method, and Ben-Hadad realised that some sort of ritual had just taken place.

The lights suddenly went out in the Hall, and the Governor knew it was not by his request. Some of the guests voiced their fears, but a panic was settled as the four Jaevisk warriors moved to stand in the exact centre of the Hall. All that could be seen was their glowing yellow eyes and the stones in their hand as they each extended their arms outward before them, recreating through their respective positions the square within which the stones had been arranged.

A beam of red light shot upwards from each of the stones, but not vertically. Each beam arrived at the same point above the centre of the aliens' square-shaped configuration, and a stronger, brighter beam continued upwards from the apex of the pyramid of light. It exploded through the ceiling far above, ripping a gaping hole in the roof as daylight streamed in and pieces of debris fell down amongst the spectators.

Ben-Hadad was not immediately impressed by this display. 'This is it?' he mocked. 'This is the great Jaevisk *secret*?'

Again, the voice sounded in his head: '*Your ignorance is unsettling, Governor.*' There was a hint of anger and the Governor swiftly conceded, saying aloud, 'Then I apologise for my ignorance. I was told that I would be given the secret to the ultimate power in the Galaxy, something that would power our ships, our weapons, even our homes and machinery.'

'As you have been,' came the reply. This time, one of the four had spoken aloud in its own language, a succession of hisses and clicks, translated into the Garran tongue by the automated system of receivers and transmitters set into the numerous pillars around the Hall. 'A Reaper Stone in one of our ships has gathered and converted the energy of the four Slave Stones, returning serviceable energy. You can place these Reaper Stones in orbiting satellites. This energy is far beyond anything you possess. No natural resource, no Garran-made power cells, nothing else will ever be needed again. This one device will produce enough energy to power this entire city for one hundred of your years.'

The lights in the Hall returned to full power and Ben-Hadad understood, as he looked in those piercing alien eyes, that the whole city had been drained of power, simply for the purpose of demonstration. 'One hundred years of energy in one device,' he told himself quietly. The four Jaevisk gathered before him and returned the stones one at a time. The Governor replaced them in the box and closed it, his hands once more stung by the icy crystals. 'How long will they last in our vessels?'

'Smaller devices have already been fitted in your own Star Cruiser as a gesture of…friendship. The Slave Stones should never be exposed to space. We have found that their use in space is…dangerous if not correctly attuned to the vessel. None of the stones should ever be exposed at length to a temperature greater than that in this container. The power in your Star Cruiser will then last indefinitely.'

Now the Governor was truly incredulous. 'Are you saying that our vessels will never again need refuelling?'

'Circumstances in the vacuum of space mean that the stones are not prone to the same depletion of power as those on a planet. Other than exposure to heat, the only thing that will cause the stones to lose power is the destruction of the ship. However, the stones will be powering your shields and weapons systems also, increasing their capabilities. Is your ignorance waning in the face of this knowledge, Governor Ben-Hadad?'

'Yes, it certainly is,' he replied, smiling. 'Tell me, how long ago did you fit the device in my Star Cruiser?'

'Sixteen hours ago, at the request of your personal envoy.'

Ben-Hadad nodded, pretending for now that he had been aware of this request. He recalled something significant within that time frame. 'Was this before or after you destroyed one of your own shuttles outside this city?'

197

There was a short silence as the Jaevisk exchanged glances. They turned back as one and the speaker replied, 'These are unconnected events, Governor. You need not concern yourself with the loss of our shuttle.'

'Under normal circumstances, the loss of your shuttle would not concern me, but these are not normal circumstances, and it was reported that one of my citizens was almost killed in the blast.'

'It is surprising that he was not, Governor.' Even the computer seemed to relay the clipped tones of this swift response, and Ben-Hadad realised that this was indeed an intuitive observation. 'I wonder...' he asked, 'do you know why this man would come near your shuttle, or indeed why your shuttle was at his home? I understand that there is nothing more than farming land out there.'

'We are aware of the limits of your understanding, Governor. This matter should be set aside for later discussion.'

Ben-Hadad held tight to his diplomatic smile, but his lips trembled with rage as he felt humiliated in front of so many people. 'Well, of course,' he replied casually. 'I wouldn't wish to complicate our newfound friendship at such an early stage.'

'Of course,' replied the Jaevisk. 'It is too early for such a thing.'

'Indeed. So, is there anything else you require? My ships are ready, my rivals have been exposed...with your help, of course. Your people are welcome to come down and enjoy some...' He struggled to imagine a Jaevisk relaxing. 'Leisure time,' he finished.

The Jaevisk turned to speak amongst themselves, and it was not lost on Ben-Hadad that the translation system around the Hall had somehow deactivated. As the Jaevisk turned back to him, it reactivated: 'To ensure that your people can become familiar with our technology, we will need you to assign a number of Garran soldiers to us. They must be strong and in perfect health.'

Ben-Hadad pointedly glanced at the closest soldier, who was clearly horrified by this suggestion. There was no telling what the soldiers would be forced to endure. 'If this is what you wish in return for your gift of power,' the Governor told them, holding the piercing gaze of the Jaevisk, 'it will be done. How many of my men will you require?'

'Ten thousand.'

Ben-Hadad's eyes widened, but the Jaevisk spoke first. 'There is much for them to learn, and you will have ten thousand men through which that knowledge may be passed on.'

This would indeed be a valuable venture, were it the truth, but Ben-Hadad could not help feeling that he was being duped. He knew, however, that ten thousand soldiers was a small price to pay for his goals to find fruition. 'I will arrange for their transport immediately.'

'A wise decision, Governor. You will appreciate the power of our alliance.'

'I'm...sure I will,' he replied, sensing a dark undertone in that statement. But they disappeared before he could question them further. The black box was left behind, its glowing contents promising great things.

Ben-Hadad looked around the room before returning to his throne. The guests began talking amongst themselves as refreshments were brought out. There was a commotion across the great room, and Ben-Hadad watched from his chair as the crowd parted to allow two soldiers to approach him. They carried between them a body, bound and gagged, its clothes stained with blood, and Ben-Hadad recognised it immediately. He rose and descended from the dais with uncharacteristic anxiety. 'Aita!' he exclaimed, looking at the two soldiers. 'Who did this?'

They set the body down on the floor, and Ben-Hadad saw the hole in the throat of his envoy. 'He was killed on Niera,' one of the soldiers replied with evident disgust, 'left there like some animal. Your Star Cruiser was stolen, Governor!'

Ben-Hadad, as he sometimes did when faced with a dilemma like this, stood still and spoke his concerns aloud. 'Aita asked the Jaevisk to install the engine,' he recalled. 'Within hours, the Jaevisk destroyed a shuttle which was apparently sent to abduct one of my citizens. Then someone took the Star Cruiser.' He turned to look across at a Senior Aide standing some three metres from the left side of his chair. 'What do we know about this man the Jaevisk were so interested in?'

The Senior Aide, a man whose job it was to know everything, replied immediately. 'His name is Malik Ki Jen, an employee at the munitions factory here in Khas. He hasn't served in the military for many years.'

'Is this still the case?'

Withdrawing a small device from his pocket, the man checked. The whole room held its breath until he shook his head and said, 'According to this, he was assigned to the command of Overseer Carak.' The Aide looked up and everyone in the room turned to Ben-Hadad as he continued: 'Governor, the transfer request was only made within the past few hours, and hasn't even been processed.'

'Carak took my ship,' Ben-Hadad realised. 'Where is he now?'

Tapping more keys on the small screen, the Aide replied, 'He appears to be heading for Earth.'

Ben-Hadad looked again at the body on the floor. 'The Jaevisk knew about this,' he declared. 'They *knew* what was happening!' He clenched his right hand into a fist and caught the angry glare of the soldier before him. 'They know something about this Malik. Find out what it is…quietly. Don't alert them to our suspicions.' The soldier nodded and turned away, as Ben-Hadad hissed through gritted teeth, 'I'll deal with Carak and his people. It's time they paid for their treachery!'

Ω

Eyla San Setta stood at the end of the path, her long grey hair moving in the warm breeze and her steely eyes watching the house while her team swept the grounds of the property. Shielding those eyes from the descending sun, she saw a young woman step out from the house. 'What are you doing here?' she shouted at the men and women of the search team. 'Get off my land!'

They ignored her, but Eyla approached her, calling for her to calm herself. 'We're here to help, my dear. It's about your husband.'

Malik's wife stared at the older woman, her eyes red and tired. 'Who are you?'

'My name is Eyla San Setta. I'm – '

'I know who you are,' the other interrupted. 'Malik said never to trust any of the High Families.'

Eyla smiled. 'I'd be inclined to agree with him. However, this situation is one which calls for a certain…leap of faith on your part.'

'I don't understand.' She looked around at Eyla's team, watching them check closely the ground and the grass. Others had passed around to the rear of the farmhouse. 'I also don't understand why the military haven't been around here. My husband was abducted by a…a Jaevisk shuttle.'

Eyla noted the hesitation, confirming her suspicions. 'Why don't we go inside? I'd quite enjoy a mug of Jersane. I heard you grow your own out here, and I've come all the way from Promies.'

Malik's wife smiled nervously and looked around again, before gesturing for Eyla to enter the house. The search of the property continued as the two women spoke in the kitchen. Eyla watched as the steaming reddish liquid was poured into the metal cups. 'Have you any idea why the Jaevisk...or anyone else...' Eyla nodded as she accepted the cup of Jersane, 'would want to hurt – '

'It *was* the Jaevisk!' the woman interjected before Eyla could finish.

'I didn't suggest otherwise.'

'But you said...'

Eyla smiled. 'What's your name, dear?'

The woman caught her gaze, and any sense of naivety vanished as she quietly and confidently replied, 'Don't pretend you don't know, Miss Setta.'

'Ah...now we're getting somewhere. Someone in your husband's situation wouldn't live with a woman for so long without divulging something and preparing her for the inevitable questions.'

'My husband's...situation? And what might that be?'

'Well, that's what I'm here to ascertain...Vella. Your husband may be in a lot of trouble.'

'I don't know what I can tell you,' said Vella genuinely. 'I know he had secrets...but he kept them to protect me.'

'Well, a woman always knows when her man is keeping things from her. So...' Eyla sipped her Jersane, 'let's see if you can remember some of those times.'

While the women were talking, one of Eyla's men spotted a recently disturbed piece of land some distance from the rear of the house and went to investigate. '*Something was taken out of the ground back here,*' he remarked over the com. In the house, Eyla listened to Vella in one ear as he explained: '*Looks like a grave was emptied and re-filled. Very recently. There's evidence of chemical burning.*'

There was the sound of vehicles approaching and a warning shout: 'The Governor's troops. Let's go!'

Eyla and Vella came to the front door as the military vehicles stopped outside the gates. More than thirty soldiers were deployed with speed and Eyla's men and women prepared to engage them. 'No!' she shouted. 'I'll deal with this.'

'A wise move, Miss Setta,' came the response as a senior officer emerged from one of the armoured trucks. He looked around. 'I do hope you haven't disturbed any evidence.'

Eyla met him at the end of the path. 'Evidence, Commander?'

201

'Oh, yes. You see, there was an...incident here recently. A man was almost killed.'

She noted the slip of information and feigned shock. 'I had no idea,' she gasped, turning back to look at Vella. Had she heard what he said? 'Will this young woman be safe here?'

'Of course. We merely wish to learn what happened.'

Eyla nodded, stepping closer. 'It's just that...I quite like the girl,' she said quietly, 'and I would be...aggrieved...should something happen to her.'

The Commander smiled. 'Well...we wouldn't want that, would we?'

'No,' said Eyla sweetly, 'you wouldn't.' She turned away from him and, gesturing for her people to follow her, she returned to her vehicle. The Commander watched them leave as the soldiers surrounded the property and began their operation. Vella came down the path as the Commander walked up to the house. 'I won't tell you anything!' she told him defiantly.

'I don't need you to.' He drew his gun and shot her in the chest, leaning down with her as she crumpled slowly and breathlessly to the ground. 'It's your traitor husband that the Governor wants!'

Ω

Senneya Tae Ahn heard the approach of the vehicle, and had just enough time to send a coded message to her husband before Governor Ben-Hadad opened the door and stepped into the entrance hall of the affluent home, followed closely by three soldiers. 'Won't you come in, Governor?' Senneya quipped as she met him. 'I'm sure you and your ruffians would like a drink.'

Ben-Hadad was positively beaming. 'My Dear Senneya, it's always good to see you.'

'I imagine it is, Governor. You should have called ahead. I might have been out.'

'How fortunate for me that you're not.'

'I'm sure that good fortune isn't shared.' She turned and walked to the kitchen at the rear of the house.

'You know,' Ben-Hadad called with good nature as he followed her, 'you should have married me, rather than that misguided husband of yours. You'd be a Governor's wife now instead of facing treason charges.'

202

Senneya laughed, but there was no humour as she replied, 'As Carak's wife, I share his loyalty to the Sieltor Confederation, a much...' she eyed him pointedly, and grinned, '*larger* institution than your short-sighted administration.'

Ben-Hadad glared at her. 'I see that we edge ever closer to truer sentiment, Senneya. But don't let concern for hiding your convictions worry you too much.' As he spoke, there was a scream from upstairs and the sound of struggling as the soldiers returned with a captive. 'You see, I'm fully aware of the extent of the conspiracy against me.'

With tears falling to her cheeks, Senneya managed to stand her ground. 'If you hurt her...' she warned through gritted teeth.

'Yes, yes...' he dismissed her, as the soldiers brought a young girl into the kitchen. The child struggled in their strong grip, kicking and biting as she did so. The Governor turned to grab the child's face and she spat at him. 'Defiant to the last,' he commented distastefully, pushing her back into the care of the soldiers. He swung on Senneya, lashing out with his fist as she lunged at him. She collapsed to the floor as he roared at her, 'Not Carak or Jakari San Setta or any of your conspirators will bring me down, do you understand? Your daughter stays with me until I am assured of Carak's compliance.' Softer, he added, 'You have my permission to inform him accordingly.'

Leaving Senneya lying on the floor, Ben-Hadad left with his men. Carak's wife got to her feet as soon as the door was closed, testing her jaw for damage as her eyes burned with rage. She went straight to her com centre and opened an encrypted channel. Eyla San Setta appeared on the screen. 'The pig took my daughter,' Senneya told her before she could speak. 'I want everyone activated, Eyla.'

Eyla nodded. 'Once you do this, there's no going back,' she reminded her. 'We take this all the way. How do you want to begin?'

'I want to speak to the Jaevisk,' Senneya replied.

Ω

Eyla leaned back in her chair as the convoy sped back to Khas. 'No going back,' she whispered to herself, feeling the excitement rushing through her body. Emboldened by the concept, she made a rash decision. 'Tell the driver to turn around,' she ordered.

The man opposite her nodded without question and tapped on the glass behind him. 'We're going back,' he said. 'Inform the team.'

As the convoy reversed their course to once again visit the house of Malik and Vella, Eyla took a communication device out of her pocket, speaking into it: 'I want an encrypted channel to the lead Jaevisk Warship. Tell them that the real rulers of the Garran wish to speak with them.'

Ω

An hour had passed, with Senneya trying not to think about the fear her daughter was experiencing as a captive of the Governor. Carak had not replied to the wordless warning she had sent him, and she had no way of knowing where he was or whether she would see him again. Eyla's son was due to meet with Carak, but he would avoid communication with home once the warning was passed on to him. A call sounded from the com system and she took a deep, calming breath as she steeled herself for the subterfuge. 'Respond,' she said aloud.

A male Jaevisk with a red cape hanging from his golden shoulders appeared in holographic form in the middle of the living room. His size had been altered proportionately to compensate for the relatively small Garran dwelling. 'Who are you?'

Senneya stood proud. 'My identity is irrelevant. The people I represent have operatives on more than twenty worlds. They are the power which allows incompetents like Ben-Hadad to maintain his tenuous position.'

'Why would they tolerate an incompetent representative of their species?'

'Everyone needs a scapegoat,' Senneya replied. 'The realities of administering an intergalactic operation can't be entrusted to the whim and ego of individuals in the public domain. It is necessary for organisations like ours to operate behind the scenes of democratic delusion. The general population only see a short distance into the future, a future almost always defined by their personal needs. If they don't get what they want, they blame it on the people they elected. Meanwhile, the reality continues in the background, alongside the rise and fall of...incompetent individuals.'

The Jaevisk appeared to consider this, although Senneya knew that her image would be scanned back on the Warship and her identity affirmed. 'You are the mate of Overseer Carak, a political rival of Governor Ben-Hadad.'

Senneya smiled. 'That's one aspect of my life, yes.'

204

Again, silence. Senneya wondered at the significance of the red cape, and filed it for later. Eyla would know. 'I, too, have many aspects,' admitted the Jaevisk, causing Senneya to blink and mentally stumble. 'I can create as well as destroy. Most recently, I created something designed to destroy something else.' This sort of concession on the part of a Jaevisk was highly unusual, and reference to the individual amongst the Jaevisk was tantamount to unprecedented, but it opened the conversation in Senneya's favour.

'What did you create?' she asked, feeling for some reason as if she were talking to a child about the latest product of its imagination.

'I created a virus.'

Senneya's stomach turned. Of course this was no child. It was a Jaevisk, a master of manipulation, deception and, when necessary, cruelty. 'Why would you do such a thing?'

'I was ordered to.'

'I know what you intend to do here,' said Senneya, changing the subject and calling their bluff. 'I know that you've sided with Ben-Hadad against my husband and his associates. And I know about the Garran soldiers the Governor gave you. Are you testing the virus on them?'

The silence was longer and louder this time, and Senneya kept glancing at the translator on the table to ensure that it was still on. 'It is not that kind of virus, and you imagine more than you know. The politics of your world only become relevant when they affect the future of ours.'

Now it was Senneya's turn to be quietened by the exchange. 'Your...what?' she asked eventually. 'I thought the Jaevisk didn't have a home.'

The hologram flickered and the Jaevisk glared at her, the translator managing to capture the clipped tones of its reply: 'Everyone has a home.' The Jaevisk vanished.

'No...wait!' Senneya shouted, cursing herself for her impatience and lack of tact.

Ω

Eyla's convoy skidded to a halt outside the home of Malik Ki Jen. The place was deserted, and Eyla was surprised that the government troops had left so quickly. 'They mustn't have found anything,' one of the team remarked.

205

'Or maybe they did,' snapped Eyla, 'and they took it with them.' The search which had so recently been cut short resumed again in earnest, and the first thing Eyla noticed was a pool of blood before the door of the house. She sighed sadly, but her curiosity was piqued by a spot of blood just short of a metre to her left, with another one following it. Gesturing that one of the team accompany her, she followed the blood trail around to the rear of the house. Farming equipment and garden tools were strewn around the yard, disrupted by Ben-Hadad's soldiers. In one of the open barns, a ploughing vehicle had been unnecessarily vandalised. Eyla's team was subdued as their survey of the property continued, and the burning afternoon sun curbed their enthusiasm. It was quiet as the blood trail ended abruptly. 'There's no sign of a vehicle,' Eyla's guard remarked. 'No tyre tracks...no emission burns.'

'So you'd agree that no one took the body away?'

The guard nodded, hunkering down to brush at the dusty ground with his gloved hand. Eyla joined him with her bare hands, each of them moving away from each other methodically to cover an area expanding from the last spot of blood. 'There!'

Eyla looked up as the shouter pointed down at an area she had just passed. She could not see it, but he was pointing emphatically, and she moved back with his guidance, catching a fingernail in a subtle edging. Her guard moved towards her, drawing a knife and scraping out the definition of an entrance hatch as she stood up and clapped the dust from her hands. 'Now how do we open it?' she wondered.

'Maybe there's a magic word,' suggested a familiar and unwelcome voice. Eyla's guards were completely surrounded and outnumbered by the government troops who had returned in silence. With weapons trained on them, Eyla gestured for her people to stand down. 'There's a good girl,' said the Commander, approaching the older woman, eyeing the disturbed ground as he did so. 'You seem to have found what I was looking for. I'll be sure to forward my appreciation to the Governor when he decides what to do with you.' A knife slammed hilt-deep into the forehead of the soldier next to the Commander and the body crumpled to the dusty ground. Then one of Eyla's men had his arm shorn off by a metallic projectile which slammed into the wood of the back door. With every man and woman thinking they were under attack from their obvious foes, the two groups opened fire on each other as Eyla dropped to the ground and the Commander tried to flee. He turned to find a tall and dark Human male, wearing a strange black cloak and wielding a knife, blocking his escape. The knife was introduced to his throat, and they hit it off immediately.

In the chaos, Eyla was kicked in the head and she began to lose consciousness. She felt herself being dragged along the ground and thought that she might be descending into the underworld. She was not too far off the mark, for when she came round she found herself lying on the floor in a dimly lit world beneath the ground. She realised, as she sat up and looked around, that this was no ordinary cellar or even a cave of any kind. There was machinery everywhere, some of a kind she recognised and more of a kind she did not. Computers which controlled robotic assembly and maintenance units were evident nearby, but most of the other objects and devices she could not begin to define. 'Where am I?' she intoned with traditional curiosity. Footsteps were heard from behind her and she turned quickly, regretting it as her head pounded and her eyes blurred. 'You're safe,' a man told her. 'Which is more than I can say for the little army you brought with you.'

She raised a hand to her forehead, closing her eyes to steady herself. 'Who are you?'

'My name is Naveen.' He was in front of her when she opened her eyes, a Human man with dark hair and eyes, and stubble mimicking the shadows of bestial incisors. 'And you are Eyla San Setta.'

'Yes, I am.'

'It wasn't a question.'

'So ask me one.'

'Why did you come back?'

'To protect Vella.'

'Now, we both know that's not true.'

'What makes you think that?' She got to her feet and he caught her as she stumbled. He held her as she steadied herself, nodding once she was confident enough to stand on her own. She stared into his dark eyes and shivered as he replied with a whisper, 'No going back.'

She stepped back from him. 'Who are you? One of Harrogate's spies...or Relland's fanatics? Or has Tesckyn finally figured out what I'm doing?'

He grinned. 'Don't you think I'm a little...conspicuous for that sort of work?'

She considered the long black cloak he was wearing and the pattern of silver and gold dragons upon it. Were they looking at her? 'I suppose you would stand out in a crowd, yes.' He laughed and walked away from her.

'You're not surprised that I know Tesckyn,' she noted as she followed him.

'Very little surprises me, Eyla.' He clearly had no intention of giving anything away, but she had a more immediate concern. 'Where's Vella?' she asked. 'Was she hurt?'

He said nothing as he led her to a coffin-like object constructed of a smooth black metal. 'I've never seen a mineral like this,' she gasped, touching its cold surface. 'It's not...'

'From around these parts?' He smiled. 'No, it's not. But that's not a conversation I wish to have.' He tapped an access code on an illuminated panel and the lid became transparent, so that Eyla could see Vella's wounded body inside, the blood from her wound coagulated on her naked flesh. 'She's healing,' he explained. 'I need you to take care of her once the cycle has finished.'

'I don't understand. What do I have to do?'

'Nothing special. Just make sure she's kept safe. She's pregnant, and she's...important.'

'She's Malik's wife,' said Eyla, 'and he loves her.'

Naveen shook his head. 'They didn't even know each other. As far as she's concerned, her husband died in that Jaevisk shuttle.'

Eyla held his gaze for a moment, wondering what he meant, but nodding her agreement before turning back to look at Vella. 'Why do the Jaevisk want him? I know he's still alive.'

There was no argument. 'Because he knows too much about them.'

'Such as?'

Before he could respond, Eyla's com unit sounded. Naveen indicated that she should answer it and she found that it was Senneya on the other end. '*I spoke to the Jaevisk and tried to get them to reveal something,*' she told Eyla, '*but they said that our operation was unimportant unless it had an effect on their world!*'

'What world?'

'*Well, I thought the same, and said as much.*'

'And?'

'*And they got angry and cut me off!*'

At that, Eyla heard Naveen emit a short laugh. 'I'll come and see you soon, Senneya,' she said, before disconnecting. 'Something amuses you about that conversation,' she noted.

Naveen re-entered the access codes on the coffin and the lid became opaque again. 'You asked me what Malik knows about the Jaevisk.'

'Unless you know what he knows, I doubt you can help.'

'Oh, I know much more than that,' he teased.

Eyla was becoming increasingly frustrated by the arrogance of this man. 'Such as?' she pressed.

'Well, for a start...' he chuckled as if some private joke had eluded her, 'the Jaevisk don't get angry.'

Eyla blinked. 'Is that *it*?' she snapped. 'That's not very helpful, is it?'

'Everything I say is helpful, Eyla. You just need to figure out how to use it.'

Eyla shook her head angrily and looked around. 'How do I get out of here?'

Naveen pointed towards a stone staircase. 'Vella will come to you when this is over,' he promised as she walked away. 'I suggest you do as I ask.'

Eyla said nothing as she made her way up the steps. When she looked back, Naveen was gone.

Ω

Senneya opened the door with a mixture of relief and disappointment on her face, and Eyla walked in as she stood aside. 'Why are you alone?' the younger woman wondered.

Eyla made a gesture of dismissal, and then drew Senneya into an embrace. 'We'll do everything possible to get Kera back. You have my word.'

Senneya's eyes filled with tears, but she drew herself up and stepped back boldly. 'I want to make sure he never hurts anyone again,' she declared. Eyla nodded, heading into the living room. Here, she was all business once Senneya joined her. 'I want you to access our deep space scopes. I need some answers before I do anything else. Once Ben-Hadad realises I'm still around, he'll push harder to have me killed. I need to have something worth bargaining with.'

209

'Where do you want to look?'

Eyla thought for a moment. 'Let me see the Kiranis system. Relland's people were talking about it before the cage severed their com links.'

Senneya located the scope best suited for the task and entered the co-ordinates. The image of a six-planet system appeared on the dark wall. 'That's the latest archive capture, but it's more than two days old. I'll run a catch-up sequence.'

Eyla nodded. 'Close in on the fifth planet and then slow it down once we see the cage appearing.' The fifth planet was isolated on the image and then magnified. It was a dark and lifeless world with no sign of any physical or chemical activity. A number of Jaevisk Warships could be seen orbiting the planet. As the sequence of shots continued, the cage appeared and the Warships retreated. At first the cage was disconnected, just as it currently was at Earth, but it swiftly came together around the dark world. Then, with a blinding flash, the planet was ripped apart as the cage opened and then vanished. What it left behind was a swirling, boiling mass of solidifying and melting crust, volcanic and chaotic. The geological processes at work were astonishing. 'What are we seeing?' whispered Senneya, awed by the sight.

'Something that makes no sense,' replied Eyla. 'It's like the planet is forming, or in this case re-forming. We just couldn't see it from the distant shots of the system.'

'How's that possible? It was a dead world. No seismic activity had ever been registered.'

Eyla nodded. 'It was certainly that way for as long as we've observed that system.' She stepped closer to the image, marvelling in the fiery activity and the gravitational instability of still scattered orbital remnants. The Jaevisk Warship was in a higher orbit with each successive image. 'Of course, we have no idea how long *they've* been watching it...or why.' With terror seizing her, Eyla considered a momentous possibility and danced around the implications. 'What if we're not seeing its after-life destruction? What if this is its formation?'

Senneya caught her gaze as she turned around. 'What are you talking about? The only time a planet could look like that other than during its formation is if its sun expanded enough to rip it apart, and even then the debris field would be significantly different. This couldn't possibly be after-life destruction.'

210

'I agree. Which leaves us with the only other option. Pre-life formation.' Her eyes burned like the planet behind her as she glared emphatically at Senneya. 'How much do you know about what our people protect, Senneya?' she asked. 'What has Carak told you about the experiments?'

Senneya hesitated, trying to catch up without looking like a fool. But she knew that much had been kept from her, and she knew why. 'I asked to be spared the details,' she admitted. 'I knew I'd never hold up against concerted interrogation. All Carak told me was that the experiments began when some people were taken from Earth to be studied, and that eventually Human scientists played a role in the genetic modifications.'

'But you've no idea why we were so suddenly interested in that at the time? Considering that we'd been in contact with them for centuries, I mean.'

Senneya shook her head. 'I'm not sure I understand.'

Eyla turned back to the image, watching the fifth planet of the alien system forming as if billions of years of galactic history had not occurred. 'I think we've just witnessed something similar to what happened to Earth more than two hundred years ago,' she said. 'And if that's the case, then Tesckyn is going to be even more convinced that he's on the right track.'

'You're going too fast, Eyla. Who's Tesckyn?'

Eyla held her gaze for a moment. 'Tesckyn oversees a long-established covert organisation on Earth. His people operate with complete anonymity and autonomy. Currently, they're intent on destroying the Church of the New Elect, something I strongly disagree with. Unfortunately, your husband doesn't see things my way.'

'He's never said anything about this to me,' said Senneya, clearly stunned. 'What's this...Tesckyn going to do? What's Carak going to do?'

'It's...complicated, Senneya, and we may be able to convince Carak to back down in time. I'll explain later, but there's something I need to see first. Jakari's fleet is out at Omneri, making preparations for the journey to the Kiranis system. He's following the orders of Governor Ha-Cxada at the moment, but he's no idea of what's in store for him.'

Within a few moments, the images were up. Scores of battleships and escort vehicles were orbiting the Garran world renowned for the supply of advanced military technology. But as the images were enlarged, the women saw the work which was underway on Jakari's ships. Senneya pointed to unusual structures being attached to the hull of each battleship. 'What are those things?' she asked.

'I don't know,' said Eyla. 'But we need to find out fast.'

THE THIRD DAY

Sieltor Teuvas, a small planet with a population of roughly six hundred million, was the outer planet of the primary system under Garran control. Rich in fuels and minerals when discovered, it was now a thriving world of fortune frequented by merchant enterprises from across the known galaxy. It also attracted fortune seekers and adventurers from many worlds, most with a mind to solve an ancient mystery. For centuries, there had been stories of strange lights in the mountains and caves, and it was said that a power source unlike any other existed deep beneath the surface of Teuvas. Crews of underwater vessels reported flashing beacons deep on the ocean floor, but like ancient reports of aliens and monsters, there was nothing substantial and the stories were dismissed as such. Today, however, those stories were proved dreadfully real as the planet began to heat at an alarming rate and waves of quakes shook the planet for hours on end. This prelude to greater destruction was followed by nothing short of the eruption of the world. Massive blasts of molten lava and toxic gases spewed into the atmosphere across every landmass, burning the air as clouds plunged the planet into darkness. Millions of people died, ships trying to leave were engulfed and blown apart. Hell had come to Teuvas and its rivers ran red with the blood of the world. Something terrible had awakened, something ancient. The ground hissed with bubbling heat, people combusted as they took a wrong step in a minefield of fire. Searing, blood-red rain hammered down in a relentless shower of death.

Many vessels escaped the phenomenon, carrying terrified people out into the relative haven of space. They watched in horror as the planet dropped away from them. Its surface had started to glow red, but this phenomenon dissipated as the ground cracked to reveal blood-like veins pulsating from deep within the world. Shards of the planet were ejected into space and soon Sieltor Teuvas was no more than a shell of transparent flesh revealing a pulsating red core which had been hidden from the galaxy for thousands of years. The Jaevisk in the Sieltor system left as they had arrived, for no amount of misdirection could obscure this phenomenon.

Governor Ben-Hadad arrived aboard a battleship to observe this destruction, too late to do anything about it. But as he stared at the devastated planet, he knew that nothing would ever be the same again. For he realised exactly what he was seeing in that blood-red core. It pulsed with energy, alien energy, taunting him with his own stupidity and greed as he recalled the Jaevisk gift which had enjoined him to their cause.

Ω

Ben-Hadad's ship remained in the vicinity of the ruined planet, and he summoned the Garran leaders of the Sieltor worlds, who had lingered at Sieltor Prime, revelling in the excitement of the Jaevisk alliance. Now, seated around a long table on the Imperial Flagship, their excitement was decidedly eroded. The room was understandably quiet, its occupants subdued, their private muttering the only sound until Ben-Hadad walked in. Ten armed guards followed him, spreading out around the room while the Governor of Sieltor Prime waited for absolute silence and attention. His face did not betray any of his churning emotions as he acknowledged the Governors of Thuros and Promies, Goruset and Omneri. These men of high influence in the growing state of Garran domination ruled the planets on which only Garran were allowed to live. Representatives of other worlds under Garran control or occupation had not been summoned, for this was an internal matter.

The Chair of Teuvas was empty, and Ben-Hadad looked at it for a moment before addressing the Governors. 'Sieltor Teuvas is a dead world now,' he began quietly, 'but sometimes death can reveal a greater truth.' His gaze moved around the table as he appeared to carefully study each of those present. There was something unreadable in his expression, some ominous reasoning behind his piercing gaze as he resumed. 'You have heard of the changes in the fifth planet of the Kiranis system.' They nodded in unison. 'I believe this hasn't happened by chance, not when the device responsible for it surrounds Earth as we speak.' They agreed, mercifully unaware of the implications. 'But let us not digress. Better we consider the events we have more recently witnessed. The Jaevisk came to us with an alliance, immediately after visiting Earth. They offered us the secret of their power and left our space when it became clear that this secret had been sitting under our noses...all the time.' He smiled, a sibilant thing. 'But there are other...more subtle betrayals occurring here. It has been brought to my attention that a potential rival for our power, Overseer Carak, has stolen my Star Cruiser and is heading for Earth. Now this – '

'Will you have Carak punished for this?' someone interrupted. It was the Governor of Sieltor Omneri, an industrial world in the Sieltor system, a planet known for its research into the most advanced of all technologies. There was a palpable silence as Ben-Hadad looked down at the floor with a dark smile. 'He will be punished in time, Ha-Cxada,' he replied. 'I believe he has a rendezvous to make at the Kiranis system. A large fleet is leaving soon to investigate the events in the system, commanded by Jakari San Setta...a friend of your family, I understand. Did you know that this fleet has also been fitted to transport some kind of structure for the Jaevisk? This work was done at Omneri at the behest of the Jaevisk, and I find all of this intriguing, Governor, considering that the orders appeared to have been rushed through my office without my knowledge.'

Ha-Cxada tried and failed to conceal his dismay. Painfully aware of the futility of lies, he rose from his seat and roared at Ben-Hadad, 'You will be the death of us all!' A guard stepped away from the wall behind him and raised his gun as Ha-Cxada continued: 'You squander our power through useless alliances and barbaric exchanges of resources...and now *soldiers!* It is *you* who are the traitor, Ben-Hadad!'

The gun was pressed into the back of the Governor from Sieltor Omneri. 'I see it differently,' Ben-Hadad replied, dismissing the man with a flick of his wrist. The trigger was pulled, and a gaping hole was blown in the man's chest. He slumped forward across the table and soon the smell of blood and the cacophony of silence filled the room. As the body was dragged away, Ben-Hadad looked around at the shocked faces of the other leaders. 'Don't mourn for him,' he warned them. 'You should know that the ten thousand soldiers demanded of me by the Jaevisk are all dead.'

'What?' one of them gasped. 'How?'

'Their vital statistics were being monitored, and they were all transferred to a Warship orbiting Omneri which had been waiting as I was speaking with the Jaevisk. And they were all dead within hours.' The Governors understood Ha-Cxada's execution and said nothing. 'Even though the Jaevisk have betrayed us,' Ben-Hadad continued, 'I will permit the modifications to Jakari's fleet to remain intact. After all, if this is another element of Jaevisk betrayal, better for Jakari's fleet to experience it than one of ours.' They nodded emphatically. 'It is time, my friends...my brothers...to declare ourselves leaders in the true sense of the word. The Jaevisk are intent on claiming the fifth planet of the Kiranis system as their

215

own. However, in light of recent events, I feel that it is the Garran people who are owed a new world. Don't you agree?'

They vocally assented this time, and Ben-Hadad delighted in their short-sightedness. 'Each of you will gather every available fighting vessel at your disposal and you will join me in showing the Jaevisk the price of their betrayal. My fleets are ready to leave, and yours will follow close behind. The fight will be difficult, of course, and if any of you don't return to your worlds I will personally appoint a suitable replacement. You will join me in retaliating against Jaevisk lies and the plans of those who bring Humans into our affairs. You will follow me in once again asserting the supremacy of the Garran race.'

Although no question had been asked, they nodded in acquiescence, aware of the ring of Ben-Hadad's loyal soldiers within which they sat. 'An excellent decision, brothers,' he commended them, sitting down. 'Now,' he said pleasantly, pressing his hands together with congenial fervour. 'Does anyone else wish to be heard?'

Ω

Jakari San Setta was an Imperial Fleet Commander from Sieltor Promies. Officially, this elevated military rank subordinated him only to the Governors. Of course, there was always room for the adjustment of allegiance, and Jakari was a man who watched the changing tides of the political ocean with the passion of a gambler who risked everything with every bet. And indeed he did, for Fleet Commander Setta was not one to back the obvious, most powerful political player, the favourite to win the coming battle. The figures upon whom he would place his trust and – never to be forgotten – his money were those whom he believed to have the best interests of his people at heart. He would never consider himself a traitor, or a defector. It was simply that he knew things that others did not; that much larger tides would soon lap at the shores of Garran supremacy. Seated in a comfortable leather chair on the bridge of his battleship, the man who looked every inch the formidable warrior watched as his First approached and sat down in the chair to Jakari's left. Jakari's First, Kaste, leaned a little closer and informed him quietly, 'There's been no message from Ha-Cxada.'

Jakari nodded, masking his concern. The meeting was over. The other Governors had left Ben-Hadad's ship. Jakari's fleet, consisting of one hundred battleships, each flanked by a transport vessel carrying fifty

216

smaller attack craft, was in orbit of Sieltor Omneri, and strange modifications were being made to every battleship. Rising from his command chair and walking to the starboard window of the bridge, Jakari could see scores of battleships undergoing these modifications. Giant robotic construction vessels sent up from Omneri were attaching some sort of structure to the hull of each ship, and it was unclear as to whether these structures were for transporting cargo, or whether they were the cargo itself. Clearly Jaevisk in design, Jakari presumed that these modifications were part of the terms of alliance. 'We need to know more about these things,' Jakari noted, his hands clasped behind his waist. 'Ha-Cxada wasn't clear on what we'd be carrying.'

'He had to make it look like the order came from Ben-Hadad's office,' Kaste reminded him. 'I dread to think he was discovered.'

Jakari turned to regard Kaste, his most trusted friend. Companions since childhood, Jakari and Kaste were of similar build. Each of them was just short of two and a half metres tall, with a lean, muscular frame. Jakari's skin was only slightly darker than that of his First, and Kaste's hair was showing signs of age, turning white along the centre of the cranial ridge. He worried more than Jakari, whose hair was still black and long, drawn together tightly and tied to hide the ridge-cut of birth. However, if the next few days did not go as planned, Jakari might find himself as bald as a *Gorim* rat. 'Has there been any word from our elusive Overseer?'

Kaste shook his head. 'Carak will probably maintain com silence until he reaches Kiranis.'

'Why?' wondered Jakari. 'If Ben-Hadad has realised what's going on, then it's already too late. He won't back down from a fight.'

'Let's hope not,' said Kaste, 'because Carak insisted that was part of the plan.' A communication alert sounded and a female officer called to Jakari: 'A message from Governor Ben-Hadad, Commander. We're to set course for the Kiranis system immediately.'

Kaste was visibly confused. 'It must be a trap. He wouldn't allow us to go ahead if Ha-Cxada is out of the picture?'

'We don't know that he is or even that we've been connected to him.'

The crew, however, did not share in their Commander's optimism, and they began to talk amongst themselves of the potential dangers to come. 'Don't speculate!' Jakari snapped at them. 'I need you all focused on your work...nothing else! You heard about Teuvas. The Jaevisk made a fool of Ben-Hadad and now he wants to retaliate.'

'Apparently, we're to be the bait,' the woman explained as she continued reading the message. 'We've been ordered to move on the fifth planet...without waiting for the rest of Ben-Hadad's forces.'

'Then he knows nothing about these modifications or Ha-Cxada's deal with the Jaevisk,' Jakari assured them. 'All he cares about is taking that world for himself.'

Kaste came up to him and reminded him quietly. 'Then where's Ha-Cxada?' He caught the gaze of his friend and saw the doubt there as he pressed, 'And why haven't we heard from your mother?'

Jakari grinned. 'Mother's silence is sometimes welcome,' he remarked.

But Kaste was not swayed by the levity. Quieter again, he whispered, 'What if the Jaevisk have betrayed us as well as Ben-Hadad? They're known for manipulating internal feuding.' Jakari could say no more, quieted as he was by the possibility, but he came to a decision, and he turned to address the crew. 'Whatever the motivations of our glorious Governor, we're still going to Kiranis,' he reminded them. 'Disobeying Ben-Hadad now is the best way to reveal ourselves.'

'He'll kill us all when he catches us,' argued Kaste.

Jakari smiled. 'He'll try,' he agreed, 'but we'll have help out there.'

'If we can still trust the Jaevisk,' Kaste pressed.

Jakari shook his head dismissively. 'If I know Carak, he won't be relying on just the Jaevisk. He always has a plan.'

THE FOURTH DAY

The Star Cruiser was heading for Earth, speeding through the relative emptiness of space at a velocity beyond anything Carak had anticipated. 'An impressive ship,' noted Tanna as he seated himself next to the Overseer's command chair. 'With an impressive engine.' Forced to maintain subterfuge due to the last minute crew arrangements, both men were aware of the risks involved in going to Earth. Carak glanced sideways at his First. 'Impressive,' he agreed. 'It occurs to me that a certain schedule is being adhered to here, as if we're being propelled towards some prescribed fate.'

'Our charming guest was certainly in the right place at the right time.'

'Recent events outside Khas would suggest that that's not always the case.'

'The reports say that a man died out there,' said Tanna, 'but of course, we have first-hand knowledge to the contrary.'

'You can be sure that we won't be alone in that knowledge for long, Tanna. Then we can start worrying.'

Tanna nodded and lowered his voice further. 'And what of the rumours about the Kiranis system? A lot of people are determined to connect the changes in the fifth planet with the device surrounding Earth.'

Carak was momentarily silent, where Tanna had expected some humorous retort. 'You *agree* with them?' he asked incredulously. Carak's head turned and it was in his eyes that Tanna found his answer, warning him to speak of it no further. Again Tanna nodded, changing the subject. 'This Malik might be connected in some way,' he suggested. 'I think we should find out.'

Carak sighed. 'I hate going down to the brig,' he remarked. 'Those cells remind me of my student days.'

Tanna grinned. 'Didn't you set one on fire?'

Carak chuckled and shrugged, replying, 'It was cold in there, Tanna.'

Ω

Jakari had settled down to read once his fleet had left the Sieltor system. Reading calmed him, and it was the concentration and focus associated

219

with reading which kept his mind sharp. He had been reading about the turmoil of the Age of Kings, two centuries of tyranny and torture which stained the history of his people, and he had just finished a chapter on the structure of the hierarchy in the Western Realm of ancient Grask when he felt the engines powering down. Turning in his chair, he reached out to his left and tapped a button on a console. 'Bridge, Report!'

'I can't explain it, Commander,' one of the crew replied. 'Our command codes are denied at every turn. The engines have simply stopped and we have no access to anything up here.'

'Keep trying,' said Jakari, his voice even. 'Let me – ' There was a quiet sound of warning and the computer announced the presence of an intruder on board. He severed the connection. 'Locate and display intruder,' he told the computer. As he stood and walked to the prow-facing rectangular window of his quarters, he could see that many other ships had also stopped, the light of power in their engines dimming and dying. A monitor on the wall flickered to life and a three-dimensional map of Jakari's vessel displayed a flashing red light to indicate the intruder. It was not moving and Jakari's heart beat faster as he took a deep breath, recognising the location on the grid. He walked back to his desk, his eyes darting around to survey his room. He lifted a glass of water as he sat back down and looked at the text on his screen. 'Are you going to show yourself?' he asked, feigning boredom.

There was a palpable, almost mocking silence for a while. Then a voice spoke in the Garran language, a male voice: 'Will you stay calm if I do?'

The Commander leaned back in his chair. He could not tell from which direction the voice had come, although he looked around and swivelled on his chair to see behind him. There was nothing there. The voice had seemed all-enveloping, as if he was lost inside its hypnotic sound. 'As long as you mean no harm,' Jakari replied, 'you've nothing to fear.'

The response to this was a shimmering of the air in front of his desk, as if liquid darkness rose before him. There was no discernible image in what had now become blue-white light. 'Oh, it's not my fear I'm worried about, Jakari.' The figure coalesced until Jakari found himself looking at a Garran man wearing a very un-Garran black cloak which concealed his body from neck to toe. This shimmering cloak teased the floor with its perfection, and upon it two serpentine creatures played in magical motion. The man appeared unarmed, but Jakari was not a fool. 'I

220

didn't think Ben-Hadad would dispatch any…visitors so soon,' he mused casually. 'You must have come on board before we left home.'

The stranger smiled. The bestial, stubble-lined face, which was also considerably un-Garran, creased with devilish humour. 'I'm not associated with your squabbling authorities,' he replied. 'In fact, I'm quite beyond them.'

Jakari held his gaze for a moment, wondering what those words could mean. The only people he knew who could claim such status were associated with his mother. 'Are you a friend?'

'You don't care to know my name?'

Jakari shrugged. 'Your intentions mean more to me than your name.'

'As well they should,' the stranger congratulated him. 'So let's move on. I'm about to take you to the Kiranis system, somewhat ahead of schedule. I want you to be ready.'

'Take me…what are you talking about? Ready for what?'

'Not just you, Jakari. Your entire fleet. The Jaevisk are there in force, and they'll be surprised to see you. Nevertheless, they'll relieve you of your cargo and you'll have time to visit the fifth planet before Ben-Hadad gets there.'

Jakari laughed aloud. 'Whoever you are, you must think I'm an idiot. Firstly, we don't have anything that I would consider cargo, and secondly, that planet out there is a boiling mass of liquid rock. No one could set foot on it, even if it had a surface to speak of.'

'One of Carak's ships has been monitoring certain individuals on Earth, as part of an ongoing operation he has inherited.'

Jakari was confused as everything he said was ignored. 'I'm aware of Carak's responsibilities, but I don't see the relevance.'

'That ship left the Sol system with one of these individuals on board. It's on its way to the Kiranis system as we speak. A young man called Cana is going to be left behind at the fifth planet. He's important to me, so I'd like you to find him.'

'They're leaving him behind? In an escape pod?'

The stranger shook his head. 'He'll be on the surface.'

Jakari was annoyed by the conversation now. 'That planet doesn't *have* a surface!' he snapped. '*Who* are you?'

There was some mocking laughter. 'You mean now that my intentions confuse you?'

'That's one way of putting it.'

221

Without replying, the black-garbed Garran held out his left hand. On his palm, something materialised and Jakari moved closer to see it. It was a brooch, on which was engraved the twisting form of a golden beast similar to one of those on his dark garment. The beast had sparkling eyes and an open mouth. 'When you see this again, Jakari,' the man told him, 'I want you to consider it...a guide. Follow it, no matter what. Your life will depend on it.' He closed his palm on the brooch as if there was nothing there. 'Go to Kiranis, find Cana and keep him safe.' The mysterious Garran vanished, leaving Jakari in an unsettled silence.

There was a disturbance in space just beyond the prow of Jakari's battleship, and he noted that it was not unlike the shimmering that had heralded the arrival of the dark-cloaked stranger. The event was growing, expanding outwards in every direction to envelop every vessel in its path. Like a sphere of nothingness, those inside the event could see nothing beyond its boundaries. Anyone fortunate enough to be outside this phenomenon would have seen this spherical void growing until it encompassed the entire arrangement of Garran vessels, before it collapsed slowly in upon itself, removing the fleet from any manner of visual and physical recognition. The fleet was there. And then it was not.

Ω

Senneya was dreaming, and it was a thing of despair and horror:

Kera, her beautiful little girl, was walking hand-in-hand with a huge Jaevisk warrior, and she was turning to look back at her mother. Senneya called to her, but the girl simply laughed...as her skin began to rot. Emanating from the hand within the alien grasp, insect-like creatures of metal multiplied as they raced along her flesh, consuming and transforming the skin and muscle beneath. Her daughter was turning black as she laughed happily. The Jaevisk turned its head to observe Senneya as they walked farther from her, one yellow eye spying her with intent and delivery. Suddenly, the giant prow of a Garran battleship came into view beyond them. It did not, could not stop, and it ploughed into them both, breaking their bodies upon its hull; upon which the insects resumed their consumption.

Senneya awoke screaming, and Eyla was swiftly by her side, a man called Raill and others standing by the door of Kera's room in which Senneya

222

had slept. 'It was just a bad dream,' Eyla soothed her, pushing her damp hair back from her forehead.

Senneya shook her head as the haze of reality cleared. 'Not that kind of virus,' she gasped, her eyes wide. 'It's not that kind of virus!'

Eyla dismissed the onlookers, but Raill remained, stepping into the small bedroom. 'What do you mean, Senneya?' he asked softly.

'The Jaevisk I spoke to told me that he'd been ordered to create a virus, but not a biological one. That's what he meant. He wasn't just making conversation.'

'Everything I say is helpful,' whispered Eyla.

'What?'

Eyla shook her head. 'Just something I heard. Do you think the Jaevisk wanted you to know?'

Senneya nodded. 'He wanted us to know. He knew exactly who he was talking to, Eyla.'

'How can you be sure?'

'You said that this...cargo...attached to Jakari's battleships was connected to their on-board systems?'

'Yes. The drone I sent out reported that each of the Jaevisk structures has self-guidance information embedded in a dormant receiver, but it couldn't identify any target coordinates or locate a control server.'

'What if it's not there?' Senneya swung her legs from the bed and sat up. 'What if the control server isn't in Jakari's fleet at all?'

'Where else would it be?'

Raill was one step ahead. 'On a Warship,' he realised. 'The Jaevisk are going to activate the guidance systems. It's their cargo.'

'Yes,' said Senneya, 'but why not carry it themselves? I don't think the systems are for guiding the cargo down to the planet...or anywhere else.'

Eyla felt out of the loop for a change, and was not at all comfortable with it. 'So what are they for?'

'I think that whatever Jakari's ships are carrying, they're going to infect the fleet with a computer virus designed to take control of their navigation systems. The Jaevisk can take control of the fleet before the armada gets to the Kiranis system, and they'll launch an attack on the Governorship using our own ships. They know who we are and they know that the Governors will defend against us. Whatever's left, the Jaevisk can clean up without breaking a sweat.'

Eyla went silent, thinking of her son caught in the middle of a Jaevisk trap. But something caught her attention. 'Why would the Jaevisk tell you about the virus at all? If they want us all to kill each other out there, why give us a chance to do something about it?'

Senneya stood up and thought for a moment. 'Maybe they don't want us *all* to die. Maybe they want to give us a chance to rescue our own people before Ben-Hadad gets there,' she said eventually. 'If they take full control of Jakari's fleet, they won't need his crews on board. Or, if necessary, a skeleton crew would do.'

'The ten thousand soldiers they demanded,' Eyla recalled. 'They're going to put them on Jakari's ships!'

'Maybe they already have,' suggested Raill. 'They could be in amongst them now, waiting for some kind of signal. They could murder our men and women in key positions and take control.'

'We need to warn your son, Eyla,' said Senneya. 'Forget about com silence. It's gone beyond that now.'

Raill took a com unit out of his pocket. 'Get me Commander Setta,' he told the unseen recipient. There was a tense silence as they waited to hear Jakari's voice. But it was not the Commander who came on. '*His fleet's out of com range,*' the voice eventually informed them. '*There's no sign of it within our territory.*'

'That's impossible!' Raill argued. 'There's no way the fleet could travel that fast. Check again.'

'*I'm sorry, Sir, but I've checked three times, and the Ops centre isn't getting a reading on the transponder. There's...*'

Eyla and Senneya exchanged worried glances, the other men and women pushed into the room and Raill was baffled as the man stopped talking. 'There's *what*?' he shouted. Silence forced them to wait again, until the voice returned to the com unit speaker. '*They've arrived!*' the voice reported with evident surprise. '*I don't know how, but they've arrived already.*'

'Arrived where?'

'*At the Kiranis system,*' the voice replied. '*Deep-space mapping just caught the image.*'

Eyla jumped up and pushed the others back as she went to the main room to activate the viewscreen. Her actions were quickly the centre of attention as she brought up the images. With the fifth planet of the Kiranis system still burning behind it in the static imagery, there was a flash of light, and then the fleet appeared in the next shot. All were silent

224

for a moment, until Senneya remarked, 'We're too late.' Jaevisk Warships could be seen moving in around the fleet.

Eyla shook her head. 'There's someone else who can help.'

'Who?' asked Raill, still holding the com unit as if the little voice inside might change reality.

'A man on Earth whose job it is to know everything.' Eyla smiled with rediscovered confidence as she settled back into the driving seat.

Ω

The Star Cruiser had entered the Sol system, and Carak and Tanna had returned to the bridge after a conversation with Malik which had been a waste of time. Tanna was still wrestling with his frustration as Carak was speaking to a representative from Earth, a man named Harrogate. The conversation brought a thin smile of amusement to Tanna's face, however, as Carak exchanged banter with the Human, enjoying the thinly-veiled riposte of diplomacy. *'Our...spot of bother appears somewhat life-threatening,'* the man was saying.

'Oh, not for me, Pontifex,' replied Carak with a grin. 'That's the whole point of this visit. But we can discuss that when I arrive. So, until then...'

The Human replied, *'Until then,'* with a frosty deliverance and the channel was closed. Carak rose from his chair. 'Cut engines,' he ordered. 'We'll wait here until they've dealt with their little delivery and we get our invitation. Move us in when it comes.' A communication request was quick on the heels of the conversation with Harrogate and Carak shook his head as he sat back down. 'Harrogate again?'

'No, Overseer,' an officer replied. 'A recorded message from Sieltor Prime. It was encrypted, so I put it through to your office.'

Carak gestured for Tanna to join him, and they retreated to the privacy of the office annex. The monitor on the wall activated and they were surprised to see Ben-Hadad's Senior Aide: *'You should listen carefully, Carak,'* the man warned them. *'The Governor holds you personally responsible for the death of his envoy and knows that the traitor Malik is with you. But I wanted to warn you about the Jaevisk gift to the Governor. It's a container of four red stones, like crystals, although they seem to be mostly comprised of some kind of frozen liquid. I've included readings I managed to get, and all I can do is leave it to you to determine anything further. I risk my life just by giving this to you, so you can't ignore*

225

it. The Governor's trying to play against Jaevisk deceit, but I think he's met his match. They've already murdered ten thousand of our soldiers that the fool willingly gave to them. Our armada is leaving soon for the Kiranis system and I've a feeling something terrible is going to happen out there.' He paused. *'Do what you can, Carak. I've tried to stay loyal to the Governors, but with these dealings with the Jaevisk they've gone too far.'*

The screen went blank, and then the image was replaced with Garran writing and symbols. 'Make a copy of those readings,' ordered Carak. 'Then purge the message.'

'Of course.'

There was a knock on the door and an officer walked in. 'We have the coordinates and the codes to dock. We're approaching the station Harrogate mentioned.'

Carak nodded. 'Get someone you trust to deal with that message, Tanna.' He smiled. 'You and I have a meeting to attend.' Tanna hesitated. 'What is it?' Carak asked him.

'I'm not entirely comfortable…negotiating with these people. We know how deceitful they can be.'

'I appreciate your candour, Tanna, but it's their very nature which makes these probing negotiations necessary.' Carak smiled. 'It's also something we have in common.'

'I just don't like giving them too much information.'

'You worry too much, Tanna. I'll be discreet. I promise.'

Tanna shook his head with mock disdain, and Carak laughed aloud. Emerging onto the bridge, the crew looked at them both expectantly. 'This isn't going to be easy,' he told them, as his smile evaporated. 'Follow my instructions to the letter and we may just get out of this system in one piece.'

Ω

'There's nothing else we can do from here,' said Raill, as everyone in Eyla's house prepared to leave. 'I suggest we go somewhere less vulnerable. Your conversation with Harrogate won't have gone unnoticed.'

'Isn't it about time we started looking for Kera?' Senneya snapped, causing them all to stop and look at her in silence. Eyla approached her. 'We will,' she promised.

'When?'

'As soon as we've found a safe place to begin.'

'Well, how long will that take?'

Eyla looked at Raill, who nodded. 'I don't see why not,' he said. 'Senneya, it just so happens that we know the perfect place to hide.'

'Where?'

'Right under their noses,' said Eyla.

Ω

Reporting to the bridge of his own volition, Malik was just in time to hear that Carak had finished his meeting with Harrogate on Earth. 'They're on their way to the North Pole,' one of the staff reported. 'Should we move in?'

The officer in charge agreed and the descent began. It was when the man turned to see their prisoner standing behind him that the situation became more complicated. 'What are you doing here?' he snapped. 'How did you escape from the brig?'

Malik grinned as the officer drew his gun. 'I don't answer to you,' he replied, dismissing the officer as he took Carak's seat. The Star Cruiser descended between two of the open sections at the zenith of the cage, but as the officer raised his weapon, the ship trembled with the sudden impact of enemy fire and he was forced to react as other vessels were moving in. 'Return fire!' he shouted as he steadied himself. The fight continued as the Star Cruiser pierced the burning clouds of Earth, and explosions rippled outwards along the white ether, illuminating their heavenly emptiness. 'Protect the shuttle!'

'Jaevisk Warship! High orbit! Fighters launched!'

They saw scores of fighter craft closing in on them, opening fire without preamble. 'The shuttle's docked!' The Star Cruiser reversed course and rose through the cage aperture to find itself immediately bombarded by the monstrous Warship. 'We don't stand a chance!'

Malik rose and smoothed his clothing as he balanced himself. 'Get us as close to the Warship as possible,' he ordered calmly.

The officer stepped up to him. 'Are you *insane*? You're not in command here. You should be in the brig!'

Malik's forehead connected with the officer's nose and the man crumpled to the floor. 'New parameters for the shield output,' he shouted, in a tone which suffered no ignorance, as he tapped some keys on the command console next to Carak's chair. 'Coordinates and speed as entered. Do it or die!'

227

With that, he left the bridge, leaving the young men and women to decide their fate. 'Do it or die!' one of them shouted. They conceded. It was the right decision, they concluded, as the Jaevisk Warship exploded in front of them and they somehow passed through the horrific destruction without damage. Carak and Tanna arrived on the bridge to witness the event through the bow window. The officer was getting to his feet as the Star Cruiser sped away from the planet, blood pouring down his face. 'What happened to you?' asked Carak.

'The…prisoner!' the man spat. 'He's responsible for this.'

Carak and Tanna exchanged glances, and the Overseer smiled broadly. 'A good man to have around, then!' he said. Tanna raised his eyebrows, hating Malik even more but remaining silent for now. He was just glad to be alive.

Ω

Some time later, Carak stood alone in his quarters, staring nervously at the black cube on the table. Reaching out for it with venomous surrender, he held it in his hands and relaxed himself against the burning cold of its exterior, slowing his breathing until the thing inside the cube was pulsing at the same rate as his heart. He had not dared open the box, as if the knowledge of what was inside would bring him to his knees. In this, the owners of the box had achieved their aim. There were secrets to be kept. His eyes remained open, but it seemed as if the world beyond them was darkening.

Tricking his mind, the energy from the black box created a gigantic room around him, its dimensions stretching away into inconceivable horizons. Rising up around him were huge pillars, each many times wider than his muscular frame and towering above him. Lines of blue light, intermingled with silver wiring and black casing ran up these pillars; some lines spiralled, some shot vertically upwards. But Carak did not focus his terrified thoughts on these phenomena, for what was directly ahead of him was even more ominous.

Stepping forward from the virtual shadows of this imaginary chamber was a towering figure, more than three and a half metres in height. It moved forward into the blue light, which cast an eerie glow upon its features. In a form reminiscent of the Jaevisk, but ultimately more powerful and monstrous, this creature was a seemingly chaotic melding of shining metal and dark blue skin. However, little skin could be seen

228

between the covering of strong black leather. It had a long snout-like head like the Jaevisk, but this was slender and smooth-skinned, more serpentine than the almost crocodilian skin of the smaller Jaevisk.

Its arms ended in three finger-like extensions, its legs in four. Each limb had four joints, giving this creature the ability to alter its height and composition at will. Carak had previously come to the conclusion that these creatures were easily adaptable, ready to run on all fours or even to jump into the branches of a great tree should the situation warrant such a thing. Of course, Carak could not imagine this thing running from anyone or anything. From here he could not see for certain, but it was said that these creatures had twin spines, connected at what had at one time in their turbulent evolutionary past been a tail bone. But as he had surmised, there was very little chance of ever seeing one of these aliens turn its back to him. 'Why do you make contact?'

Carak gritted his teeth, for the alien language was painful to hear, and the translation took a moment as the agonising hissing and clicking sound dissipated. 'We're on our way to Kiranis now. I activated the device at Earth as you ordered, and I sent the message to the Church, but I still don't fully understand the implications.'

'You will, and you will be offered a reprieve from your bargain. Destroying the Jaevisk Warship was a formidable act.'

Carak's head came up, high up, so that he could look the alien in the eyes. 'What will they do now?' he asked, reluctant to credit a man who had escaped him. 'Surely this will have repercussions for my people?'

'Your alliance need not suffer. You will explain the position you were in. You will offer them the man responsible.'

Carak paused. They knew. Of course they knew. Yet Malik was gone. 'I should surrender the man who saved our lives?'

'This Garran is more than he appears. He escaped us on Sieltor Prime. If it had not been for the Jaevisk presence, we would have been revealed.'

Carak thought for a moment, looking down again. Then he smiled, aware of a slight victory over these people. 'He's gone,' he said quietly, secretly revelling in the fear of retribution. 'I'm told that he had hidden his own vessel on the hull of the Cruiser. With that in mind, I'm not really surprised that he escaped our brig.'

'He is a man of considerable talent,' the creature agreed. 'We will find him. But you will still present his body to the Jaevisk at the Kiranis system. They will identify it positively, and its condition will suit the circumstances of your lies.'

'I don't understand.'

'You will.'

Frustrated by the ever cryptic nature of these conversations, Carak looked up again and sneered. 'Are you sure my feeble Garran mind can comprehend all of this?'

'Where there is time, there is hope,' replied the massive alien. Carak found himself grinning, and there was silence for a moment. A sound from behind Carak caused him to turn, seeing Tanna through the psychic projection. His friend stared at him, clearly distressed. He appeared to be calling him, and the image around Carak began to fade. Before it evaporated completely, Carak heard the last words of the alien. 'No one must know of our dealings, Overseer,' it warned him. 'No one must know that we have been here all along.'

Ω

Tanna stopped calling to Carak, for the man had not yet turned to acknowledge his presence. He still appeared lost in a trance-like state, the black box held tightly in his hands. He made no sound or movement, and Tanna wondered whether this was truly the meditation in which he so often indulged these days. Or whether it was something else.

Carak set the black box down on the table next to him, still refusing to acknowledge Tanna. He remained silent, seeming to regain his composure as his First cautiously approached. 'I seem to have done it again,' he apologised. 'I know I should have waited for permission to enter, Carak, but...'

Carak nodded and turned to regard him. 'One day, I'll explain exactly what you should do,' he replied in English. 'Now, why are you here?'

Tanna noted the threat and dismissed it, attributing it to fatigue or stress, for not once had Carak spoken to him in such a manner in all the years they had known each other. He took up the conversation in English. 'I was analysing the data sent from Prime,' he explained as he took a slender rectangular device from his pocket. 'These...crystals the Jaevisk gave to Ben-Hadad.'

'Well...what did you find?'

'A problem.'

230

Carak held his gaze. 'Get to the point, Tanna. I was hoping for a rest before we get to Kiranis.'

'You may find that difficult once you hear this.' He handed the small scanning device to Carak, and continued. 'The stones are most definitely comprised of organic material. In fact, unless I and these readings are very much mistaken, they are essentially frozen flesh and blood.'

'Blood?' Carak perused the readings on the device's screen and acknowledged the conclusions there. 'From what?'

'I have no idea. It matches nothing in our database, and I'm reluctant to liaise with anyone at home...considering the situation.'

'Of course. I'm sorry, Tanna, but I don't see how this poses a problem for us.'

Tanna took the device back and tapped a few keys before returning it to Carak. 'These are the results of a scan performed aboard this ship.'

'But...they're identical!' Carak looked up. 'Where are these readings from?'

'They're from our engine room, Carak. I found out that the Jaevisk put an engine in this ship as part of their alliance gift. Shortly before we were called to the shipyards.'

'You're suggesting that this ship is fuelled by blood?' Carak scoffed. 'That's ridiculous!'

'I didn't say I could explain it,' Tanna replied, 'but have you been down to the engine room lately? It's freezing down there! You may have found Earth cold, but that was like a volcano compared to the conditions in which the engine core needs to be kept. And the Jaevisk instructed Ben-Hadad to keep those stones in freezing conditions. The Jaevisk have supplied us with a bio-fuel unlike anything we...' He stopped as he noted that Carak was not listening. Instead, he was transfixed by the black box on the low table. 'Carak?' There was no reply, and Tanna reached down to grab the box. 'No!' Carak snapped, but it was too late.

Tanna felt the chill in his hands and he gasped, shocked as much by the sharp icy sting on his flesh as by the implications in their context. 'What is this, Carak?' he asked quietly. 'Where did you get it?'

'It couldn't be connected to the Jaevisk,' Carak replied, seeming to stare through his friend. 'They don't work with the Jaevisk.'

'Who?' pressed Tanna, softly and cautiously.

Carak blinked. 'Why would they both have the same power source? How could two different species have the same source of power with this...*blood* in it? It doesn't make sense.'

Tanna could feel his heart pounding in his chest, and he lost his patience. 'What have you done, Carak?' he snapped angrily. 'What did we do back on Earth? And who are you working with? You need to tell me!'

Carak found himself swiftly, reaching out to snap the box from Tanna's grip. 'I don't need to tell you anything!'

'I deserve to *know*, Carak! I'm as deep in this thing as *you* are!'

Carak appeared to consider that, and he replied finally as he set the box back on the table. 'They call themselves the Kwaios Council.'

'I've never heard of them,' admitted Tanna.

Carak nodded absently, feeling a different sort of chill rush through him. 'Pretty soon, you're going to wish you hadn't.' He pushed past Tanna and headed for the door, knowing he had been duped. 'We all will.'

Ω

Under the home of Malik Ki Jen, the conspirators gathered and welcomed others to their fold. Senneya found that she cared little for their dissent and their scheming, and she decided to explore the enormous chthonic lair of the mysterious man who had escaped the wrath of the Jaevisk and who was now apparently enjoying refuge with her husband. Senneya had not gone far when she came across the black coffin. She was drawn to its surface with the wonder of a child and both her hands were on it as Eyla stepped up beside her. 'His wife is in there,' she explained. 'Ben-Hadad's men shot her and...someone brought her here to be healed.'

'Healed? What is this thing?'

'I'm not entirely sure.' Eyla pointed to the access panel. 'There's a code to open it, but I don't know it. The...person who was here didn't tell me.' To forestall any questions on the matter, Eyla quickly added, 'Whatever happens, we have to take care of this woman. It's the right thing to do.'

Senneya nodded, too distracted to argue. 'Why did they want her dead?' she wondered.

Eyla shook her head as Raill came up next to her. 'I've no idea,' she replied, 'but there's already been permission granted to demolish the house and clear the land. A number of buyers have shown interest, but someone else has laid down such an incredible bid that none of them will get to touch it.'

'Who?'

'It must be someone within Ben-Hadad's circle, because we've had no luck with any of our usual contacts. It saves the Governor from making a public affirmation of involvement if it's done this way.'

'He's not the idiot we hoped he was,' noted Raill.

'He's still a pig,' said Senneya.

The older man smiled sympathetically. 'That he is, my dear. But he'll regret taking your daughter, I can assure you.'

'Have you located her yet?'

Raill shook his head. 'My operatives are closing in, but the palace compound is enormous. There's a lot of ground to cover.'

Eyla laid her hand on Senneya's arm. 'We'll find her.'

Senneya nodded and took a deep, calming, breath. 'I want to look him in the eye when I get her back,' she said coldly.

Raill was taken aback. 'Senneya, we can do this without confronting him at all. The armada has left the system, so he's likely to be out at Kiranis when we find Kera. And if we're correct in thinking that the Jaevisk intend to kill every Garran out there, there's not much chance of him coming back.'

Eyla's com sounded and she moved away to take the call. 'Calm down,' she was saying as she walked away. 'When is the surgery due to begin?'

Senneya was quiet for a moment, and Raill shared her silence. When Senneya finally found her voice, her words were filled with such hatred that he could not bring himself to deny her her request. 'I need you to find a way to get him back, Raill,' she said. 'I want him to stand before my family and pay for what he's done!'

Ω

An officer approached Carak as he emerged onto the bridge. 'There's a high-priority call from Sieltor Prime. I don't think our plans for com silence are going to work with this one.'

Carak covered the top of his face with his right hand, massaging his temples. 'Let me guess. Ben-Hadad?'

The com officer nodded. 'I put it on a private channel.'

233

Carak shook his head. 'No going back now,' he stated in English, gesturing for the activation of the main monitor. Tanna arrived and the two men were seated as the Governor's image appeared before them all.

'*My personal envoy is dead.*' These were the first words the Governor spoke as he appeared on the screen, and Carak was clearly unsettled by this. 'I'm truly sorry for that,' he replied genuinely.

Ben-Hadad waved the pointless gesture aside. '*Where's the fugitive?*'

Tanna shifted uneasily in his chair, but Carak remained calm. 'He was killed destroying a Jaevisk Warship. They attacked us and your...fugitive took it upon himself to plant some sort of device. I've no idea how he did it, but he certainly didn't come back from it.' He decided to try a little tangent of deceit. 'Why would the Jaevisk attack us in the middle of nowhere? Wouldn't they presume that you were on board?'

Ben-Hadad was prepared for outright lies, but this was an interesting collaboration of half-truths, and he suppressed a grin of twisted admiration. '*The Jaevisk have betrayed me,*' he explained, and Carak noted the reference of self, realising that the Garran people meant nothing to this tyrant. '*My presence on that ship would have been irrelevant, but then you and I both know they were after Malik.*'

Carak smiled. 'Do we?'

'*Did you find his body?*'

Carak hesitated and Ben-Hadad laughed softly. '*No, I should think not. After all, he escaped the Jaevisk at Khas and I've recently learned that he was once a guest on one of their prison worlds. Cenin-Ta, no less. Now what sort of a man escapes from Cenin-Ta, Carak?*'

Tanna glanced at Carak, whose mind was working overtime as he commented, 'There's clearly more to this man than meets the eye, Governor.'

'*If indeed he's the same man our records declare him to be. I suggest you compare your most recent education with the archived personnel files.*' He smiled. '*Oh, and I do hope you enjoy my ship, Carak, because it will be your tomb. I'll personally see to that.*' Carak said nothing as he continued. '*For now, however, you'll answer my questions directly, before the Jaevisk Society deprive me of this unique opportunity. I know where you're going, and where you've just been. I know where the Jaevisk attacked you, and it wasn't in the middle of nowhere, as you so poetically put it. I also know that you wouldn't have wanted to murder Aita. I believe the man actually admired you...although I can't think why.*'

234

'It was an accident, Governor,' stated Carak. Beside him, Tanna rose and headed for the com station.

'*You may believe that,*' Ben-Hadad replied, '*but I believe that this man who calls himself Malik was responsible, and that nothing is an accident where he's concerned. I believe someone is trying to make a fool of us all, Carak. Whoever this man is, his past is most definitely a lie. Were you aware that Bounty Hunters from Axceb, Nassoie and even Sieltor Thuros were looking for him? And they're still looking, Carak!*'

'*Still?* He's dead!'

'*That won't stop these people from chasing a man accused of violating Cloning Codes and dabbling in temporal mechanics. Tell me, did you even look for his body?*'

Carak shook his head slowly. Of course he had entertained varying suspicions of Malik, but nothing such as this had crossed his mind. He recalled with a sinking feeling in his stomach the words of the Kwaios: *You will present his body to the Jaevisk at the Kiranis system. They will identify it positively, and its condition will suit the circumstances of your lies.* Carak realised that the Governor was waiting for a response. 'He would have been incinerated in the blast,' he said. 'He was inside their shield wall.'

'*Quite a feat of daring for a man of humble descent working in a munitions factory,*' noted the Governor.

'I had little time to question his motives. If it wasn't for him, I wouldn't be sitting here having this delightful conversation.'

'*The pleasure is all yours,*' Ben-Hadad assured him. Yet he remained unconvinced. '*What sort of damage did you suffer at the hands of an incomparable Jaevisk Warship?*'

Carak's mind whirled. What was he suggesting? 'Minimal,' he confirmed quietly, knowing that this was exactly what Ben-Hadad had surmised. 'My crew tell me that Malik provided them with new shield parameters.'

'*It would seem that this man is nothing less than a military genius, don't you think? Did he tell you anything about the technology you stole...about the engines on that ship?*'

So Ben-Hadad also knew about the strange bio-energy. 'Nothing,' said Carak. 'But he knew a lot about it. I have no idea how.'

'*Nor do I.*' Ben-Hadad's thin smile was malevolence manifest, an attempt at levity beaten back by hatred. '*If I ever see your face again, Carak, it will be because someone has failed to carry out my orders. Do*

235

you understand? I have enough to fill my plate without a course of Humanity's sympathisers, genetic mistakes and religious fanatics!'

Carak recognised the cessation of all falsities. 'And if I ever see you again, Ben-Hadad, it will be for one of two reasons: one, because good fortune has allowed me to kill you myself...'

'*And the other?'*

'Because you wish to admit that we...genetic mistakes...have won.'

'*Let the games commence,*' the Governor replied. The screen went blank. Regardless of Carak's preparation over more years than he cared to remember, his nerves were slightly jarred as it became all too clear that the game was, most certainly, afoot. He turned to Tanna. 'Be so kind as to search for Malik's body, would you?'

Tanna was not amused. 'What?'

'Humour me, Tanna,' Carak said quietly. 'This is a time for covering all eventualities, wouldn't you say?'

Ω

Jakari watched in silence from the bridge of his battleship as the Jaevisk shuttles pulled their cargo from the Garran hulls. They had moved in as soon as the initial shock of the sudden appearance of the fleet had passed, and it most certainly appeared that the structures attached to the Garran ships were, indeed, the items of cargo themselves. There had been no communication from the Jaevisk and requests for such were ignored. 'What are they doing with those things?' Kaste wondered as he came up beside his Commander. 'There's no planet to bring them to, and no indication of a staging area.'

Jakari wanted to agree, as he saw the churning world beyond the Jaevisk and Garran vessels, but something stopped him. 'Perhaps there's something we're missing,' he mused. 'We already know that this planet has suddenly reverted to some primordial state of formation. I'd be correct in stating that such a thing doesn't happen too often, would I not?'

Kaste nodded. 'I never heard of such a thing. But all of our readings confirm what we can see out there. It's not an optical illusion of any kind.'

'But could there be something else out there? Something...obscured by the forming world?'

'Such as?'

236

Jakari was silent for a moment. Then he said quietly, 'Do you trust me, Kaste?'

'Right up until you asked,' he replied, without skipping a beat.

Jakari chuckled and turned to the crew. 'Set a course for the planet,' he ordered. They hesitated, but his eyes took no prisoners. As the battleship turned and began its approach, Kaste asked formally, 'Might I ask what exactly you're doing, Commander?'

Everyone waited until Jakari replied, 'I'm trying to get someone's attention.'

Ω

'I'm sure this is a waste of time,' said Tanna, as he headed a search team looking for Malik's body. 'However, we can assure Carak that there is no body to find by doing our jobs well. Understood?'

He did not even look back at the six men as they walked the corridors. 'We'll start by eliminating the exit points of the ship from our search and working inwards from there. You each have your allocated search areas. Once you've covered every possible place a body could be, make your way to the engine room.' The team split up and Tanna headed straight for the engine room. He had no intention of looking for anything. He spent the hours wrapped up in a heavy coat and gloves and checking the engine performance and other vital systems and taking more readings from the strange Jaevisk bio-fuel. He did not know what to make of the red stones which he knew were harboured deep inside the mechanism, but he was less than comfortable around such technology. He heard someone calling him and he turned around. One of the men from the search team had come to him, his breath visibly rising from his lips and nose. 'Where are the others?' asked Tanna. 'You should all be finished looking by now.'

The man stepped closer and told Tanna quietly, 'We found a body.'

Tanna stepped back and eyed him suspiciously. 'Where?'

'In the brig…in Malik's cell.'

'Have you told anyone else?'

'No. The rest of the men are down there, but they won't touch the body.'

'Why not?'

'It's been completely burned, and two of the guards are dead.'

237

Tanna closed his eyes and sighed. 'Get the Overseer...quietly. I'll meet you there.' He glanced at the engine as the man walked away. 'I should have stayed at home,' he said.

Ω

Carak soon shared the sentiment as he joined the search team in the brig, passing the covered bodies of the two dead guards. There were eight separate detention suites, four of them smaller and less welcoming than the others. Malik had been interned in one of the larger units. The men parted to allow the Overseer access to the body. It had been hidden under Malik's bed, and had been uncovered once the sheets were stripped away. The men had removed the bed before Carak arrived, so that he was able to hunker down beside the blackened corpse. 'Well...' he looked back to Tanna, 'unless someone really turned up the heating, this man burned to death.'

Tanna was in no mood for Carak's levity. 'There's no way that this happened on board, Carak.' He pointed to the ship's doctor, who had arrived before the Overseer. 'Our good friend here thinks he was dead some time before he was burned.'

Carak rose and looked at the doctor. 'I really could have done without hearing that,' he said. 'You men, get back to your stations. We'll be at Kiranis soon and I need everyone ready.'

Tanna and Carak were left with the Doctor, who moved back to the body again. 'I didn't want to say anything in front of the others, Overseer,' he began, as he examined the corpse further, 'but I don't think this is the same man you had locked up in here.'

'Oh, I hope you're wrong, Doctor, because when we get to the Kiranis system, I'm handing our crispy friend here over to the Jaevisk.'

Tanna was horrified. 'What possible reason could you have for doing that?'

'A reason of my own!' Carak snapped. 'Don't you have anything to do? Commanding this vessel, for example?'

Tanna held Carak's steely stare for a time, but backed down with stinging sarcasm. 'Of course...Overseer.'

Carak felt as if he had been slapped in the face by his closest friend, but he regained his composure as Tanna walked away and he turned back to the Doctor. 'How fast can you answer my questions?'

238

'Give me four hours,' said the Doctor confidently. 'I'll know everything there is to know about this man.'

Carak looked back at the burned corpse. 'I really don't think you will,' he said.

THE FIFTH DAY

Heading for Kiranis now, Governor Ben-Hadad read the reports with growing concern. The bridge of the battleship he now commanded was silent as he considered the implications of what had happened. His Aide approached him and Ben-Hadad looked up quickly. 'You have no reason to doubt this?' he challenged.

'Absolutely not,' his Aide assured him quietly. 'Commander Setta's fleet appeared to have simply vanished. Now the fleet is at the Kiranis system, two days ahead of schedule.'

'The reports say that a disturbance in space swallowed the fleet.'

The man nodded. 'The readings are all too familiar, Governor.'

'The Jaevisk have accelerated their plans,' he agreed, 'possibly even changed them. It is unsettling that I was not informed of this alteration in light of our recent agreement.'

'Indeed it is. This suggests collusion between the Setta family and the Jaevisk. And Overseer Carak is heading for the Kiranis system as we speak.'

Ben-Hadad threw the tablet across the bridge. 'I am tired of these traitorous animals!' he roared. 'My head is spinning with all of this deceit and lies. Can I trust no one?' He leaned forward and grabbed the arm of the man in front of him, dragging him closer. 'Do you realise what all this means?'

'Yes, Governor,' said the shocked Aide. 'The allies of the Setta family extend beyond our own worlds and their sympathisers on Earth, but only if we are right about this. Why would the Jaevisk ally themselves with us *and* with the Setta's own rebellion? It makes no sense!'

'Nothing makes sense with the Jaevisk Society,' Ben-Hadad reminded him. 'They are the greatest deceivers of all.' Such a statement was like acid on his tongue. It was like admitting to being second best. 'How long until we reach the Kiranis system?'

'Ten hours, Governor,' someone replied from behind him.

Ben-Hadad swore and stood up, his impatience evident. As he did so, an alarm sounded as he heard an officer shout, 'A Jaevisk vortex!'

Ahead of the massive armada from the Sieltor worlds, a single Warship emerged from the synonymous phenomenon and Ben-Hadad found this audacity terribly unsettling. 'It's a trick!' he declared. 'An ambush!' Before any action could be taken, a Jaevisk hologram appeared directly in front of the Governor, who almost fell back in shock. The only difference between this Jaevisk and those with whom he had spoken on Sieltor Prime was the pale blue cloak hanging from its shoulders. 'I am not your enemy,' the intruder quickly assured the Garran, all of whom had drawn weapons and were prepared to fight, fully aware of Jaevisk tricks. Yet this one was unarmed, remaining alone at the front of the bridge.

Ben-Hadad scowled at the alien. 'Your people have lied to me, reneged on our agreement to locate and remove my political enemies. *And...*' he summoned what courage he could muster to move closer, 'you destroyed a valuable world in my system, killing millions of my citizens. Why should we not open fire on your ship?'

Through the intercom system, the Jaevisk replied. 'The destruction of Sieltor Teuvas was not my doing. There are more powerful players in this game of ours, and not all Jaevisk are on the same side. You made an alliance with my people, and we were in turn betrayed. I am here to re-commit to that agreement by restoring the balance in your favour.'

Ben-Hadad took a deep breath, looking around at the men and women who would kill for him. 'And how do you propose to do that?'

A rectangular datakey appeared in the Jaevisk's open hand as the image flickered with the replacement of the hologram by the real thing. 'The cargo brought to Kiranis by your advance fleet have infected their computer systems with a virus. It is a program designed to launch their ships in an attack against you, Governor. This contains the access codes so that you may take control of the fleet yourself...with or without their crews aboard. You will also be able to distinguish our vessels from our own...political enemies, thus ensuring that no further errors befall our alliance.'

He hated the Jaevisk, but could never fault them on their ingenuity. He particularly liked this ploy. Taking the datakey, he looked down at it and asked, 'How will I know *your* ships?' But when he looked up, the Jaevisk had vanished and the Warship had disappeared from view and from sensors.

Ω

All was silence and dread as Jakari's ship ploughed the madness of the forming world. Moving as slow as a painful death, the pilots applied all of their skills to the evasion of coalescing masses of land and rogue formations of solidifying rock flows and volcanic expulsions. They were

241

amidst an all-encompassing minefield of stone and fire, energy and mass, as elements of the fifth planet of the Kiranis system pummelled each other and tested the forces of creation and destruction. Nothing more than releasing spent gases from the exhaust and minimal manoeuvring thrust systems were used to propel the battleship, and nano-shielding was intensified to compensate for the impacting rock. The tension was claustrophobic, and Jakari had to remind himself to breathe from time to time.

'Commander,' someone called quietly from the rear stations, 'I'm getting a landmass up ahead.'

'And?'

'It's thousands of times larger than any we've encountered so far, and I think it's…stable.'

As Kaste continued to stare straight out the window, Jakari rose from his seat and asked, 'What do you mean…stable?'

'I've launched some probes to be sure, but there seems to be gravity across a relatively level surface. I suppose it's possible with a formation so large.'

'I suppose it has to happen somewhere and at some stage,' Jakari agreed, 'but wouldn't this particular land mass be in the centre of the planet?'

Another officer put in, 'Sir, we're no longer sure of our own position within the formation. We may be close to an area which will come to form a polar region or any other landmass.'

Jakari nodded. 'Well, considering that we shouldn't even be able to make this particular journey of ours, I suppose anything's possible.'

'There's a lot of supposing going on back there,' called Kaste. 'Anyone got any facts?'

The landmass in question came into view before them, and no one had any words, let alone facts. Like some upturned mountain floating in space, the spectacle of a forming continent teased their wonder. Nothing collided with its upper reaches, but merely passed above to be drawn back into the melee of the rock storm. The land appeared levelled with the orientation of the battleship, and rocks and flaming boulders were drawn to its underbelly, exploding and being consumed by the new world. The closer the battleship came to the land, the more chaotic their surroundings, until the pilots could no longer avoid the millions of pieces of debris whizzing past them and slamming into the continent.

242

Closer still they came, pummelled now like the rest of Creation, alarms wailing, lights flashing, people falling and injured, officers shouting orders and crewmen struggling to obey. Jakari was stunned by the sight before them, and it fell to Kaste to conduct the bridge-crew through their panic and trials. 'We have to get out of here!' he shouted. 'We'll be torn apart!'

Jakari heard something, but understood nothing. He felt like a child in one of the vessels they used back home to bring families up into orbit and show them the cosmos. This was Wonder. This was Creation. There was nothing more amazing in all the universe. Someone grabbed him by the sleeve and turned him away from the window. He tried to keep his eyes on the majesty of their impending destruction, but Kaste had other plans: 'If we don't change course, we're all going to die!'

'No, this is where we're going to live,' said Jakari, more sure of that fact than anything else in his life.

Kaste stepped back from his Commander's insanity and ordered the pilots to find an escape route. They tried. But the rocketing pieces of the new world tore everything to shreds and the battleship was breaking apart as it hurtled towards the forming continent of mountain and flame. Suddenly, everything went black. There was nothing beyond the window, nothing beyond their hands and no power anywhere to illuminate their doom. But everything went red as two giant points of light outside regarded them. Two great eyes, as of a beast, taunted them as some unworldly silence enveloped the complete destruction of their ship, the last pieces of metal pulled away into the emptiness. A black-cloaked Garran appeared before Jakari as the floor beneath him was whipped away. 'I found you,' Jakari congratulated himself.

'Yes, Jakari, you did,' Naveen replied in perfect Garran. 'Welcome to Kiranis.'

Ω

The stolen Star Cruiser dropped its speed as it approached the Kiranis system, as much for caution as to facilitate navigation. Carak and Tanna had shared nothing more than the discomforting silence of colleagues forced to work together, and Carak was sure that he found this more unsettling than his friend did. 'We've just crossed the path of the outer planet,' a crewman reported.

243

'Cut engines,' Carak ordered. 'Locate the nearest Jaevisk vessel and make contact.'

Tanna stepped up beside him and asked quietly in English, 'You were happy with the Doctor's conclusions?'

'I'm not sure "happy" is the right word,' Carak whispered. 'All we can hope for is that the Jaevisk didn't know what age our guest was when he set foot on this ship.'

'We could always tell them we got lost.'

Carak turned to see a smirk on the edge of Tanna's otherwise immovable expression and his heart lifted. 'I'm sure I could blame your navigation skills if we were talking about a few weeks, Tanna, but our dead and crunchy friend was nearly fifteen years older than Malik.'

Tanna nodded. 'But we're sure it *is* Malik?'

'It is. Ben-Hadad mentioned the violation of some cloning laws. Probably on Thuros. But if we've got a clone down there, then how exactly would it be older than the man we met?'

'So we met the *clone*?'

Carak sighed. 'I have a headache.'

'Sir, I have the Jaevisk,' said an officer. 'For some reason, they're only communicating in text.'

'Then write them a letter.' Carak turned round as Tanna smiled and sat down. 'Apologise for not being in touch sooner. Tell them that we've got the body of the man responsible for destroying their Warship at Earth, and that we wish to hand it over.' He returned to his command chair. 'Oh, and tell them how much we've missed their warm smiles and charming voices.'

'Permission to paraphrase, Sir?' Everyone laughed, a welcome release of tension. They were given coordinates by the Jaevisk once the message had been sent. 'There's some sort of flagship at the outer planet. They want us to meet it there.'

'Well, let's not keep them waiting,' said Carak. 'It won't be long before Ben-Hadad gets here.' An officer called Tanna to his station and there was some discussion about sensor readings. 'Something I should know about?' Carak called back to them.

Tanna looked up from the monitor. 'A ship from Earth is fast approaching. The *Nostradamus*.'

'Nothing to worry about, I trust.'

'Not on its own, no. But there's a fleet of battleships closing the gap behind it. Wait...something's happening.' Carak stood up and turned to face him as he explained: 'The *Nostradamus* seems to be under attack. Some sort of...electrical storm has just picked up around them. They're completely enveloped.'

'The Jaevisk?' Carak knew better, and his heart pounded as the officer shook his head and Tanna replied, 'Whatever this is...it isn't the Jaevisk.'

Ω

Less than an hour later, the Star Cruiser came into orbit around the outer planet, where a number of Jaevisk Warships appeared to be doing nothing more than waiting. The transponder codes of the ship to which they had been directed were identified and, as they made their way, Carak left the bridge with considerably less confidence and a humour subdued by revelation. He knew now that the Kwaios were most definitely here. He knew they were watching. And for all the Jaevisk power around him, he knew that he would not be safe should the Kwaios decide to cease their dealings with him. 'There's a vortex on the dark side,' Tanna reported as he joined him in his office, 'with a Warship emerging every ten minutes or so.'

'So, this is where it's all happening,' Carak remarked, 'whatever "it" is.'

'Don't you know?'

'Not from their point of view, no. My...friends in the little black box aren't particularly forthcoming with information.'

'So why would you work with them?'

Carak held his gaze for a moment and then gestured for him to be seated. 'How long have we known each other, Tanna?'

'Sometimes I think too long, Carak.'

Carak grinned. 'It's amazing how long one can know someone and yet never know what really drives them...what their life is really all about.'

'I feel I'm somewhat aware of your ambitions, Carak.'

'Yet you don't agree with them?'

'I...understand them.'

'That's hardly the same.'

Tanna shook his head. 'No, it's not. But we're part of something larger than your personal goals, Carak.' Tanna cursed inwardly as the words came out, but it was too late. Carak raised his eyebrows and stared

245

at him for a moment. 'What we're part of, Tanna,' he said finally, 'is a misguided attempt to seize power from someone who will be as much at the mercy of the Kwaios in a few years as anyone else. Ben-Hadad isn't even aware of their existence!'

Tanna took a deep breath. 'You really believe they're that powerful?'

'I've seen it,' said Carak. 'And so has Tesckyn on Earth. He's well aware that he's dancing with the devil on this one, and yet he's been naive enough to think he's going to come out on top.'

'And you know different?'

Carak shrugged. 'Not specifically,' he admitted. 'But I know that there is no way that the people of Earth are going to live happily ever after once the Kwaios take the people of the Church. Even if the Kwaios do come through for Tesckyn and they deliver their part of the bargain, there'll be outrage on Earth once they find out what Tesckyn did.'

Tanna leaned back in his chair, looking at Carak and knowing there was more. 'Is this really about the Kwaios, Carak?' he asked shrewdly. 'Are your motivations purely those of survival?'

Carak would not meet his gaze. 'What else is there?'

'Revenge.'

When he finally looked at Tanna, there was dark humour on Carak's face. 'You think I'd do all this for revenge?'

'I remember the meeting, Carak. You forget I was there. And I saw the way you looked at Eyla and her sycophantic followers. I could sense your rage for hours after.'

Carak's eyes narrowed as he glared at Tanna. 'I am an Overseer in the Garran Command,' he reminded him. 'She is an old woman who has outlived her usefulness!'

There was a tense silence, until Tanna asked, 'Why are we out here, Carak? I'm guessing that whatever you did at Earth has ensured that the Kwaios are in control of things there, and the Jaevisk are clearly all over this system. So why haven't you taken us home to wait for the outcome?'

Carak shook his head. 'I need to know about Malik. No one knows who he was, but he knew about the Kwaios, and my dealings with them. Both the Jaevisk and the Kwaios want him dead, and the Kwaios told me to come to this...Jaevisk war-camp and hand either him or a clone of him over to them. If there's a chance that he's still alive...and he makes it back home...'

246

'He'll expose you.'

'Precisely.'

'Things aren't exactly going to plan, are they?'

'No, they're not,' Carak admitted, 'but I wouldn't be so quick to mock, Tanna. You're as deep in this as I am, remember? Now, we need to find out the truth about this Malik, because I have a feeling that something has gone seriously wrong. And the Kwaios know it!'

'What do you mean?'

'I think the plan has run away from them, and I believe that Malik is symptomatic of that. There's an unseen factor here, a player who's been eluding everyone for quite some time. Whoever it is, he doesn't want Earth back the way it was.'

'What makes you say that?'

'The information gathered so far on Malik. It appears that he arrived in the Kiranis system shortly before the cage appeared there. Now, his means of arrival are reminiscent of a phenomenon known as a Temporal Intersection Event. And when was the last time such a thing was observed, Tanna?'

Tanna was stunned by the implications, and his eyes were wide as he replied, 'When the war ended. When Earth changed!'

'Exactly. Isn't it strange that the Kwaios have promised the use of the cage to undo the damage caused by the last recorded T.I.E., and that our mystery Garran traveller...whom they want dead so badly...arrived here by the same means immediately before the cage appeared?'

'You think he's here to stop them?'

'It's one possibility,' Carak agreed. 'But I'm starting to think that that cage is capable of a lot more than moving a planet, and that Malik will have the answers.' There was a knock on the door and they heard a voice saying, *'We've docked with the Warship.'*

Both men made for the door, and Tanna quipped, 'You'd think that moving a planet was enough for the Kwaios.'

Carak laid a hand on his shoulder as the door opened. 'No, Tanna, you don't understand. I never said that the Kwaios were in control of the cage, although what we did back there may have permitted them certain access to it. This is why I think they're not only going to betray Tesckyn, but that the choice was never theirs to make. As far as I can see, our unseen player controls the cage.'

Tanna blinked. 'That's possibly the most disturbing thing I've ever heard.'

247

Carak nodded. 'That's why we have to find Malik.'

Ω

Senneya watched the monitors and listened to the operational chatter. A team of twenty men and women had been sent to search for Kera in the Governor's palace, an enormous complex of buildings for state, military, religious and private use. 'How long do they have?'

Raill was the only person she knew of those remaining in the underground chamber, and three other men stood with them as they oversaw the rescue attempt. This mission was only one part of a massive operation on many fronts, and Eyla had left to take control from elsewhere. 'About another six minutes,' the older man replied. 'The guard rotation is tight, and the bodies will be found quickly.'

'And once they are?'

'We can still see what they see, but external communication will be severed and they'll be on their own.'

The team had split into pairs, and ten monitors displayed images from a camera set into the headgear of one of each pair. The voices Senneya heard were calm and low, sending shivers through her as they reported in: "*Team One cleared Section Three.*" "*Team Six cleared Section Four-Two.*" The reports continued, and Raill was marking each passed section on a map projected onto the wall. With each touch of the pen, the relevant section was highlighted in red. Each team had been assigned a number of sections through which they would pass during their search. The grid was huge, and the search would take hours. Raill was relying on the swift penetration of the teams into the lower and less well guarded areas of the palace complex. That way, once the alarms went off, the palace guards would spend a lot of time on the upper floors, giving his men and women the time they needed to get to the extraction point. 'They're risking their lives for me,' said Senneya, as if she had only now realised this.

'They're doing this because a desperate man is using a scared little girl to protect himself,' Raill reminded her. 'Don't lose focus, Senneya.'

She nodded, but could not shake the guilt she felt. 'I haven't even told Carak.'

Raill was brought up short by this. 'What? I thought you warned him what was happening.'

248

Senneya shook her head. 'Before they took Kera, I sent an encrypted message to his ship. Then I found out he took the Governor's ship and I presumed he'd get the message once he used his own access codes. He was supposed to reply. That was our arrangement. When he didn't, I decided not to pursue it further, so he doesn't know about Kera. He probably has enough to deal with out there.'

Raill thought for a moment, glancing at the monitors as the search continued. 'He's bound to have logged into the ship's systems. No matter whose ship it is, it needs someone with his level of access even to start the engine.'

'Unless he trusted someone else to do it for him...someone who knows his access codes.'

'Who serves under him?'

'A man named Tanna Ga Han.'

Raill's eyes widened. 'Oh, Senneya, you should have told us earlier. Ben-Hadad took your daughter as leverage to try to get Carak to fall into step, and now you're telling me that the only person out there who knows that the Governor came to your house is a Ga Han.'

Senneya felt tears in her eyes. 'I don't understand...they've been friends for years! Who is he?'

Raill shook his head. 'The Ga Han have been indebted to the Governors since the Colonial Rebellion. There's been a blood pact for decades.'

'But wouldn't Carak know that?'

'Yes, he would, which makes it all the more baffling. Maybe he thought that having one of them on side would gain him inside access.'

'But you don't think he's on side?'

'We have no way of knowing. But what we do know is that your message didn't get to your husband. Otherwise we would have heard from him. This...Tanna must have intercepted it.' An alarm sounded across the speakers, and attention once again turned to the rescue attempt. 'Here we go,' said Raill.

Ω

The alarm sounded and the searching pairs immediately switched off their com units. Spread out across the complex as they were, they had no way of knowing if their counterparts had been engaged by guards or if they were even still alive. Although they had until now been moving swiftly

249

around the palace, they picked up the pace even more, sure that they would soon encounter resistance. Some of the pairs came to the areas in their respective search grids which led to the underground levels, and they descended without delay. These levels were not officially used nor did they officially exist, even though many people knew that the palace had been built on top of older areas of the city. What lay beneath was a maze of abandoned homes and commercial districts, warehousing and construction facilities, and the search team had been furnished with plans stolen from the city archives. But those plans were about to prove useless. As if to highlight this, one man was tapping the screen before him for the camera to see and then raising his head to show Raill his surroundings.

'What's going on?' asked Senneya.

Raill rubbed his face with exasperation. 'It's been changed!' He looked at the other monitors, noticing that many of the search pairs were encountering new buildings and even construction in progress by automated machinery. 'He's building under the palace.' He turned to Senneya. 'They don't have a chance of finding her down there.'

'No!' Senneya shouted, staring at the screens. 'Don't say that!'

'I'm sorry, Senneya, but I'll have to recall...' A monitor turned to static. There was a flash of light in another, quickly followed by weapons' fire and one of the pair went down. Another camera lens shattered and Raill shouted, 'No, no, no!'

'Get them out of there, Raill!' one of the other men snapped.

Every pair was quickly under attack, and there was little chance of saving them. Still, Raill made the call. 'Get them out,' he shouted over the com. 'Do whatever it takes.'

Over the city of Khas, three shuttles dropped through the clouds and immediately opened fire on the palace. Anti-air guns returned fire from the battlements, and the damage to the shuttles was heavy. One was blown apart and its pieces hurtled towards the palace, destroying a wing of an administration building. The other two concentrated their fire and blew holes in the assigned section, boring through to the underground levels and opening up the extraction point. With other vessels closing in, the shuttles were hard pressed to defend themselves and were losing power and control fast, until a battleship opened fire from orbit and started taking out the palace defences. It was engaged in turn by other military vessels, but the strongest ships were with Ben-Hadad's armada, leaving these small ships to defend Sieltor Prime.

Lines descended from the rescue shuttles, but were drawn back up with only five survivors, clinging desperately while returning fire to the guards in the palace. One man was shot and fell to his death, and only four made it to the safety of the shuttles. Somehow, the two shuttles escaped the melee, and Senneya and Raill stared in shock at the images of the aftermath. Eyla had said it before, but Senneya felt the strength of her words as she whispered to herself, 'No going back.'

THE SIXTH DAY

The Star Cruiser was still docked with the Jaevisk Flagship, and Carak's impatience was showing. Unlike most people, who would be pacing to and fro or snapping at colleagues and friends, Carak was a man who went still when he was anxious. The usual rush of chemicals through the Garran body which anticipated action was quelled by years of training as the Overseer stood at the forefront of the bridge, staring straight ahead. The view was less than beautiful. In fact, it was no more than a bolted bulkhead on the starboard side of the Jaevisk vessel, and staring at it for any length of time was never going to provide any insight into how the situation was progressing. By now, the crew surmised, Carak must have familiarised himself with every bolt and construction line in the frame. It was possible, they mused through whispers and carefully passed screen messages, that he fancied himself capable of building a Warship, or at the very least repairing the hole he felt like blasting through it.

Tanna stepped up beside him. 'I think you've been standing here too long. Any minute now your legs are going to give way.'

There was a twitch of humour on Carak's face, but he suppressed it to maintain control of his state of peace. 'Tell me something new, Tanna,' he requested in hushed tones. 'There must be something else happening out here.'

Tanna nodded. 'Ben-Hadad's armada is in visual range. If he sees us sitting here with the Jaevisk...'

'Yes, well, we've already established that our cover is well and truly blown.' He took a deep breath. 'Why are they delaying so much? They've had the body long enough to verify its identity.'

'Perhaps they have.'

Carak raised an eyebrow. 'And they're trying to decide what to do with us for deceiving them?'

Tanna shrugged. 'Why not? I'm sure they knew more about Malik than we did.'

'You think a retreat would be in order?'

'I don't think it would do any harm at this point...apart from running into Ben-Hadad on our way.'

'Then plot a course to the contrary, Tanna. Jettison the docking port.'

Tanna turned and relayed the orders to the crew. When he had done so, he came back to Carak, who was still staring straight ahead. 'I need to dismiss myself for a short time,' he said.

Carak came out of his nirvana. 'I'm in no mood for jokes.'

Tanna smiled, but there was something behind the expression that Carak could not fathom. 'Do you trust me, Carak?' he whispered.

'The tables have turned, I see.' Carak held his gaze and then nodded. 'Without reservation.'

'I won't disappoint you.' And that was the last thing Carak heard him say. The Star Cruiser broke away from the docking port and retreated from the Warship as Tanna left the bridge, and Carak had no time to pursue his curiosity. It certainly appeared that Tanna had been correct in his assumptions regarding Malik's body, for the Jaevisk opened fire as the Garran ship moved away. A shuttle launched from the Star Cruiser and escaped the attack, but Carak's ship was swiftly overwhelmed as a second Warship moved in. Not even the shield modifications made at Earth could withstand the concerted assault, one which was focused with educated ferocity on the engine and its housing, and the Star Cruiser was soon breaking apart. As the stern section exploded, the forward section was thrust towards the planet. From his shuttle, speeding away from the Kiranis system, Tanna watched the sensor readings until the Star Cruiser impacted with the surface.

$$\Omega$$

The armada moved across the orbital path of the outer planet, pointedly avoiding the growing number of Jaevisk Warships at the planet itself. Ben-Hadad was handed images of the destruction of his Star Cruiser and he smiled grimly. 'One less thing to worry about,' he commented. 'I want to know as soon as any of those Warships leave that planet.'

He returned to his office and poured himself a drink as the armada headed for the fifth world of the system. Constantly updating images of its formation process were displayed on three large monitors on the wall and he watched them as he sipped the fiery liquor. 'Astonishing,' he commented thoughtfully. But something else was in the images which he found even more astonishing. It was Jakari's fleet, maintaining a safe distance from the chaotic phenomenon. 'Magnify Sector 3,' he commanded the computer. The image was enlarged and Ben-Hadad saw the Omneri fleet. 'Locate the Flagship.' There was an error sound and

253

Ben-Hadad looked closer at the image. 'Access the transponder codes for the battleship under the command of Jakari San Setta and display location.'

A green-lined grid appeared on the image and the transponder codes were shown next to a red circle. 'I don't see a ship,' said Ben-Hadad, realising that the circle encompassed nothing more than some of the moving debris of the planet. The computer buzzed again. 'Magnify transponder location until the battleship is visible.'

The image was once again enlarged, and again, and a third time. However, all Ben-Hadad was seeing was enhanced images of the forming world and the rock and flame and dust which ensued. The magnification stopped and Ben-Hadad realised why. Moving even closer to the screen as if he could peer through the molten melee, he said quietly, 'How did you get in there?'

There was an entry request at his door and he moved back from the screen. 'Return to original images,' he said, before calling, 'Enter.'

Three Governors were quickly standing before him and it appeared that they had found the courage to question him. Good, he thought. A bit of excitement. 'Well, what is it?'

Their reluctantly nominated spokesman, the Governor of Sieltor Thuros, stepped forward from the centre, glancing pointedly at the images on the wall. 'You brought us out here for *this*,' he said. 'Of what possible value could this world be to us? Or is this just about avenging your humiliation at the hands of the Jaevisk?'

Ben-Hadad was pleasantly surprised by the man's audacity. 'Our humiliation,' he replied.

'What?'

'*Our*...humiliation, my dear Governors. We are all here...together, to face the Jaevisk and to show them that they cannot simply vanish from sight after betraying us and expect us to forget about it. You've seen how many Warships they have out here, so clearly this place is of some significance to them. Now whether it's of economic or strategic significance...well...' he raised his hands, 'I don't know. But our probes and sensors are currently scanning the system for this...power source they tried to buy us with, the same thing they had hidden in Teuvas. Now we know where it is.'

They exchanged glances, their interest piqued. 'Where?' asked the middle man. Ben-Hadad grinned and pointed at the three screens, holding his hand in place until the proverbial penny dropped. Now they were back on side. 'How do we get it?'

'We are here for more than a power source,' he reminded them, 'considering that a world in our own system is practically made of the stuff.'

'Well, if you think we can defeat so many Warships, Ben-Hadad, then you really have gone insane.'

Ben-Hadad glared at him until he visibly deflated. 'I have been promised help,' he informed them through gritted teeth, 'which is a word I would hesitate to apply to your input right now...Governor.'

The man sighed, exchanging glances with the sheep on either side of him. 'I apologise,' he said. 'I don't have your...faith, it seems.'

Ben-Hadad nodded and softened. 'We are going to go down in Garran history, my brothers,' he promised them. 'This is a time for celebration.' He gestured for them to help themselves to drinks. They needed little persuasion.

'So,' another of the three asked, 'when should we begin deployment?'

One thing at a time,' said Ben-Hadad. 'There's something I need to deal with first.'

'Jakari?'

Ben-Hadad nodded. 'Somehow, he's managed to find his way right into the heart of our new enterprise. Luckily, I have the means to drag him back out.'

Ω

Jakari was awed by the sights around him. The edge of the continental shelf upon which he stood was on a distant horizon, and there was no sky or other atmospheric impediment to stop him seeing the gigantic pieces of rock which were being drawn towards the world. They slammed into the land, but Jakari experienced not a thing. Far behind him, a mountain range had been thrown up by the compressions of the planet's crust, and he saw what appeared to be a giant black creature in its shadow. It was difficult to define shape and size in the disconnected darkness, but even from where he stood, Jakari could feel the intensity of the beast's red eyes. He turned away from it, and watched the strange Garran in the black cloak. He was gazing upwards, and Jakari wondered if he was as fascinated by the sight as any ordinary person might be. 'What are you looking at?' he asked him.

Naveen turned to him. 'I want to see it arriving. It's always quite breath-taking to see it from this perspective, but...well, this will be a sight to remember.'

'You're talking about the cage,' Jakari realised. 'That thing around Earth. It's coming here?'

'It's coming *back* here, Jakari. And it's bringing some playthings for our big black friend over there.'

'I don't understand.'

'You will. I don't want to spoil the fun.'

Jakari looked around again. 'How is any of this possible? I'm standing on a landmass...which shouldn't be stable in any way...in the middle of a planet that hasn't formed yet. I mean, stop me if I'm being melodramatic.'

Naveen laughed. 'Believe me, Jakari, you haven't seen anything yet.'

'I don't like the sound of that. You said that I had to find someone when I got here.'

'Yes. A young man called Cana. He's...lost.'

'You really expect me to believe that you don't know where he *is*? You brought him here, didn't you?'

'It's not that simple. You see, I'm not in complete control of this place now, no matter how much I'd like to be.' He pointed at the black creature. 'That thing over there is.'

'What is it?'

'The Humans call them dragons. They played a part in a lot of ancient religions and myths and fantasy stories.'

'Really? And there just happens to be one here...so far away from home?'

Naveen chuckled at the mockery. 'That's where Cana comes in. You see, he...brought it to life. What you're really looking at is a manifestation of the...spirit or essence, if you like, of this planet, a sort of conduit through which this world is forming. It calls itself Leviathan, and Cana gave it that form simply by subconsciously recalling his own fears and imagination.'

'Who is this Cana?'

'He's a member of the Church of the New Elect on Earth, but out here he's...' Naveen shrugged, 'something else. And Leviathan took him from me. I can't help him right now, because I'm...tied up with other things.'

256

Jakari stared at him for a minute, and it hit him. 'You're doing this, aren't you? You're...*creating* this world?'

Naveen grinned. 'What do you think? It's my first.'

'This is insane!' Jakari snapped, holding his head and looking around wildly. '*I* must be insane. This can't be happening!' He recalled the journey to this system and then ordering the ship into the chaos. 'We must have died,' he gasped. 'I must have died. How could we have survived?' He stared at the dark Garran and asked hesitantly, 'Are...you...?'

Naveen laughed loudly to sway the question. 'If you think this is Garran Heaven, Jakari, you can think again. Of course, if you think you're in Hell...' he shrugged. 'Have you been bad, Jakari?'

Jakari swung at him in a rage, but Naveen caught his arm with unnatural strength and twisted, so that the powerful Commander was forced to the ground. On his knees now, Jakari felt helpless and lost. 'What am I doing here?' he begged. 'Tell me.'

Naveen released his arm. 'I told you already. I want you to find and protect Cana. Where he goes, you go.' He helped Jakari to his feet. 'Your destiny is greater than you can imagine, Jakari. I will make you pre-eminent among your species, a hero to your people.'

Taking a deep breath, Jakari steadied himself. Luckily for him, his mind was still working perfectly. 'You said "*your* species"...not "ours".'

'Yes, I did. But that's a mystery for another day.' Naveen moved closer to him. 'Are you ready to embrace your destiny?'

'What do I have to do?'

Naveen reached out to him and turned him around. The black dragon was glaring at them from the distance, daring them to come his way. The answer, Jakari knew, was inevitable: 'You'll have to face the dragon, Jakari. It's the only way you'll ever get off this world.'

Ω

Jakari's fleet had been completely stripped of its cargo, but the Jaevisk still appeared to have no plan as to where the cargo was going. One of the Battleship Commanders, a wise old Garran named Gerra who decided he must have left his wisdom at home, had his bridge crew monitoring the movement of Jaevisk removal teams. 'Every piece has been brought to the same point, Commander,' an officer explained. 'I could describe their position as maintaining a synchronous orbit if I could identify a surface point to synchronise with.'

257

The Commander nodded. 'With the planet not even formed, there isn't even polar orientation to put it into context.'

'Yes, Sir. However, there are readings of a considerable land mass in there, not far from where the cargo was moved to.'

'Really? So the planet is forming from the inside out?' He thought for a moment. 'I suppose it makes sense. Are there any electro-magnetic readings from that region?'

'Nothing definitive, Sir. Polar magnetism wouldn't be stable until the complete formation of the planet.'

Again he nodded. 'What are we seeing here?' he mused aloud, staring out of the forward window. 'This is happening hundreds...if not thousands of times faster than it should.' He turned to the officer. 'Speculate. Do the Jaevisk know what's going on? Could they be aware of a time-frame here?'

The officer looked beyond his Commander to the alien world, its debris still seeming to reverse the course of explosion in order to solidify and define. 'If they do,' he began carefully, 'then they might be waiting at a specific point for the emergence of a specific region of the planet.'

'But why?' the Commander pressed. 'It would be complete fantasy to expect the geography of a previous world to reassert itself in this new one. Wouldn't it?'

The officer laughed, pointing at the image beyond the window. 'We're looking at complete fantasy in action, Commander. Our science may as well be childish imagination here, because it's completely incompatible.'

'Is it? Or is it just that all of this is happening too fast? Get a few people together and apply what we understand to a comparatively shorter time-frame. We might get some answers.'

The officer nodded and left the bridge, while another approached the Commander. 'Sir, some of the engineering crew have reported structural damage from the Jaevisk modifications.'

'Well, we don't need those cargo clamps anymore, so get rid of them. In fact, tell everyone in the fleet to remove them.'

'Yes, Sir.' He nodded to a subordinate beside him, who set off to carry out the orders. 'Also, the Governors' armada is less than an hour away. I don't understand why they haven't made contact yet.'

'Maybe they tried Commander Setta's ship and they aren't aware that we've taken Point. Has there been any word from Jakari?'

'None, Sir. I hate to speculate, but...'

258

'Then don't. Ben-Hadad is not to know.'

The younger crewman returned, his anxiety evident. 'What is it?' asked the officer.

'The cargo clamps aren't detaching remotely, and...' he hesitated.

'Spit it out,' snapped the Commander.

'They've infected our systems with a virus!'

Ω

Ben-Hadad was handed an imaging sheet with new information concerning the command structure of Jakari's fleet. 'Another ship has taken command?'

'Yes, Governor. Commander Gerra Noth Kan leads the fleet now.'

Ben-Hadad scowled. 'A Noth Kan! Animals!' He turned to the other Governors. 'Return to your vessels and follow my deployment plans. I'm taking this ship after Jakari San Setta, who has clearly found something worth relinquishing his command.'

'Do you think it wise to network our systems?' asked the Governor from Thuros.

'Yes, I do,' Ben-Hadad replied patiently. 'Our strategies will be more easily controlled and maintained by allowing a central computer complete access across the fleet. My only concern is that the computer in question is on your Flagship, Governor, which is why I am sending some of my own people to oversee the network setup.'

'You honour me, Governor,' the man replied sarcastically, turning to leave before Ben-Hadad could reply. Watching them leave, Ben-Hadad took a deep breath and turned to his Commander. 'At the first sign of dissent, kill them.'

'Yes, Governor.'

'Now get me this Noth Kan.'

Ω

The virus was quickly spreading, and Gerra Noth Kan had been informed that the entire fleet was losing control of vital systems. As the engines powered down, the lights went out on the bridge and emergency power kicked in after a few seconds. 'Governor Ben-Hadad wants to speak with you, Commander,' someone called.

259

'Put it up,' replied Gerra. The Governor appeared on screen, his image decidedly demonized by the dim emergency lighting of the bridge. 'It's good to see you, Governor.'

'I doubt that very much, Commander,' Ben-Hadad replied with a smile, his voice dripping venom. 'However, I may be able to assist with the problems you're having.'

Gerra paused. 'You know about the Jaevisk virus?'

'I know many things,' said the Governor, not a beat missed. 'And because I wish to deal with certain things…internally, I'm willing to purge your systems of the virus.'

'Most gracious of you,' noted Gerra. 'And once you have?'

Ben-Hadad pondered that with dramatic expression. 'Once I have,' he said, 'we'll talk. A pity Commander Setta isn't around to speak with me.'

Now Gerra grinned. 'You're welcome to go looking for him, Governor. I believe he found something of interest.'

There was a tense silence as the huge face on the screen hardened. 'Oh, I do hope so,' said Ben-Hadad. 'You'll receive a datastream from Governor Rann-Jen of Thuros. The anti-virus program will be on it. I suggest you use it immediately, Commander. You wouldn't want to be a sitting target, now would you?'

'Absolutely not, Governor,' said Gerra. 'There are so many enemies around.'

'Indeed. These are such…dangerous times.'

The screen went blank and Gerra looked around. 'How close are they?'

'The armada is splitting up into three forces, Sir, but Ben-Hadad's ship is heading straight for the planet. I think he's taking you up on your suggestion.'

'Well, there's nothing more we can do for Commander Setta now. Isolate a workstation with the virus on it. As soon as that datastream arrives, I want it broken down, analysed and tested. If there's no sign of an anti-virus on it, throw the workstation out the airlock.'

An officer called Gerra to a console and offered the Commander a headset. 'There's a priority com request from a Captain Harris. He's heading a battleship fleet from Earth.'

Gerra looked at the man for a moment, before saying, 'Put him through.' He held the earpiece to his ear and listened with a grim expression on his face: '*I've been ordered to facilitate an evacuation of your fleet. The virus in your systems is designed to take control of your navigation and weapons systems.'*

Gerra replied in reasonably good English. 'It seems, Captain, that everybody knows about this virus except us. We have received an anti-virus from Governor Ben-Hadad.'

There was a pause. *'Check your navigation systems, Commander. Have they been re-programmed?'*

Gerra moved to a monitor on his left, perusing the co-ordinates listed on the right-hand side of the screen. 'Who entered these numbers?' he demanded. Three men and a woman looked at the screen, shaking their heads, clearly confused. They attempted to regain control, but the station would not allow it. Gerra replied to Harris, 'I don't recognise the co-ordinates. What are we looking at?'

'According to my information, the Jaevisk are going to use your fleet to attack the Governor's armada to weaken the entire Garran force in their favour.'

Gerra looked at the numbers again. 'These co-ordinates...' he gestured for someone to plot them, 'aren't for the armada, Captain. They're not...' He stopped as he saw the location on the monitor. 'They're for the outer planet.'

'What?'

'Just beyond the planet's current position, to be precise.'

'But that's where we are,' replied Harris. *'There's some sort of massive electrical phenomenon out here and it's closing in fast. You need to stay where you are and we'll come for you.'*

The engines of the battleship suddenly powered up and every ship in the fleet started to move away from the fifth planet. 'I think the decision has been made for us, Captain,' Gerra explained. 'I hope you have something else in mind.'

Ω

Governor Rann-Jen could see Jakari's fleet moving away. 'What are they doing?' he asked his Commander.

'I can't get anyone on com, Governor,' the man replied. 'I don't think they're in control.' An alarm suddenly sounded and the Commander rushed over to a workstation to see what was happening. The bridge crew were frantically trying to gain control of their own stations.

'But we sent them the solution, didn't we?' the Governor pressed, glancing around desperately and shouting over the alarm. 'What's that alarm about? What's happening?'

When the Commander turned back, Rann-Jen felt his stomach turn as he recognised the expression of utter defeat in the man's face as he explained, 'We never had the solution. When we opened a connection to send the datastream, it took the virus from Jakari's fleet and threw it back at us.'

'What?' The Governor was horrified. 'But we're networked to the entire armada!' Moving to the port window, Rann-Jen could see his ships and those of the other Governors manoeuvring into parallel vectors. 'They're all doing the same thing!' He spun round. 'Override the network commands. Close the channels. Whatever it takes, sever the link!'

But nothing worked, and every single ship from the Sieltor worlds was moving away from the fifth planet and following the same course. The Commander sank into his chair, as calls for guidance and direction from the crew overwhelmed him. 'There's nothing we can do!' he roared. Silence descended and he said, 'We're going wherever the Jaevisk want us to go.'

Disgusted by the Commander's surrender, Rann-Jen shouted in return. 'Well...find out where that *is*!' He looked at the bewildered crew. 'Where are we going?'

At the navigation centre, a woman looked up from her console. 'To the outer planet,' she told them. 'Towards the Jaevisk army.'

Ω

As his ship moved cautiously through the veritable minefield of a world under construction, Ben-Hadad found his mind wandering. He remembered his childhood on Sieltor Prime, that beautiful world of innocence and disconnection, where consequence and accountability were nothing but big words for an even bigger world. A face sprang to mind, a beautiful girl with whom he had played and grown as the years defined his manhood. He smiled softly, with his back to the crew, wondering when last he had thought of her. Everything had seemed so wonderful back then, and the life he had mapped out for himself included her at every turn. It was not war which had changed that plan, nor disease nor time.

'Governor, there's an urgent message from home. Teuvas was attacked by the Jaevisk! They've completely stripped the bio-fuel from the planet!'

An accident in her workplace, the munitions factory of Khas City, had seen her beautiful face scarred beyond repair, mutilating her terribly. No matter how much the young man of Ben-Hadad's memory had tried, he could not bring himself to look at her for any length of time. He had been swiftly filled with self-loathing and he had projected that hatred upon her, until the poor girl had taken her own life in despair. But the young Ben-Hadad knew that it was he who had killed her, no matter the circumstances of her death.

'Governor, can you hear me? The armada has been infected with the Jaevisk virus. They're moving away and we've been left on our own. It's a trap!'

He was a murderer, and he never allowed himself freedom from that expression of his darkness. It defined him in every way as he grew into a political animal, and it helped him to become the man he was today. A murderer.

'Governor, did you hear what I was saying? The armada's gone!'

He turned to the officer, blinking, realising that the man had been addressing him. Yet amidst his reminiscing, he had heard it all. 'I've killed us all,' he declared. 'Ha-Cxada was right. How could I have trusted the Jaevisk?' He laughed, but there were tears in his eyes. 'Nobody in their right mind would trust the Jaevisk.'

 'Governor, there's no reason to look for Commander Setta in this chaos. We'll die in here.'

 Ben-Hadad nodded. 'Get us out of here, Commander.'

 The man tried his best, but everywhere they turned, the path was treacherous. 'We've lost our bearings,' he reported, desperately searching the navigation readings for a way out. 'There's no...wait, what's that?'

 Ben-Hadad was quickly frantic. 'What is it? A way out?'

 'A stable surface. If we orientate ourselves...yes, there it is.' He pointed ahead and everyone looked out of the window. There was definitely land ahead, and it seemed as if the rocks were parting like some geological curtain to allow them safe passage. 'Can we land?' asked Ben-Hadad.

'I believe so.' The Commander was stunned and excited by the possibility, and he moved the ship now with new purpose. However, everything was about to change.

Ω

There was a massive gravitational shift all around the forming fifth planet, and the small Jaevisk ships whose mission it was to protect the structures carried by Jakari's fleet moved into a higher orbit. They did so to avoid destruction as the cage materialised in its disconnected state. Slowly, the many sections moved in towards the chaos...

Ben-Hadad almost fell over as something rocked the ship. 'What was that? What hit us?'

'There's no damage,' shouted the Commander. 'I'm staying on course.' The ship shuddered and there was an ear-splitting sound as if something was scratching the hull-plates. Then there was a number of thudding impact sounds, although the ship had not collided with anything. The Commander was oblivious as he piloted the ship himself, but Ben-Hadad edged towards the exit as soon as someone else reported, 'We're being crushed by gravitational compression!'

'We can make it!' the Commander argued. As Ben-Hadad left them to their fate.

An unseen energy forced the debris to move faster and faster, heating it up until the definition of a planet could finally be seen. With crackling lines of volcanic dissent, the planet fought this unnatural compression to no avail. From the inside of the cage sections, hundreds of thousands of torpedo-like capsules were launched towards the churning surface, passing through dark gaseous clouds and disappearing into the madness...

Governor Ben-Hadad, on the other hand, was launched in the opposite direction by way of an escape pod. It rocketed upwards, outwards...the direction was completely irrelevant, he considered...through flaming pockets of trapped gas and molten rock. He was pinned to the seat and he screamed wildly as his flight continued, even though he could not see anything. The pressure and heat was so intense that heavy protective panels had closed around the escape pod, enveloping its occupant in a dark and terrifying cocoon. Ben-Hadad could not even bring himself to observe the instrument readings. He simply prayed, muttering with his eyes closed as the computer reported, *'Gravitational forces unstable. Unable to calculate escape velocity.'*

Ben-Hadad screamed anew, and continued to do so long after the escape pod had passed through the closing cage.

Ω

Gerra Noth Kan sat helplessly in his command chair. The virus had taken control of every system, and the fleet was now hurtling towards the outer orbital ring. An officer sat down next to him. 'I've been trying to figure this out,' he said.

'You'll drive yourself mad doing that.'

'Maybe, but there's nothing else to do.' He leaned in. 'Why would the Jaevisk take over our systems to bring us to them? An alien race that can just appear and disappear in space doesn't need to go to all this trouble if it wants to wipe us out.'

Gerra considered that for a moment. 'You think they have other plans for us?'

The officer nodded. 'In a few moments, we'll be in visual range of what that Captain from Earth called an electrical phenomenon. It's been growing...' he lowered his voice, 'and it will soon encompass the entire system.'

Shocked by the implications, Gerra stood up. 'Give me a virtual shot of our destination.'

The forward window was replaced by an image of the darkness in the distance, but it was far from empty. Enormous lines of crackling energy, blue in colour, lashed at the space around, as if warning of impending doom. In the corner of the image, the outer planet could be seen, but the magnification was such that no vessels could be identified in its vicinity. 'The fleet from Earth should be on an intercept course.'

'Maybe they took a circuitous route,' the officer suggested.

'Or maybe they decided to leave us to our fate.' Gerra moved closer to the image. 'What in all the gods' names is that?'

The officer shook his head. 'The Jaevisk must have found a use for their power source.'

'No,' said Gerra, feeling a chill run through him. 'Whatever that is, it's not the Jaevisk. But if the *Jaevisk* need help dealing with it...' He

265

turned his back to the screen as the blue lines continued to snap across the darkness. 'Then we don't stand a chance!'

Ω

Carak opened his eyes, but there was little he could see through the haze of smoke. It was coloured orange by fires in the vicinity, and it launched itself with conscious purpose at Carak's mouth and nose as he tried to catch his breath. With his eyes streaming, he coughed and managed to get to his feet, pushing some metallic debris aside and trying to get his bearings. Was that his chair? Had he been thrown across the bridge? He remembered little of the moments before impact.

'Tanna!'

Then he remembered Tanna abandoning him, and he roared with anger, his fury fuelling his resolve. As he stumbled towards the exit, he saw disfigured and dismembered bodies in various poses of expiration, some slumped over workstations, others crushed by pieces of the collapsed roof, an aspect of the damage which allowed intermittent light to scream in through gaping holes. It was not natural light, Carak knew, and he imagined a Jaevisk search party ensuring that every member of the Garran crew was dead. The light illuminated scenes of horror which would be forever seared into Carak's memory, and he ran from the bridge.

Twice he fell, once he lost consciousness and came round again, and the journey to the closest airlock was torturous. Yet he made it, his lungs protesting and his heart emitting blades of anguish, his body pushed beyond its limits. Eventually, he fell out of the crashed section of the Star Cruiser, and the ground beneath him was cold and dark. Booted feet he heard as he groaned, his mouth half pressed into the alien soil. The Jaevisk were upon him, he thought. It was all over.

'This one's alive!'

'Get him out of there. We're gonna have to let it burn. The Jaevisk are coming!'

Carak felt himself being lifted, and realised then that the voices were Human. 'Who are you?' his gravelled voice asked.

'We're from Earth,' a woman told him. 'We're from a ship called *Nostradamus*.'

INTERVAL – PROPAGATION

Jennifer woke suddenly from a lapse of consciousness. Fresh pain, dull and bone-grinding in her skull, reminded her of her fate. Back on Earth, when she had been standing on the balcony of her apartment, she had felt the horror course through her as friends and colleagues below were consumed by the rising red tide of the cage's energy weapon. She heard their screams as they tried to no avail to run or climb to some higher level of their surroundings. And she had stood transfixed as the crimson wave rose to embrace her. That was the last thing she had seen on Earth, the last thing she would ever see on her home planet. Her silent reminiscing was abruptly vanquished by screams of pain and fear.

All she could see was a dark wall in front of her, and she came to realise that she was standing in an open capsule. Sweat trickled into her eyes and she blinked it away, just as the clamps on her ankles, thighs, wrists and neck released her. The wall opposite her was then illuminated, blue strips of soft light running horizontally along the top and bottom. She heard a skittering, snapping sound from behind her head and she gasped with breathless agony as tendrils from the metal device on her brain retracted through the holes it had drilled. Blood ran from the wounds, but she was free.

Stepping forward from the capsule, she looked around to see in both directions that countless capsules ran the length of a corridor stretching on into the darkness. And in those pods were captive people, men and women familiar to her in most cases. There were some strangers, and she was sure there would be many more, once she had time to explore. It appeared that there was another, larger corridor running alongside this one, and intermittent groupings of windows permitted a view into that corridor. Finding no access points, Jennifer chose to walk on, spending some time helping other captives who had been freed. Many were not allowed such liberty, it seemed. Although the clamps had released them, the device in the head of each of these people latched firmly to the tiny ports behind. Jennifer watched their agonised struggle, as they tried desperately to drag themselves free while roaring and screeching in terrible anguish. The metal tendrils would not let go, and some people lost consciousness as blood poured down the back of their necks. Jennifer was sure that some died from the shock of the struggle.

After some time, with a group of more than twenty people following her, Jennifer found him. Tears ran silently down the face of Patriarch Mannix Relland, and he appeared defeated as he was held firm. For some reason, even the metal clamps for his body remained in place. 'Patriarch Relland,' Jennifer whispered softly. 'Can you hear me?'

Staring blankly at the massive windows behind her, Relland tried to swallow his self-pity behind the neck-clamp, refusing to focus his eyes on her. 'What have I done?'

'This isn't your doing, Patriarch,' she assured him, trying to undo the clamps. 'It couldn't possibly be.' Another man assisted her, while others marvelled at seeing their Patriarch for the first time.

'I've been so arrogant,' he continued. 'So blind.'

'You wanted the best for us,' said Jennifer. 'Renewal and rejuvenation.'

'I don't want to die,' he whimpered. 'Help me. Someone help me.'

'You're not going to die,' Jennifer told him, surprised by his attitude. She had never heard him speak like this. 'The Sentience has a place for you...for all of us.'

Relland laughed darkly, and the sound echoed up and down the dimly lit corridor. 'Everything I've done, all of my sacrifices and prayer...everyone I betrayed and lied to...this can't be the renewal I worked so long for.' He groaned with anguish. 'Our *place*?' he mocked. 'Our place is in Hell!'

There was the sound of mechanical movement and the man helping Jennifer dragged her back just as a convex glass door was closing over the capsule. 'No!' shouted Jennifer. All along the corridor the same thing was happening to all those who were still held in place. A second transparent covering moved into place and it snapped shut while Relland stared in horror at Jennifer, struggling as she was against the others who stopped her from helping him. 'There's nothing we can do,' the man told her. 'Get back!'

Patriarch Mannix Relland mouthed the words, 'Help me...'

The sealed capsule was launched from the cage and Jennifer screamed as she watched it descending towards the molten world far below. It passed through dark clouds forming amidst a mocking atmosphere of volcanic mayhem. And no-one ever saw Patriarch Relland again; in this form.

Ω

The components of the cage were closing inwards around the alien world. Thousands of sealed capsules, carrying captive Church members, hurtled through roiling clouds of dark unknown as the rate of the formation process was increased. Descending towards the planet's questionable surface at terrible speed, each victim could see only the deadly promise of a sky above and imagine the searing curse of a fate below. As the last stages of the planet's creation reached their climax, small and wayward pieces of matter slammed against the capsules, causing some of them to spin uncontrollably in a nightmarish affair. Other tiny pieces, impacting at such speeds with some of the capsules that they breached the glass and protective casing, brought about the depressurisation of the capsules. Many people died before impact.

The impacts themselves were varied, depending on the varying geological stages of creation waiting to embrace the captives. Some of the capsules crashed into mineral so hard that they exploded, others passed through permeable surfaces so that their occupants were caught inside the planet's crust. The balance of hydrogen and oxygen molecules which had been precipitated by the circling bands of planetary matter was altered by the energy of the cage and water collapsed to the surface, drawn by gravity to create rivers and seas which welcomed many occupants of the capsules. Wherever the captives fell, their environment determined the form of their mutation, but not before the Garran blood had been introduced with all its accompanying agony to their midbrain.

Just as Cana's imagination had been the catalyst for the manifestation of the black dragon, that same perception of life pervaded every new introduction to this world. In dark caves and deep valleys, atop mountains and beneath oceans, the captive Church members experienced the horror of rebirth as defined by the young man sent ahead as an emissary of their terror. The waiting entities of disassociated energy sought out their respective hosts and the capsules were rent apart by expanding Human bodies; whose flesh pulsed and split; whose bones grew and snapped and twisted; and whose consciousness became trapped in the monstrous form of a primordial reptile. Their Human consciousness was absorbed and overwhelmed by the other conscious minds which had awaited physical definition, facilitated by the re-awakening and re-prioritising of what had at one point in mankind's evolution been the brain of their reptilian ancestry. Some of the creatures spread giant wings of glory, others no more than stubs of despair. Of

269

every colour they were, their size and characteristics defined by the geological womb of their birthing. But not all were exposed to the outer realms of the world, for some of the capsules had penetrated deep into the planet's crust.

These ones grew in protest, suffocated by the gaseous and molten heat and pressed against the rock which surrounded them. Many of them managed to escape into the upper reaches of the subterranean world, there to live a chthonic subservience to the greater beasts above. Others, however, could not escape, and still the alien minds were inescapably drawn to them. These creatures were misshapen, blind and furious and their anger would ever be immense. Their curse was simply that they survived this horror.

As the cage eventually closed, the fifth planet of the Kiranis system had become a world of monsters. Its first victims were the crews of two Garran battleships, the first of which had been beaten and torn apart, the second crushed, burned and liquefied within its molten layers. Its first visitors were a terrified young man named Cana, whose dark surroundings caused his childhood nightmares to shine in comparison; and a Garran Fleet Commander, who was soon to discover that his mother's concept of divine intervention belonged to the category of bedtime stories when compared to the forces at work in this place. For if this had once been a Jaevisk world, Jakari dreaded to think what they must have done to bring forth this Hell.

PART 3
JAEVISK

TWO YEARS BEFORE ARRIVAL

The Jaevisk Society had long occupied what one might call a space station, yet it was really a world of metal and muscle, a gigantic network of once autonomous habitation modules positioned close to an ancient star for reasons an outsider would kill to comprehend. Hundreds of Warships were coming and going by way of their vortex technology, and countless millions of Jaevisk lived their lives here, praying for the restoration of their ancestral home. In a relatively small room deep within one of the many habitation areas, a red-caped Jaevisk male stood before two ancients, his head lowered and his eyes closed. A dual-prayer was being recanted by the Old Ones, each reciting his lines simultaneously in an ancient form of the Jaevisk language, so that the mystery of the supplication was lost amidst the twisting and overlapping words. The prayer ended, and the Old Ones remained silent for a short while. Then one said, 'Raise your head.'

The red-caped Jaevisk did so, replying with his eyes closed, 'My heart gives thanks for the dual-prayer of Restoration.'

'Your heart beats solely for Restoration,' the second Old One replied. They rose from their seats and approached their initiate, each of them holding a golden cylindrical implement. Standing on either side of him, they raised these devices to his shoulders and proceeded to push them into a corresponding depression in each of the golden clamps holding his cape in place. The initiate braced himself as the devices were activated, drawing out the bolt which was set deep into the bones of his shoulders. The agony was indescribable, a dull interior pain of marrow-deep fire. As the piercing sound died out and the bolts fell to the metal

271

floor, the Old Ones stepped back and waited. The initiate drew himself up to full height and shrugged his shoulders backwards, releasing the clamps to the floor with the red cape still attached. The Old Ones returned to their seats as one declared, 'You are no longer Tu-Han.' Turning back to the sweating and bleeding initiate, they waited while icy water was released from the ceiling and the blood was washed away with the force. 'You are cleansed of the blood and the gold,' said the other.

Two different elders emerged from the darkness behind him, carrying a long blue cloak with tarnished silver rings ready for attachment. They lifted the cloak to the shoulders of the now shivering initiate, inserting the bolts into the metal threads set in his bones. Producing two rusted devices, they fitted the new cloak to their subject and said together, 'Days of water and rust await you. You are a Warlord.' When they had retreated to the shadows, the ritual was complete.

After some silence, there was a voice from the shadows: 'I expect great things of you, Krell.'

'I will not fail you,' Krell replied, suppressing the agony he felt. 'When the time comes, I will prove my worth.'

'The time is now, Krell.'

'Now? What has happened?'

'The Kwaios have contacted Earth, and an agreement has been made. The Kwaios have promised the use of the cage to return the Humans to their own universe.'

Krell was shocked by the implications. 'We cannot allow it. That universe is a Source.'

'The Kwaios do not control the cage. They will betray the Humans, for their activities are ever centred upon the Harvest. We have learned that their quantum forecasting has predicted the arrival of the cage at Kiranis.'

Krell felt a joy swelling in his heart. 'Then Restoration is at hand.'

'Yes. Kiranis will return.'

'What would you have me do?'

'Revive the myths and create zealotry amongst our people which has never been seen before. Every Jaevisk must be willing to die for Restoration.'

'It shall be done,' said Krell. 'What else?'

Krell strained his eyes to see the speaker, for only the elders were permitted to see the Guide. But nothing could be seen as the Guide replied, 'Prepare us for war.'

THE DAY BEFORE ARRIVAL

In a high synchronous orbit above a seemingly inauspicious place on the dark and lifeless fifth planet of the Kiranis system, the crew of a Jaevisk Warship were ever observant. On the brightly lit Operations Centre, four Tu-Han, identified only by the red capes clamped to their shoulders, fell silent as the blackness along the orbital path of Kiranis was torn open. They watched intently as a small vessel with a glistening reflective hull emerged from the portal. 'We know this vessel,' one of them remarked.

'The World Killer has arrived in our time,' another confirmed.

For a moment, the small ship drifted aimlessly, but then it fired its engines and raced away, rapidly vanishing from sight. 'He has set course for Sieltor Prime,' a lesser crew member informed the Tu-Han. 'Should we intercept?'

'No,' the Tu-Han replied, pointing to the still open tear in space. 'We will monitor this event. How long until Kiranis reaches the portal?'

'Seven days.'

'This is the time of which the Warlord spoke. We will prepare. The World Killer will remain in this time until Kiranis reaches the portal. It is the only means by which he can escape.'

Ω

On a hidden vessel which would have dwarfed the Warship had it been in proximity, a Kwaios Administrator also monitored the portal and the orbit of the fifth planet. Tapping pulsing blue light-keys, the hybritech alien opened a channel to the command centre of the Kwaios Council. 'There are seven days until the Harvest,' it reported. 'The Jaevisk are preparing to fortify the outer planet and the World Killer is approaching the Garran home world. We must mobilise the colonies before the Humans see the signs.'

There was a short delay: '*Dispatch a ship to Sieltor Prime to take the World Killer. Contact our Garran asset and provide him with the means to accelerate the process at Earth. The cage will soon arrive.*'

ARRIVAL

Now on numerous Warships around the fifth planet of the Kiranis system, the Jaevisk were stunned by the events transpiring before them. The dark planet of grey and death was alone and silent one moment, and surrounded by the components of the gigantic cage the next. As the Warships closest to the phenomenon retreated to escape the gravitational echoes, the pieces of the cage closed in upon the planet until, just before connection, they drew back to tear the planet apart in a terrific flash of light. The alien world was at once in tumultuous disorder, its elements whipping around in apparent chaos. But, as the components of the cage retreated farther into the vacuum of space and then passed into inter-dimensional absence, the Jaevisk knew better how to interpret this event. 'Kiranis has returned,' they said as one, initiating a long-awaited mantra. 'The old world has passed. Restoration is at hand.'

'The Kwaios will be watching,' a Tu-Han reminded them.

A voice from behind them interjected, 'They are already here.' Turning to see who had spoken, the Tu-Han found themselves looking at a tall and unusually garbed Jaevisk. They were less disconcerted by the sudden appearance of this stranger than by its clothing. It wore a full black cloak which trailed to the polished metal floor, on the fore of which were two winged beasts, one of gold, the other silver. Mocking them with their dreams of the future and their nightmares of the past, these beasts moved freely across the dark cloak, snapping at each other across the breadth of the mighty Jaevisk chest beneath. Their bestial eyes glared with hatred at the Tu-Han as if some aeons old vendetta warmed their flaming hearts. As the Tu-Han noted that this stranger cast no reflection upon the metal floor, the grey eyes of the black-cloaked Jaevisk sparkled with the secret knowledge of untold and unmatched mischief.

'What are you?' one of the Tu-Han asked shrewdly.

'You doubt your eyes?'

'You are not Jaevisk.' The reflective surface was indicated. 'You are not here.'

'I am what I am,' came the cryptic reply. 'Where I am is unimportant, but what is happening is of the utmost significance to the survival of your species. Restoration will not occur without a price.'

They conferred within the apparent privacy of their minds before the first one said, 'We will listen.'

The visitor wasted no time. 'A new Harvest is upon you, a new kind of Harvest, but it will be contested and others will play a part. You will wait for a signal from Earth and you will cooperate with the Humans.'

'We do not require alliance.'

'You are mistaken,' the visitor snapped in their sibilant and clicking language. He stepped closer to them, enjoying their uncertainty at his identity, sensing the gradual erosion of their arrogance. 'Did you think you could watch Kiranis so intently without attracting attention? The Kwaios Council has long noted your interest and your presence here complicates their plans. They have facilitated the concealment of a fleet at the fourth planet, as part of their agreement with the Humans. They have even equipped the fleet with some of their technology.'

'We have seen the ships from Earth. They do not concern us, and the Kwaios Council has no further interest in Kiranis. Their cloning capabilities have ensured that their store is renewable and theoretically infinite.'

'That *was* true,' the visitor delighted in explaining, 'until two years ago, when their cloning plants were destroyed, their reserve supplies infected, and their last major production facility was obliterated. They have been left with no source of renewal other than the Harvest. Did your Old Ones not think to ask why the Kwaios want those people from Earth?'

They glared at him, knowing what he was saying and how he had positioned them on his board. One of them stepped forward aggressively, on the verge of attack. Changed suddenly to his Human form, Naveen simply gestured with outstretched palms and the huge Jaevisk was thrown back against its fellows. Naveen pursued, snapping in English, 'Know this! Everything I do here is written in the pages of *my* history. The Kwaios are coming in force, and you need much greater defences than you have. Your storehouse at Sieltor Teuvas will need to be stripped of its fuel. Without the power of the stones out there, you won't survive a concerted attack. The Kwaios Council is considerably more powerful than the last time you faced them!'

He vanished, leaving the bewildered Jaevisk Tu-Han to absorb what he said and to consider their options. 'We will wait for the communication from Earth before proceeding.'

'Then we will not succumb?' one lesser Jaevisk bravely asked.

The red-caped Jaevisk made a snorting sound of derision. 'The Jaevisk succumb to no one,' it said, turning to face its three colleagues.

'We will find a way to destroy this creature who mocks us with our own faith. He is only Human, and Humans always underestimate their enemy.'

'What of the Kwaios?'

'We will permit them to know that this Human is responsible for the destruction of their facilities. He is a false prophet, using the World Killer to further his cause. Once the Kwaios know that a Human is responsible for his actions, their anger will be incalculable.'

They returned to a state of observance, noting that the fleet from Earth of which Naveen had spoken, a fleet some two hundred strong, had just emerged from its hiding place at the fourth planet. It occupied a strategic position between that planet and the broken remnants of Kiranis, waiting for events to unfold.

THE FIRST DAY

The signal from Earth came as predicted, yet it was on the frequency of a prototype communication network, a fledgling concept of Jaevisk intra-dimensional summoning. No one outside the highest echelons of the Jaevisk Society should have had access to it. And yet the Tu-Han were being ordered by their superiors to consider this the result of technological espionage the likes of which they had never experienced. This was why five heavily-armed Warships were dispatched to Earth to respond to one little signal.

While the meeting with Councillor Messina was underway, the Jaevisk scanned the cage, noting the buzzing around of countless vessels from Earth as the Humans attempted to understand this immense structure. They noted also the broken and burned remains of scores of satellites and military stations, the aftermath of the arrival of the cage. Through an interconnected com system, the commanding elements of each Warship were able to listen in on the conversation with the Humans which was taking place on one of the fully operable stations. When the alien and advanced nature of the tiny device presented to the Jaevisk Speaker was recognised, the representative in question was immediately transported into the rendering of its own hologram, whereupon it snapped up the device. Nothing else mattered at that point, and all Jaevisk eyes and ears were fixed upon this device. '*There are…Jaevisk elements in the device*,' the Human female was saying. 'What is this?' every other watching Jaevisk was either saying or thinking. 'Where did it come from?'

The Speaker on the station was quick enough to feign knowledge of the technology and ignorance of the magnitude of its discovery. The Tu-Han on the Warship farthest from Earth were relieved by the improvisation and realised that this was the catalyst for alliance of which the black-cloaked Human had spoken back at Kiranis. Their impatience was monumental but they knew that they must not appear too enthusiastic. Now the Human was speaking of the small ship which had emerged from the portal event some time before the return of Kiranis. She was ignorant of the identity and significance of the Garran pilot, and she was mistakenly convinced of a connection between the Garran and the cage. It was a conclusion of nonsensical proportions, but there was no call to correct her. As the Jaevisk Speaker reminded the Humans of Garran military strength, one of the Tu-Han said, 'Perhaps a visit to Sieltor Prime is now necessary.'

'Perhaps,' said another. It tapped a key on a floating console of light and ordered the Speaker, 'You will agree to produce the devices. We will liaise with the Axcebians.'

They heard Councillor Messina demanding action, and they practically held their breath as the Speaker was so bold as to offer the device back to her. The Humans conferred and the agreement was made. But whether or not the Humans would be friends to the Jaevisk, as the Speaker dared to put it, remained to be seen. The Speaker was brought back to its Warship, and the Jaevisk force left Earth. They entered their respective vortices, leaving as they had arrived. While two returned to the home station, three emerged at Sieltor Prime.

There was an immediate reaction from the Garran military, but it was simply strategic and defensive posturing as a score of battleships positioned themselves around the three visitors. The Jaevisk made no aggressive move, and messages were sent to the palace of Governor Ben-Hadad requesting an alliance. 'The Governor is a power-hungry fool,' one of the Tu-Han explained to its fellows. 'His rise to power was facilitated by brute force and corruption, rather than intellect and diplomacy. He will be easily manipulated.'

'Many are wary of exposing the Stones to him,' another admitted. 'Do you think it wise?'

'The Warlord thinks so,' the first argued. 'The Stones we have prepared for Ben-Hadad are old and limited, but they are sufficient to interest him, making them a worthy sacrifice.'

There was a warning sound and attention shifted towards an approaching vessel. In the distance, a small craft approached the Garran blockade and was recognised instantly by the Jaevisk as that which had emerged from the portal at Kiranis. Without slowing, the vessel continued towards the planet as it was scanned openly by the Garran battleships and covertly by the Jaevisk. To open fire on it here would jeopardise everything, so they chose instead to watch. The mysterious craft was coming to ground too fast, but the pilot did not adjust his speed. The Jaevisk watched in amazement as the ship disappeared beneath the ground, passing through the soil and rock as if it were insubstantial. And they were not the only ones who found this intriguing. It was not long before a shuttle detached from its place of concealment on the belly of the same Warship, alerting the Jaevisk to a new factor. They watched it approach the planet, ignored for some reason by the Garran security forces. And then they understood: 'The Kwaios are here.'

'Let them take him first,' said another Tu-Han. It was a wise decision, for an opportunity had presented itself. On their monitors, they observed as what appeared to be a Jaevisk shuttle landed at the farm outside the Garran capital city of Khas. After a while, a Garran emerged from the house and walked calmly towards the shuttle, his reasons mercilessly unclear. As the Garran boarded the shuttle and it rose from the dusty ground, the Jaevisk Warship opened fire from orbit, knowing they could kill two extremely dangerous birds with one stone.

Even seen on their monitors, the image of the shuttle flickered to momentarily reveal its true form, a relatively small Kwaios single-decked reconnaissance vessel. But the illusion of the twin-decked Jaevisk shuttle returned as the ship sped westwards, perhaps intending to break atmosphere and rendezvous with a larger vessel hidden on the current night side of the planet.

Garran battleships descended from their security detail, down into the atmosphere to chase the fleeing shuttle. They bombarded it with their weapons, but found that their attack was futile. In orbit, the remaining Garran vessels moved to engage the Jaevisk, convinced of betrayal. But the Jaevisk ignored them, intent as they were upon destroying their enemy. All three Warships synchronised their weapons' lock and fired simultaneously at the shuttle. It was blown to pieces, and the devastation, the smoke and the dust obscured the events transpiring beneath it. For the Jaevisk could not see that the mysterious Garran had survived.

Ω

In the giant home station inhabited by many millions of Jaevisk, only two had been entrusted with the secret appraisal of the strange metal disc upon their return from Earth. It was suspended in the air before them above a sterile metal square atop a computer console in the centre of the dark room. The disc rotated slowly in the light shining down upon it, and one of the Jaevisk reached down to tap a red light-key beneath the sterile surface. The disc began to pull itself apart as the rotation continued, and the array of miniscule parts was revealed for their scrutiny, each one slowly turning in the light. Holographic cubes, composed of red lines and varying in size, encased each component and next to each cube were data readouts of the nature and composition of each piece. One of the

279

Jaevisk pointed. 'Some of these components are Jaevisk,' it said. 'The Human female was correct.'

The other altered the position of the floating pieces so that they formed a vertical line and a pulse of green light made its way slowly upwards from the console. The results were displayed in larger text hovering in the space to their right. 'Quantum scans suggest instability.'

'It is not of this time,' the other concluded.

'This is of great significance. By such means are victories achieved.'

'We should learn more of the Human who first possessed it.' As they spoke, a drop of dark liquid began to form at the end of a tiny rod about a millimetre in length which had been at the centre of the device. At first it had appeared that this liquid had coagulated and was part of the design to keep the device together. But the liquid dropped out of the rod, and the tiny glistening blob was suspended amidst the pieces, its image magnified and scanned. Both Jaevisk looked closely at it, and stepped back as the results were displayed on the opposite side of the console to the previous results. 'This is blood.'

'Garran blood,' agreed the other. It tapped more keys and a hologram of a Garran body was displayed. The computer isolated the part of the body from which the blood came, clearly indicating the point at the base of the skull at which the cranial ridge was cut at birth. 'Cranial Stem Fluid is present.'

They were silent as one performed some calculations to determine how much of this fluid would be needed to produce the amount of devices requested by the Humans. The Jaevisk text displayed the answer. 'Ten thousand Garran will be needed,' one of the two announced. 'I will inform the Tu-Han.'

THE SECOND DAY

In a dark and cold room on one of the Jaevisk Warships orbiting Sieltor Prime, four black hollow poles extended diagonally from where they were embedded in the floor. Leaning inwards towards a large red crystalline stone suspended at the apex of this arrangement by means unknown, they were usually used as conduits for power transfer. However, the Slave Stones were too far away to enter the conduits, situated as they were on the planet below. The meeting with Governor Ben-Hadad was underway, and the time for display was fast approaching. There were no Jaevisk in this room, for the freezing temperatures required to store a Reaper crystal were too extreme for them to withstand. All of the stones involved were cold, as Ben-Hadad was currently learning, but the larger ones were kept even colder, a vital aspect of the transfer process.

From the planet below, shooting up from the Hall of Governors in Khas City, a single composite beam of red light was directed towards the Warship. While it tore a hole in the roof of the Hall, it passed through the hull of the Warship without any damage, continuing through every deck and insignificant room before reaching the Reaper storeroom. Bypassing the standard configuration which would utilise the four sloping black poles, the beam made contact with the base of the Reaper crystal. The Reaper vanished, facilitating the energy transfer which returned powered to Khas City. The ultimate source of that power was a truth fiercely protected by the Jaevisk; one which Ben-Hadad did not concern himself.

Ω

Across the system at Sieltor Omneri, a Warship emerged from a vortex and came to a stop just short of the military shipyards. A large Garran fleet was stationed here, but it was currently leaderless and no move was made to engage the Jaevisk. A single shuttle launched from a nondescript Garran vessel and the docking bay of the Warship opened to permit access, the tiny Garran shuttle entering the belly of the beast. In the rumbling silence of the docking bay, four Tu-Han stood and waited as their guest arrived. The shuttle depressurised and a ramp extended from the side as the door opened. A tall, male Garran who was relatively thin for his position was dressed in robes of state, and he stopped halfway down the ramp. 'I am here for the good of my people,' he declared, clearly trying to convince himself as much as anyone else.

'Of course, Governor Ha-Cxada,' one of the Tu-Han replied. 'We would expect no less.'

'What is it you want me to do?'

'First you should be aware of the rewards.'

Ha-Cxada maintained his composure, although his heart was beating rapidly. 'Go on.'

'You are a man who appreciates the balance of power, Ha-Cxada, and so we have decided that you should be the new overlord of your people. Your conspirators amongst the Setta family and the Tae Ahn Affiliate will not survive what is to come. Nor will Governor Ben-Hadad and his supporters.'

This time Ha-Cxada could not mask his excitement. 'That is excellent news. If of course it's true.'

'It is true if we say it is.'

The Governor drew himself up. 'I am not the idiot you take me for!' he snapped. 'Ben-Hadad may kiss your feet, but I will not!'

They hesitated, pretending to be thrown off-guard. Yet the passion of Ha-Cxada was exactly what made him perfect for this deceit. He hated Ben-Hadad like no other. 'We are aware of how much trust you place in Jakari San Setta,' they said, diverting his anger with confusion.

Ha-Cxada stared at the speaker for a moment. 'Will *he* survive?'

'His fleet will be spared, and returned to you as your personal guard. Jakari will never suspect your involvement.'

'How will you ensure that his fleet is spared?'

'You will assist us. We wish for his fleet to collect a consignment at the Kiranis system. The collection will require some structural modifications to his battleships.'

'What sort of modifications?'

'We will attach dedicated collection units to his ships. However, it is through the guidance systems that the collection will be controlled. Regardless of what happens at the Kiranis system, our consignment will find its way to Jakari's ships using its own navigational network. The fleet will then return here.'

'Why would you want your consignment brought here?'

'This is how the Jaevisk and the Garran will begin their new alliance, Governor. Ben-Hadad thinks he has obtained the secret of our power. But we will bring the real secrets to you.'

It all sounded too good to be true, but sometimes the desire to believe the unbelievable was sufficiently overwhelming that logic evaporated in its wake. Ha-Cxada focused on the practical matters of such an arrangement. 'Although I oversee the shipyards out here, orders of this magnitude go through Ben-Hadad's office. How would I convince him to approve this?'

'You will make contact with Ben-Hadad's Senior Aide, and he will rush the orders through the administration.'

Ha-Cxada's eyes widened. 'His Senior Aide?'

'Not all of Ben-Hadad's opposition are as...overt as you, Governor.'

'Apparently not,' he replied. He stood for a moment, waiting for more. But there was no more, and they were clearly finished speaking with him. After an uncomfortable silence, he turned and headed back up the ramp. He felt a shiver run through him, as the anticipation of triumph overwhelmed his suspicions. Had he known that his actions would see him shot dead the following day, he might have given those suspicions greater analysis.

Ω

Krell was on a Warship in the Kiranis system observing the eponymous planet, fascinated by its continuing re-formation. Lost in his thoughts for a time, he failed to notice the lesser Jaevisk who had approached him. This messenger stood and waited behind Krell, for one such as he could not address a Warlord directly, and had simply to wait until he was noticed. Eventually, Krell turned. 'What word?'

'Lord, there is a communication request from Sieltor Prime.'

'It is highly unlikely they have asked for me.'

'Of course, Lord. The request has come from the Setta family, and my Tu-Han has suggested that you might wish to coordinate the response.'

'Your Tu-Han was correct. Inform him that he shall speak with this Garran personally and that I shall direct him. Connect me immediately.'

'Yes, Lord.'

In Senneya's room on Sieltor Prime, the hologram of the Tu-Han in question appeared and the conversation began with an unnecessary probe into Senneya's identity. Her image had been scanned and Krell was supplied with all the information required. He knew that the Setta family

283

and their associates were political rivals of Ben-Hadad. He spoke to the Tu-Han without interfering in the conversation: 'They are merely attempting to disrupt our proceedings with their Governor. You will make them aware of the presence of a systems' virus in their associate's fleet. This will distract them from their immediate goals.'

The Tu-Han did so, but Krell noted something which the Tu-Han had simply breezed over. This female was the mate of Carak Tae Ahn, whose dealings with the Kwaios Council were known to the Old Ones of Sieltor. As a result, Carak was no friend to the Setta agenda, and it was interesting that Eyla San Setta would take the man's mate under her wing. Krell found himself admiring the multivalent deceptions of Garran politics, until something despicable caught his attention, the transcript of a conversation between Eyla San Setta and the woman to whom the Tu-Han was currently speaking. 'It appears that Governor Ben-Hadad has abducted this woman's child,' said Krell. 'This is her motivation for contacting us. Sever the com link.'

The conversation with Senneya ended abruptly with the cryptic reference to Kiranis, and the hologram of the Tu-Han appeared before Krell. 'You did well,' Krell commended him. 'We will take steps to punish Ben-Hadad for his actions. This will permit the Setta and their associates to take control of Sieltor.'

'How shall we proceed, Lord?'

'We shall wait until Ben-Hadad is close to Kiranis. I will speak with him personally.'

'But, Lord, no Warlord has ever revealed himself to an outsider.'

'My presence will convince him of instability amongst our people, and I will tell him that he can take control of the fleet of Jakari San Setta. This will facilitate the transfer of the virus to their entire armada, and we will use every Garran ship to attack the Kwaios. In his last moments of life, Governor Ben-Hadad will share the fear of the child he holds captive.'

THE THIRD DAY

The Warlord Krell had ordered the revealing of Sieltor Teuvas, based on the warnings the Prophet had delivered to the Tu-Han. Krell was sure that the Human was manipulating his people, but his logic concerning the might of the Kwaios Council could not be overlooked. The process of Revelation was a relatively simple one, but it had never before been undertaken on an inhabited world. Undetectable by Garran sensors or the satellite grid of Teuvas, a single short pulse of energy raced across the Sieltor system. It passed through celestial bodies, ships and satellites before striking the crystalline core of Sieltor Teuvas.

The spectacular event was monitored by the crews of the Warships still orbiting Sieltor Prime, and four Tu-Han stood in the Operation Centre of one ship in awed silence as they observed. Sieltor Teuvas, which had until today been a greatly populated centre of commerce and a monument to Garran diversity, was melting, burning, and breaking apart. 'There can be no return from this,' one of them said solemnly, watching the rivers of fire.

'This is an unprecedented Revelation,' another agreed. 'The Kwaios will be enraged.' It turned away from the window and the others followed as it left the bridge. They entered an elevator and made their way to the lower decks. As they silently walked the corridor, there came to them the smell of their deception and the price of war, a disgusting thing which filled the corridor. Although tainted by its presence, they also felt justified, for there had been no other way to achieve their aim. They stopped at a door on their right and hesitated. 'We should look upon this,' said one, 'if for no other reason than to understand the path upon which we tread.'

'There was no choice,' said another. 'The devices needed to be made to the exact specifications. This was a vital ingredient for the Harvest.'

'There is always a choice,' the first one reminded them. 'It is the consequence that confirms whether the right one was made.'

'It will become apparent in time that this is the Garran lot in this galaxy,' said the third Tu-Han. 'Until that day, we should protect them from annihilation. The Humans will soon be the greatest threat we have ever faced.'

'First we will have to survive the Kwaios,' said the first one, reaching out to open the door by pressing the adjacent panel. Stepping into the room one by one, they spread out into their customary line of four, withstanding the overpowering stench. 'We should look upon this,' the first one repeated. 'It is our hope for the future.' They stared for some time, heroically ignoring the reek of death and corruption. For in the centre of the giant room was a huge pile of Garran bodies, male and female soldiers given up by Ben-Hadad. Ten thousand Garran bodies there were, still in their uniforms. Each with a hole in the back of its head.

THE FOURTH DAY

The Jaevisk were rarely taken by surprise or shocked by inexplicable phenomena, for they were usually the masters of such things. Yet, as Warships were monitoring the events at Kiranis, a gravitational disturbance just beyond their position activated alarms and weapons' systems searched for target locks. Had it not been for the identification of the Jaevisk structures attached to Jakari's fleet at Omneri, the Garran battleships would have found themselves under attack as they emerged from the strange portal activated by the Prophet.

The initial shock of the arrival of the Garran fleet passed, and the Tu-Han issued orders to the gathering Warships. More and more vessels were moving in from the outer ring of the system, and the gathering process began. An order came down through the Jaevisk ranks: 'The virus will activate as soon as we detach the components of the tower. Once the planet stabilises, locate the mountain and begin construction.'

Ω

Krell had previously been informed that no remains had been found following the failed attempt by the Kwaios to capture the Garran calling himself Malik: *'Both the Setta group and the Garran authorities searched the destruction site as well as the home of Malik Ki Jen. There was no trace of a dead Garran.'* During the meeting with Ben-Hadad, the confusion of the Garran surrounding this incident was clear. However, Jaevisk monitoring of the activities of Carak Tae Ahn had paid off in this regard, and an update on the matter was delivered to Krell: *'We believe that the World Killer is at Earth. He is on board the ship stolen by Carak Tae Ahn.'*

Not one to underestimate the World Killer as many in the past had done, Krell decided to send a Warship with a skeleton crew and devoid of Tu-Han. In essence, a ship solely in the hands of lesser Jaevisk was dispatched to Earth. 'Attack the Garran Star Cruiser without delay,' Krell ordered them. 'Do not engage the Humans.'

Krell watched the events unfold at Earth by remote connection to the Warship. He was fascinated by the actions of Carak down on the planet, as the blue beam of light shot upwards from the surface and Kwaios energy interacted with the mechanics of the cage. 'The Kwaios are using him well,' he noted. Sixteen Tu-Han in the room with Krell acknowledged this observation, but had little time to consider the implications. 'Lord, there is an intruder aboard the Warship!' a lesser Jaevisk reported from the middle of the Operations Centre. Krell turned to this Controller, who then said, 'It is the World Killer!'

'Order them to stop him!'

'He is in the engine room.' They accessed the networked cameras and watched in horror as the mysterious Garran activated an explosive device, blasted open the engine core and ripped out one of the Slave Stones. The alarms would be sounding on board as the engine room reported instability, but Krell could see that there was no time for the crew to react. The Garran intruder took from a pack on his shoulder a black device similar to a Kwaios communication module, yet smaller and with slight variations in shape. Krell did not recognise it, and all gathered in the Operations Centre watched as the Garran threw it into the engine core. He turned to the camera with a hateful glare and raised his hands outwards and above his head. There was a blinding blue flash before the network feed went dead.

Every Jaevisk in the Operations Centre fell silent, and Krell suppressed his rage. 'He has three days to get back to Kiranis,' he reminded them quietly. 'We will find him there.' Turning back to the great window, Krell could see the scores of Warships vanishing through vortices in their journey to the Kiranis system. 'And where we find the World Killer...we will find the Prophet.'

THE FIFTH DAY

There were now more Jaevisk Warships in the Kiranis system than any other race would have seen in one place, and Krell knew that he was taking a huge risk by committing such force and such a vast number of his people to this operation. However, the ultimate goal of Restoration was worth the sacrifice, and the Kwaios Council would fight hard for their Harvest. A Tu-Han approached Krell, informing him that Carak's Star Cruiser was closing in on their position at the outer planet of the system: 'They claim to have the man responsible for destroying our vessel at Earth. They wish to deliver his body to us.'

Krell was momentarily confused. 'This is a Kwaios trick,' he declared. 'Supply them with our transponder codes. I want to see this...body.'

'Then you do not believe that the World Killer is dead?'

'No, I do not. But the Kwaios will not have supplied Carak with a poor fake. It will be interesting to understand their motive.'

An alarm sounded and holo-imaging systems displayed the electrical phenomenon occurring beyond the outer ring. 'The Kwaios are here,' a lesser Jaevisk reported. 'They are attacking a ship from Earth.'

'Identify the vessel.'

'It is called *Nostradamus*. An insignificant ship.'

'Nothing is insignificant. The Kwaios Council have distracted us with this story of the World Killer's body while they attack it.'

The incredibly powerful computer systems on the Warship raced through the information gathered by the Jaevisk at Earth, cross-referencing this ship with recent events. The lesser Jaevisk who found the information shuddered with fear and decided to pass the burden on to his Tu-Han. After all, that was what they were there for. The Tu-Han in question felt the same fear as he approached Krell with the news. 'Lord, it appears that the Human who was on the cage when it arrived in our time escaped Earth aboard the *Nostradamus*.'

Krell glared at the red-caped subordinate. 'This is the man from whom the first neuro-implant was extracted!' he roared. 'The very implant we replicated for the Humans and which was then stolen by the Prophet!'

'Yes, Lord,' the Tu-Han replied humbly.

'I am disappointed,' said Krell. 'You will take the blade.'

'Yes, Lord.' The red-caped Tu-Han turned to walk away, and Krell approached the lesser Jaevisk who had been too afraid to deliver the bad news. 'You will join your Tu-Han,' he ordered. With two honour suicides on his hands at the brink of battle, Krell fought to quell his disgust. But as he turned around, a black-cloaked Human stood in his place of command. 'Do you know who I am?' the man asked.

'You are the Prophet,' Krell replied calmly. 'You are in my place.'

Naveen grinned and stepped aside. 'My apologies, Krell,' he mocked, gesturing that the assigned circle be filled by the feet of someone more worthy than he.

Krell did not move. 'Why are you here?'

'To bring you good news.'

'From what I have heard, that would surprise me.'

Naveen laughed aloud, a horrible sound for the Jaevisk ear. 'I don't doubt that. Still, it's the truth. You see, you're worried now that the Kwaios have in their possession the man from the future who had the original implant.'

Krell regarded the Human for a moment, noting with distaste the dragons playing on his dark cloak. 'Are you suggesting that they do not?'

'No, but I'm suggesting that I have something better to offer you.'

'You will return the original implant?'

'I will. Let's just say that I...saved it for you.'

'Why would you do such a thing?'

Naveen grinned again. 'Because your goal on Kiranis...is my goal.'

Krell did not believe him, for the man was known amongst many species to be a consummate liar. 'Where is the implant?'

'It's in Councillor Cassandra Messina, whom I've taken the liberty of sending your way. You will have to send a ship immediately to extract her shuttle from light-travel. This must be done outside the electrical boundaries which the Kwaios are erecting as we speak.'

'The boundary restricts our vortex travel.'

'Then send someone from home, Krell!' Naveen snapped. 'If you want her...go and get her!' He vanished, and Krell immediately sent the command to the Jaevisk home station: 'Take Cassandra Messina captive and bring her back to the station. Examine her implant and its applications. If our initial findings were correct, it might be used to break through the Kwaios boundary. If this is so, then bring Messina directly to Kiranis. Bring her to me at the mountain.'

THE SIXTH DAY

Approximately halfway between Earth and the Kiranis system, a Warship appeared and its crew immediately activated a pulsing net of energy, waiting like fishermen along a specified transit vector. The Jaevisk anticipated considerable difficulties in this operation, unprecedented as it was. A vessel racing towards the Kiranis system at multiples of the constant would prove a very dangerous catch to their space-going trawler. Structural damage was expected and fatalities were likely, but the prize was worth the risk and the Warlord had demanded it.

Incredibly precise sensor equipment detected the approach of the small craft in the great distance, and the calculations were begun with earnest. They confirmed the accuracy of their assumptions, and there was no need to re-position the energy net, so well known was this safest of routes across the stars. Within seconds, the speeding craft slammed unceremoniously into the energy net, dragging it from the altered reality of light-speed back into the real time of the galaxy. As anticipated, the damage was significant. The energy emitters at the prow of the ship were torn out and a hull breach followed the resulting explosion. Jaevisk bodies drifted out into space. The Warship quickly moved into place above the tiny craft, and the catch was hauled in as a cargo arm took hold of it, taking it up into the belly of the Warship. Inside the massive Jaevisk vessel, the small craft swayed from side to side as the arm manoeuvred it onto a deck. Here, Jaevisk soldiers waited to bring the occupant of the craft to their medical decks, where a special facility had been prepared.

She kicked and twisted, punched and screamed and cursed them all, but Cassandra could not escape the strong grips of her captors. 'What do you want with me?' she demanded. Although she could hear their inner voices in her head, she did not understand the language and nothing vocal was offered. With their massive hands, they examined the back of her head as they carried her with her feet hanging limp above the polished floors. They were fascinated by the metal tendrils pushing through her hair, some of them stuck to it with the blood from the scores of openings in her skull through which they had emerged. As one of the Jaevisk investigated with too much force, the pain set Cassandra to screaming, before she passed out.

Ω

When she awoke, she lay on a surgical table, cold metal against her naked flesh. They had wasted no time or thought for her dignity, leaving her feeling vulnerable and violated. Four of them gathered around her, each one with its nose and mouth covered by metal objects attached to convenient contact points on its exoskeletal frame. Cassandra found herself considering what other tools or peripheral objects these aliens could make use of via their hybrid organic technology, but her distraction was temporary, for she saw another Jaevisk at the end of the room. This one was clothed differently, with a red cape attached to its shoulders via exoskeletal contact points which were not found on any of the others. 'What...are you?' she asked in a rasping voice. To her surprise, this Jaevisk approached her and replied as the others moved aside in obvious deference. To Cassandra's greater surprise, she understood clearly what it was saying, as if it spoke in English. 'I am Tu-Han, a level of leadership amongst my species.'

'Why am I here? And how can I understand you?'

'Your brain is altering your auditory receptors to compensate for our language. I am speaking in my language, but you are hearing me in yours.'

Cassandra shook her head slowly, feeling the pain at the back of her skull. 'That's not possible,' she argued.

'It would seem that the device in your head has made many things possible which once were not. For this purpose, you might consider it a type of translation implant.'

She was silent for a moment, recalling the Jaevisk with whom she had spoken on Matthews' station. *This interests us*, it had said. From nowhere, the revelation made horrific sense and she groaned as the implications assaulted her. 'You had never seen the device before,' she whimpered. 'I gave you something you haven't even invented yet.'

'That is correct,' replied the Tu-Han. 'Although it is not altogether clear if we would ever have invented it. The presence of Jaevisk elements and design signatures may be a result of some form of technological assimilation in the future. There is no way for us to know. However, we have this technology now, and so there will be no initial invention in the future. It exists in our time and we intend to use it.'

'Use it for what?'

'The device appears to have been designed to act as a catalyst for a process which would otherwise have taken millions of years to occur.

The hybritech tendrils attach themselves with precision to parts of the brain left dormant by millions of years of Human evolution. They also force the drawing together on both an organic and psychological level of the two sides of your brain. The device presumes that the logic and the intuition centres of the Human brain will become fused at some point in your evolution, and it anticipates that condition.'

Cassandra held the fierce gaze of the alien, sensing its intellect; sensing it reading her. 'We know that you were aware of this, Councillor,' it duly informed her, 'and we also know of your dealings with the Prophet. We are curious as to whether you would have permitted the surgery had you known about the Garran blood in the device. That was the ingredient which led us to visit their Governor and promise an alliance similar to that promised to you.' The Jaevisk leaned in closer. 'What sort of leader simply hands over thousands of his own people to another race without understanding why?'

She understood the inference, knowing that it was not Ben-Hadad the Jaevisk spoke of. But how could they know about Tesckyn's deal with the Kwaios? The implications were momentous, but she could not find the words to respond as the Jaevisk straightened and resumed its explanation. 'We extracted the cranial fluid from the soldiers given to us by Ben-Hadad and we completed the devices, all the time curious as to how these devices would help your people. Of course, not all your people were suffering, Councillor.'

'No,' she said quietly. 'Just the Church members.'

'Yes. A relatively small proportion of your population, but significant in its genetic heritage. Do you know why the experiments began?' She did not reply. 'Of course you do,' it continued. 'You are a keeper of secrets on your world. But you were occupying two worlds amongst your people.'

'I'm not the one responsible for all this,' she argued. She was referring to Naveen, but the Tu-Han misunderstood based on what it had learned. 'No, you are not,' it replied. 'But you worked for Tesckyn long before declaring yourself a member of the Church of the New Elect. We have managed to put your entire story together, Councillor, by intercepting communications made on seemingly dormant networks on Earth.' The red-caped alien leaned in again. 'We know everything, Councillor.'

Cassandra heard its thoughts now, and realised that it truly did know everything, and maybe more than even she did. 'Why is there Garran blood in the device?' she whispered, terrified of the answer. 'If everyone in the Church is descended from cross-breeding with the Garran, why would it need more Garran blood?'

There was a strange sound that may have been laughter, and the Tu-Han exchanged warning glances with the lesser Jaevisk standing nearby. 'You need to know what you have done, Councillor,' it replied eventually. 'You are responsible for the manipulation of my people. The implantation of these devices has provided our enemy with the means by which they can rebuild their energy reserves.'

'I...I don't understand.'

'Of course you don't. Your people blindly agreed to do what the Kwaios Council asked of them, so desperate as they were to get home. But you will all pay the price for dealing with them, I can assure you.'

Cassandra looked around at the other Jaevisk, who were preparing surgical tools and waiting for their superior to permit them to begin. 'What are they going to do? What do you want with me?'

'As we speak, Councillor, the Garran cranial fluid is causing mutation in your midbrain, a part of your evolution remaining from your reptilian phase.'

'What?' Cassandra was horrified. 'What's going to happen to me?'

'You will avoid the fate in question, Councillor, because another awaits you. The device in your head was taken from a man from the future, and as a result it is in a state of temporal flux. We are going to use that circumstance to our advantage.'

Cassandra felt tears rolling down her cheeks and she closed her eyes as the red-caped Jaevisk leaned in closer to tell her the rest. 'You are going to be our greatest weapon, Councillor. You are going to help us regain control over our gods and our home.' It backed away and gestured that the work begin, saying, 'And then we can kill the Prophet.'

Ω

Krell watched as the charred Garran body was examined. Quantum scans were being performed on the remnants of the boiled and blistered organs, and it was not long before the report was brought to the Warlord: 'Lord, this Garran is exactly the same as the World Killer, but he is not a clone. This Garran was older than the one we seek, and scans show considerably more temporal damage to the organs.'

294

'So this is a future version of the World Killer?' Krell approached the empty husk on the table. 'This Garran has travelled through time many more times than the one who came through the portal at Kiranis.'

'That is the most likely conclusion, Lord.'

Krell laughed darkly, an unsettling sound for even the Jaevisk ear. 'It appears that this time-travelling maniac has found himself in the past and then murdered himself.'

'We are dealing with a truly insane individual then, Lord.'

'Or an individual of insane intellect.' Krell stared at the body for a moment, considering his next step. The Kwaios Council also wanted the World Killer, and it was they who arranged the delivery of this body through their Garran puppet. What were they trying to prove? Perhaps the answer lay with Carak Tae Ahn himself, for the Kwaios had ensured that the man become familiar with the World Killer. Krell tapped a button on his right arm, saying, 'Bring Overseer Carak to me.'

There was a short delay, until he heard, *'The Garran ship has just broken away from the airlock.'*

That was unfortunate, and it called for immediate reassessment. 'Destroy the ship,' Krell ordered. 'I want Carak dead.'

Ω

In the distant Sieltor system, twenty Warships emerged from vortices close to Teuvas. Perimeter defence at the ruined Garran world had recently been increased in order to protect the valuable bio-fuel, and countless orbiting weapon modules opened fire on the approaching vessels. The huge ships, however, destroyed this nuisance with ease. They moved into orbit around the glowing planet, and hundreds of shuttles were launched. While the Garran battleships of the reserve fleets closed in and the Jaevisk Warships held them off, the stripping of the planet's core began in earnest. There was no call for subterfuge now, for the Kwaios had revealed themselves at Kiranis, and the Jaevisk would need all the power they possessed to defend their world once their enemy began their attack. All they needed now was assurance that the Human weapon they called Messina could breach the Kwaios wall.

Ω

Cassandra could not feel any pain, although she was experiencing intense cold. The tendrils of her implant had once again pushed through the holes in her skull and they had connected with the control panel next to the engine core of the Warship. Four Tu-Han observed in silence as the first jump was made without Cassandra's assistance.

Scientists on many worlds had spent decades considering the mechanics of the Jaevisk vortex. Some had offered theories concerning artificially created wormholes linked directly to a specific source of energy on the ship. Others had suggested that perhaps the Jaevisk used a powerful tachyon-based weapon to disrupt the elemental fabric of space, ripping it open to reveal a pathway through space itself. Of course, this would also have an effect on dimensional time, having distorted the conditions of motion through the vacuum, essentially ignoring the constraints of time and space. Ignorant of existential displacement, the Jaevisk vortex was a problem causing discomfort to scientists and philosophers alike. Within moments, however, Cassandra knew that they were all wrong, and that it was at the same time infinitely more complex and more incredibly simple than they could possibly imagine.

There was no journey, no passing through a hypothetical short cut. The Warship was swallowed by the vortex and its prow pushed out through the fabric of space at its prescribed destination. One moment, they were in an area of space which Cassandra knew was not on any grid map, and the next they were emerging with the outer planet of the Kiranis system in view, the crackling blue of the Kwaios boundary blocking their advance. She knew that the Jaevisk had considered this the safest area of the system in which to emerge before trying their newly adapted version of a dimensional jump. However, as a dark and monstrous Kwaios vessel many times larger than the Warship began to materialise just outside the boundary, it opened fire, pummelling the Warship with intensity, and Cassandra knew that the Jaevisk had been wrong. And, as the Tu-Han ripped the hybritech tendrils out of the console and carried her to an escape pod, she prayed that she would either wake from this terrible nightmare...or die within it.

INTERVAL – FOUNDATION

Colle had never liked gas masks. Just seeing someone wearing them gave him the creeps. Of course, he would never admit that, and so he had to swallow his fears as Naveen handed masks to each of them. Sandra and Jason put theirs on, and they waited for Colle to do the same. 'Remind me again,' he said, avoiding looking at them and turning to Naveen. 'How come we don't need protective suits, but we need these masks?'

'It's an airborne virus,' Naveen replied impatiently. 'We're not dealing with radiation here. All you've got to worry about is what you're breathing in. Now, remember that the pods are for their own protection, so make sure you get everyone back into them.'

Colle nodded, yet still he hesitated. Sandra was about to say something when Naveen stepped forward and, in one swift motion, snapped the mask from Colle's hands, forced the strap over his head and set the mask in place. Colle looked fit to panic, but Naveen grabbed him by the shoulders and looked into his eyes. 'It's just a mask,' he said calmly. 'I can still see you, and you can still see me...and everything else. The world is still the same. Okay?'

No one noticed the sudden rumbling throughout the cage which had accompanied Naveen's physical actions, and Colle held his gaze for a moment before nodding slowly. Naveen stepped back. 'Remember,' he said. 'Don't talk to any of them. They're probably delirious...hallucinating and paranoid. Whatever they say...ignore them.' They nodded in unison, too afraid to argue. Then Naveen vanished and the door to the central thoroughfare opened.

This was a vast corridor, many times wider and longer than the one by which they had entered the room at the top of the cage. This was now a single corridor connecting the north and south poles, and Sandra and the others tried not to think about the length of time it would take to reach the other end. Essentially, they figured, one could walk the entire circumference of the cage without ever making a turn. But why walk?

Colle was the first to notice the huge transport pads set into a track on the wall to their right. 'Why don't we use one of these?'

Sandra shook her head. 'Because he said we don't have to go far. It's only the most northerly ends of the corridors that malfunctioned.'

'I don't get this,' said Jason. 'What's the point in bringing all these people out here if they've got this virus? Who's gonna help them out here?'

'Couldn't agree more,' said Colle. 'I'm starting to think that someone back home arranged for this to happen. There's no way it could all be brought together without some inside help.'

'For what?' Sandra argued. 'Like you said...what's the point?'

Neither man could offer a viable hypothesis, so they stayed quiet as they continued. After a while, they heard banging from up ahead. This section of the corridor was different. From here on, there were window sections to their left, looking out into another corridor running parallel to their one. They could see the pods along the opposite wall, as well as people who had been taken from Earth in those pods. Some of the pods were clearly missing, but those which immediately concerned them were empty. 'HELP US!'

Someone was suddenly at the window, a woman slamming her fists against the heavy glass. Clearly horrified to see three people wearing gas masks, she was probably even more horrified to see that they were as shocked to see her as she was to see them. Jennifer slammed harder against the glass. 'What do you *want* with us?' she screamed.

The three masks exchanged glances, and Jennifer could not hear them talk amongst themselves. 'She doesn't look sick to me,' said Jason, stepping closer to the glass as if at a zoo. 'Well, we've no idea of the symptoms,' Sandra reminded him, joining him at the glass. Colle moved farther down the corridor. 'There's more of them down here,' he called. 'Some of them are just slumped against the glass. Others look like they've passed out. Hey...look at this...what the hell is *that*?'

They moved back from Jennifer's hysteria and came down to see. Of the six people who were in sight, one man lay face down, and metal tendrils were protruding from his hair at the back of his head, gathered there like exploded cable. 'What...*is* that?' Sandra stepped closer, but a man jumped up to the window and shouted, 'You have to get us out of here! Please! They fired the others down to the planet!'

'Fired them *down*...?' Jason shook his head. 'Hallucinating much?'

Colle nodded. 'Must be. Unless they're stuck in the artillery hold.'

'Not funny, Colle,' snapped Sandra. 'These people have gone through Hell! They've been infected, abducted and now they're stuck in *this* thing.'

298

'Well, *excuse* me...' Colle snapped back, 'but apart from the infection part, doesn't that remind you of anyone? We're not exactly here of our own free will either!'

Sandra shook her head angrily and moved back, but as she did so, she could hear a hissing noise. And then an alarm sounded. They watched in silence as the corridor beyond the glass filled with gas and the people dropped like flies. After a while, the gas dissipated and the dividing glass panels opened upwards to permit access. Some remnants of gas drifted lazily into the larger corridor, and Colle felt his heart racing. 'These masks...' he said. 'Were they for the virus or the gas?'

Jason shrugged. 'Maybe both.' He crossed the threshold into the outer corridor and the others followed. They gathered up the fallen infected and returned them to the remaining open pods. 'Where did the other pods go?' Jason wondered, daring to step towards the transparent panels and lean forward to look out. He heard Sandra shouting, 'Get back from there, Jase!' and he decided that was probably wise. When the work was done, they stepped back into their corridor and waited for the glass partitions to close down. Colle was the first to take off his mask, anxious to be relieved of it. Sandra and Jason followed suit, and they had just started to laugh with the breaking of nerves when a sudden force threw them back towards the inner wall and the transport track. 'What the hell was that?' shouted Colle.

Jason stood and pointed silently towards the outer corridor, his earlier question answered. All of the pods were gone, and they realised the result of Naveen's latest manipulation.

Ω

The dark, rippling waters of the tides of creation lapped against the shores of a formative nightmare. Landscapes had for the most part been defined, with aspiring rock formations asserting their goals of domination as they reached upwards and outwards with geological purpose. The seas were hostile areas of membranous discontent, promising sweet oblivion in a sleep of welcoming abduction. The sky, roiling with combatant clouds of unrest, was still some kind of gaseous confusion, unsure of its place and purpose in this placental world. What was needed was the definition of a firmament, a significant proclamation of the divisions of this place. What was required in this place of chaos...was order. It just so happened that a creature in possession of the necessary skills was present.

Leviathan, a fully formed dragon of the deepest black, powered through the tumultuous underworld like an armoured plesiosaur, his wings folded against his back as he felt and sensed his way through the forming planet. He recognised the proximity of many thousands of souls, distorted beyond their original form to populate his world with suitable subordinates. Still they writhed in agony and torture, their internalised humanity sinking ever deeper amidst the psychological strength of their dark, spiritual twins. 'They will come soon, my children,' Leviathan called out across the gathering world, his voice ablaze with grating fire. 'They will seek to devour your hearts and souls. But I will protect you.'

The great landmass which had formed in the centre of the world had risen to prominence as the north pole of the planet, and the geological upheaval had erected a mountain peak at this zenith. Beneath this landmass, the chaos was slowing down and melding together, cooling and hardening, defining and determining. Leviathan forced his way into a vast cave network beneath the polar mountain as the rock layers behind and beneath him compressed and solidified. All around the world, the other dragons were emerging onto the land or occupying the settling oceans and rivers and lakes, as the ground beneath them forced itself into a distinctly layered body, from the upper reaches of the planet's geological heights to the solid electro-magnetic core of life's protection. Kiranis had truly returned to the galaxy.

Ω

It may have been a dream, but of such things Cana could no longer be sure. Was he the dragon? Surely not, for it looked down upon him. Not the black terror he had previously seen, but a white one, similar in size but variant in presence. Feeling weak and disoriented, Cana attributed his impression of this seemingly ghostly creature outlined by a hazy aura to his memory of having his blood drawn from him by Leviathan. So had that been a dream...and this the sequel of his subconscious?

'You're not dreaming, Cana,' a female voice assured him. It was soft and soothing, but Cana could think only of being hypnotised into submission in time for feeding. He scrambled back from the giant beast, grazing his palms on loose stones until he felt rock against his back. His panic was met with gentle laughter before the white dragon said, 'None of us will harm you, Cana. You gave us life.' The laughter again. 'At least...in this form. But I like it,' she added. 'I feel stronger than I've been in a long time.'

'Who...' Should he say "What"? '...are you?' he decided.

'None of that matters now, Cana. And names are fleeting things.' The giant head appeared to vibrate, and Cana was transfixed by the vision of multiple heads overlapping within the violent iridescence surrounding the dragon. 'RUN, CHILD!' a different voice shouted. 'Get out of the mountain!'

A rumbling began inside the beast and it threw back its huge head to blast flame up from the depths in which Cana found himself. He got to his feet and turned to climb the rock wall. The white dragon was roaring furiously, but a human voice was screaming with it, resulting in a twisted sound of possession from which Cana sought desperately to escape. He reached a ledge and pulled his tired body up onto it, rolling to his back as he regained his breath. Looking towards the dragon, he saw that although the great bulk of its body was seated in the depths below where he had just been, he was still not above its head. He had to escape, and as the dragon began to rise and its movement disturbed the rock around it, an opportunity presented itself. It was not the opportunity Cana would have chosen, however, for as the ledge upon which he lay crumbled beneath him, the rock wall from which it hung opened up and swallowed his tumbling form. Sliding and rolling helplessly amidst the debris, Cana descended a natural chute which opened into another cave. This one, however, was far from natural, which he saw even as he lay on his back coughing the dust from his throat. The ceilings and wall bore the impressions of laser-cutting, and metal scaffolding supported precarious formations. It was not until the rock and dust settled that Cana heard the humming of machinery and decided that the light in this cave was somewhat greener than it should have been. Before he could determine the source of that eerie glow, however, a shadow fell over him and he shouted with fright. But it was not a dragon.

Looking down at him and, surprisingly, offering a helping hand, a Garran man with a shock of red hair along his cranial ridge looked suitably maniacal in the green light. 'Can't say I'm overjoyed to see you either,' said Malik.

Cana was too confused to respond, and he stared at the strange machine as he rose and steadied himself. 'You should probably be moving on,' Malik told him as he moved back to the machine. 'You certainly don't want to be down here when I flick the switch.' He gestured towards an exit from the cave. 'Come on, I'll show you the way out of here.'

'What's going on?' Cana asked, still staring at the machine, which was the size of a small shuttle, as it hummed and vibrated. The sound would reach a soft crescendo before fading away and then repeating itself, and the green light grew brighter in concert with the sound. 'What is that thing?'

Malik regarded him for a moment before observing, 'You're one of those...Church people.' There was a hint of disdain as he added, 'You're descended from the cross-breeding.'

'I...' Cana turned to him. 'What?'

'Not entirely human. Not entirely Garran. Must be confusing for you.'

'What are you talking about? Who *are* you?'

Malik chuckled darkly. 'Do you really want to know what's going on?'

Cana nodded and said emphatically, 'Yes.'

The vibrations caused the cave to rumble and sand and stone fell intermittently to the floor. Cana could not be sure, but it appeared for a moment as if the machine was not really there. And then it was. 'I wouldn't be too sure about that,' said the Garran, 'because people like you tend not to take it very well.'

'What do you mean...people like me?'

'You know...people who think their version of a higher power calls the shots.'

Cana straightened himself. 'The Sentience is the *only* true power!' he declared. 'It controls everything!'

Malik laughed scornfully. 'You really believe that, don't you?'

Cana nodded, but his conviction was clearly in conflict. Malik stepped up to the young human and stared fiercely into his eyes, and Cana became aware of the rage and anguish therein as he replied with a certain satisfaction: 'I can fix that.'

PART 4
KWAIOS

TWO YEARS BEFORE ARRIVAL

Councillor Cassandra Messina was escorted along the corridor by two guards whom she had never met before, and this made her uncomfortable. She liked to at least know the name of the man or woman who was duty-bound to take a bullet for her, even if it would not be she who wrote the sympathy card when it happened. Cassandra found the venue for the meeting suitably ostentatious, the pretentiousness of the place promoting a certain reverse psychology in light of the nature of the meeting. This was no Council affair, nor was it organised by the Church of the New Elect masquerading as Central Command. No, this was an impromptu gathering of a more select nature. Elaborate doors were opened to welcome Messina into the room and she took note of those present within seconds. There was Marrahaim, looking particularly uncomfortable in an ill-fitting suit of deep blue. Rendorff was here, as were Tennon and Lynam and twelve others whom she had learned were all Church members serving on the Council. Men and women with conflicting political interests acknowledged Cassandra with varying degrees of amity and apathy. All were as concerned and confused as she about the purpose of this meeting, yet not all disguised it as well. They sat in two neat rows of comfortable chairs as the man who had called them here entered through another door and stood before them.

Anev Tesckyn was a master of deceit, as much as it galled Cassandra to admit it, and it was usually difficult to gauge his emotions. Today, however, the solemnity of defeat on his rough features was enough to send chills through those seated before him. He took a moment to listen to the reports in his ear confirming the situation safe for him to proceed. 'Thank you for coming on such short notice,' he opened. 'I trust the security implications were not too testing.' It was completely rhetorical, for he cared little for what they had to go through to dissuade those closest to them from asking questions or following them. As his agents, they were expected to handle such situations speedily and with the utmost professionalism. 'I'll get straight to it, because we've a lot of work to do. We've been contacted by a species called the Kwaios Council. Although we'd never heard of this species before yesterday, they are apparently fully aware of our situation. And I mean...*fully*...aware.'

Some whispers and glances were exchanged and discouraged just as quickly as Tesckyn continued: 'They've offered us a solution.'

It was Cassandra who asked, 'They can get us back?'

Tesckyn nodded. 'So they say. They're building something they say can do it.'

'What do they want in return?'

'That's why I called you here. Why I'm speaking to you as a group. We all appreciate how difficult it's been for you as members of the Church to continue to work for us while maintaining your positions on the Council. Many operatives can't handle the conflict of interest.'

'Are you testing our loyalty, Sir?' Cassandra asked.

Tesckyn nodded again. 'I need to know that our goal takes absolute priority over everything in your lives.'

They all looked at him, feeling that chill in the room once more. Each of them assured him of their loyalty, either by nodding or affirming it vocally. Cassandra hesitated, and all eyes turned to her. 'I prefer to see the hand I've been dealt before throwing in,' she said.

There was silence for a moment, before Tesckyn replied, 'Normally I wouldn't tolerate your attitude, Messina, but I need you in this, and I'm also grated by the commitment I'm expecting of you all.'

'Which is?'

Again there was a short silence. 'The Kwaios have demanded that we hand over the Church.'

'*What?*' Messina jumped up, incensed. 'The *Church*? *Everyone*? Why?' The others were mostly stunned to silence.

'You're fully aware of your genetic heritage, Messina!' Tesckyn reminded her. 'You know the history of the experiments and you know the danger posed from within the Church as Garran political problems escalate. We need to remain focused on our goal.'

'How? By declaring the Church subhuman and dealing with us like animals? We're not some commodity to be bartered with!'

'The decision's been made!' Tesckyn snapped. 'We've agreed the terms. I asked you all here merely as a courtesy.'

'To do what? To tell us we're all cannon fodder for your backroom deals?'

'No,' said Tesckyn. 'To give you an out.'

'So we'll be protected?' asked Marrahaim. 'I mean...as your operatives?'

Tesckyn could not look the man in the face. 'I'm afraid not. The method of removal will incorporate your genetic...uniqueness.'

Cassandra gasped, horrified. 'What the hell's gonna happen to us?'

'I'm...not entirely sure. Which is why I would suggest...an alternative.'

She realised what he meant and she sank back into her seat. 'You want us to kill ourselves,' she said quietly.

'I imagine it would be better than what these aliens have in store for those they take. Their technology is, in a word, unbelievable. We've no way of knowing what they want these people for.'

'But you want us to accept that the greater good is worth the price?'

Tesckyn felt sick to his stomach. 'I truly believe it is,' he said. 'We don't belong here. The Garran permitted the initial phases of the genetic experiments with the understanding that we'd be capable of leaving once the situation presented itself. Now, these...Kwaios assure us that their technology will allow everyone *except* the Church to make the journey home. They say that the genetic modifications did nothing more than isolate the Church from the rest of the population.'

'So, instead of the descendants of the experiments going home...the majority of people will be going?'

'That's exactly it. We can't afford to ignore this opportunity. The Garran Governors are fighting amongst themselves and it won't be long before they launch another invasion. They're getting tired of pandering to our requests for more time. Also, our counterparts on the Sieltor worlds are talking about assisting in a military coup that we believe is bound to failure. If it fails, they're bound to be discovered, and it's most likely that the Governors will want to wipe out the Church and any evidence that the

305

experiments ever happened and that they colluded with our leaders back when all this began.'

'You really believe this is our only option?' asked Marrahaim.

'I do. But we've got two years before the Kwaios come for the Church, and we'll continue to consider all our options before that happens. If we're left with no choice, then we'll give you the option: either risk being part of whatever the Kwaios have planned for the Church, or one of our assets will ensure that doesn't happen.'

'You're not even leaving us with the dignity of doing it ourselves?' Cassandra asked.

'And risk your security services putting the pieces together as you start dropping like flies?' Tesckyn shook his head. 'We'll send someone to do it quick and clean.'

Cassandra fell silent, and the rest of the meeting became nothing more than background noise as she dealt with what she had just heard. Taken by aliens or being shot in the head was not much of a choice. But Cassandra believed that another option would present itself. It was simply a matter of faith.

ARRIVAL

Two hundred heavily armed vessels comprised a fleet sent to the Kiranis system by Anev Tesckyn long before the cage appeared there. Maintaining position within the upper reaches of the atmosphere of the fourth planet of the system, the fleet had spent two weeks monitoring the activity of the Warships of the Jaevisk Society, whose crews were in turn monitoring the desolate fifth planet of the system. Of course, the Jaevisk were aware of the fleet from Earth, but they considered its presence unworthy of their attention. Had he been aware of this, there would have been no one more relieved than Commander Eli Chane of the flagship, *Grant*. Unfortunately, he was not, and so he projected his tension across the fleet in the form of constant combat readiness and simulations. There had been no word from his superiors and the absence of a timeline for his orders consigned Chane and the fleet to the murky world of the unexpected. To obtain some brief respite from that world, Chane had retreated to the arboretum, settling himself into comfort upon a folding seat he had brought with him. The greenery around him encouraged swift relaxation, caressing his soul with its serenity and its scent, which would waft intermittently as the climate system introduced fresh oxygen to the expansive enclosure. Chane closed his eyes for a short time, but was denied sleep by the approaching footsteps of another officer. 'I'm sorry to bother you, Commander.'

Opening his eyes and raising his head slowly, Chane's soul cried out from within as serenity fled from its grasp. 'There must be a good reason for you to come down here, Patrick.'

'Yes, Sir.' He looked around him. 'Although I should have done so before. I can see why you like it here.'

'Well, hopefully it won't be too long before I can visit a real rainforest again. And I mean a real one, not the synthetic kind they had to create back home after the move.'

'I've gotta say, Sir, I really admire your faith in this. I mean, I know Tesckyn's people are brilliant, but...'

'But what?'

'Well, this is the Kwaios Council we're talking about, Sir. We're not even supposed to know they exist, cos no one back home's seen them yet, that's for sure.'

Chane nodded. 'You think they won't come through for us?'

The officer shrugged. 'I dunno. I suppose it depends on what this cage thing can do. And the price is pretty high.'

'Yeah, I know. But the Church has been stirring things up lately. If something isn't done about them, we could be talking war. Who knows? Maybe the Kwaios will settle them somewhere they'll be happy.'

Patrick looked at him, knowing full well that he did not believe that. Chane nodded. 'Any movement from the Jaevisk today?'

'Nothing, Sir. Same as ever. They just watch.'

'Well, if what the Kwaios told Tesckyn is true, the Jaevisk are waiting for exactly the same thing as us. And when it gets here, we gotta be ready.'

'Holding back the Jaevisk isn't gonna be easy, Commander. I don't know why the Kwaios wanted us here at all.'

'Cos they'll be coming through at the outer planet, Patrick, and the only way we get to control the cage is by keeping the Jaevisk busy long enough for the Kwaios to get all their ships through. Then they get over here and back us up.'

'May I ask, Sir...what's the latest estimate on losses?'

Chane took a deep breath, loath to consider it. 'I've had a team going over the Jaevisk tactical reports the Kwaios gave us. As long as they're predictable, and as long as defence systems the Kwaios gave us hold up, we'll be looking at losing no more than half the fleet.'

'You make that sound like a good thing.' The words were out before the officer could stop himself and he shook his head. 'I'm sorry, Commander.'

Chane nodded, replying, 'Better than losing it all.' He rose and stretched, and had no sooner put one foot in front of the other than something powerful rocked the ship. Alarms sounded and the two men ran from the arboretum. It took them three minutes to reach the bridge, and the reports were coming in from across the fleet. A communications officer summarised for them: 'The cage is here. The Jaevisk are moving into higher orbits to avoid the gravitational pull. Apart from that, there's no other reaction from them.'

Chane took it in rapidly and ordered a com channel opened to the fleet. 'This is Commander Eli Chane,' he announced confidently. 'Prepare to break atmosphere and move to your assigned coordinates. This is what we've been training for. Remember what's at stake.'

As the fleet ascended into the darkness around the fourth planet, the crew of the *Grant* were just in time to witness on the VR magnifier the cage components rising from their positions around the fifth planet. There was such a tremendous burst of light from the cage that everyone had to look away. When it was safe to look back, they could see that the entire planet had been torn apart. The cage continued to retreat from the event, until they saw the disconnected pieces vanish into the darkness. 'It's gone to Earth,' Chane noted quietly, horrified by the chaotic remnants of the fifth planet of the Kiranis system.

Patrick nodded, equally transfixed. 'God help them,' he said.

Ω

Chane's people were not the only ones from Earth who had been occupying the space of the Kiranis system for some time. An enormous ship called *Dragon* had been hidden at the innermost moon of the third and largest planet of the system, and its crew were only made aware of events transpiring in the wake of the cage as sensor information was processed. They were, however, more concerned with waiting for a message from home which would direct their next move. The Captain of this ship, Seth Hand, had devoted his life to serving the will of the Church of the New Elect, and would do whatever it took to bring about the dreams of Patriarch Relland. He could feel the zealot's rush of anticipation as the reports concerning the cage were brought to him. 'This is it, Sir,' an officer told him, unable to keep an entirely unprofessional grin from his face. 'It's actually happening.'

Captain Hand found himself returning the grin as he took the nanosheet. 'Patriarch Relland was right,' he said. 'The Church's renewal won't go unnoticed.'

'It's about time we were noticed.'

'I can't say I disagree, Lieutenant. We've spent too long hiding behind the coat-tails of Central Command and operating behind the scenes.' He rose from his chair and the bridge crew turned to listen as he declared with fanatic zeal, 'We are the New Elect! And it's time to embrace the true destiny of our Church!'

THE SEVENTH DAY

Outside the buildings in which Harrogate had very recently set up shop, he stood and watched as the convoy pulled up. Three heavily armoured vehicles were followed by a veritable bulldog of urbanised warfare, with another three vehicles on its heels. Harrogate was flanked by four of his men, whose composures bristled with distrust. 'Wait here,' he told them, walking forward to greet his guest. The door of the massive vehicle in the centre was opened and a surprisingly wiry man stepped out. He was clean shaven and wearing a crisp navy blue suit, with a white shirt left unbuttoned at the neck. The man looked as if he was going to a dinner party. 'Mister Tesckyn?'

'Yes,' the man lied with ease, offering his hand. 'It's a pleasure to meet you, Mister Harrogate. I'm looking forward to working with you on our little problem.'

Harrogate ignored the understatement, and pointedly eyeballed the convoy. 'I thought you might have preferred to arrive by air.'

The man shook his head. 'Too conspicuous, I decided.'

'Of course. This is just everyday traffic, right?'

'Precisely.' The man grinned, and then gestured towards the doors. 'Shall we?'

'No.'

'I beg your pardon?' Guards on both teams were alerted by the change in tone, and hands moved towards weapons.

'I understood that I would speak with Tesckyn,' said Harrogate. 'Not one of his lackeys.'

The grin was most certainly absent as the man replied, 'I assure you, Mister Harrogate...'

'You assure me of absolutely nothing...whoever you are. Tesckyn wouldn't be so stupid as to step out of a car in broad daylight looking like he'd booked the VIP room at a nightclub.'

'And you would know this because...?

'Because I wouldn't if I were him.'

'Maybe I'm not as paranoid as you are.'

Harrogate stepped closer to the man and weapons were more overtly brandished. 'I have a feeling that Mister Tesckyn is considerably more paranoid than I am. He would have to be if he's managed to stay off my grid for so long.'

The man held Harrogate's steely gaze, but did not concede until there was a voice in his earpiece and he said, 'He's decided he's ready to see you.'

'Wonderful. Where is he?'

Turning around, the man got back into the car and his operatives followed suit. The window descended and the unidentified man eventually replied, 'He's in your office.'

Harrogate could not help but grin. 'A dangerous man.'

'Dangerous doesn't begin to describe him,' said the man, very seriously. 'You'd do well to remember that.' The convoy moved away. Turning back and joined by his guards, Harrogate returned to his new building. And his new office.

Ω

As he approached the office, Harrogate gestured for the two men who had accompanied him to wait outside. They nodded and turned their backs to the door as he opened it. A broad-shouldered man in his fifties rose from Harrogate's chair, reaching out with his suited arm to offer his hand. 'Mister Harrogate!' he beamed. 'A pleasure to finally meet you.'

Harrogate shook the man's hand and found himself sitting on the wrong side of his own desk before he knew what was happening. 'A pity we didn't have the chance to meet before all of this,' he noted dryly.

'On the contrary, Mister Harrogate,' Tesckyn replied. 'Had we met before all of this...' he smiled, 'all of this wouldn't be happening.'

'Am I supposed to take that as a compliment?'

Tesckyn shrugged. 'Let's just say that I acknowledge how...difficult you might have made things.'

Harrogate glared at the man. 'Look...one of your people came to me last night and cast a line. Now, I'll admit that I'm curious, but quite frankly, the bait is a little hard to swallow, if you know what I mean.'

Tesckyn laughed. 'Well, despite your terrible fishing analogy...the bait got you here, didn't it?'

Harrogate leaned back and looked around. 'Why this building? Why tell me to choose this office?'

'Sentimentality on my part, I have to admit.'

'Really? Nothing to do with the fact that this entire floor is encased in lead?'

311

'Well...that...*and* sentimentality. I used to work from this office.' He looked around. 'But that was a long time ago. Another age, it seems.'

'Just tell me what's going on, Tesckyn. I need to at least understand what it is I've no control over.'

Tesckyn nodded sympathetically. 'I can appreciate that,' he said. 'Okay, here we go.' He stood up and began to walk around the room while he spoke: 'Two hundred and thirty years ago, everything changed for Humanity. There was an anomalous gravitational shockwave rushing towards Earth and no one had any idea where it came from or what it would do. They also had no time to do anything. It hit the planet, but...nothing seemed to have happened. Until they realised that global communication systems were down. They'd grounded everything in the air, but satellites weren't responding. It wasn't long before they realised there weren't any satellites.'

'What happened to them?'

'This will take longer the more questions you ask,' Tesckyn replied, pausing in his incessant circling of the room, which was driving Harrogate crazy. He resumed both his talking and his walking. 'The satellites weren't there, but nothing had happened to them. They weren't gone. The planet was.' Tesckyn raised a hand to stop the inevitable uttering of disbelief. 'It was the astronomers who noticed it first, and they were careful to keep it quiet. Entire star systems and constellations had changed. None of them were familiar. Systems we had long deemed uninhabitable had planets we hadn't even seen before. To cut to the chase, Harrogate...there was life in places where our greatest minds had long said it was impossible. But they discovered that long before any observatories were fired up, cos the Garran were sitting on the doorstep, and they were as stunned as us about what had just happened. You see, the way they saw it was that one minute they're ready to sweep up what was left of us on Earth, and the next...' he threw his hands up, 'the universe pulled a rabbit out of its ass!'

'I prefer the hat trick myself.' Harrogate stood up and shook his head. 'What are you trying to tell me, Tesckyn? That for two hundred plus years, everyone on Earth's been lied to about our history? That we just...jumped from one place to another across space and time and...' He stopped, feeling like a fool. Tesckyn watched the penny drop, nodding and smiling. 'You've got it, John,' he congratulated him. 'Now reel it in.'

Harrogate felt somehow light-headed. 'But they would have noticed the cage, right? I mean, it just picked up the Earth and...what...*merged* it with the original one?'

Tesckyn shrugged. 'We think there was some kind of...swap.' He noted the expression of disbelief. 'Look, we don't know what happened, okay? But it's unlikely that the cage was used for the original event. It's just that...well, it's going to be used for the next one.'

'The *next*...' Harrogate felt a shiver run through him. 'What have you done?'

Tesckyn actually had the decency to appear shameful. 'On the surface, the experiments with the Garran began with a view to maintaining peace between our two races. Our governments were stupid enough to believe that the Garran would leave us alone if we helped them, when all they really wanted was to find a way to infiltrate us, seeing as their plan to wipe us out had been delayed by our sudden...reinforcement. When their infiltration plan was uncovered and it fell apart, the Human scientists who'd been part of the original experiments were...contracted to work on a new program here on Earth.'

'Let me guess...eugenics. Manipulated breeding.'

Tesckyn nodded. 'The powers that be decided that if we were to be stuck in a perpetual war with the Garran, then we would appropriate their physiology into a new breed of soldier. Unfortunately, things didn't go as planned. Let's just say that the files don't exactly make for bedtime reading. There were some benefits to the program, however, and so it was refined for medical application. And you know the rest of the story, considering what Doctor Greene figured out.'

'The members of the Church are the ultimate descendants of those experiments.'

'Yes. But the irony is that it was the Garran who contributed to their self-identity as the Church of the New Elect. They found out that the experiments had been altered and that Humans were going around wearing Garran DNA, and they didn't like that. So they took a whole bunch of people to Sieltor Prime, where...guess what...they found religion. Some new movement out there talking about a universal power called the Sentience, controlling everything that happened everywhere in the universe and pervading everyone's lives.'

'And they came back to spread the good word?'

313

'Precisely. Over time, every single person identified as a descendant of the experiments was located, and the Church of the New Elect was born.'

'You'll have to excuse me, Tesckyn, but I've noticed that the words "they" and "we" are interchangeable when you talk about the people behind all this.'

'Well, of course. I represent the powers that be...those who were in control back then and are still in control now.'

'So what you're saying is that...essentially...you created this mess?'

'Now you're up to speed!' Tesckyn slapped him on the back. 'So you see why we had to do this?'

'This?'

'Clean up our mess, Harrogate.' He finally returned to the chair, sitting back and looking up at the ceiling. 'We made the Church...and now we're getting rid of it.'

'And how exactly did you arrange this...purging?'

'We were approached by a race called the Kwaios. Two years ago. They promised us the use of the cage to get Earth back where it belongs. It's a dimensional shift device...' He raised his hands defensively. 'Don't ask me, I'm not the techie.'

Harrogate could not believe what he was hearing. 'And you promised them...?'

'The Church,' said Tesckyn as he nodded.

'What do these...*Kwaios*...want with them?'

'No idea.'

'Did you bother to ask?'

Tesckyn actually looked blank, and Harrogate was horrified. He slammed his palms down on the desk and leaned in, glaring down at the man. 'You arranged the mass abduction of millions of our people to...a race I've never *heard* of, and you didn't ask what they *wanted* with them?'

'Certain elements in the Church were stirring things up within Garran political circles. They had begun to fund their religious counterparts on the Sieltor worlds in their fundamentalist activities. When we heard a couple of years ago that a major coup was being planned against the Governors, we knew we had to disassociate ourselves from the Church.' Tesckyn laughed with heartfelt humour. 'You know, when the Kwaios came to us with their offer...I mean, it was like *Christmas*! Talk about two birds with one stone! We even managed to convince that nut-job Relland that what was coming was part of some great plan of their universal god, and he filtered this on down through the ranks as if some esoteric knowledge was being doled out. Believe me, when people are sucked in by this stuff, it's not hard to bring them into step.'

Harrogate felt sick now, disturbed by the callousness of this man and his willingness to exploit people of faith and hope. He straightened and held Tesckyn's glare. 'Who are the Kwaios?' he asked. 'What do you know about them?'

Tesckyn's smile fell. 'That they're not the sort of people you say "No" to, Harrogate. I'm warning you...don't interfere.'

'Do you really expect me to roll over for you?'

'I hope you do, because what's going on out at the Kiranis system has drawn everyone in. Now, I've got a fleet out there ready to defend the cage from the Jaevisk so that the Kwaios can keep their word and bring it back to us, but the Garran are also out there in force, and they've got their own things to sort out. It seems that Ben-Hadad didn't like what the Jaevisk served for dinner, and Overseer Carak appears to be working for the Kwaios.'

'How do you know that?'

'Because they told me. The Church sent a ship out there weeks ago and, courtesy of a little message to Relland from Carak, the Kwaios have set a trap for it. Trust me, Harrogate, these people want the Church members so badly...'

'Makes you wonder why they didn't just come here and take them,' Harrogate interrupted. Tesckyn did not reply, clearly uncomfortable with the implications, and Harrogate pressed on. 'I can't let you do this. I can't just stand by and allow millions of people to be taken like that. God knows what they're going to put them through.'

Tesckyn gave a dark laugh, pushing back the chair as he stood. 'God?' he mocked, moving around the desk. '*God?* You haven't been *listening*, Harrogate!' He came right up to him, his pockmarked face further creased with venomous humour. 'We're in another *universe* here! And God can't hear us!' He slammed the door behind him as he left, but Harrogate followed, shouting at his back, 'What about the rest of us?'

Tesckyn stopped and turned, glancing at Harrogate's men, who remained silent and still, for all intents and purposes ignorant of what was being said. 'What are you talking about?'

315

'If the Church members needed those Jaevisk implants to survive the journey in the cage, aren't we going to need them for this magical trip you're planning?'

'We're not going in the cage, you idiot!' Tesckyn sneered. 'The whole planet's going back.'

Harrogate laughed and addressed his two guards. 'You hear that, lads?' he mocked. 'Earth's going to disappear from this universe and end up in another one!'

They grinned somewhat tentatively, but any potential levity was cut short by Tesckyn's response: 'It disappeared yesterday, Harrogate...or have you forgotten? Why don't you ask Matthews what he saw up there?' He turned back and left, leaving the three men in an uncomfortable silence. But Harrogate was far from done. He pulled an old cell-phone out of his pocket, the likes of which people on Earth might collect as ornaments; if they had ever seen one so old. The beauty of this device was that Harrogate could patch a call through a network of cell towers kept operative by only his most trusted people. He hit speed-dial 1 and waited as the phone rang. '*This network is no longer available,*' a monotone voice told him. Still, he spoke into the phone, saying, 'The grass is green.'

'*The sky is blue,*' came the reply, in the same monotone computer voice.

'Yeah, well...lately it's been sort of grey. I want the evac cancelled immediately and our people brought home! Pull back everyone with so much as a slingshot and have them meet me at Matthews' station. And get me the fastest, most dangerous son of a bitch ship we've got!'

There was a short silence until a man with a much more Human voice on the other end asked, '*Where are we going?*'

'The Kiranis system,' said Harrogate. 'There's a whole lot of people out there who need our help!'

Ω

Cassandra was one of those people. As she came round, she had no recollection of what had occurred in the past few hours, and she found herself stuck between two dead Jaevisk inside a shuttle laying twisted and broken like some rotting beast. Only three of the thirty Jaevisk were alive, and they struggled to free themselves from their safety restraints in an area which reminded Cassandra of the interior of a military drop-ship. She watched them, remaining silent even as she felt the pain coursing through

316

her body. The two Jaevisk had slammed into her as the shuttle crashed, their heavy bodies enveloping and crushing her in a deadly embrace of ironic salvation as they were tossed around the shuttle. Listening to the hiss and click of the Jaevisk language as the three survivors assisted each other, Cassandra managed to push one of the bodies aside so that she could free herself from them. Gradually, the translation of their language came to her via her strange implant: *We must get to the processing floor. The Warlord will be there.*

What about the Human?

One of them sniffed the air, and Cassandra froze behind the other body. *She is either dead or has escaped. There is nothing we can do now.* They made their way to an airlock and Cassandra stole a glance to see them leave. Still, she kept her movements slow and staggered, in case there were others alive. There was room to stand, but she chose to keep low and out of sight, crawling to a second airlock. Standing on top of a dead Jaevisk, she reached for the emergency handle and opened the door. With no power on the shuttle, electronic panels were useless. As she climbed up into the airlock passage, she heard the clicking sound of a Jaevisk from behind her. Too panicked to close the inner door, she reached for the outer one and turned the handle. The door was pulled from its hinges by the change in pressure and it leaped out into the dark air. A risen Jaevisk grabbed her ankle weakly and she kicked back to free herself. Emerging from the broken shuttle, she took little time to consider her surroundings as the other three Jaevisk came around the shuttle from her right.

There were caves in sight, and she ran across the blackened, stony ground towards them. The Jaevisk were behind her and the unknown lay before her. High above her, a battle was raging, and explosions and weapons' fire filled the night sky. As the cave mouth beckoned and the Jaevisk behind her mysteriously gave up their pursuit, Cassandra realised to her horror that she did not even know what planet she was on.

Ω

Inside the mouth of another cave on that same planet, Adam was trying to get the tracking system working while Anya looked around and Carak rested himself against the dark stone wall. He sat back with his eyes closed, trying to assimilate everything that had happened. Here he sat with two Humans without whom he would have been killed by the Jaevisk clean-up crew who turned up within minutes of his ship crashing to the surface of this desolate planet. And there was no way for him to contact his Kwaios allies, because the communication device had been left behind on the Star Cruiser. Of course, the way things were going, Carak had difficulty in defining the Kwaios as allies. Their assistance had been notably absent as the Jaevisk attacked him, and it had been the Kwaios who sent him into the Jaevisk camp in the first place. Then again, he thought, it had all happened so fast that the Kwaios may simply have had no time to intervene. For some reason, that thought eased his encroaching despair, and he pushed himself to his feet. 'We need to find the Kwaios,' he declared.

Anya was far out of earshot, as her exploration of the cave took her deeper into the beginning of a subterranean network. Adam turned to Carak. 'Who the hell are the Kwaios?'

The huge Garran stalked towards Adam, who held his ground more out of stubbornness than courage. 'They're the people I was working for,' Carak explained. 'They're behind all of this. The cage at Earth, whatever happened to the fifth planet out here...' he gestured expansively within the cave. 'And whatever's going on in this place.'

'You may not have noticed,' Adam argued, his concentration returned to the handheld tracking device, 'but it's the Jaevisk who are all over this place. I have it on good authority that whatever went on at Earth with the cage drew us all into some major Jaevisk offensive.'

'Then this...good authority of yours is an idiot!' Carak snapped.

Adam grinned, still not looking up. 'I'm beginning to think they're all idiots where he comes from.'

'And where would that be?'

'More like when. He said he came from the future and that he was looking for a Garran called the World Killer, who also came from the future! So you'll forgive me if I'm reluctant to believe everything I hear these days.'

Carak was stunned. 'A Garran? Did he tell you his name?'

'The *Garran's* name? No.' Adam finally looked up from the device, noticing the concern in Carak's voice. 'What's going on?'

Carak stepped back and thought for a moment. 'A man called Malik Ki Jen was...assigned to my crew, but there was something strange about him. He knew things...more than he should have. But it was also like he was waiting for something to happen. He ended up destroying a

318

Jaevisk Warship single-handedly and apparently escaped the blast. It was like he could...'

'See the future?' Adam offered.

Carak nodded. 'One on your ship...one on mine. That has to be more than coincidence.'

'Like they both knew they had to end up here?'

'Or they wanted us to end up here!'

'Why?'

'I have no idea.' Carak looked at the tracking device. 'What's that?'

'My crew are tagged.' He pointed to the edge of the cave, where a small metal sphere was flashing intermittently. 'I set up that beacon to guide them here, but I'm trying to get this tracker working so I can be sure I've got them all.'

'Leave no one behind?'

'Something like that.' Adam looked out of the cave where they could still see the glow from the burning Star Cruiser in the distance. 'I'm sorry about your crew.'

Carak nodded. 'Let me take a look at that.' Adam gave him the tracker and he examined it for a moment. Then, with one strong slap on its side, the tracker was activated. He grinned and handed it back to Adam, who said, 'Old Garran trick, I imagine.'

'Ancient knowledge,' the Overseer agreed. 'You Humans wouldn't understand.' Anya could be heard returning from her impromptu reconnaissance. When she was close enough, she saw the two men scrutinizing the monitor on the tracker. 'What's happening?' she asked.

'Pretty much everyone who landed is closing in on our position,' Adam explained, 'but there's a signal coming from somewhere else. Underground, by the looks of it.'

'Well, who could that be?'

'No idea. But we should find out.'

Anya nodded and watched Carak agreeing with Adam. 'Well, looks like you boys are getting on. What were you talking about?'

Adam smiled. 'Well, he was talking about finding some race called the Kwaios. Personally, I think he's nuts.' He looked back at Carak. 'Probably banged his head in the crash.'

Anya shook her head. 'He's not nuts, Adam.'

Carak approached her. 'You found them?'

319

'I found something,' she said. 'And it's definitely not Jaevisk. These guys stand head and shoulders above the Jaevisk.'

'That's them.' Carak headed back the way she had come, unconsciously checking that his gun was still strapped to his hip. 'Let's go.'

Adam and Anya exchanged glances of renewed fear. With a deep breath, Adam steeled himself and offered his hand, saying, 'I've a bad feeling about this.' Anya took his hand and smiled nervously. 'Come on,' she said. 'Things can't get much worse.'

Ω

Jakari San Setta had decided that when he got home he would become a fan of monotony. Not for him the inexplicable jump across the galaxy from one point in space to another; nor the suicidal flight into the molten interior of a forming planet; nor the obligation of finding an idiot Human boy who had ended up on that same planet, where it seemed that monsters of childish imagination lay in wait for wandering Garran Fleet Commanders. No, not at all. The return to monotony would be akin to the immersion of one's soul into a bath of fragrant asylum. And there would be a book to read, of course. Jakari could sit back and read about some other poor soul embarking upon treacherous adventures, instead of actually risking his own life.

The planet had begun to quieten down, geologically speaking. In fact, its settlement had occurred as if a magician had enchanted the world with a spell of calm. Jakari found himself wishing that his mother could be here to see this, for she would be truly enthralled. Of course, he was sure that his mother currently had her hands full with her own problems. The landscape here certainly would have fascinated her. In the greatest distance from where Jakari stood and becoming more obscured by forming clouds, a towering peak was white with snow and ice. This was the mountain to which he was destined. From there back to here, that snow gradually broke in intermittent areas across fissures and depressions and rolling hills and valleys until it relinquished its grip on the land upon which Jakari now stood; a stony, dusty and dry place spotted with courageous greenery in its earliest throes of life. Jakari felt the dryness of his throat keenly as he looked upon the vegetation, for he was certain it would not survive long in this place. Both he and the plant life could sense the moisture in the cold air far ahead, but Jakari was not looking forward to experiencing that air. Garran did not do cold air.

As the cage turned in synchronicity with the planet and the sun illuminated the land, Jakari was bathed in heat and light. But he also saw the flash from up ahead. The sun had bounced off something reflective, and he hurried on to see what it was. It was not long before he found one of the pods which had launched from the cage. It was fully intact, which was enough of a miracle, but it was embedded half way into the ground and standing slightly to one side. He guessed that it must have struck the ground at the moment of cooling and solidification, thus ensuring that one end had been trapped in the surface. Drawing out his knife, Jakari tried to pry open the seal which had closed across the opening of the cylindrical pod, and suddenly there was banging and shouting from within. 'Help me!' a woman shouted. 'Please!'

'I'm trying,' he shouted back in her language. 'I can't open it!'

'Shoot it! I'm running out of air!'

Jakari agreed that that was probably the only way, and he stepped back and drew his gun, aiming for what he hoped was the position of a locking mechanism about halfway down the door. He fired. Nothing happened, and dust filled the air. He fired again. And again. Some damage had been done along the seal, and he fired twice more. The seal gave way, and the door flew off into the air. There was a second glass panel across the pod, but it had been broken from within, and the woman reached out with bloodied hands, crying with relief as Jakari rushed over to haul her out. 'Oh, thank you,' she sobbed as she collapsed into his arms, completely unfazed by the fact that he was Garran. 'I thought I was going to die in there.'

'You're safe now,' he told her. 'What ship are you from?'

She pushed back from him and looked up at his face. 'Don't you know what's going on here?'

He shook his head. 'I wish I did.'

Pointing up, she said with tears in her eyes, 'I was taken from Earth in that cage. Everyone I know is gone, or down here somewhere.'

Jakari looked up, and was horrified by the thought as he regarded the shadows cast by the massive structure around the planet. 'What's your name?' she asked him. 'Jakari,' he replied as he turned back to her.

She nodded and offered her hand. 'I'm Jennifer,' she said. 'And I would really like to go home now.'

Jakari grinned ruefully. 'Then I'm probably not the best person for you to be with.'

'Why not?'

He pointed to the distant snow-covered peak. 'Because I'm going there.'

Ω

Governor Ben-Hadad of Sieltor Prime had no idea where he was going and was unaccustomed to such helplessness. He was the sole occupant of an escape pod measuring only eight metres in length and speeding through the emptiness of the Kiranis system. The pod was filled with supplies and facilities to keep him alive and healthy for no more than twenty days, give or take a few days of self-inflicted rationing, and there was no way that the pod would make it home before those supplies ran out. Ben-Hadad had a large appetite, always had, and the thoughts of starving to death in a metal tomb was less than appealing. Reaching out with his left hand, he tapped a button on a console, praying that he was not close enough to a star that he would blind himself as the view panel opened. He squinted his eyes shut, holding his breath apprehensively. Feeling no pain on his lids and sensing no light through the unveiled window, he let out a long breath as he opened his eyes again. He was met by darkness at first, but he swiftly realised that it was not the void-black darkness of space. Reaching out with both hands now, he used manoeuvring thrust to move his pod back from what he gradually recognised as the hull of a Garran battleship. 'Praise the gods!' he gasped.

He made contact with the vessel. 'This is Governor Ben-Hadad. Identify yourself.'

'This is the *Takada*, Governor. We will bring you aboard.'

Ben-Hadad laughed with relief and self-satisfaction. Of course they had come looking for him. His people would not leave him alone to die out in this terrible place. Guiding lines were fired from the battleship and they latched to the pod, drawing it into a recovery bay. When the pod was righted and set down upon the floor, Ben-Hadad rushed to the airlock and hurried out. Soldiers were there to assist him, and the Commander of the vessel welcomed him. 'We're relieved to see you alive, Governor,' said the man. 'I have relinquished my quarters for your journey home.'

'I would expect no less, Commander,' said Ben-Hadad, reaching the floor and steadying himself. His head swam from the change in pressure, but he took a deep breath and blinked as he looked around. 'I

322

don't recognise the configuration of your ship, Commander. I've never heard of a ship called the *Takada*.'

'This is a recently commissioned vessel, Governor,' the Commander assured him. 'You'll be more comfortable once you get to your quarters. I'll have some refreshments brought to you and you can rest in peace.'

The Governor hesitated. Had the man actually used that Human funereal expression? He dismissed it, seeing no deception in the Commander's respectful demeanour. 'Please, Governor,' he said, gesturing towards the open corridor, 'follow me. I'm sure you'd like to get back on top of things.'

Ben-Hadad realised that that was exactly what he needed to do. Out there in that pod, he had been mercilessly cut off from the progression of events in the system. 'I most certainly would,' he replied, heading to the corridor. 'I trust I will have complete privacy in your quarters.'

'Absolutely, Governor,' the Commander lied.

Ω

Cassandra was shivering uncontrollably as she walked through the dark tunnels, mesmerised by how high above her were the ceilings, and how smooth was the stone around her. Her teeth were chattering and her muscles were tense, and she recognised the symptoms of panic setting in. Stopping for a moment, she struggled to settle her breathing, leaning her hand against the wall. As soon as she did, she saw in her mind terrible flashing scenes of horrific butchery and surgery. But this was surgery on some alien creatures, and she was reminded of childhood pictures of dragons and monsters. She felt the pain and terror of these monsters, however, a terror expressed in Human terms, and tears filled her eyes. Knowing where this nightmare was occurring, she ran on, channelling her overwhelming adrenaline, noticing for the first time that there was a light in the distance. As she finally came upon the source of the light, she hesitated, wondering if she truly wished to see the reality beyond. Then, steeling herself, she walked on.

Ω

Carak slowed down as the cave became darker, and Anya and Adam were able to catch up with him. 'Are we close?' asked the Garran.

323

Anya nodded, pointing to a soft blue glow at the edge of the next turn. 'Just up there.' The light was coming from an arc of energy emanating from some kind of portal guard or limit marker. The strip of blue light connecting the cave floor on either side reached up in a high arch designed to facilitate the passage of someone or something up to five metres in height. Carak stopped them from getting any closer. 'Once we pass this,' he told them, 'we're in Kwaios land, and all I can tell you is that these people don't take kindly to intruders.'

'So remind me again why we're doing this?' Adam asked. 'My people are closing in on the beacon back at the cave, and for all we know...' he looked at Anya, 'the other signal could be just a glitch in the readings.'

'Well, apart from this being our best chance of getting off this rock,' said Carak, 'I'm hoping my dealings with them will keep us alive.'

'Unless they're finished with you.'

'That's definitely a possibility,' Carak agreed. 'But we've no choice. The Jaevisk will probably figure out pretty soon that I'm not dead, and they'll come looking for me.'

Anya chuckled. 'You're not exactly popular in these parts, are you?'

Carak smiled and shrugged. 'I like to make a lasting impression on people.' Without another word, he passed through the glowing blue portal into the tunnel beyond. He was immediately scanned by systems embedded in the cave wall, and a hologram of his Garran Military Service record was displayed. 'Well, at least they'll be expecting me,' he quipped.

Anya glanced at the alien text on the wall on her side of the door. A complex integration of what in Human terms would be called hieroglyphics and cuneiform, the Kwaios writing was similar to Jaevisk, but with subtle distinctions. Anya took Adam's hand again and they walked through together. Both were scanned, and their information from home was displayed in the same way. 'How do they have this information?'

'The Kwaios know everything,' said Carak, moving on. The journey brought them deeper underground, and the tunnel network opened up before them. They stuck to the main thoroughfare for a while, but strange noises brought them to a halt at a junction. Coming from their right and echoing eerily along the stone tunnel were sounds of bestial roaring and pathetic, horrific whining. Carak made to go that way, but Anya grabbed him, whispering harshly, 'You can't be serious!'

'I need to know what's happening here,' he replied, shaking her free and walking away. They were compelled to follow him, and they eventually saw a welcoming source of light coming from around a bend farther along the tunnel, although it was being blocked out intermittently. Combined with the cacophony of blood-curdling roars and howls as of animals in anguish, the light was not as welcoming as it should have been, and the shadows appeared to be cast by huge passing forms. Carak stopped: 'Okay, I need you two to wait here.' They nodded as he drew his gun and stepped forward, realising as if for the first time that he had never seen one of these aliens in the flesh before. He rounded the corner, and Anya held Adam's hand tight. Both of them shouted out in terror as Carak was flung back against the stone wall at the corner. He collapsed and passed out. Anya ran to him as Adam shouted, 'No!' but it was too late. The Kwaios came into view.

Both Anya and Adam fell back as if they had run into glass, scrambling back with their hands on the ground as the massive alien approached them. Encased in an anatomical suit of shining metal, black leather and blue light, a Kwaios nearly four metres in height looked down on these Humans. Its elongated face was like some genetically altered alligator, but its skin – as much as could be seen – was made more blue than it really was by the technology around it, and there was an almost shimmering effect as its limbs moved and its torso expanded and retracted with each deep, powerful breath. It extended an arm and Adam was rooted to the spot as a second Kwaios stepped into view. Slightly shorter than the first, this one approached Anya, who lay wide-eyed and terrified as it reached down towards her. With its massive palm spread out, a blue glow emanated from it and bathed her abdomen as her heart pounded and her breath came in short gulps of panic. A third Kwaios joined its kin, and now only pinpoints of light escaped from the exit beyond them. With her terror absolute, Anya heard a calming voice in her head: *'Be at ease, Human. Your child is safe. You will return home soon.'*

As Anya cried with relief and Carak started to come around, there was the sound of something approaching from the way they had come. A Jaevisk came into view and opened fire on the Kwaios standing over Anya. It was knocked back by the force of the impact, and Anya screamed as the other Kwaios stepped over her and Adam to engage their intruders. An alarm sounded and, as they helped Carak to his feet, more Kwaios rushed past them to join the fight. 'Now what?' Adam shouted over the gunfire.

Carak groaned, one hand holding his head and the other pointing towards the source of the light and the chilling howls and roars. 'We find the way out,' he said.

Ω

Jakari and Jennifer were both shivering as they ascended a hill; Jennifer, because she still had the same clothes she had on when taken from her home by the cage – a light, long sleeved, white cotton top and her navy uniform trousers; and Jakari, because he was Garran and their worlds were not as cold as this. Still, his mother had raised him well and he removed his jacket and put it around Jennifer's shoulders. She smiled with frozen gratitude and put the jacket on properly, savouring the warmth of the Garran's body heat. 'So how do you know this Cana person is up here?' she asked.

'You wouldn't believe me if I told you.'

'Oh, I dunno about that. Right now, I could believe...' There was a sudden roar from behind them, and they spun round to see three huge winged beasts in the air, two of them with blue-black skin and one green and brown, speeding towards them. But these beasts were not hunting. A different roar preceded the appearance over the horizon of five vessels travelling at immense speed. Both the beasts and these pursuing vessels were flying dangerously low, and Jakari pulled Jennifer to the ground as he rolled onto his back, recognising the racing ships. 'They're Jaevisk shuttles!' he shouted as the sound of engines rushed over them. They got back to their feet in time to see the shuttles opening fire, projectiles tearing through the wings and bodies of the flying reptiles. Jakari and Jennifer could hear their cries of agony, cries which were answered from the east as Jennifer shouted, 'They're *dragons*!'

Two massive red-skinned creatures dropped from the sky above the shuttles, slowing down in mid-air as their four limbs were held out before them and their great wings played with the wind. The shuttles did not hesitate to meet this resistance, opening fire on these red beasts, which responded by spewing flames across the bow of the ships and reaching out to tear at them with their claws. The shuttles were almost the same size as these giants, but they seemed no match for the ferocity of the attack. With their massive tails smashing vital operational areas of the ships and their teeth and claws ripping at the metal hulls, the doom of the Jaevisk on board was sealed. Even still, Jaevisk soldiers could be seen

326

standing amidst gaping holes, firing repeatedly at the beasts with massive projectile weapons.

Three shuttles went down, but Jakari could see terrible holes in the animals' bodies. Blood poured from their wounds, and they glanced at the two fleeing animals, heading for the enormous mountain in the north. The hesitation of these bestial saviours cost them their lives, for the remaining two shuttles tore them to pieces with lasers and missiles, descending to the ground with them as they fell. Even from such a distance as they were, the impact of their ruined bodies shook the hill upon which Jakari and Jennifer stood in awe. Jennifer let out a cry of shock and horror, while Jakari found that there were tears in his eyes. Once again he looked to the distant mountain. And for some reason, it felt a lot closer than before.

Ω

Ben-Hadad reclined on a large couch in his newly acquired quarters, sipping a tall glass of Jersane and enjoying the heat of the drink coursing through his body. His calloused hand savoured the warmth from the glass, and he felt momentarily at peace. But there was no time for peace. Jakari San Setta was dead, as was Carak Tae Ahn and the Governors of the other worlds who had accompanied him on what seemed to have been a fool's errand. It had been reported to him that his entire armada was now engaged in a furious battle against both their will and an enemy greater than the Jaevisk Society. Of course, it was now obvious that the Jaevisk had anticipated this great enemy, and had used the Garran military as a frontline assault force, keeping these...Kwaios people occupied while they concentrated on whatever they were doing on the fifth and sixth planets. It was all too much for Ben-Hadad, he realised. All he cared about now was returning home and taking control of whatever was left for him. With that and his more domestic enemies in mind, he turned to one side to activate a console. 'Interface with my palace in Khas City,' he commanded the computer. The connection was made. He trusted nobody now, and he had to be sure that his bargaining chip was still in play. 'Display location of item number one-zero-one.'

The schematics of the massive palace complex were displayed on the screen and floor after floor was penetrated and bypassed as the computer located the room, deep underground, in which the item in question was being kept. Upon confirming its presence, Ben-Hadad smiled. 'Good to see you haven't gone anywhere, child,' he said quietly. 'I'm going to need you even more now.'

On the bridge of the battleship, the Commander turned to someone standing in the shadows and reported, 'We have it, Lady Setta.'
Eyla stepped into the light and smiled. 'Good.' She tapped a com device and waited for the response before explaining, 'I'm sending you the location now.' She nodded. 'Just get her back safely. And be careful, Senneya.'

Ω

Cassandra stood as if in shock, unwilling to accept what she could clearly see below her and around her as she stepped out onto a balcony running for many hundreds of metres in either direction. Giant winged creatures, a mere impression of which she had been offered in her vision in the tunnels, were tied down and held captive, and there were Jaevisk everywhere around them. Of many different colours were the beasts, their cries of pain stifled by muzzles and bonds. In the centre of the enormous chamber, its four great limbs chained and surrounded by hundreds of Jaevisk soldiers, a blood-red creature the likes of which Cassandra could only ever have imagined struggled to break free. Its massive tail was pinned to the floor, its head was covered with metal and leather and its jaws were clamped shut. Its wings were spread out by winches on hooks in the stone ceiling. It dwarfed every other creature in the room, and Cassandra felt both fear and sorrow as she witnessed its plight.
She could hear Jaevisk voices in her head, amplified by her implant. Down in the dizzying depths of this place, they worked furiously and efficiently around the scores of creatures, aware of some sort of deadline. She could not understand how she knew, but she could almost sense from many of the Jaevisk below that what they were doing was an atrocity, and that some kind of law was being broken. Looking down to her right, she could see even more of these creatures being dragged into the chamber, struggling against their bonds and their captors. These magnificent beasts were nothing but prey to Jaevisk hunters. From her left, someone approached, and she turned to see a blue-robed Jaevisk, tall and muscular. 'Who are you?' she demanded. 'And what's happening here? What are you doing to them?'

'I am Warlord Krell,' the newcomer replied. 'And this is the Harvest.'

Cassandra was horrified. 'I don't understand any of this. What has this got to do with the cage...and the Kwaios...and the Church? And why would you bring me out here?'

Krell came closer. 'Without the cage and the people it took from Earth...' he gestured towards the beasts below, 'there would be no Harvest. That is all the Kwaios wanted. The people of your Church...like you...were ready to evolve into something greater. And the device you brought us facilitated that evolution.'

'*Evolution*? This is *mutation*!'

'Our gods may take many forms. This form was determined by one of your people.'

'Your...*gods*?'

'The Kwaios and the Jaevisk ultimately share the same history, and the same gods. They have lain dormant on the planet Kiranis for millennia, awaiting resurrection.'

Cassandra could not take it all in. 'You still haven't explained what you want with me,' she declared, as she looked down again. She felt the Jaevisk tapping on the back of her head as he replied, 'This is the original device, remaining in a state of temporal flux since it was taken from the man in the cage. I will take you to the planet Kiranis and you will use it there.'

'For what?'

'To confront the Prophet. And to remind him that our gods are not his to toy with.'

Ω

But it was not the way out. In fact, when Adam reached what they had hoped might be an exit, he was stopped in his tracks by the scene before him, terribly sure that they were heading even deeper into the Kwaios facility. As Anya and Carak joined him in his emergence from the short passageway, they came out onto a balcony of sorts, a walkway leading to left and right. It led away into the distance on either side, and they saw countless exits from it to other such suspended paths which connected across the gigantic subterranean chamber, either supported by massive stone pillars from beneath or hanging by strong metal cables from above. But all this was secondary information. All this was no more than a viewing

329

area compared to what it was that one could see below. They gathered together at the edge of the balcony, gripping the railing with white knuckles as they looked down in horror.

Hundreds of glass containers, many stacked atop each other, filled the floor. Inside each was a hideous beast, grey and vicious and angry. At first glance, they looked to Adam like overgrown and mutated rhino, but these were not creatures from Earth. On their flanks were small, calcified and useless wings of transparent tissue. Instead of one or two horns atop their heads like rhino, these creatures had two sets of massive horns protruding from the sides of their heads. One set curved upwards, the other down.

The bellows and roars of these monsters could not be drowned out by the alarm announcing the intrusion of the Jaevisk, and they butted their heads and tried flapping their flightless wings to no avail in their glass prisons. Many of them scraped their prodigious horns against the glass, causing no more damage than a pebble might cause to a window, but creating an ear-splitting noise that irritated the Kwaios as much as the Human watchers. The Kwaios punished the creatures by activating an energy field which made its way upwards through the container. Still, this did not deter these maddened beasts, for they knew that a more terrible fate awaited them.

Adam turned to Anya, seeing that she was still transfixed by the scene. 'Are these...*dragons*?' he asked her. She took a moment to respond, shaking her head. 'It's not possible,' she replied, despite what she was seeing.

'What are dragons?' asked Carak. He was more concerned with the fact that they had been spotted by the Kwaios, and that four of them had been dispatched to intercept the intruders, heading towards a makeshift elevator on the far side of the chamber.

'Well, they're supposed to be mythical creatures, but...' Adam chuckled with the madness of it all. 'Here they are!'

Carak grabbed them both and dragged them away from the passageway behind them just as the Jaevisk came in. Immediately, the Kwaios ascending the distant elevator opened fire, and the Jaevisk were forced to respond rather than chase Carak. As he and the others ran along the high walkway, Anya stole a glance back to see more Jaevisk pushing in. Some of them broke off from the main group to follow her and the two men. 'They're coming for us!'

'*Everyone's* coming for us!' shouted Adam. 'Keep moving!'

They ran as fast as they could, keeping low as shots from Jaevisk weapons struck the bars on their left, the stone on their right, and whizzed by over their heads. As more Kwaios arrived up onto the walkway in their path, Carak found another exit to their right and the three of them got out of the way just as the two alien groups opened fire on each other. With the sound of the gunfight echoing behind them, they went down a slightly descending tunnel into a deep and ominous silence. When they finally reached the end of it, sure that there was no one on their heels, they exited to their left and emerged into another chamber which was occupied by only a small number of Kwaios. Although this chamber was smaller than the last, it was still large enough to house thousands of small containers, only a fraction of the size of those they had previously seen. Inside each of these containers, suspended and swinging from a metal hook, were transparent bags of membranous skin, like some cocoon of transformation. And inside them…

'They're breeding them!' Anya gasped.

'No,' said Carak. 'Look.' He pointed to a distant section of the floor, where they could see a number of Kwaios working at tall, cylindrical containers from which vapour wisped lazily into the already cold air.

'They're cloning them,' Adam realised. 'And accelerating their growth.'

'Why?' asked Anya. 'What possible reason could they have for creating so many of these monsters?'

Carak recalled the readings Tanna had brought to him, the chill of the Kwaios communication device, the strange and freezing engine core of the Star Cruiser, and the seemingly benevolent gift of the Jaevisk to Governor Ben-Hadad. The chill he now felt had nothing to do with the temperature in this place. 'I think I know,' he told them, seeing an exit on the opposite side of the room. 'Stay down and follow me.'

Ω

The ground was now snow-covered and becoming treacherous to traverse, and Jakari had to catch Jennifer a few times to keep her from falling. A fleet of Jaevisk shuttles raced by above them, some of them breaking off to head for the clouds, where Jakari saw some dark shadows moving. Weapons were fired and cries of anguish and anger echoed across the barren land as more of the dragons were attacked. A brightly coloured dragon escaped the melee and headed towards the two travellers as if they were part of the threat. They dropped to their faces, hearing a cry from the animal and the roar of engines from beyond it. Jakari risked a glance and watched as the weapons of the ship tore chunks of flesh and bone from the creature's wings and blew a hole in its throat. Only its momentum kept it heading towards Jakari and Jennifer, and it barely missed them as it slammed into the ground behind them and bounced and rolled across the hostile land, sharp stone ripping and tearing at its body.

The shuttle caught up quickly and Jakari and Jennifer stood up and turned around to see it hovering over the dying animal, even as the beast still snapped its great jaws in futile defiance. A different weapon was fired then, and the animal lay suddenly still. As the shuttle landed, great nets were thrown out and the dragon was gathered up and dragged back into the shuttle. As it lifted off again and headed away into the distance, shadows fell across the pair and they looked up to see scores of larger Jaevisk vessels descending through the clouds. These ones, however, were not here to hunt. With strange devices attached to the underside of their hulls, their purpose here was entirely different. Jakari immediately recognised the devices they carried, gasping as he shuddered with the implications. The huge vessels headed for the frozen mountain, and Jakari was ever more appreciative of the scale of this astonishing deception and the game into which Naveen had placed him. 'What is it?' asked Jennifer, as the expression on his face drained the warmth from her bones. 'What are those things?'

'I don't know,' Jakari replied. 'But I brought them here.'

Ω

Ben-Hadad could feel the welcoming embrace of sleep when a knock on his door snapped him back to reality. He groaned first, and then snapped angrily, 'Who is it?'

'*I have urgent news, Governor,*' the voice outside his door announced.

He sighed and slowly got to his feet. Urgency or not, nothing got Ben-Hadad out of bed at any rate faster than a crawl. He gathered his voluminous gown around him before opening the door. The young man outside burst in past him, looking around furtively. 'How dare you!' Ben-Hadad roared. 'I'll have you whipped and – '

'This isn't one of your ships!' the man snapped in a desperate whisper.

Ben-Hadad blinked. 'What? What do you mean?'

'Eyla San Setta is on board. She's colluding with the Commander!'

The Governor felt sick, realising he had been duped. 'To what end? Why keep me alive?'

'I heard them say something about a girl you took. Is it true?'

Ben-Hadad backhanded the man across the face. 'You do not question me, boy!' he shouted. 'Now tell me what happened!'

The young man straightened himself, noting with a certain triumph that he looked down on the fat Governor. 'They were waiting for you to check something. I think it's the only reason they rescued you. I heard them mentioning Overseer Carak…and his wife.'

He had been tricked and he felt like a fool. So they had monitored his computer access. Of course they had. It was all so simple that he cursed himself for being so naïve. Still, they could not have been successful already. Too little time had passed since he pulled up the schematics. Rushing to the computer faster than he had rushed out of bed, he commanded it to once again interface with the palace, and said, 'Get me palace security.'

After a short delay, a man said, '*Yes, Governor?*'

'Get down and get the girl. I want her moved to the secondary location as discussed.'

'*Of course, Governor.*'

He drew in a deep breath and turned to the young man, but any words they may have shared were cut off as two soldiers burst in and shot the unknown informant. He collapsed to the floor at Ben-Hadad's feet as Eyla San Setta walked in. 'It's so difficult these days to know who you can trust,' she said smugly.

Ben-Hadad scowled at her. 'You're too late. There's no way you can mobilise your people again before she's gone.' He held her angry glare and continued. 'Oh yes, I heard about your last desperate attempt. I think it's about time you accepted – ' He was cut off as a voice from the open com channel reported, '*The girl is gone, Governor!*'

Both Eyla and Ben-Hadad shouted, 'What?'

'*Someone was already here. Hours ago. The tracking chip was removed from the girl.*'

Ben-Hadad stepped up to the computer as if it was to blame. 'What do you mean…*someone*?' he snapped.

'*Just one man, Governor. He killed eleven of my men and wounded three. One of them claims to have recognised him, but...I'm reluctant to believe him.*'

Eyla let Ben-Hadad do all the talking, because it was clear that the situation was beyond her control. 'Just tell me the name!' the Governor ordered. 'Now!'

'*He said it was a man who serves under Overseer Carak. He said it was Tanna Ga Han!*'

Eyla could not help but laugh at Ben-Hadad's defeat and the simplicity of it all. After all the effort she had put in to create this elaborate ruse, it appeared that Carak had been one step ahead of them all the time.

Ω

Krell was practically dragging Cassandra along the high walkway, and she was stumbling and tripping in her attempt to stay upright and to keep away from the edge. Still astounded by the huge dragons below, her most potent struggle at this time involved coming to terms with what she was witnessing in this place. 'What's the name of this world?' she called to Krell as he hurried on with her in tow.

'We have called it Einnor for a long time,' he replied. They were approaching the end of the balcony, and an elevator housing awaited them. Cassandra felt a greater fear course through her and she set her feet to the floor, managing to stop Krell from dragging her by sheer force of will. Or maybe something else. He turned to her. 'How are you doing that?'

'I don't know,' she said, 'and I don't care. Something's very wrong here. I can feel it.' She snapped her hand from his grip and looked around. 'I don't want to die,' she whimpered.

Krell looked at her for a moment. 'What do you sense?'

She closed her eyes and steadied her breathing. When she opened them, she gasped. 'The Kwaios are coming!' No sooner had she said it than there was the sound of combat from below, and they both looked down to see scores of Kwaios breaking in as they blasted through the cave walls of the Jaevisk facility. Krell grabbed Cassandra again, taking her to the elevator. 'I have to get you off this world!'

'How? The last time I was in one of your shuttles, the Kwaios shot us down. They're everywhere!'

They got into the elevator, and Krell drew a gun and a sword as the car began its descent. 'You're not going by shuttle,' he told her. 'We have another way.'

Ω

The tracker Adam was carrying started buzzing, and he took it from his pocket to check the screen as they were creeping out of the cloning chamber. One or two Kwaios looked up from their work, but they either did not see the intruders or did not care enough to stop what they were doing. 'Whoever it is, they're close,' Adam whispered as they found themselves in another tunnel. This one was relatively short, and they quickly reached the next room, feeling the dreadful cold emanating from it. They could each see their breath as they walked in, ducking down behind a large metal container as they saw that the Kwaios here were using sterile tools like those in the previous room. However, there were no embryos here, and the cloning process was long passed by the time the subjects got to this stage.

Standing at shining metal tables from which blood dripped onto the floor and ran into a network of sluice channels, these Kwaios surgeons worked on huge pulsing things of dark red and black flesh, pulling transparent films of unnecessary tissue from them until they were a bright, pristine red. Anya stifled a gasp and felt like she would vomit, realising what they were. 'Hearts,' said Adam. 'These must be the hearts of those…creatures back there.'

Carak pointed to where one of the Kwaios surgeons was lowering one of the still-pulsing hearts into a steaming container with long forceps: 'And they're freezing them.' *Of course they are*, he thought. *This is what it was all about. I've been such a fool.*

Adam looked at the tracker again, and realised that the signal was coming from this very room. He risked standing up to look around. The only place in which one of his people could be held was behind a tall door in the wall to their right. Adam pointed to it, saying, 'I have to go.'

Anya was crying, realising that they were hiding behind one of the massive freezer units which held the hearts of the dragons, and she had never wanted to wake up from a nightmare more than she did right then. Carak grabbed Adam by the arm and shook his head. 'Stay here with her,' he whispered, giving Adam little chance to argue as he pushed him back and made his way across the floor. As he did so, a huge Kwaios entered

335

the room from behind them, glancing at the two Humans on the floor and ignoring them as he followed Carak. Adam shouted, 'Look out!' and Carak spun around with his gun raised. He fired as the Kwaios bore down on him, and two shots slammed into the alien's torso. Still, it came on, grabbing Carak by the neck and hurling him across the room as the surgeons continued their work. One of the tables was knocked over and Carak found himself laying in a mess of blood and tissue that was not his.

Adam and Anya ran across to the door in the wall and it took both of them to open it. There was a great hiss of released pressure and vapour clouds rushed out from behind the door. As they cleared, Adam was shocked to see who had been held in this frozen chamber. 'Conner!'

Their stowaway looked up, too cold to reply as Anya rushed in past Adam and dragged the man to his feet. 'Are you okay?' she cried. 'What have they done to you?' They got him out of the freezer just as the Kwaios guard was about to crush Carak's throat. Conner broke away from them and stumbled towards the Kwaios, reaching out to place his palm flat on the alien's back. Releasing Carak and throwing its arms up, the Kwaios howled in agony. Adam rushed in to grab Carak's gun and fired repeatedly at the alien, eventually taking it down with a bullet between its eyes. Now the surgeons stopped working, gathering up massive knives and turning on the intruders. But Conner, his strength returning as his temperature was rising, turned upon them all and unleashed his unique power. The Kwaios, all eleven of them, were thrown back as one, their bones and skulls crushed against the cave walls as they collapsed to the blood soaked floor. Surgical tables and oversized organs were strewn around the room, and Carak was shocked by the sight as he got to his feet. Handing him his gun, Adam grinned, saying, 'You'll get used to it.'

'We have to leave...now!' shouted Conner, heading towards the exit beyond the fallen Kwaios surgeons. 'The Kwaios and the Jaevisk are killing each other all over this place, and we're caught in the middle.'

They followed him without question, and another tunnel led them into the last room of this place that any of them wanted to see. The howls and roars of terror and agony were pitiful and heart-wrenching, and they swiftly saw why. At first, they passed trolleys of pulsing dark hearts waiting to be brought into the room they had just left, and then they saw the grey dragons, strapped to huge tables as Kwaios butchers worked on them. Although Conner led the others at a run, caring little now for being spotted, they still managed to witness the application of huge serrated knives cutting open the beasts before their hearts were ripped out of their living bodies. The scene was horrific, and Anya tried her best to keep her gaze averted and focused only on their path of escape. What they could not know was that this path would bring them into even greater danger.

Ω

Jakari and Jennifer were walking through an icy canyon, where rocky walls rising up on either side were occupied here and there by snow-covered vegetation. For some time Jakari had felt that they were under observation, and the sensation came to him again, that tingling feeling up his spine as secret eyes bore into his back. 'Jennifer,' he called. 'Stop for a moment.' She did so, waiting for him to catch up with her. 'What is it?' she asked quietly.

He gestured that she remain silent and they both listened carefully. They could hear in the distance the sound of fleeing dragons and hunting shuttles, but there was nothing imminent. Then some stones broke away from the top of the rocky heights to their left, a short distance ahead of them. Here, a dark shape moved into view, looking down on them as more stones fell from the precipice on which it dared to stand. It was a dark grey creature, much smaller than the ones they had recently seen, but heavily built and made for hunting and killing. On either side of its long and stony reptilian face, two sets of horns protruded horizontally, one set curling upwards, the other down. Scaled wings were folded flat against its back, but Jakari could distinguish the lines of bones and almost transparent flesh, even from this distance. 'I think we should move.'

Jennifer did not need any further warning, and the two of them picked up their pace, keeping watch on the predatory beast as it moved along the top of the canyon wall to keep up with them. Some distance ahead, the canyon turned sharply to the right. Jennifer kept her eyes fixed on that sharp turn, hoping that nothing lay in wait. But she could not watch for long. From the other side of the canyon, a second grey dragon appeared. The first one roared, as if challenging the newcomer. 'Run!' shouted Jakari, as the challenge was accepted and the second beast leaped from the edge, spreading its flightless wings for balance as it crashed down to the ground just behind Jennifer. She was already moving, but Jakari was so close behind her that he was forced to leap headlong over the dragon as it thrashed about in the ice and dust, clearly injured and disorientated by the desperate leap. Rolling and getting quickly

337

to his feet, Jakari caught up with Jennifer as the first dragon let out a roar of rage, still reluctant to jump such a great distance.

They headed for the blind turn up ahead, and the reluctant dragon changed its mind, running along the canyon wall before launching itself into the air. Coming down into heavily packed snow, it barely missed Jakari's legs as it lashed out with massive claws to tear his trousers, drawing the slightest hint of blood and the scent of impending victory. By now, the other dragon had joined the chase, and it was clear that Jakari and Jennifer would not outrun them. Two dragons behind them and the risk of ambush ahead, Jakari drew his gun as the snow and dust was thrown up around them by a great impact. Something shook the land, the rumbling nearly knocking them to the ground as the canyon walls seemed to rain stone. Jakari and Jennifer grabbed each other and looked back to see if something else had joined the chase, and were shocked to see the two beasts, clearly sedated or stunned by whatever weapon had been fired, being lifted from the ground by forces unseen as a black vessel hovered silently above.

Neither of them knew that this was the Kwaios, and they looked up in wonder as the ship passed by above them and then rose towards the clouds. The silence in which they were left was not completely empty, however. It was surreptitiously occupied by a low-pitched growling noise as of a devil's breath. Jennifer and Jakari stared at each other, their expressions asking the same question: *Do you hear what I hear?*

From up ahead, their question was answered as the head of a massive red creature moved into view, looking at them from around the bend in the canyon. Each breath it released rumbled through the snow-covered stone and Jakari and Jennifer could feel its warm breath flowing over them. Despite their fear, they welcomed the heat in this frozen place and found themselves moving closer to the beast. The huge red dragon had a long snout, with vicious curved horns protruding from each side. A pair of menacing tusks curved downwards from the front of its upper jaw and, atop its snout, a row of ivory horns progressively receded in height as they traced their way back to its spiked crown. Its entire body was heavily armoured, its massive wings were thickly scaled and each of the bones in these wings ended in a split pair of talons, their wicked curve alternating up and downwards within the pair.

Although he had seen one of these creatures in the air attacking the Jaevisk shuttles, Jakari was dumbfounded to see one so close. The grey dragons taken by the black shuttle were at least ten times smaller than this creature. It turned its head and regarded the two tiny creatures standing in the shadow of its own head, glaring at them as its sparkling emerald eyes assessed the situation. The skin of its mouth rose up to display a row of killer teeth at the rear of its jaw, and Jakari backed away. Jennifer, however, did not. In fact, she stepped closer, looking far up into those huge eyes. 'What are you doing?' Jakari snapped.

She waved away his objections, so sure of what she was feeling. 'Patriarch Relland?' she asked, as tears filled her eyes. 'Mannix...is that you?'

The dragon looked directly at her, and Jennifer knew without a doubt that she was right. 'Help us!' she said. 'Please.'

The beast growled in response, and then rose to its full height on its hind legs, spreading its wonderful wings up and out above the rocky walls of the canyon. Its shadow fell across the entire clearing as it bellowed a call to others of its kind, and Jakari stumbled backwards, dropping his gun, marvelled and unmanned by the enormity of the beast. Jennifer turned to him as tears ran down her face. 'It's Patriarch Relland,' she sobbed. 'He's in there. I know it!'

'How? How is that possible?'

Jennifer shook her head. 'This must be why we were brought here. This must be what the Jaevisk wanted all along. This is the result of those things we got stuck in our heads.'

'What are you talking about?' asked Jakari as he retrieved his gun from the snow.

'It's a long story.' She gazed in wonder at the red dragon. 'But this must be the result of some kind of mutation brought about by the Jaevisk technology.' She pointed at the beast. 'These are my people, Jakari! And the Jaevisk betrayed us all!'

Jakari was beyond scepticism at this point. He was beginning to feel that everything was possible in this place. 'What...so that they could...*hunt* them?'

'I think so.'

'But why? What do they want from them?'

The great head came down to regard the bewildered Garran, and Jakari closed his eyes as the heat of its breath rushed over him. He had to open one eye to ensure that he was not in danger. When he did, he saw teeth revealed which were larger than he. Inside the bestial mind of the dragon, Mannix Relland still screamed with anguish and fought for supremacy, and he longed to answer Jakari's momentous question.

However, the dragon was in control, and it understood very different priorities.

Behind Jakari and Jennifer, the ground shuddered in rapid succession as numerous beasts arrived to join the giant Red. Jakari swung around in shock, taking in the fantastically monstrous scene as Jennifer's attentions remained on Relland's new form. The sheer bulk of the beasts would not allow Jakari to determine their numbers as they filled the canyon, their individual bodies lost amidst the chaos of wings, tails, talons and teeth. They were every colour and shade, blues of an evening sky mixed with the verdant hues of woodland; rusted metal bleeding into a melee of dappled darkness where browns, greens and yellows frolicked along rippling muscles of prophetic terror. They were at once beautiful and revolting, terrifying and humbling. Jakari recalled the words of his mother as she had spoken of a god at work amidst the unfolding of recent events, and he knew now that she was absolutely correct.

Two of the smaller dragons pushed forward through the bestial gathering, lowering themselves on their haunches and waiting as they regarded Jakari and Jennifer. 'I think they want us to get on,' said Jennifer, eagerly approaching the closest animal.

'I'd be happier walking.'

Jennifer laughed as she stepped up onto the dragon's back, using its foreleg as a step. She sat atop the beast as if a reptilian Pegasus were under her command. 'This'll be much quicker,' she called out to Jakari. 'Come on.'

The red dragon moved in as if to nudge Jakari onward, and he shook his head as he headed towards his very own dragon. 'I must be insane.'

The other dragons moved away as Jakari mounted the beast, jumping from the ground before spreading their wings and lifting themselves higher into the air. And that was how Jakari and Jennifer became airborne. There was no dramatic build-up to some monumental departure. The sudden leap to the air meant that the travellers were slammed against the tough scaled skin of the dragons' backs, and the air exploded from their lungs. Dazed and bruised, Jakari closed his eyes and gripped with all four limbs as he lay flat on his chest, more frightened than he had ever believed possible.

He had, in his time as one of the most decorated Fleet Commanders in the Garran military, faced some undeniably terrifying situations, in which Death laughed in his face – and Jakari spat back. But here and now, clinging for his life to the reptilian neck of this alien creature, he felt an unfamiliar lack of control and confidence. Only when he heard – and felt right through him – a bestial scream coming from his dragon did he open his eyes, knowing instinctively that danger was imminent. He lifted his head slowly against the forces of gravity seeking to deny his movement and saw, some distance ahead, a fleet of Jaevisk shuttles blocking their path. The...*pack* – Jakari decided to call it – of thirty or more dragons spread out in every direction, Jakari's dragon rising higher as Jennifer's dropped towards the distant landscape. Looking down as they rose, Jakari watched as the shuttles compensated for this evasive action, and then his attention was drawn by black shapes to the east. The Kwaios shuttles were closing fast.

The Jaevisk opened fire on the approaching dragons, fanning out as much as tactically possible while ensuring that no space was left uncovered by weapons' range. Six Red Dragons launched the attack on the shuttles, while the smaller creatures rushed by around them, above them, below them. There were thirteen shuttles, and they opened fire in every direction, desperately trying to suppress this inexplicable coup. And then suddenly they had to contend with the Kwaios as their vessels entered the mile-high fray, determined to protect these particular dragons. The scene was chaos as Jennifer and Jakari were flown beyond this fight, heading inexorably towards the mystery of the mountain.

More Jaevisk shuttles burned through the clouds, descending into the battle even as the Kwaios, too, were reinforced. Great blasts of energy and projectile weapons seared through the clouds from above as the gigantic Kwaios Colony ship in orbit targeted the Jaevisk shuttles, even as that same ship was being attacked by five Jaevisk Warships. Unbeknown to Jakari, the Kwaios were furious with the Jaevisk for the atrocities they were committing in the name of the Harvest. For Jakari, all that mattered was getting off this winged creature. He could see an open ledge in the towering mountain up ahead, and he could make out the relatively tiny shapes of Jaevisk soldiers moving around. Desperately trying to calculate his options amidst the madness, he then saw something which distracted him so greatly from the terror around him that all sound and motion seemed to halt as he followed its path through the air. The small silver ship which had come to Sieltor Prime from this very system within hours of the arrival of the cage at Earth was descending rapidly towards the northern face of the mountain. Jakari had heard of the rumours regarding this strange vessel and its Garran occupant, and the presence here and now of this new variable provoked so many questions that he was taken off guard.

The Jaevisk soldiers occupying the ledge opened fire with powerful mounted guns, and dragons around them were ripped apart as holes were blasted through wings and limbs. Jakari's dragon tried to spin and dive to avoid the sudden attack, but it was too late. As the sun was blocked out by a Kwaios shuttle, Jakari felt the impact of the weapons as they shredded his dragon in mid-air. It cried out in pitiful agony, and Jakari was thrown from its back, roaring in fear and desperation as he plummeted to the ground below and anticipated the impact. But the impact came sooner than he expected, once more slamming the air from his lungs as he struck a larger dragon, its skin seeming gold and brown in the haze and blur of such rapid movement as he slid down its back, desperately grasping for something to halt his demise. Somehow, he managed to catch hold of something, realising in the chaos that he was hanging from the tail of the beast. Unable to steady himself enough to see what was happening around him, he was suddenly thrown up and around by the whip of the dragon's tail as it directed him to exactly where he wanted to be and the dragon rose high into the sky above the mountain. With Jakari delivered to the mountain, the other dragons also retreated. The Jaevisk and the Kwaios may have continued to fight each other, but Jakari was detached from that now, entering as he was into a new world of mystery.

He rolled head over heels a number of times as he struck the ledge, intermittently hearing weapons' fire and the roaring of dragons before he lay on his back, still and stunned as he caught his breath. A shadow fell over him and he reacted immediately, drawing his gun and firing up into the face of a bewildered Jaevisk. Another stepped in, but a powerful gun took it from its feet and Jakari heard Jennifer shouting, 'Over here!' He got to his feet and steadied himself as he saw her standing at one of the mounted guns, turning it to fend off an attack by more approaching Jaevisk. But as Jakari neared her, his gaze was drawn beyond her, for here, in this arena of curiosity to which everyone was being inexplicably drawn, was yet another answer to another mystery. He walked purposefully past Jennifer as she protected both of them, and his eyes were wide and fixed ahead even as Jaevisk gunfire tore the air around him, until he came to the inside of the ledge which ran around the entire inner circumference of this mountain hollow. His stomach lurched as he looked down, where the strange warmth of subterranean winds rose to his face and the sheer depth of this place made his senses reel. Here in this enigmatic mountain, a massive feat of construction was underway, a towering thing of alien metal rising from the dark depths of the mountain to grasp for the sky-reaching peak above.

The Jaevisk were working furiously around this tower, thousands of them like ants in the deep distance, the sound of their machinery echoing throughout this vast chamber of stone. Jennifer stepped up beside Jakari, silently appreciating his wonder. 'Are these the things you brought here?' she asked.

He gazed at the Garran military insignia which was still visible on some of the structures; structures which had been fixed to his fleet at Omneri. His mind reeled as he nodded dumbly and Jennifer took his arm. 'We have to keep moving,' she said. As more Jaevisk took notice.

Ω

Harrogate was considerably frustrated, so close as he was to discovering what was going on in the Kiranis system. 'What do you mean...we can't get in?'

The Commander of the ship held his ground. 'Whatever kind of energy field this is...it's stopping us from penetrating the system beyond this point. The current position of the planets puts Kiranis 3, 5 and 6 almost in line with each other, and this...electrical field is being generated from the third planet.'

Harrogate thought for a moment. 'Where's the other fleet?'

'Captain Harris reports that he'll be with us within the hour. Let's just say he had to take the long way round.'

'Tell him to set course for the third planet.'

'The...you want us to go to the *third* planet?'

Harrogate eyeballed the man. 'It amazes me, Commander, that you find that surprising. If the energy field is being generated from the third planet...where else would you expect to go to put it out of action?'

The Commander leaned in, whispering harshly, 'Mister Harrogate – '

'*Pontifex* Harrogate,' he was smoothly corrected. 'I'm aware of the dangers. Now if you can't follow my orders, I'll appoint someone who can!'

The man stepped back, saluting with no little sarcasm. 'Yes, Sir!'

343

Harrogate smiled. 'That's more like it. Now spread the word across the fleet. We're attacking the Kwaios generator. Our people need our help.'

Another officer approached Harrogate and handed him a nanosheet as the Commander moved away. 'I think you should see this, Sir,' he said, pointing to the image on the screen. Harrogate looked at it and raised an eyebrow. 'What exactly am I looking at here?'

'Some sort of...tunnel, Sir. It's connecting the fifth and sixth planets.'

Ω

The fantastic tunnel did indeed connect the two worlds, but it was not a thing of material stability or energy fluctuations. It was something...different, and it would soon be perfectly straight as the fifth and sixth planets of the Kiranis system moved into a precise alignment.

Deep in the underground of the sixth planet, Krell had taken more than one bullet as he protected Cassandra, still dragging her through the bizarre installation in a desperate attempt to keep her safe and to fulfil his role as Warlord. This act would be his greatest feat as representative of his people, and he endured the pain of Kwaios bullets as he fought to bring this climactic weapon into play. Leaving the scene of battle behind them as the massive red dragon began to break free of its chains, Krell and Cassandra descended deeper into a dark tunnel to escape the chaos. Cassandra could feel a terrible cold from further ahead, and a blue glow filled the stone corridor.

Ω

The blue glow of Kwaios deception filled the corridors of Eli Chane's mind as he listened to the ever-updating damage reports. The battles around both the fifth and sixth planets of the Kiranis system were unlike anything he had ever experienced, and the only difference between the experience of his fleet and anyone out at the sixth planet was that he was not currently engaged in a fight to the death with the Kwaios Council. No, instead of the relentless attack of the mighty Kwaios, Chane's fleet was enduring the fanatical rage of the merciless Jaevisk. Of the two hundred ships of his fleet to which the Kwaios had added their own technological

344

upgrades, only seventy-three remained, and a Kwaios Colony ship had only recently arrived to reinforce them. This thing was enormous, many times larger than any ship he had imagined and armed to its hybritech teeth with countless forms of weaponry. However, despite its presence, Chane was not assured by haunting Kwaios promises. 'Has anyone got Tesckyn on com yet?' he shouted as the ship was rocked by the impact of a Jaevisk missile. No one had, and Chane had stopped thinking that things were beginning to go wrong. Because things were far beyond beginning.

'Then get me the Kwaios Colony ship!'

In the centre of the bridge, a black cubic box rested on a pedestal, and Chane rushed to it and gripped it tight as the ship trembled again. Immediately, his mind was transported to a Kwaios communications' room, and he was facing one of the giant aliens: 'Speak, Eli Chane.'

'What the hell have you done with the people you took?' he shouted angrily. 'There's only a handful of life signs left down on that world and the cage is empty!'

'Your masters did not require an explanation. Nor do you.'

The link was severed from the Kwaios end and Eli roared with anger as he stepped back from the cube. 'Get us out of here!' he ordered the crew.

Patrick turned to him. 'But...the cage,' he argued. 'Tesckyn was adamant that we bring it back.' He stepped up to Chane. 'YOU were adamant!'

Chane held his angry glare, and the two men felt the dreadful weight of their naivety and the deaths of thousands of men and women in their fleet. 'Look me in the eye, Patrick,' he replied, 'and tell me that you believe in what we're doing.'

Patrick was silent. And Chane nodded.

Ω

The chains and bonds of the large dragons held in the Jaevisk chamber were at first weakened and then broken by either stray shots or zealous and miscalculated attempts on the part of the Kwaios to free them. They jumped from their holding platforms to grab Jaevisk and Kwaios alike in their great jaws, whipping bodies aside with their tails and tearing flesh with teeth and claws. They cared little for who protected them and who butchered them, and it was when the giant red dragon broke out of its restraints that a chill of fear fell upon the combatants.

It ripped away its muzzle and spewed flame around the upper chamber, engulfing the Kwaios and Jaevisk on the balcony and weakening the supporting structures. Bodies fell burning and screaming to the floor below and the high surrounding walkways began to break apart. The floor shook as the dragon dropped to all fours, its bulk filling the room, this simple motion crushing scores of fighting aliens as well as trapping smaller dragons beneath it. The red dragon slammed its tail against the stone wall and it started to crumble, parts of the high ceiling breaking away as the vibration spread throughout the chamber.

It was out of the Kwaios tunnels and into this madness that Conner led his rescuers, and Anya's scream as the massive red tail swept across the chamber just short of their position was suitably loud enough so that as the men screamed…they were mercifully drowned out. Both Adam and Carak were quick to retrieve Jaevisk weapons from the nearby dead, noticing with some disappointment that the Kwaios guns were too unwieldy for them to operate. Conner looked around quickly, determined to avoid running deeper into the fight. 'There!' he shouted, pointing at a black exit along the wall to their right. They ran, hugging the wall and ducking as another sweep of the giant red tail slammed against the cave wall, bringing debris raining down upon them. There was a tremendous roar from the Red as Conner disappeared through the exit and Adam and the others looked back in time to see a blast of blue light spearing the ceiling to strike the terrific beast. It collapsed in death, shaking the entire underworld as the Kwaios Council chose to destroy it rather than have its majesty violated by the Jaevisk, and Carak had to drag Adam and Anya away from the breath-taking scene. Hundreds of Kwaios were now clambering over the dead dragon, and with the Jaevisk facility destroyed, they now had in their sights the people who had seen too much. Deeper into the subterranean network these unfortunates ran, feeling a terrible chill and seeing a blue glow ahead of them in the tunnel, a portent of the one final surprise this world had in store for them.

Ω

Jakari dived out of the path of a Jaevisk laser, wishing he had just ducked. He did not land well, slamming against the stone wall and scraping his side before landing on the stony path which spiralled upwards along the inside of the dark mountain. Jennifer was farther ahead, as she always seemed to be, but now one of her legs was injured and she was making her way up the path with considerable difficulty. They had chosen to go up, not just because it was a shorter journey than going down, but also because Jaevisk occupation of the heights was considerably thinner than that of the depths. There were no mounted cannons here, and not a lot of Jaevisk security, but every now and then one of the wily aliens would take them by surprise, the fact that it had them in range from the opposite side obscured by the density of the massive structure filling the interior of the peak. Jakari caught up with a groaning and bleeding Jennifer, thinking that her right leg might be broken. She screamed as she instinctively put pressure on it in her attempt to stand up straight, and Jakari supported her as they continued their ascent.

A dull, thrumming sound began from deep in the mountain, and the tower reverberated like a tuning fork. Jakari and Jennifer cried out as the tone rumbled through their brains. Holding their hands to their ears, they found it difficult to stand up straight, but Jakari noticed an opening up ahead and nudged Jennifer with an elbow, gesturing that they go there. She nodded and they stumbled farther upwards to a small ledge high in the mountain. As they stepped out into the light and the scene of perpetual battle between dragons, Jaevisk and Kwaios which was spread out as far as the eye could see, Jennifer looked to her right to see a young man sitting on the snow-covered ledge, transfixed by the view. 'Hey!' she called. 'What are you doing up here?'

Cana found that it was a question for which he had no response.

Ω

Harrogate could see it beyond the forward window, the monumental power of the Kwaios Council, a power of which Tesckyn had warned him and which was now pulsing and crackling outwards from a generation facility on the surface of the third planet. If they could do something like this, he thought, why did they need to make deals with people like Tesckyn? Why not just take whatever they wanted?

'This isn't going to be easy,' the Commander reported. 'There's about a hundred ships approaching. They're small compared to the others we saw, but...they'll hurt.'

Harrogate nodded. 'There's also a considerable array of S-to-O weaponry around the generator.' There was silence for a moment, until the Commander said, 'About earlier, Sir...'

'There's only now, Commander. Let's make it count.'

The Commander nodded, and then turned to address the bridge crew. 'Begin the assault!'

Ω

Cassandra was silent and fearfully appreciative of what stood before her. The blue glow which had beckoned her had been emanating from an archway embedded in the wall of the cave. It was made of black and shining silver metal, a hybrid technology which did not belong to the one who stood next to her. The pulsing blue of active hybritech energy filled the empty space within the archway like a glowing, transparent film of alien flesh. 'You didn't build this,' said Cassandra.

'No,' said Krell, 'they did. But we have activated it because the time is right. An alignment of this planet and the next allows for its use on rare occasions such as this.'

Cassandra turned to him, the blue glow throwing one side of her face into shadow. 'Why do they hate you?' she asked him. 'The Kwaios.'

'They hate us because we no longer adhere to their obsolete laws. They hate us because we use the bio-fuel obtained from the higher gods as well as the lower ones. With this current restoration of Kiranis, they will use in massive numbers the weak and subordinate creatures you call dragons before they begin to clone them in even greater numbers. The Jaevisk Society will make itself strong by hunting the stronger and dominant ones, using only pure and raw energy.'

Cassandra found that she was crying, and her breath caught in her throat. 'You used us all,' she sobbed. 'You and the Kwaios took advantage of us to make all this happen!'

'Yes,' said Krell. 'The Kwaios deal with your people alerted us to a new beginning. Without it, we would not have been prepared for the return of our world. But without your intervening with the man on the cage, we would not have had the device which allowed for the abduction of your people.'

'And that doesn't *concern* you?' she snapped. 'Don't you realise who *told* me about that device...that he facilitated my coming into

348

possession of it? Don't you care that by drawing the Jaevisk into this, the Prophet helped the *Kwaios* as well?'

'The Prophet engineered events so that the Harvest was necessary for the survival of both of our species. There was also no other way to regenerate Kiranis and to ensure its reconnection to the Sentience.'

'The...Sentience?'

'The source of all power and life in the galaxy. It is the only true god.'

Cassandra gasped. 'That's what the people on Sieltor Prime were talking about! The fundamentalists the Church were supporting!'

'And the reason that the Prophet is active in this time.'

'In this time? I don't understand.'

'You were never supposed to.' Krell reached out for her and she struggled in his grasp as he said, 'And you never will.' A shot was fired and it struck the wall next to the pulsing archway. Krell spun round to see Carak and Adam taking aim, but Conner pushed past them. 'Let her go,' he said calmly.

Krell found himself doing so, but Cassandra had quietened down and she stood still, staring in wonder at the newcomers. For some reason Anya could not fathom, the Councillor had fixed her glare on her. 'Come over here, Councillor,' Adam called to her, lowering his gun. 'You'll be safe.'

Cassandra blinked and turned to him. 'Safe?' she mused quietly, before laughing aloud. '*Safe? With you?*' She shook her head. 'I don't think so.'

Carak kept his gun on the blue-robed Jaevisk, who recognised him and said something in the Jaevisk language. Carak did not understand, and Cassandra had to act as interpreter. 'Are you Carak Tae Ahn?' she asked him.

Carak nodded, and she explained. 'He said he has some news for you.'

'If it's about Malik,' Carak replied as he watched Krell closely, 'I've heard enough.'

Krell replied and Cassandra said, 'It's about your daughter.'

Carak stepped closer with greater intent, but Anya shouted, 'Don't! It's a trick!' She looked to Conner, but he shook his head, saying, 'It's not. Governor Ben-Hadad kidnapped his daughter a few days ago.'

Carak turned on him. 'What? You *knew* about this?' Horrified, he turned back to Krell. 'Where is she?'

'The Jaevisk rescued her,' Cassandra translated for the Warlord, knowing instinctively that he was lying, 'and he says he'll make sure you get her back safely.'

Conner glared first at Cassandra and then at Krell, knowing that he had to protect the lie and hating them for it. If what was about to happen did not proceed as he had learned, everything he had ever known in his own time would cease to be. Carak lowered the gun, and Anya pointed at the glowing portal. 'Is this the way out?' she asked. 'Because the Kwaios are right behind us.'

'We can all go this way,' said Cassandra, her eyes once more fixed on Anya. 'The Kwaios won't be able to follow us.'

Adam was still confused by the Councillor's earlier outburst, but he dismissed it for now and approached the archway as the sound of the approaching Kwaios could be heard by all. 'Well?' he said. 'What are we waiting for?'

$$\Omega$$

While Harrogate's fleet engaged the Kwaios defence grid at the third planet, and Harris' fleet used an opposite approach vector to reinforce them, the space around the sixth planet was already filled with shipyards of destruction. The huge Garran armada was almost completely wiped out, but the Jaevisk control virus had taken its toll on their real targets, and many Kwaios vessels of various shapes and sizes were out of control, crashing into their counterparts or drifting aimlessly in the vacuum. Still, the Kwaios fought with the Jaevisk who were defiling their gods and perverting their beliefs, both here in orbit of the outer planet and down on the surface. It was truly a warzone.

And from far beneath the disputed cave network, a Jaevisk, a Garran and four Humans were transported by means beyond their understanding and control, shot through the glowing blue tunnel of Kwaios technology with bone-shaking speed as the two worlds aligned. They were thrown out of the tunnel at the other end, covered in a disturbing film of transparent tissue, and all except Krell collapsed vomiting and heaving to the stony ground beyond the exit. Krell turned and threw the Jaevisk equivalent of a hand-grenade back into the portal, and the blue glow of pulsing bio-energy collapsed in upon itself, killing the many Kwaios soldiers who had attempted to follow.

Adam was the first to gather himself, helping Anya to her feet before standing with her to look around. They were in another cave, yet this one was different. The stone was reddish brown, rather than almost black, and it was hot here. Very hot. Cassandra had fallen alongside Carak, and he failed to notice as she took from him a small knife concealed in his boot. Everyone was standing as Adam wondered, 'Where are we?'

'Kiranis,' said Conner, backing away from Adam and Anya as Cassandra moved closer. 'It's the Jaevisk home world.'

Conner's movement had not gone unnoticed, and Adam felt a chill run through him as he saw, in the corner of his eye, the Councillor drawing silently and suspiciously nearer to Anya. 'How are we going to get home?' Anya asked.

'You're not!' Cassandra shouted as she lunged at her with the knife. Adam, however, was already there. In the way. The knife went deep, too deep for hope to remain, and Anya cried out in dreadful shock as Adam was forced back against her by Cassandra's sudden attack. Carak dragged Cassandra back as Conner and Krell looked on; Krell, because he did not care so long as Cassandra was alive; and Conner, because he knew that this would happen, and that it had to happen. Krell took the struggling Cassandra from Carak, who had disarmed her, and he held her still in his grip. 'You failed,' the Warlord told her.

Even if Carak did not understand it, he knew that something had been shared, and he swung on them as Anya cradled her dying lover in her arms. 'Why?' he roared. 'Why did you do that?'

Tears ran down Cassandra's face, but she steeled herself against his fury. 'It should have been her!' she shouted back. 'She's pregnant with his child!'

'What?' Carak was truly disgusted. 'What is wrong with you?'

'She wanted to stop all this from happening,' Conner explained, as Carak turned to him. 'After they took the Jaevisk device from my head...the one they ended up putting in hers...they discovered that there was a genetic line between me and Captain Echad. In short, I'm descended from him...from both of them.'

Carak struck out with the back of his hand, taking Conner by surprise and lifting him from his feet to slam him against the stone wall of the cave. 'You *allowed* this to happen!' Had he decided to continue his assault on Conner, who was now well beyond surprised, Carak might have been killed on the spot. But Anya's terrible sobbing stole his attention and

351

he came to her, dropping to his knees as Adam was coughing blood and struggling to hold his head up. Carak tore open the man's uniform, but he knew of the damage his blade could inflict. He knew before seeing the horrible wound that the Human was not long for this world, and his expression told Anya as much. 'He was going to be a father!' Anya whimpered, her hands covered in blood as she kept his head from lolling to one side. 'We were going to start a family.'

'I'll get you home,' Carak told her. 'You have my word.' He took Adam's hand. 'I'll get you both home.' He held Adam's dying gaze as the last spark of consciousness left him and the strength of his grip was gone. As Conner suppressed the hatred he felt for the one who had put him in this horrific situation, and Krell took the opportunity to drag Cassandra away with his hand over her mouth, the Captain of the *Nostradamus* died. And, as if the event might have caused a reverberation on a cosmic scale, the planet rumbled.

$$\Omega$$

Yet it was no such romance which caused Kiranis to rumble. The cage was beginning to close, ignorant of dying men in caves and ferocious battles on and around the planet. For there was a schedule to adhere to, and a strange phenomenon lay in wait for the planet along its orbital path. The hole in space, the fissure in reality through which the mysterious Garran from the future had arrived, threatened the destruction of the planet should it continue along its course. Both the Kwaios and the Jaevisk had calculated the length of time allotted for this momentous Harvest, and they knew that their time was almost up. The Jaevisk, however, had one last trick up their malicious sleeves, and Naveen was all too aware of what was to come.

Deep beneath the mountain at the north pole of Kiranis, to where all were being inexorably drawn, Naveen appeared. Growls of fury and hatred greeted him, but he ignored the lesser dragons, turning his back on them as the great black head of Leviathan emerged from a huge cave mouth. 'Do you like my work?' asked Naveen with a grin.

Leviathan's growl accentuated the rumble of the world. 'You have manipulated my children. They think they are at war with only each other.'

'I am Human. It's what we do best.'

'I will find you in your time,' Leviathan promised him. 'And I will kill you.'

Naveen chuckled. 'First...my scaly friend, you'll have to survive what the Jaevisk have in store for you. They succeeded in distracting the Kwaios long enough to build their machine here.'

'No *machine* can threaten me. I am a god!'

Nodding, Naveen pointed upwards. 'Then show them,' he dared.

Ω

Cana rose from his place in the snow, shivering and pale. 'Who are you?' he asked, too cold to be afraid of the tall Garran soldier.

Jennifer removed her jacket and Jakari passed it to Cana. 'My name is Jakari,' he said. 'And this is Jennifer.'

Cana looked at her. 'Are you from the Church?'

She nodded. 'Yes. You?'

'They lied to us,' he replied despondently, pulling the jacket closed across his chest.

'I know,' said Jennifer, moving closer with Jakari's help. 'Did your pod crash here?'

He glared beyond her to Jakari. 'No. A Garran ship brought me here. It was up on the moon and I was sent up to find out why they'd been spying on the Church.'

Jennifer turned to Jakari. 'Do you know anything about this?'

He shook his head. 'It might have been something to do with Carak,' he mused.

'Who?'

'Look, none of this matters now. Are you Cana?' He nodded and Jakari offered him his hand, saying, 'I was sent here to rescue you.'

'Let me guess,' Cana replied as he got to his feet of his own accord. 'A man in a weird black cloak with dragons on it?'

'Yes, but...he was Garran.'

Cana laughed. 'I'm sure Naveen can be whatever he wants. I think he's a god.'

Jakari shook his head. 'I think he wants us to believe he is. Now let's get out of here.'

'You don't get it, do you? If he brought you here, it was for a reason.'

'Yes, to rescue *you*. He said that that black...monster was keeping you here and that he couldn't come here himself.'

353

'And you *believed* him?' Cana chuckled darkly. 'The way I understand it, there's nothing he can't do. He's the one who promised the Church to that monster you're talking about! He's the one who delivered me right to it!'

Jakari felt the intrusion of fear. 'So...you don't exactly *need* rescuing?'

Cana walked past him, back into the mountain, and neither of them saw it coming. He gestured towards the great Jaevisk structure which had been facilitated by Garran complicity, calling back to the others, 'Look around you, guys. Did you really think you could make a *difference* here? Everything is happening for a reason. Every...little...detail. And that reason is Naveen.' He turned back around as Jakari and Jennifer joined him, feeling some slight respite from the biting wind as the Jaevisk tower activated with a hum of bone-chilling power and Cana shouted, 'You're the ones who need rescuing!' He spun round and ran towards the edge of the spiralling stone path, screaming at the top of his lungs as he leaped off into the depths of the Jaevisk tower.

Jennifer screamed in horror and Jakari rushed to the edge, seeing Cana plummeting into the now active machine. But he also saw, as if in slow motion, the emergence from the deep of the giant black dragon, its red eyes illuminating its ghoulish ascent. Jakari shouted, 'No!' as the dragon opened its jaws wide and Cana disappeared into its great throat. The beast roared with a deafening ferocity as it rose higher and higher, up through the skeletal tower towards Jakari and beyond. Jakari fell back as the massive black form rushed upwards to occupy the tower, and he saw, standing amidst those great heights, a blue-robed Jaevisk...and a Human female who struggled in his alien arms. But something else caught his attention, for the inside of the mountain was starting to crumble.

Ω

Carak lifted Adam's body and slung it over his shoulders as Anya looked on with tears of anguish and exhaustion. As Carak turned to face Conner, he noticed the empty space where Krell and Cassandra had been. Conner anticipated by pointing upwards and saying, 'He took her up there.' He also had to anticipate Carak's anger by adding, 'Look...I know you hate me and whatever you believe I represent in all this, but things have to happen here that you just can't change!'

Anya was dumbfounded, feeling only now the enormity of trusting this man. Conner was weary with guilt as he turned to her. 'All I can do is apologise for not telling you, Anya,' he said. 'But I know for a fact that you'll get out of here. Both of you.' He glanced at Adam's form draped across Carak's shoulders and said, 'All of you.' The ground was trembling again, and a terrible thrumming sound was coming from nearby but reverberating throughout the cave system. 'Well, this would be a good time to tell us how!' Carak snapped.

Conner nodded, pointing to the tunnel behind Anya. 'Go that way,' he told them. 'Ignore what you see...whatever you see...and get as high up as possible as fast as possible. There should be some sort of elevator system that the Jaevisk are using.'

'Where are you going?'

'There's...something I have to deal with.'

Anya blinked from her absence, and asked, 'He's here, isn't he? The World Killer.'

'Yes,' said Conner. 'Whatever happens, I have to find him. I have to stop him.'

'You're talking about Malik,' Carak realised.

'That's not his real name, but...yeah. It's ironic, really, that if it wasn't for everything he's done, you wouldn't have the future you're gonna have.'

'Why is that ironic?'

Conner smiled thinly, looking first at Anya, and then back at Carak. 'Because just as I'm descended from her...he's descended from you!' Without another word, Conner turned and left them, heading away down another tunnel from which emanated a soft, pulsing green glow.

Carak gathered himself from the shock of his words, and shifted his weight to deal with the body across his shoulder as the ground shook and a slithering crack ran across the floor of the cave. Then he turned to Anya and said, 'Let's go home, shall we?'

Ω

The two fleets from Earth under the command of Harrogate and Harris were being decimated by the Kwaios defence at the third planet, and Harrogate knew that they would all be dead soon as his ship oversaw the assault. What galled him most was that he would not get to see the look on Tesckyn's face when he returned to tell him that all he had worked for

355

was gone. 'Sir, there's another fleet moving into flank us!' an officer shouted. 'We're getting the same energy readings from it. It's Kwaios!'

Harrogate turned to the Commander, who gave a nervous smile before sinking back into his seat and saying, 'Can I ask you a question?'

Harrogate sat next to him and grinned. 'You mean...seeing as it's open season on confessions?' He shrugged. 'Sure. Go for it.'

The Commander hesitated for a moment, like a nervous child. Then he asked, with comical frustration, 'Why *Pontifex*?'

Harrogate laughed aloud, and the bridge crew were mystified. But before Harrogate could respond, his laughter was cut off as scores of battleships sped past them towards the battle, opening up on the Kwaios shuttles and tearing them to pieces. 'There's a com request!'

'Put it up!' shouted Harrogate, as both men rose from their chairs. Across the speakers, they heard an unfamiliar voice: *'This is Commander Eli Chane of the Grant. We decided not to let you guys have all the fun.'*

Harrogate felt tears of joy and relief in his eyes as he responded, 'I've no idea who you are, Commander, but you're very welcome to the party.'

'Look, you don't wanna know why we're out here, but if we don't get this generator down, no one leaves this system. You should set course for the fifth planet and pick up some people we left behind.'

'How many life signs?' asked the Commander. 'We've a lot less capacity now.'

'Shouldn't be a problem,' said Chane. *'There's only two. Now get going.'* The rest of Chane's fleet joined the fight just as a huge Kwaios ship emerged from a crackling blue storm. As the two weaker fleets retreated and Harrogate wondered aloud, 'Did he say *two*?' a Kwaios colony ship appeared and they could only pray that Chane would make it. All was silent on the bridge of Harrogate's ship as they moved farther away and the report came in that the energy field was down, the generator and the emitters destroyed. The next report confirmed that not one of Chane's ships had survived.

$$\Omega$$

The crew of the *Dragon* monitored these events with muted trepidation. Captain Seth Hand was a lot less passionate and confident about his role in Church events and their triumphant seizure of power and recognition. In fact, he was downright pessimistic. 'Get us the hell out of here!' he snapped as they witnessed the arrival of the giant colony ship and the subsequent destruction of the generator on the third planet, a destruction facilitated only by the suicidal race to the surface of Chane's flagship as the others covered him. 'Go to the coordinates Relland gave us!'

The *Dragon* altered its position and orientation and prepared to move away from the moon, the planet...the whole cursed system. Of course, Captain Hand had no way of knowing that Relland's coordinates had been passed on to him by the Kwaios themselves and had come through Overseer Carak during his visit to Earth. The *Dragon*, a ship staffed exclusively by Church members, genetically altered Humans who were untouched by Jaevisk brain implants and ripe for experimentation, headed towards the outer moon of the third planet. It was a grey and soulless body, yet Hand was the first to see that it was far from uninhabited. Evidence of ongoing industrialisation caught his eye, long lines of construction across the face of the planetoid. 'Are you sure these are the coordinates we were given?'

'Yes, Sir.'

But all could see the intensity of activity on the moon as they came around to its night side, and shuttles and large vessels were coming and going everywhere. Before they knew it, the crew of the *Dragon* had wandered aimlessly into the den of the wolf, for they were surrounded by Kwaios ships within minutes. Weapons' fire disabled their engines, their defences and their life-support system, a precision attack designed solely to cripple them in unconscious apprehension. Once everyone on board had lost consciousness, the Kwaios set about taking them captive. It seemed that, for the Kwaios at least, not all had been lost.

Ω

Cassandra looked around and above her in terror as dust and stones began to fall and the inside of the mountain began to disintegrate. They were at the peak of the Jaevisk structure, a massive tower-like device made of strong metal and powered from far below. Channels of energy pulsed upwards through it like blood pumping through metallic veins, and there were emitters at the top where the skeletal metal curved inwards like a great claw. It was to this point that the head of Leviathan, the great black dragon and recently re-animated god of Kiranis, reached in his rage and determination and his defiance of Naveen's damnation. However, the climax of his ascent was accentuated by the activation of the Jaevisk

357

machine, and beams of red light shot out from the metal claw around his head to penetrate deep into his very being. And down along the depths of the tower, more and more of these beams had activated, resulting in the entrapment of Leviathan and the encroaching triumph of the Jaevisk.

The dragon snapped its great jaws and roared and screamed in its fury, ensnared as he was by the intricate Jaevisk weapon as Krell stepped towards him with delight. 'Did you think we would be content to gather only others of your kind and to ignore the power you possess?' he roared at the monster. 'We will win this war only by sacrificing the greatest of our gods!'

Leviathan replied, growling in the Jaevisk language, 'There is no war but the one you perceive. You have all been tricked by the Prophet. He is Human and his kind should have been destroyed by the Garran centuries ago.'

'We are aware of the extent of his manipulation,' Krell answered with false confidence. 'Which is why we must do this.'

'You fool!' Leviathan roared. 'I am no Reaper Stone for you to drain. I am the very essence of this world!'

'Which is why we are sending you to another.'

Cassandra saw it, the dreadful fear in the eyes of this monster, and it chilled her to the core. Anything that scared this thing must be horrific indeed. She began to back away as the dragon growled, 'That is not possible.' But he must have known, Cassandra realised, as those red eyes fixed on her and she read its despair and Krell reached back for her. He dragged her closer to the edge as she fought and clawed and screamed. 'No!' she whimpered desperately, even as the dragon bellowed its own fury. 'Please don't do this!'

'It is done,' said Krell, as he lifted her from the back of the neck and squeezed until he felt the compression of the vertebra necessary to paralyse her. She collapsed in his strong grip, and he lifted her higher as the implant at the base of her brain stem was activated and the tendrils shot out. As they made contact with the points from which the red beams of energy had been fired, Krell released her and the tendrils took over, supporting her weight as her limp body was elevated above the head of the dragon. Leviathan tried to consume the woman, snapping up with his jaws, but she was beyond his reach and the machine was holding him in place.

'This Human,' Krell shouted, 'has in her head a device from another time, a device designed to facilitate cross-dimensional travel. It has been in a state of flux since its arrival here, and we have programmed it to return to the time from which it came, taking you with it.' Krell stepped back. 'We will collect your energy from the very place and time this thing belongs and we will destroy the Prophet from right here!'

Leviathan howled, as his physical presence began to ripple with the uncertainty of its place in the universe. He would vanish from sight, and the Jaevisk machine would draw all of his power in one great collection of energy. Despite his protestations, he would become the ultimate Reaper Stone, and the ultimate weapon against the Prophet. But the Jaevisk plan was not to be. In his Human form, Naveen appeared close to Krell as he stared at the unfolding process, and the Warlord turned to him and immediately opened fire. The bullets went through the Prophet and Naveen stepped in to punch Krell in the abdomen with some unseen force. The Jaevisk was thrown back and Naveen moved in to stand over him. 'I'm going to let you live, Krell,' he told him, 'because you need to bring a message back to your Old Ones. But first, I want you to understand what's happening here, and what you overlooked amidst your fanatic plan. Get up!'

Naveen walked towards the edge of the precipice even as the stone beneath him began to split and crumble, moving close to the now inconsistent form of Leviathan as the quantum uncertainty of Cassandra's implant was amplified, and Krell got to his feet to pursue him. Naveen stepped aside to avoid further confrontation, and he pointed down, saying, 'You forgot about someone.'

It took a moment for Krell to see it as he steadied himself on the trembling path, but as he gazed down into the black depths and his eyes gradually adjusted to the darkness, he saw a green glow, pulsing with alternating intensity and directed towards the base emitters of the tower's collector array. He could not see the machine by which this glow was being produced, but he understood the implications. 'The World Killer!' he hissed. 'You brought him into this!'

Naveen laughed at Krell's fury and defeat. 'Brought him *into* this?' he mocked. 'The World Killer *is...this*, Krell. He is *everything*...and *everywhere*...at *every* time!' The Prophet stepped closer, shifting into his Jaevisk form so that he could look Krell in the eye and say in the Warlord's own language, 'And so am I!' Then he vanished, and Krell stumbled back, looking up at Cassandra as she awoke into a nightmare, screaming anew with a terror so great that her heart almost exploded in her chest. Krell roared with rage as Leviathan's body began to solidify, and the great scheme of the Jaevisk was being torn apart from within the very bowels of its inception, torn apart like the world around it.

Far down in the deepest caves of the mountain, the machine of the World Killer had tapped into something so much more powerful than anything the Jaevisk could generate. It was the one thing with which both the Jaevisk and the Kwaios were afraid to tamper. But Malik, his chosen name in this time, was in possession of knowledge and power which would not be invented, discovered or put to use for centuries to come. And he was not afraid to tamper with anything.

Ω

Kiranis was dangerously close to the temporal fracture now, and the planet was at risk of being torn apart and drawn into the phenomenon in a way which would have a devastating effect on the time-line on the opposite side. However, this was not the greatest danger, for the mechanics of the cage around the planet now posed a magnificent threat to all life in the Kiranis system and beyond. The science involved in the creation of an artificial wormhole, a tunnel through time and space, was hampered by a type of feedback loop which prevented stability and would quickly cause the collapse of such a creation. In short, it was not possible to maintain a connection between two distinct points in space and time under the laws of physics as they were understood in this time, and any temporal tunnel designed in this way would implode as a result of its own stresses. Those who designed the cage had managed to correct this problem.

At regular and specific intervals along the insides of the longitudinal arcs of the cage, large circular apertures opened, and within each aperture, a glowing and spinning ring of blue fire surrounded an abyss of empty space. There were hundreds of these artificial wormholes, but they were interconnected, their power sources and their power emitters integrated, so that the instability of feedback was passed onto the next wormhole below. Forming a continuous dispersal array, the powerful energy rushed down from the north to the south along the cage, until it was ready to be released in one massive controlled burst from the unseen and unoccupied south pole of the great device. If the emission was not activated at the correct time and at the correct rate of release, it would blast a hole in space large enough to swallow the entire star system. And the spatial rift was threatening to tear the cage apart even as it fought against its gravitational pull.

Ω

The Jaevisk tower began to crack from bottom to top, and then the section holding Leviathan and Cassandra captive suddenly collapsed to one side, throwing her like a broken doll to the breaking ground while Krell fled to find a way out and Leviathan broke loose of the energy stasis, intending to retreat to the depths below. Yet, as he did, great chunks of rock and metal began to rain down upon him and he howled in pain. When it seemed as if he would become trapped amidst the twisted, collapsing Jaevisk tower, a flash of green light from below shot up and engulfed him in its eerie glow. As Cassandra watched on, laying in her broken paralysis and feeling only the tears of her despair, the great black dragon vanished from sight as the tower crumbled down upon itself.

Cassandra knew that the ground was breaking beneath her as she saw spider-web cracks racing out from beneath her head, and she waited for her death with helpless surrender. But then she rose from the ground, feeling someone lifting her head and hearing a voice saying, 'It's okay. I've got you,' as she was turned around to see that she was in the arms of an unfamiliar Garran man. Jakari looked down at her, smiling with endless pity. 'I'll get you home.' Cassandra's relief and confusion and exhaustion was such that she lost consciousness. And she never got to thank this stranger who had saved her life.

Ω

Carak and Anya stepped out of the Jaevisk elevator even as the line was breaking and the housing threatened to give way. They hurried across the crumbling pathways, and Anya pointed to where a woman was huddled against a wall close to an opening in the mountainside. 'Hey!' she shouted, waving across to her. 'What are you *doing*?'

The woman, stunned by the approach of anyone not trying to kill her, pointed up, and both Carak and Anya followed the gesture. Descending along the treacherous paths was a tall Garran with a woman in his arms. She looked for all the world as if she was dead, but it was the Garran in question who caught Carak's attention. 'Jakari!' he shouted.

361

Jakari looked down as Carak hurried across to the opposite side, to where Jennifer was too afraid to move away from the wall. It was that moment of distraction which doomed the Fleet Commander from Sieltor Promies, for he lost his footing and stumbled, losing hold of Cassandra. She fell to the stone path as it broke away beneath her, and her body slipped out and down towards the gaping Jaevisk structure which was collapsing in upon itself. With a desperate cry, Jakari threw himself after her, grabbing a flailing hand within which no strength was found. Her head was lolling to one side and she could not even look up to see him. 'Please!' he begged, whether of her or of the universe in general. 'Don't fall!' He had anchored his feet in a fissure in the stone on which he lay, but it would not support him for long.

Jakari could not have known that the planet was on the verge of being torn apart but for the counteractive power of the cage, and the north pole of Kiranis had by now come into contact with the edge of the fracture in space. This was the phenomenon Jakari saw as he held tight to Cassandra's limp hand. A terrifying, gaping mouth of inter-dimensional blackness was now drawing the pieces of the Jaevisk tower into it, and it would soon consume the mountain itself. As Cassandra's body twisted around within Jakari's grip, he saw the necklace Nell had given to her after her surgery, and his heart skipped a beat. For there, hanging above the breast of this woman whom he had never met, was the golden dragon from the brooch Naveen had shown him. 'When you see this again, Jakari,' he had said, 'I want you to consider it...a guide.'

The path beneath him was breaking farther away from the great inner wall of the mountain, leaning inwards as if to confirm Jakari's conclusion. He could hear Carak's roars as if from far away, he could hear the groaning of the metal above him and the cracking and crumbling of the stone around him, and he could see the threat of emptiness far below. Until only days ago, he had never met the strange, black-cloaked Garran or had ever considered himself part of the greater scheme of things, at least not in a way his mother would understand it. 'A god exists and operates outside the realms of our comprehension of space and time,' she had told him. 'Reality, as we know it, is less of a boundary for such an entity than it is a challenge.' Her voice was coming from the very essence of the darkness below as she added, 'Such an entity is at work here.'

'I believe you, mother,' he said, as he released his anchored feet. As he fell, he took Cassandra in his arms and closed his eyes. Neither of them felt any pain.

362

Carak was horrified as he watched them fall, but Anya grabbed him and they made it to the open ledge, coaxing Jennifer away as everything was about to give way. Gigantic cracks raced down the inside of the mountain, but rescue was closer than they could have imagined. Next to the ledge, soldiers jumped out of a waiting shuttle and helped them on board. With the doors sealed, it raced upwards as great crevices opened up in the world beneath and the cage above was finally closed. No sooner had the shuttle passed through the northern arcs of the cage than it had vanished, taking Kiranis with it. The vessel momentarily lost control, but a battleship moved in to assist it, manoeuvring over it to drag it in. On the bridge, Harrogate felt the bittersweet triumph of this tiny rescue. With the Jaevisk gone from the fifth planet and the Kwaios energy field disrupted, the remainder of the ships from Earth turned around in safety. And they headed home.

THE FINAL DAY

As Harrogate's bedraggled fleet came within visual range of Earth, he was dozing and the Commander had to tap him on the shoulder to wake him. 'You have to see this,' he said. Blinking and rousing himself, Harrogate was quick to see what he was talking about. Hundreds of unfamiliar vessels, which looked more like automated construction units, were moving about in orbit of their home planet, and sporadic areas of construction could be identified. 'I think they're building something,' said the Commander.

Harrogate felt his heart race and his stomach turn. 'And I think I know what,' he replied. 'Get me down there as fast as possible.'

They passed the military station where Matthews was most likely as much in the dark as they were, and it was not long before Harrogate was in a shuttle heading for the surface. And heading straight for his office. He knew he would be there, overseeing whatever scheme was underway, but also waiting to confront Harrogate and probably to mock him by opening with a nice, big, "I told you so".

Anev Tesckyn gestured for his men to allow Harrogate passage into his own office. 'How magnanimous of you,' Harrogate sneered, glaring at Tesckyn's guards as he passed them. Harrogate's men were stopped from following him, and he conceded with a nod as Tesckyn rose to greet him. 'I'd say I was glad to see you,' said the man, 'if I thought it's what you wanted to hear.'

'All I want to hear from you is that you know you've failed.'

'On the contrary...' Tesckyn came around to the front of the desk to square off to him. 'We have simply adapted to the circumstances.'

'The *circumstances*?' Harrogate roared. 'Do you realise how many people have *died* because of the circumstances *you* created?'

Tesckyn held his ground with frustrating composure. 'I realise that many more will live because of the sacrifices we were forced to make.'

Harrogate laughed scornfully, pushing past him to take his rightful place behind his desk. He stood with his hands on the back of his chair as he said, 'Funny...I don't recall seeing you out there...abducted or dying or anything at all. You were sitting here in your ivory tower watching it all unfold.'

Tesckyn turned around with a smile. 'I believe this is *your* ivory tower, Mister Harrogate,' he reminded him. 'And I've done a little more than sit here. In case you haven't noticed, there's some work going on up there.'

How could he fail to notice? he thought. 'What's going on? What grand scheme have you concocted now?'

'Oh, I can't take all the credit for this one. I was told about a species called the Illeri. They're far beyond our safe flight range at the moment, but we anticipate great changes in that regard. Anyway, because they have as much hatred for the Kwaios as we are now justified in entertaining, they've come to us with an offer to help us with our defences.'

Harrogate could not help but be intrigued, and hated himself for it. 'So...what...they're building ships for us?'

Tesckyn grinned. 'No...no, not ships. Here, let me show you.' He took a Data Slip from his pocket and held it over the console on Harrogate's desk. A hologram was activated, the three-dimensional image leaping up from the table and rotating right before their eyes. Harrogate stared at it in wonder and horror, seeing a patchwork of metal enclosing a planet. 'You...you can't be serious!' he gasped. 'It's another cage!'

'Not exactly. It doesn't do what the cage does. It's for defensive purposes only. We've decided to call it the Shield. And it will be our most vital weapon against the Kwaios.'

Harrogate was shocked. 'Don't do this,' he pleaded. 'Don't leave us at the mercy of yet another species. We don't even know that the Kwaios will come back.'

'Look...you may only be capable of seeing the small picture here, but we are stuck in a universe in which we don't belong and are most certainly not welcome by those with the power to do anything about it. And if that means using another species for our own ends, then so be it. Why shouldn't we do what the Kwaios did to us?'

The twisted logic of this man was almost seductive, but Harrogate looked again at the hologram and saw only imprisonment, marginalisation and isolation. 'No,' he said. 'I won't let you do this.' Still standing behind his chair, he drew his gun, but Tesckyn was already, and always, one step ahead. He stepped aside and fired as Harrogate's shot whizzed by him, and Tesckyn's bullet went through the chair. There were shots from outside as Harrogate's men were taken down and then Tesckyn's men burst in. He held up his hand and shouted, 'Hold your fire!' as he walked around to Harrogate, who was clinging with fading strength to the chair.

'I'm sorry to have to do this, John,' said Tesckyn as Harrogate finally let go of the chair, gasping for air as the blood pumped from the hole in his chest. He lay on his back, looking up at his killer, experiencing a terrible sense of betrayal. This was not right. This was not fair. He was a good man. How could this be happening?

'As you were told once before...' said Tesckyn, brandishing his gun for the final shot, 'you never had the ball.' The shot rang out as the others looked on.

Ω

Governor Ben-Hadad was flanked by eight heavily armed men as he made his way up the steps of his palace. A large crowd was gathering around the complex, and people were demanding answers regarding the destruction of Sieltor Teuvas, the failed alliance with the Jaevisk Society and Ben-Hadad's activity out at the Kiranis system. There were even rumours that the man had taken a young girl hostage in order to manipulate his political rivals and to deter a coup. From the palace gates, the crowd were about to witness something they would never forget, for waiting at the top of the steps for their illustrious Governor were those very rivals, and the girl in question.

Ben-Hadad stopped as they stepped into view above him, and his men readied their weapons. However, from all around them emerged men and women loyal to Overseer Carak and the Setta family. The Governor's men lowered their weapons as, looking down on him, Senneya stepped forward with her daughter by her side. Behind her were Carak, Tanna, Eyla and Raill, and all wore stony expressions except for Carak, whose anger and disgust was clear. Ben-Hadad shouted up to them, 'What do you want from me? You got the girl back.' He resumed his climb up the steps, pointing at Tanna. 'How is it that a Ga Han finds himself working for traitors?' he hissed. 'Have you forgotten where your loyalties lie?'

Tanna moved up to stand next to Senneya. 'My loyalties lie with my people!' he argued, shouting so that the crowd beyond could hear. 'They are not defined by some ancient tribal affiliations. My loyalties lie with the Garran!'

The crowd cheered and it grated Ben-Hadad to hear their support for these people. He came farther up the steps and looked at Senneya. 'And *you!*' he spat. 'Married to a traitor. Not only to this government but to his entire race. You cannot tell me that Carak's loyalties lie with the Garran!'

Carak was about to step forward but Eyla stopped him. 'She needs to do this herself,' she told him quietly. He nodded and watched as Senneya covered Kera's eyes and held her closer with one arm as she withdrew a gun with the other. 'What are you doing?' snapped Ben-Hadad. 'Lower that weapon!' He looked back to his men, who had wisely chosen not to follow him up the steps. 'Kill them!' he shouted. 'Kill these traitors!'

Senneya pushed Kera back behind her, and Carak called his daughter to him as Senneya descended the steps towards the Governor. As she shouted, 'Carak's loyalty is to his family!' she squeezed the trigger. Then she squeezed it again. And again. And again. Ben-Hadad stumbled backwards with each impact, and then lost his footing and fell back down the steps as his soldiers parted to clear the way and the crowd watched on in muted wonder.

Senneya was trembling and she dropped the gun as she watched the Governor tumbling down the steps, stopping short of the end. Carak came to her and drew her to him, pulling her into an embrace with Kera between them. 'It's over,' he told her. 'I'll never leave you again.'

That evening, as their meal was finished and Senneya was putting Kera to bed, Carak found himself standing outside with the Kwaios cube in his hand. He did not recall taking it up nor where it had been, and he gritted his teeth with the anticipation of the conversation he was about to have. His environment changed around him and he was standing in a Kwaios communications' chamber, looking up at one of the huge aliens. 'You tried to kill me out there,' he accused it.

'Objectives change rapidly during war.'

'Have they changed again?'

'You will receive a gift from our High Council.'

'What sort of gift?'

'There are many on your worlds who seek our gods and our power, and who wish to change the way your people see the universe. But those on Earth who knew the truth can be valuable in our fight to maintain its secret.'

'I don't understand. Who are you talking about?'

'The people we took from the *Dragon*. You will use them to undermine the credibility of these extremist Garran.'

Carak's eyes widened. 'You're...*giving* me some of the people you took?'

'We will instruct you on how to apply what we are learning from them. You will continue to work for us.'

'What if I choose not to?'

'Then your species will be annihilated.'

The simplicity and enormity of the threat chilled him completely as the conversation was abruptly ended. He turned back to his house and saw through the windows Senneya moving around inside. She was free, Kera was free, but Carak would never be. He wept for the world he loved. And the cage in which he was held.

Ω

The funeral was over, and Anya was left standing by the open grave. A mixture of flowers and dirt obscured the Eurasian Council drape which had adorned Adam's coffin, and it was a visual effect for which Anya was grateful, considering who had killed him. The journey back from the Kiranis system had been filled with rumour, conjecture and wild theories, but it was Harrogate who gave her the information and the peace she needed. In hearing of the great scheme of things into which Cassandra Messina had been drawn and within which she had been manipulated and used, Anya found it difficult to hate the woman, despite what she had done.

All Anya could do now was ensure that the child she had conceived with Adam was brought up safely and was given the best possible life. Holding her hand to her abdomen, she found herself thinking of Conner and the magnitude of this birth to come. As she looked down at the coffin again and tears came to her eyes, a darkness fell across the grave. The sun was low in the sky and she looked up to see a tall figure in a dark cloak with a hood obscuring its features and its form thrown into shadow by the sun at its back. Anya felt a shiver run through her as she asked, 'Who are you?'

When there was no reply, she asked, 'Did you know Adam?'

Still, nothing was forthcoming, and all Anya could hear was a rasping breath from the strange silhouette. As the sun descended farther, the shadows lessened and the hooded head could be seen with greater detail. Anya saw then that this thing had no discernible features whatsoever, for it was not even Human. There was nothing but burning fire

368

within the hood, and Anya gasped and stepped back in fear. 'What do you want?' she shouted.

The figure remained silent, and suddenly the cloak burst into flames. The flames rushed out towards her, enveloping her as she screamed. But there was no fire, and no pain. And, before the flames dissipated into nothingness and as Anya fell to her back on the grass, she heard a voice of burning coals saying, 'I will come for you!'

Ω

Tesckyn looked up at the sky, seeing the shadows of the gigantic construction which he knew would be underway for many years to come. He understood that this protective shield might not be finished within his lifetime, and he accepted that. He was a man who always saw the bigger picture, a man of great patience who savoured being part of something which would ring through Human history for years, decades or even centuries to come. He seated himself on a park bench as the sun was going down, watching the people in their complacency and ignorance, enjoying the power of secrecy and the sense of control and superiority which accompanied it. There was a call on his com and he tapped the sub dermal button in his earlobe. 'Go ahead.'

The tone of the voice on the other end brought him upright: *'Sir, there's been a breach in the global firewall. Someone's broadcasting a message.'*

'Who is it?' He took a handheld computer from his pocket and accessed the global net. Immediately, he saw Harrogate there, and he was addressing the world. 'I see it. Clearly, killing this guy wasn't enough. Stop the broadcast!'

But it was too late. Harrogate's people had covered every angle, and it took hours to stop the broadcast. Until then, it played on a loop:

'This is a message for the people of Earth. You should know that we do not belong in this universe, and that your governments have lied to you all for centuries. A secret organisation led by a man named Anev Tesckyn arranged for the abduction of everyone in the Church of the New Elect in an alliance made with a race called the Kwaios. You all know people in the Church. They are your friends and colleagues and people you have lived alongside all your lives. They are not different because they believe something you do not. Their hopes and dreams are just as relevant to

369

them as yours are to you. Many people of the Church are still here on Earth, and they deserve to be treated with respect as much as you and I. We may not belong here, but that doesn't mean that we should behave like animals!

'I urge you all to join together against this covert organisation who makes decisions against your will and without your knowledge, because in the end…we all suffer the consequences. There are very real enemies out amongst the stars, but some of the most treacherous of all live right under our noses. So find Tesckyn's people, make them pay for what they did to your friends and colleagues…and what they intend to do to your world. It is up to you all to fight back!'

EPILOGUE

Outside the universe, it was dark as pitch and devoid of dimension. There were no stars here, and as such, there was no life. Into this place without form or certainty, a planet appeared, a world recently rescued from another place and time by the cage within which it was housed. This planet became the only source of light in this place, and although it filled every available emptiness, this planet was also lost amidst a vastness beyond comprehension.

In a control centre at the zenith of the cage, three people struggled against the onset of despair and despondency in the wake of recent events and the situation in which they found themselves. Sandra and Colle sat quietly watching the equipment around them, while Jason stared out the window, desperately trying to locate a point of light which might announce the presence of someone else. Anyone else. 'This isn't possible,' he muttered to himself, squinting and trying to convince himself that he was imagining the black emptiness around them.

'*Seriously*, Jase?' said Sandra as she turned to him. 'You're going to try dealing with this within the realms of *possibility*? I wouldn't recommend it.'

Jason kept his gaze on the darkness. 'You two may be willing to give up, but I'm not.'

Colle shook his head. 'Well, let us know when you've got a plan, won't you?'

Slamming his fists against the window, the younger man swung on them both, shouting, 'We can't just sit on our asses, for God's sake! Why aren't you *doing* something?'

'Because there's nothing they can do.' Naveen stepped out of the shadows like a demon, clearly pleased with himself. 'Nothing any of you can do.'

Jason immediately ran at him while Colle and Sandra got to their feet. For some reason, Naveen permitted the attack, and Jason threw a heavy punch which knocked the Prophet to the floor as the cage emitted a slight rumble. Colle was quickly there, and he grabbed Jason to stop him moving in for more. Jason, however, was in no state to continue his physical outburst. He was sobbing, and Colle released him silently as he asked, 'What do you want from us?'

Naveen got to his feet with ease, and a bruise on his face faded away to leave no trace of the violence. 'I need you to monitor the survivors on the planet,' he replied as his long black cloak straightened itself.

'That's it?'

'That's it. Soon you'll be able to go down to the surface yourself, but I don't want you to interact with the people you come across. Just watch them.'

'Why?' asked Sandra. 'And why us?'

Naveen smiled. 'I find that it's best never to ask oneself that question. It's you because it's you. Simple as that.'

'That's not good enough!' Colle snapped.

'And it never will be.' Naveen turned his back to them, but he looked back as he returned to the shadows, saying, 'You're not prisoners here, you know. In fact, you're quite the opposite.'

'What's that supposed to mean?' asked Sandra.

'Well, you're up here...looking down on all the people of the world. Trust me, it won't be long before you feel a certain...superiority.' He moved further into the shadows as Sandra shouted, 'We'll never be like you! None of us are gods, you know!'

'Maybe not,' Naveen replied from the darkness, 'but we all want to be.' That was the last they ever heard from him. But those words resonated with them for the rest of their lives.

Ω

The planet Kiranis still rotated as any other planet might, although it did so in synchronicity with the cage, and it had no star by which it might be illuminated and heated and nourished. But in this place of starless obscurity, of absent dimension, the cage gave this world everything it required. It created atmospheric and climatic expressions of reality, and it helped to form a world of great diversity and greater mystery. At the north pole of this world, a snow-capped peak appeared to have crumbled from within, and it no longer reached for the sky as once it had.

Considering this change, Naveen stood on a nearby hill. Looking momentarily upwards, his dark eyes regarded the charade of a sky, this perpetual night. Artificial in every way, twinkling lights could be seen, a mimicry of starlight. Yet no starlight was such as this, set in mathematically determined lines along the blackness of night, curving in turn to compensate for the shape of the planet. Only through his own

372

unique method of viewing his surroundings could he see beyond the lies to the horrendous metal arms embracing the world, reaching upwards along the horizon, the mocking legacy of his great game. Cloaked as always in black, he stood tall and defiant, for here and now, in the very womb of his ambitious plan, he could still hear the horrific cries of his past.

His surroundings were suddenly altered as his grey eyes pierced the darkness. Sounds roared through his head, of fighting and killing and the screams of the dying and tortured. As some ethereal power illuminated the world around him, a verdant valley stretched away before him, running towards rolling hills. Sweeping wraithlike across the valley, a scene of battle blanketed the land, where dragons torched the ground and soldiers on foot and horse decimated the huge settlement through which they passed. In the background and overlooking the settlement from the opposite side, a castle-like building was shattered and flaming. Although populated by hundreds of people, this magical setting was oblivious to the small fair-haired child walking from this building. Only Naveen could see this boy, and his jaw tightened as he drew in a deep, calming breath and the boy spied him across the great divide of time and space.

There was a bestial, blood-chilling cry, and the black-cloaked man was snapped from his reverie. The lighted scene vanished as he faced the reality of an approaching nightmare, hiding his actions and his emotions like the fleeing child of his vision. Illuminated only by the pinpoints of false stars, a gigantic white shape moved gracefully and purposefully through the air towards him. Great wings manipulated the thermals, gorging upon their purpose. Yellow eyes pierced the darkness, spying the tiny man on the hill. Again this creature opened its mouth to announce its presence to the night, revealing to any who had the misfortune to see it a threatening array of sabre-sharp teeth, wickedly curved and pointed. Set at regular intervals along its giant wings, tapered bones of silvery-grey protected this monster. Most living things would be stunned to incapacity at the sight of this beast, but Naveen was unlike most living things. He watched dispassionately as the giant white dragon changed its form in mid-flight, passing over him and coming to rest in the form of a white-cloaked woman, at the same time ancient and beautiful, silver-haired and strong. 'Why do you haunt yourself like this, child?' she chided him gently, knowingly.

He took a deep breath, turning to face her. 'Because this is what keeps me going. These are the memories which fuel my determination. Your betrayal was next on my list.'

'You're no longer that little boy, Naveen.'

'I will always be that little boy. If you accepted that...you would understand all this.'

She nodded. 'Perhaps. But I wonder sometimes if you forget that you brought us here. That you snatched us from our moment of revelation.'

'I rescued you from obliteration as a point of necessity. There was no paradise to be found at the end of your universe.' He held her gaze pointedly. 'But I think that maybe you knew that.'

She was silent for a moment, until she said, 'I didn't expect you to imprison Leviathan like that. We'll need him as the people of this world evolve.'

'His arrogance frustrated me. I needed to remind him of what he faces.'

'And when will you release him?'

'That's already in hand.' He smiled malevolently. 'I can feel how confused you are, Asherah. You've no idea what I'm capable of. And by the time you realise, it will be too late.'

Asherah stepped closer to him, her beautiful features suddenly creased by a bestial fervour, her silvery hair rushing through with white, her magical aura pulsing with anger. As she spoke, her voice echoed with a chilling growl. 'I'll do whatever it takes to stop you, Naveen, but you should also know that what you've done hasn't gone unnoticed. When that boy resurrected us, it sparked our connection to the Sentience here. And then this...cage severed it again. There are others watching now, and they are more powerful than any of us. They won't stand for your interference in things which don't concern you!'

'I'm fully aware of who...or *what* is watching!' snapped Naveen. 'And I don't care. In fact...' He raised his hands out like a holy man on a height and declared, 'Let them come and try to stop me. And I'll show them what it means to be a god!'

374

KIRANIS HAS RETURNED

kiranis.net

Read on for the prologue of the next exciting instalment of KIRANIS, coming in 2013

PAWNS OF THE PROPHET

KIRANIS BOOK 2

RONALD A. GEOBEY

PROLOGUE

Hear, my child, your father's instruction, and do not reject your mother's teaching; for they are a fair garland for your head, and pendants for your neck. My child, if sinners entice you, do not consent. If they say, "Come with us, let us lie in wait for blood; let us wantonly ambush the innocent; like Sheol let us swallow them alive and whole, like those who go down to the Pit. We shall find all kinds of costly things; we shall fill our houses with booty. Throw in your lot among us; we will all have one purse" – my child, do not walk in their way, keep your foot from their paths; for their feet run to evil, and they hurry to shed blood. For in vain is the net baited while the bird is looking on; yet they lie in wait – to kill themselves! and set an ambush – for their own lives! Such are the ways of all who are greedy for gain; it takes away the life of its possessors. **Proverbs 1:8-19**

Samuel Vawter was a narcissist, fully aware of the fact and ultimately proud of it. He was a man of intellect and imagination, ambition and resolve, skill and talent. The perfect combination of traits for his line of work. Of course, without the legacy into which Samuel had been born, his talent may well have been overlooked. Less than a century earlier, during the fallout from the cage event, his grandfather had capitalised on the inevitable political and economic chaos. He had used his then considerable financial weight to bribe, scare and promise all the right people in all the right places into using his company like a safety deposit box. He then set about reminding all the wrong people in all the wrong places that his company was a manufacturer and purveyor of some of the most advanced weapons' systems on the planet, thus ensuring that bad people bought his product line and contributed to the security of the funds submitted by the good people. Of course, all of that depended upon the subjective nature of right and wrong or good and bad, but old Grandfather Vawter cared little for such...flexible designations. Times had always changed, but money was power, and when that money bought and sold weapons, it was the most powerful kind. Old Grandfather Vawter was moved to action by the words of a certain John Harrogate, the man who had revealed, in his posthumous address to the world, the subterfuge and betrayal of a covert organisation overseen by Anev Tesckyn.

It was Tesckyn's people who had, in a fool's deal made with the Kwaios Council, arranged for the abduction of millions of people by way of the cage. Tesckyn had believed that he could use the cage to return Earth to the universe to which it belonged. This had been implied by the Kwaios as part of the deal, but they had failed to mention that they were not in control of the cage. The abductees had been taken to the planet known as Kiranis and they had suffered a terrible fate. Not death, but not life either, for they had found themselves subsumed physically and psychologically within the form of monstrous creatures born out of the primordial chaos of the forming planet. And when the cage had finished its work at Kiranis, it had vanished from sight, taking the planet with it. Kiranis was never seen again, and the people of Earth were infuriated by the incident. Tesckyn's people were hunted down and killed, an operation which took decades but which had a strangely unifying effect upon a population haunted by the reasons. But as their proverbial backs were turned and hopes for world peace filled the airwaves, something else was going on, for the legacy of Anev Tesckyn would not be so easily obliterated.

In the aftermath of his terrible error and the return of the mighty Kwaios Council to this part of the galaxy, Tesckyn had seen fit to involve in the affairs of Earth a species called the Illeri. They had offered to construct the Shield around Earth. It was an enormous undertaking and Tesckyn knew that he would not see it completed in his lifetime. And that was without considering the assassin's bullet which passed through his brain twelve years later. Unfortunately, it was too late to stop the Illeri. The construction work was undertaken by automated machinery, highly advanced and seemingly impervious to the weapons of the day. Numerous attempts were made by autonomous militant groups and people calling themselves freedom fighters, but it seemed that the more the people of Earth tried to obstruct the work, the harder and faster the Illeri automatons worked. More of them arrived as the years went on, dropped off in Earth orbit like migrant workers. The closest things came to a work stoppage was short of forty years into the project, when a Kwaios vessel raced into the Sol system, destroying ships and outposts in an attempt to get to the Shield. When it reached Earth, weaponry and defensive systems of which the people had not even been aware were activated around the perimeter of the Shield, and the Kwaios ship was crippled. The Illeri robots towed it away, leaving the dying ship at a position just inside lunar orbit. The Kwaios never came again. This incident made it clear that construction of the Shield would not and should not be stopped, and the people of Earth became resigned to its shadowy presence.

As the decades went on, the progress of the work was akin to someone gradually blocking up every window in the house, but it soon became clear that the windows could be opened as the Shield came closer to full functionality, and politicians swiftly found the rhetoric of optimism which led to their taking control of a panicked people. For the first time in human history, one single entity, the Senate, ruled Earth. At least, that was how it appeared. In truth, what had always been known remained so: the rich ruled Earth. They controlled the resources, the food and, most importantly, the weapons. And Samuel Vawter stepped up to take control of what his father and grandfather before him had long known would become the most powerful corporation on the planet. Each of them had often been asked the question, 'So what's your secret? What have you got that your competitors don't?' but they would simply smile and change the subject. Because there was something else of which Old Grandfather Vawter had taken control.

As part of the deal Tesckyn had made with the Kwaios Council, his organisation had come into possession of Kwaios technology. When Tesckyn had retreated from the furious response of the people to Harrogate's call to arms, he had taken the secrets of Kwaios tech with him, keeping them as close as a dragon guarding its treasure. But the backlash of hatred against his operatives not only saw them hunted down and killed; it also saw their finances frozen or appropriated and the organisation was financially crippled. Grandfather Vawter just happened to knock on Tesckyn's secret door at exactly the right time with an offer he could not refuse. The fact that the old man walked out of the secret lair of the most wanted man on the planet with Kwaios technology minutes before a bullet went through Tesckyn's brain was surely a coincidence. As was the beginning of the end for all of Vawter's competitors in the weapons' market.

It is a powerful truism that the enemy of one's enemy is one's friend. As mankind looked out into the dangerous stars around them, the Shield became a more comforting prospect, and the legacy of Grandfather Vawter found itself attached to government interests. By the time Samuel Vawter took over the company, the days of operating behind the scenes like a black-op contractor had passed, and he was very much in bed with the Senate. It was a comfortable bed, but Samuel thought it wise on occasion to keep the covers on and to sleep near the edge. Exposure equalled vulnerability, and Samuel had no intention of becoming vulnerable. He saw the Illeri as a threat to the security of Earth, a theory only strengthened by the relentless progression of the Shield and the complete lack of communication from the Illeri since construction began.

Samuel was baffled by the Senate's refusal to send a fleet to the Illeri home world to get answers, which was why he had sent someone himself. Because of the nature of the operation, the mercenary he had sent had been ordered to keep off all communication channels until he reached his destination. Two years had now passed, and there had been no word from the mercenary. Samuel resigned himself to the failure of the mission and the loss of a trusted ally. The Illeri remained a mystery, a situation which would not last much longer, for the Illeri were on their way to Earth.

As he stood in the darkness, he tried to push all other concerns from his mind as he focused on the most important operation of his life. For the briefest of moments, he wondered what his grandfather would think if he could see his progeny now. The irony had the potential to bring laughter as much as it did tears. Wearing one of his favoured grey suits, Samuel stood in a darkness of his own design. He had deactivated all lighting in the room, and he waited with growing impatience as the minutes dragged on. There was silence but for his even, sometimes protracted breathing as he held the cold black cube in his hands. They had told him to come here so that the communication would not be detected. He hoped they were right, but knew better than to argue with them. He was not entirely sure whether he feared them or not. Certainly, they were more powerful than any of his other business associates, but this was a business of mutual benefit to both parties. Even if he did not understand their gain, still he appreciated their payment.

The cold box grew gradually warmer in his hands, but he knew that this was simply due to his sweating palms. Then the room changed, stretching outwards in every direction, a virtual sensation that challenged his perspective and his senses. The ceiling rose, great columns of blue and the shimmering metal of hybritech lifting it high beyond his ability to focus upon it. Flashing lights, integrated bio-technical cabling and alien console systems surrounded him. But he was not alone.

Tall, so tall that he felt the need to step back to comprehend its enormity, a figure of shimmering silver, black and blue stood facing him. 'You are not required to speak,' the Kwaios told him, the words first coming in that dreadful language that hurt Human ears, before it was translated by the device in his hands and transmitted to his brain. He nodded dumbly, respecting their requirements. Any businessman knows that there are compromises to be made during negotiation. The Kwaios continued: 'Our work is advancing to a further stage. We require an increase in supply. You will ensure that the influx is increased by a factor of ten.'

Samuel was about to argue, but the image of the huge Kwaios moved closer towards him. 'This is not open to negotiation,' it reminded him. 'You will increase our supply, and we will provide you with the payment you seek.' Samuel smiled as the Kwaios confirmed what he was hearing. 'You will live forever,' it said.

With the conversation ended, Samuel came out of the small antechamber and looked around the larger room in which it was situated. Giant windows overlooked a great city, and sunlight bounced off the surface of a massive glass table. Samuel stared into the reflected light for a moment, allowing his eyes to lose focus as he revelled in the temporary escape from reality. From the door through which he had left the antechamber, another figure appeared, a man in a black cloak of dragons. Naveen looked solemn, focused and driven. 'Are you ready?' he asked.

Samuel nodded as he turned, his eyes readjusting to the unnatural light of the room and his resolve strengthened by the presence of this enigmatic figure. 'They won't know what hit them, will they?'

Naveen grinned as he replied, 'That's the general idea, yes.'

15454150R00223

Made in the USA
Charleston, SC
04 November 2012